COAST GUARD BLUES

A MARTY GALLOWAY ADVENTURE

KENNETH ARBOGAST

All rights reserved. Published in the United States by Vigilant Newf Books.

Cover art by Christopher Mitchell.

Production design by Mariah Mason.

ISBN: (978-1-7348721-6-3) (eBook)

ISBN: (978-1-7348721-7-0) (Paperback)

Library of Congress Cataloging-in-Publication Data has been applied for.

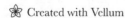 Created with Vellum

*For the dedicated members and veterans
of the U.S. Coast Guard.*

August 1991

I can tick off about two dozen reasons why I dreaded every visit back to Headquarters.

At the top of my list is National Airport, a narrow asphalt strip tucked between the Potomac River, the bridges, and the cement cliffs of Crystal City office buildings. Each flight into D.C. brings back that familiar tight-chested dread I felt five years ago on an H-3 helicopter out of Kodiak, swooping toward a capsized fishing boat off the Alaskan coast. Forty-five-knot winds handled the helo as brutally as the 25-foot seas punished the small life raft below us. The pilot held us in a steady hover long enough to hoist up five half-frozen crew members from a rubber raft. Two others were lost; a deckhand was swept over the transom when the storm blew in. The skipper was trapped in the wheelhouse when the boat rolled on its side and sank in the rough seas. An ugly stench filled the cabin when the two college kids we hoisted from the raft thawed enough to be scared sick.

Those stormy flights never worried me so much as riding commercial airlines. On a helicopter aircrew, you sit about six feet from the pilot. You trust him because you've seen his wife in the commissary, and you know he's determined to get home again. But from back in Seat 22-D, you wouldn't know if an airline pilot was free-basing bleach.

A close second complaint about my visits to HQ is wearing a uniform; the Coast Guard blues. I outgrew the old gabardine many years ago but didn't wear it often enough to justify buying the new serge version. I am forced into uniform only during infrequent visits to Headquarters. In my current line of work, I usually wear cotton and tweed. Conducting a discreet investigation would be compli-cated by bright gold buttons, spit-polish shoes, and seven rows of military decorations over my left pocket.

My remaining complaints include a shortage of parking and an excess of officers.

With all those things in mind, I was not amused when a message came to report to Washington by direction of "Commandant, U.S.C.G." on a Tuesday morning in August during a two-week stretch of leave in Maine. The message waited at the motor lodge when I returned from early morning fly-casting in a trout stream that feeds the Arundel River. Two hours later, I parked the Firebird in the long-term lot at Boston's Logan Airport. I carried three pieces of luggage; a suit bag with my "bravo" dress uniform that I always keep in the car's trunk for such unfortunate occasions, a rucksack full of real clothes, and a black leather valise I call my little bag of tricks.

When the commandant requests your presence and wants you NOW, his staff spares no expense. The admiral's office had purchased a first-class ticket on the 11:55 shuttle. Evidence indicated this was the last available space on that particular flight; otherwise, an enlisted man like myself would have been stuffed into coach or even baggage. All the clues indicated urgency. I received no travel orders, no accounting data; maybe they charged the ticket against the commandant's credit card or, even more likely, an aide's plastic. When I told the freckled redhead at the ticket counter that I was military and traveling priority, she tapped my name onto her keyboard, glanced at the screen and immediately yelled into the back office for another clerk to hustle me down to gate 7B. She also checked my black bag due to firearms laws, promising, again and again, that she would get it loaded on the same flight I was boarding.

OK, I'm an oddball. I may be the last passenger on the planet who watches the flight attendants pantomime their pre-launch safety demonstrations, their arms fluttering toward the exit windows like game show hostesses. I figure it's an excellent chance to determine who will serve my section and establish eye contact since I'm the only person looking their way. Once we leveled off at cruising speed, the young woman handling first class came down the aisle to see if I needed anything. I asked Monica for my suit bag and headed to the lavatory.

Luckily the DC-10 encountered no turbulence while I scraped a five-day bristle from my chin. With two dozen lemon-scented towelettes, I wiped away the lingering smell from wading into the trout stream, then went a touch strong on deodorant and cologne until my skin felt prickly. Then into uniform, though badly wrinkled from riding 1,400 miles in the trunk of the car. With name tag and ribbons fastened on the jacket over my shoulder, I headed back to Row 2.

High brass wanted me in the commandant's conference room at 1345.

The flight touched down at National Airport on the tail of a little commuter jet moving slowly into the taxi lane. Air traffic around Washington was stacked like a blackjack deck. We were delayed reaching the terminal due to a backlog of jets waiting for take-off. Ignoring the steward's instructions, most people unbuckled and began unloading their baggage from the overhead compartments so that pandemonium erupted in the narrow aisle when we finally reached the gate. Remaining seated, I waited it out and continued reading a novel about a shipwreck on Boon Island off Maine's coast.

Monica's eyes registered surprise as she gave my uniform a quick once-over when I thanked her outside the galley door. The gold chevrons and three gold stripes on my left sleeve are a nice contrast against the royal blue of the jacket. Before making chief petty officer, I often complained the uniform could look great on a bus driver. Somehow the sleeve adornment and a pair of gold anchors on the collar felt like finally taking off the training wheels. Monica's smile made me wish I was still on vacation.

Washington's late summer swelter caught me off guard when I came out of the cool terminal and headed for a taxi. No wonder Congress takes recess and bolts town every August. I have felt less discomfort watching molten steel poured into the furnace at the mill where my grandfather worked. When I came to the taxi stand, a mustard-colored Ford pulled up from the line of waiting cabs that stretched out of sight. The shaggy-haired driver had terrible body odor, but he seemed to recognize both 2nd Street and Fort McNair, though Coast Guard Headquarters was a mystery to him. By the time we reached the 14th Street Bridge, sweat had soaked through the back of my shirt. The lunch crunch clogged Maine Avenue, and the cabbie cursed like a bosun's mate on a drunk. This performance was for my benefit because he ignored several opportunities to cut around the inept, confused or sightseeing.

From Maine Avenue, the cab turned due south at Waterside

Mall, skirted the brick walls of Fort McNair and made another right. The street down to Headquarters borders a neighborhood that is economically challenged. Every home has iron bars set over the windows. Two burned-out hulks sat among the cars parked along Second Street. My diver's watch nudged 1335 when the cabbie dropped me in front of Headquarters, a squat brown building on a blunt jut into the Anacostia River, called, without irony, Buzzards Point.

Outside the front entrance, a gaggle of officers in their summer short sleeves waited for the shuttle bus to go downtown, milling in small clusters on the sidewalk. Conversations paused as they watched me, sweating in my dress uniform and hauling expeditionary luggage over my shoulders. I stopped to set down my black bag and execute a sharp salute, forcing a group of about eight to straighten up and salute back. Saluting is a silly tradition, but I enjoy the feeling of control it gives me: All I have to do is wave my hand, and officers hop like marionettes.

The rent-a-cop at the front entrance wouldn't accept my military ID card or my well-polished Special Agent badge. Headquarters designed their unique security system during one of the Persian Gulf crises of the Reagan years when the Coast Guard reflagged Kuwaiti oil tankers to move them through the Persian Gulf without threat from Iranian gunboats. On occasion, and without warning, the guards demand to see the special HQ badges. We both heard the screaming response when she called the central security office on her hand-held radio at 1341. My name had been posted at every door with instructions to hustle me upstairs immediately to the commandant's office. She apologized and offered to lead me topside. I waved her off and started for the elevators.

No, the layout of the building wasn't much of a puzzle. I had been stationed in a controlled-access office of the Intelligence branch on the third floor for about six months – many years earlier.

When the elevator doors opened on the second deck, a tall, gangly ensign greeted me and led the way at a jog toward the commandant's suite. Funny, but the longer you're in the service, the slower you walk. Ensigns and seamen go everywhere on the run; captains and chiefs comport with a distinctive saunter.

A pair of burly seamen in well-starched uniforms guarded the door of the commandant's secure conference room. Both snapped to attention as we approached. The ensign instructed one of them to take my luggage into the admiral's main office. Then Butterbars opened the door, reminded me about the importance of proper protocol around senior officers, and went to tell the admiral that I had arrived.

The place looked rather unremarkable for the Coast Guard brain center; pale yellow wallpaper, fluorescent light panels in the white drop ceiling, the room maybe 20 feet by 25 feet split by a long, dark-maple table faced by a dozen matching leather chairs. More chairs lined the walls. Blue curtains framed a transparent screen on one wall; the screen was set up for rear-projection video. Four lamps and eight ashtrays could have come from any hotel's meeting room, with a faux oil painting of a Coast Guard icebreaker escorting a freighter through a field of chunky brash ice.

Two doors, opposite sides of the room. I sat in a corner, about halfway between the two, back against the wall. It sounds silly, but you learn to pay attention to exits if you get in enough rough spots. In the engine room of a Panamanian freighter, you need to know a fast escape if you're surprised by somebody wielding an AK.

The room was soundproofed. Any listening devices would have been detected by the weekend sweeps scheduled on a sporadic basis. That had been one of my duties on that brief tour five years earlier, so I knew the second deck's layout quite well. About 15 feet from the conference room was Flagplot, a bank of telephones, computers, and televisions that are the cortex of all significant Coast Guard action. When any operation requires Headquarters or commandant approval, Flagplot gets the call.

I relaxed a few seconds before the hefty seaman shoved the door open and announced the arrival of the official party. I rose to attention. Seniority is important to those guys. They came through the door in exact precedence; first, a nervous-looking lieutenant, then two paunchy captains and finally the commandant, each pressed, polished, and all wearing summer shirts with short sleeves. I felt awkward in my wrinkled jacket, but the shirt underneath looked worse, so I elected to stay buttoned – though hot, sweaty, and a little claustrophobic. The commandant's aide, a lieutenant commander, identified by a blue and gold aiguillette around his left shoulder, came a moment later and motioned for me to join the group at the table.

Quick introductions followed, strictly for my benefit. One of the captains headed the operations division; the other four-striper and the lieutenant worked in Intelligence. When Admiral Thorne described me as "the sumbitch who came close to starting a war with Mexico," the others took a more extended survey of me than my unkempt uniform merited.

Thorne, a short, wiry man in steel-rimmed eyeglasses and a buzz cut, remained standing. It took an embarrassing few moments for anyone to realize that he meant for the rest of us to sit. I'm not big on military etiquette, but I wasn't going to be the first to plant my butt. Finally, his aide motioned again, and we all dropped on cue.

"Thanks for taking time to come down this afternoon. I wish to hell it wasn't necessary, and I know none of you like this any better than I do." The commandant turned to his aide and motioned toward the video screen. "Let's see that chart. For the benefit of Special Agent Galloway, I'd like Lieutenant Andrews to recap the situation."

A large chart emerged on the screen that I identified as Lake Superior. I'd earned a lot of gold stars in geography back at St. Stephen's Elementary.

The admiral gave up center stage as the lieutenant stood and ran a hand over his close-clipped curls. Perspiration dotted his forehead. After clearing his throat several times, he began. "Monday afternoon the Royal Canadian Mounted Police found one of our 44-foot motor surfboats adrift in Lake Superior, well inside Canadian waters. There was no sign of the crew, no indication of an accident, and no sign of violence. The station in Sault Sainte Marie had lost contact with the boat about seven hours earlier, and they were searching the St. Mary's River, about 50 miles southeast of where the boat was found."

"Here's the bottom line," one of the captains interrupted,

turning to face me. "Four crewmen have been missing more than 24 hours, and nobody has a clue why."

Everyone in the room turned to stare as if I would magically reveal the crew's location like the Amazing Kreskin, but I was stumped. A boat adrift sounded more like a search and rescue case – not the usual case requiring criminal investigation. I wondered why I had been summoned away from good trout fishing.

"I see you're a little puzzled," the commandant said to me, breaking the expectant silence. "That's OK, I was too at first. But hear Andrews out; it gets very interesting. Go ahead, Lieutenant."

"Thank you, Admiral." Andrews began again, now facing me, a little more relaxed than at first. "Well, from what we know, it seems unlikely there was an accident. The weather was calm; seas ran about three feet. In any event, the coxswain went through Cape D. The 44-footer had no apparent damage, and RCC Scott reported no EPIRB hits in the region during the 24 hours after the boat's departure from the station."

To put all that in its simplest terms, something rather odd indeed had happened in Lake Superior. Those 44-foot motor surf-boats were designed so they could sail over Niagara Falls and not suffer much more than chipped paint. They have steel hulls built especially for bad weather and heavy surf, and they're so seaworthy they can capsize and pop right back up for more. The coxswain had graduated from the service's National Motor Lifeboat School at Cape Disappointment in Oregon, where he learned to push a small boat through the wildest surf on the Pacific coast. Neither he nor the boat would have any problems in good weather and calm seas. As further proof, the Rescue Coordination Center at Scott Air Force Base had received no distress signals from the boat's Emergency Position-Indicating Radio Beacon. The commandant was right; this was getting interesting.

Andrews continued: "The boat left the station before muster on Monday. There was no distress call, and the four aboard were not the duty crew. According to the group operations officer, the boat left without authorization."

The other captain spoke up, the taller of the two, with a gray widow's peak breaking his forehead. "When the lieutenant brought all this to my attention, the admiral wanted you in to investigate." He glanced from me back to the commandant. I figured he was looking for a gold star of his own.

Andrews walked to the screen and moved his hand across the chart, covering the north shore of Lake Superior – the coast of Ontario. "Since yesterday afternoon, the search has concentrated where the boat was found, up here. Ottawa was a little reluctant to allow the Air Force into Canadian air space. RCC Toronto interceded on our behalf. We won't have results from that overflight until the film is developed and analyzed, so we can't expect anything from them until sometime tomorrow. Meanwhile we've got a helicopter from Traverse City, a pair of 140-foot cutters and a small boat from the station in Sault Sainte Marie covering the area."

While the Coast Guard cutters and boats scoured the surface, an Air Force spy plane flew overhead in a very exact grid, photographing every square foot of the search area. When the film – sometimes literally miles of it – was developed, trained analysts would go over it with magnifying glasses. In one case off New England, they discovered a sunken fishing boat, submerged 25 feet below the surface, that had eluded the Coast Guard's search for a week.

Many things were becoming really clear fast. First, this meeting had been called because of Andrews' intuition about the message traffic, which explained the lieutenant's nervousness. Junior officers put their careers on the line every time they speak to a captain or admiral because captains sit on their promotion board, and admirals approve the board's recommendations.

Second, nobody in the room thought this was a simple disappearance. The weather and sea conditions were too calm to challenge either the boat or coxswain. And the early morning cruise may not have been authorized, but it was no thrill; nobody goes for a joy ride that early on a Monday morning.

The shorter captain turned to me, removed his black service-issue eyeglasses, and tapped them on the table pensively. At the air station, we called them birth-control bifocals because guys who wear them look like geeks and never get dates. "So, what do you think, Galloway?" he asked.

9

"Well, sir, like Dorothy said, things just seem to get curiouser and curiouser."

The commandant scowled at me. "You've got the basics, and Lieutenant Andrews has prepared a briefing folder for you. Any other questions?"

I shook my head, feeling well chastised for joking; it was one tough room.

"Good, I'd like to see you in my office before you leave for Michigan." Thorne turned to his aide. "Pete, I want Galloway on 01 by 1500. Arrange a car and tell the pilots to get ready."

I felt flattered that the admiral would put me on CG01 – his private aircraft. Still, if I had known I was heading for the Upper Peninsula of Michigan, I'd have brought my fishing gear along instead of leaving it locked in the trunk of the Firebird back in Boston. It occurred to me that I was on authorized leave, my first time off in more than three years, but it is useless to argue with the man who wears the stars. I nodded and followed the admiral down the hall, through the glass doors, and into his private office – the Coast Guard's Inner Sanctum.

The commandant's office walls were covered with plaques from all the Coast Guard units he had visited, more than 200, I guessed, the engraved souvenirs hung in a simple grid on the dark paneling. A large lens from a lighthouse, an antique beveled-glass optic circa the 1860s, was the base of a round table set between two sofas. A long, oak work table filled one corner; its broad surface covered with neat stacks of voluminous reports.

Admiral Thorne let me enter and slammed the door behind me.

"You insolent bastard!" he snapped, "this isn't the time for jokes."

Then he smiled and held out his hand. I liked Admiral Arthur Thorne; he was a tough but good-natured guy, one of the few Coast Guard officers with combat experience still on active duty, experience he acquired as skipper of a patrol boat during Operation Market Time. He had safely brought his crew and cutter through several brutal firefights with armed junks moving supplies and munitions south along the coastline to aid the Viet Cong. Thorne earned more military decorations during his three decades of service than any Coast Guardsman still on active duty. He wore only the three highest commendations in a single row over his left breast pocket, including a Silver Star. He wasn't flashy, and I admire modesty in an admiral.

"Sorry, Admiral," I said as contritely as possible without groveling.

"You know, not every officer has my good sense of humor. Keep that in mind before you quote old movies in staff meetings."

"Yes, Admiral." Always the safest response.

Thorne leaned back against his mahogany desk and folded his arms. The long tattoo of a tall ship looked conspicuous on his forearm. I'd wondered for years where he'd wound up under a paint needle because it's rare to see such skin art among the officer corps. Had a younger Lieutenant Thorne taken an extended, intoxicated R&R in Saigon?

"Look, Marty, I'm sorry to pull you off leave – I hear you haven't had much time off lately – but this is damn important to me. I knew you'd feel the same way."

"I'll do my best, Admiral," I said.

"I know you will, that's why I asked for you. This couldn't have happened at a worse time. We're having a helluva budget fight this year. And there's been a bunch of crap on the network news lately about Coasties in Florida helping drug smugglers. They've got reporters digging up cases that are five years old and talking to guys we court-martialed and put in jail. It's all bullshit, but these reporters keep pushing it. So, until we know what the hell's going on, I've told the folks in Sault Sainte Marie not to say anything to the press or the families. One of the crew is married, and his wife was told. That's as far as it goes." He sounded angry and frustrated at being under regular attack from all quarters. "I don't want to look like some jackass who can't keep track of his own folks. That means I can only give you 72 hours to work this out. And I can't give you any help. If I sent a dozen special agents charging into Michigan, it'd be the same as holding a press conference in my skivvies."

I fought hard to push that particular image out of my mind. "Well, sir, I like a challenge."

"I know that; I read the Morgenstern case file." He reached

back on his desk and found a rigid blue folder. "I suppose you should have a ceremony with this, or a court-martial – I don't know which, but there isn't time. You should wear the uniform more often so you could show off your decorations," he joked. Since I wore the Coast Guard blues at Headquarters only by his personal direction, I wasn't amused. "Good work on that, even if you did piss off the Mexican government. Nailing Morgenstern was worth the heat."

"I don't guess I got this job on the basis of my diplomatic skills," I observed.

"No, and try not to annoy the Canadians. I want you to find the crew, not cause another international incident." He moved around behind his desk and settled into a leather executive chair. "If the State Department calls, I'm gonna say, 'Marty who?'" The admiral tugged off his steel-rimmed glasses, let them fall onto the desk blotter, and pinched his eyes shut between his thumb and forefinger. He sat motionless, his breath short and shallow. Finally, he lifted his shoulders and looked up again. "You look just like him. Except he always kept his uniform neat, even in that damn jungle." He frowned. "How's your mother doing?"

"She's good, Admiral. I went to see her last week."

Thorne nodded. "I'll see that you get some time off when this is done." He held out his hand, and I shook it again. The muscles of his forearm flexed, billowing out the sails of the tattoo schooner. "But remember, 72 hours."

I thanked the admiral and headed out to his aide's desk when Thorne called me back. "I think you screwed up back there, Marty. Seems to me it was Alice who said things get curiouser and curiouser in Wonderland, not Dorothy in Oz," the admiral said.

I nodded. "I'll be more careful in the future."

Thorne waved me off in dismissal. "Be careful in Michigan. Your mother needs you."

The commandant's aide stood at his desk outside the commandant's door, talking with Andrews. A sharp-looking seaman – from the Ceremonial Honor Guard, judging by her starched edges and polished surfaces – stood near the glass doors, guarding my luggage. The Lieutenant Commander referred to as "Pete" beckoned with a crooked forefinger for me to join them at his desk.

"Mr. Andrews will brief you on the way to the airport," he told me. "The pilots have started the pre-flight check, so you should be in Traverse City well before 1800. Your travel orders are in your briefing package. They authorize any reasonable expense but keep receipts; it'll make things easier for everyone." He paused to think if he'd forgotten anything, loudly cracking the knuckles of both hands. When he shrugged, I started toward the door. "Good luck, Marty." Pete reached across the desk to shake my hand. "The admiral is depending on you."

The seaman led the way out to the elevator and down to the underground parking garage, where a long, black Chrysler sat in the NO PARKING zone. The lieutenant and I settled in the back seat. Within a few minutes, the sedan was out in the daylight, moving north toward the city.

Andrews sat close against my right side and talked into my ear. "I haven't been in the Intel branch long, but this one sounded funny when I read the message traffic. Four people come in early for duty, take the small boat without permission, lie about where they're going and then completely disappear after seven hours of radio silence. So, last night I did a little digging into personnel records, and it was very interesting. You've got copies in here along with your travel orders." He laid a bulky brown envelope on my lap. "Look at the performance evaluations of the missing crew. They all took a nose-dive about a year and a half ago, about the same time the station got a new officer in charge. And the coxswain was brought up on charges along with another bosun who was booted out of the service."

I was impressed; this lieutenant had done his homework. "So why aren't you going to Michigan?" I asked.

He frowned, then smiled over it. "Three reasons, none of which I liked very much. First, my captain wanted a cowboy instead of the agents from the district office, and everyone named you right off, even the commandant."

I laughed. "It's nice to be popular; it's hell to be the rage."

"Second, it may be a problem among enlisted people, and you'll get more cooperation than an officer. And last, in case you haven't noticed, I'm black and if things got rough up there I might not get the, uh, support I needed."

"I'll admit I don't stay current on census figures, but aren't there a lot of Blacks in Michigan?"

"Down around Detroit sure, but where you're going is 300 miles and 100 years from Detroit. I was on a summer training cruise aboard the *Mackinaw* out of Cheboygan back when I was a lowly cadet. I came close to going home in a box."

"Nobody warned you about ship's food?" I once made the mistake of eating galley goop; lucky for me, the corpsman onboard was more proficient than the cook.

"The crew was having a party in the woods south of town. A few townies showed up, and then a few more. I made the mistake of talking to a white girl cause there were no black girls in town. On my next trip out to the little boy's tree, I had a lot of company." Andrews' voice came in a low rumble, like slag down a coal chute. "I ended up with a concussion and three broken ribs."

"How did it get settled?" I asked.

"I went to the skipper the next morning and got my butt transferred out of there that afternoon. There are some fights you can't win." He turned and smiled at me. "But I'm a black belt in karate now."

By then, the Chrysler was rounding the ramp from the 14th Street Bridge to head south toward National Airport, the tan hulk of the Pentagon out the left window. We headed south on the George Washington Parkway – directly back the way I had come from National Airport an hour earlier. Except for the heartwarming chat with my father's former commanding officer, the whole visit could have been covered in a three-minute phone call.

Andrews leaned back to my ear. "I live 10 minutes from Headquarters, so I can go in any time, day or proverbial night. Just call my office. But you've seen the neighborhood around there, so please use some discretion after midnight."

I looked at him in shock. I usually couldn't even expect bail money when I went on a case, and here was a fellow – an officer, no less – volunteering to play backfield. Andrews might be good in fieldwork; he seemed to understand that most of the game was about background investigation – tedious computer checks and time-consuming file searches. Very little law enforcement is done in the Hollywood style, with lots of gunplay and high-speed chases. But somehow, I managed to get myself assigned to the rough and tussle.

Andrews continued speaking in low tones so the driver could not overhear. "I have to warn you that the commandant is very serious about this 72-hour time limit. There was a big go-round at the staff briefing because the 0-6 in public affairs wanted to make a release. You know – bad news doesn't get better, blah, blah, blah. That captain was pissed when the commandant shut him down in mid-sentence."

"I thought that was standard policy," I observed, nodding. "What's the expression; 'Maximum disclosure, minimum delay'?"

"Not this time. The commandant figures it's better to release the bad news at the same time as the good. He's betting that you'll find them before we're forced to go public."

"Why the gamble?" I wondered aloud, knowing admirals do not become admirals by taking unnecessary risks.

"He didn't tell you?" Andrews sounded surprised. "Next Monday, the admiral goes before the Senate Appropriations Committee to ask them to restore a twelve-percent bite they took out of our operations budget for next fiscal year. They also cut out funding for our new icebreaker. Next day he's in Hawaii for a sit down with the Navy's top brass about high-seas interdiction of aliens. From there, he goes to Hong Kong to raise hell about the Chinese fishing fleet poaching in the Bering Sea."

"And bad press won't make any of that easier," I observed.

Andrews grinned as he saw the realization dawn on my military mind. "Yeah, so when I heard all that, I wasn't so upset. I'll get the credit for spotting the problem, but you'll get the blame if things don't work out."

"How did you guys pick me? Doesn't it say in my record that I get nosebleeds at high latitudes?"

Andrews chuckled. "I didn't see your personnel jacket, but from what I hear it's plenty full. Did you kick a lieutenant commander in the face?"

"Well, yes, sir, but there's a lot more to the story." I paused and thought about what he'd hear if he asked around among my fellow special agents. "And there's a lot less to it than what people'll tell you."

We entered the airport traffic maze and drove to a hangar south of the air freight companies. Coast Guard Air Station Washington has only one aircraft – CG01 – and one mission: to be ready to launch at the commandant's instant summons. Inside the terminal, Andrews introduced me to the pilot and crew. At the same time, the driver hustled my bags from the Chrysler's trunk, through the open bay door, and out to the tarmac. One of the aircrew took my baggage from her and hoisted it aboard.

Andrews shook my hand, and I gave him a quick salute, wondering how long he'd remain in the service. The problem with the Coast Guard's rank pyramid is that many bright junior officers soon realize there's only so much room at the top.

I climbed aboard the sleek Gulfstream twin-prop and strapped myself into a plush seat. It could have been any corporate aircraft except for the distinctive Coast Guard red and blue racing stripes around the nose.

We taxied out to the main airstrip and were in the air within minutes, cutting ahead of three commercial airliners waiting for a clear runway. Had Admiral Thorne called the control tower to arrange priority clearance for CG01? The Coast Guard and the FAA fall under the Department of Transportation, and rank has privileges.

I could relax after meeting the pilots at the controls. Dinner that afternoon was one of those infamous box lunches for which air stations are notorious: Slick bologna and dry cheese between two slabs of stale white. The service promises three square meals a day, but it usually refers to the shape of the box. I suspected that the admiral received a little more refined cuisine when he flew.

During the flight, I took out my eyeglasses and read through the copies of each personnel jacket that Andrews had put in the thick envelope. The missing boat's coxswain was Henry Pelligrini, a boatswain mate with eight years of service, all at small boat stations. He finished at the top of his class at both heavy weather coxswain

16

school at Cape Disappointment and maritime law enforcement school in Yorktown, Virginia. His record swelled with citations. The boat's engineer was Paul Desharnais, a recent arrival at the station after six years on the West Coast. He'd served on an icebreaker and, more recently, a patrol boat. Desharnais was the only one married among the four. The seaman aboard was Patricia Lucas, who had been at the station just a year while waiting for orders to health service technician school.

The fourth crewman was Walter Kunken, also a boatswain mate. Kunken and Pelligrini were both second-class petty officers, but Kunken was almost five years senior. As I read the file, I felt Kunken was like myself – a bit of an outlaw. His record contained plenty of reprimands and poor evaluations. On the other hand, he'd earned some impressive awards, including a Silver Lifesaving Medal. An eight-year-old girl had fallen through the ice while skating. Kunken tied a rope around his waist and plunged through the hole after her. As I read the account in the file, I shook my head in astonishment; you have to admire that kind of courageous foolhardiness or foolhardy courage.

Andrews was right about their performance marks. I wished he had included more about Raymond Drucker, the new senior chief boatswain's mate and officer in charge at the station. Still, the personnel office on base would have that information. However, the lieutenant had saved me hours of mind-numbing background work by asking the special agents at Headquarters to do quick background checks on each of the missing crew, which Andrews had summarized for me. Kunken and Pelligrini held secret clearances; Lucas' background check had been initiated but was not yet complete. Desharnais had held a top-secret clearance while serving on the Ceremonial Honor Guard. The TS is required for every member of the elite squad who performs at White House functions.

Police checks showed no outstanding warrants for any of the four. Desharnais and Pelligrini had spotless records. Kunken had two speeding tickets over the previous five years. Eight months earlier, Lucas had bounced a rent payment when her paycheck was deposited into the electronic ether after a computer at the Pay and Personnel Center erased her from its mind. Otherwise, their credit records were solid, though Kunken carried a heavy debt burden for his income. Andrews wrote a note in the margin indicating that Kunken was still paying alimony and child support.

The package the lieutenant had prepared also contained a thick stack of message traffic from the case, organized chronologically according to Greenwich Mean Time, or Zulu. On top of the stack was the initial report from the small boat station in Sault Ste. Marie informing the Group Operations Center in Sault Ste. Marie that their 44-footer had been found adrift by the Mounties.

FM COGARD STA SAULT STE MARIE MI//
TO ZEN/
INFO ZEN/COGARD GRU SAULT STE MARIE MI
BT
UNCLASS//N16130//
SUBJ: DISTRESS SITREP ONE: CG44323 ADRIFT
1. SITUATION:
A. RCVD REPORT FM RCMP OF A USCG 44-FOOT UTB ADRIFT IN AGAWA BAY. RCMP REPORT 0 POB. ISSUED SHOTGUN BROADCAST CH-16 VHF-FM. CONDUCTED PRECOMS, EXCOMS. NEGRES. REQ DIVERT BUCK-THORN AND NEAH BAY. REQ LAUNCH OF READY SAR AIRCRAFT.
B. SEARCH AREAS: LEACH ISLAND TO SAULT STE MARIE.
C. O/S WX: CEIL 5000/SCT, VIS 10NM, WND 200/5KTS, SEAS 1-3FT.
D. VSL/PER INFO: 44-FOOT UTB, STEEL, WHITE W/ RED-BLUE STRIPE
O/O: STA SAULT STE MARIE
E. SMC: STA SAULT STE MARIE
2. ACTION:
A. 141224Z RCVD INITIAL RPT FM CG44323 UTB U/W 4POB.
B. 1235Z ATTEMPTED TO CONTACT CG44323. NO JOY.
C. 1918Z RCVD RPT FM RCMP OF VESSEL ADRIFT.
D. 2020Z RCMP ADVISED VESSEL IS CG44323. NO CREW ABOARD.

E. 1955Z CG STA SOO RELIEVED RCMP OF TOW AT
GROS CAP LIGHT.
3. STA SAULT STE MARIE SORTIE DATA:
2.4 HOURS TOW RELIEF
4. FUTURE PLANS/RECOMMENDATIONS:
A. CASE PENDS.
B. REQUEST APPROPRIATE SAR ASSETS TO
CONDUCT PIW SEARCH BETWEEN LEACH ISLAND AND
MONTREAL ISLAND.
BT
NNNN

Most of the time, I work in plain English, so it took me a while
to decode the cryptic shorthand of message traffic. The string of
acronyms, "RCVD INITIAL RPT FM CG44323 UTB U/W
4POB," translated to "Received initial report from the Coast Guard
44-foot utility boat, hull number 44323, that it was under way with
four people on board."

In the following messages, the group commander in Sault Ste.
Marie informed the district office in Cleveland of the disappearance and requested assistance. The District Rescue Coordination
Center sent additional messages, instructing cutters to get
underway and ordering the air station in Traverse City to launch
sufficient aircraft to cover the designated coordinates. On separate
pages were the responses of each unit as they completed a phase of
their instructions. Every four hours, the cutters issued SITREPS –
situation reports – that provided search planners with the ship's
location, their activities for the previous four hours and their plan
of action for the next four. Each time an aircraft landed, a message
from the air station described its search pattern, the weather on
scene and the results of the sortie. Every message from Air Station
Traverse City in the stack ended with the same NEGRES – negative results.

After reading first for comprehension, I studied the Operational
Summaries, or OPSUMs, to examine the detail, even sketching out
the coverage patterns as best I could on scrap paper. According to
the operations summaries, the search was so intensive it had a 92
percent chance of locating bodies in the water, and that's about as

thorough as you can get without running Lake Superior through a strainer.

Many folks think search and rescue is based on good luck: the boats go out, the crews look around, and hopefully, they spot what they're hunting. But searches are almost mathematical equations, all based on weather, visibility, sea conditions, the size of the object and the direction the wind and waves would push it. The boats use radar, the aircraft carries infrared, and everything moves in precise geometric patterns plotted by computer. You don't save 4,500 lives a year with dumb luck. But sometimes, a little luck is a good thing.

Search and rescue is no longer my regular line of work. I'm now in Special Investigations, roughly equivalent to the internal affairs department of a metropolitan police department. Some folks in the service look at me like a ratfink, squealing on my kind. I've arrested deserters, embezzlers, drug dealers and child molesters; I don't consider them my kind. Most of the job is spent conducting routine investigations for security clearances and taking fingerprints, but sometimes a case gets interesting like this one. I'm no Sherlock Holmes, but I enjoy a little chase and a bit of action. That's why I enlisted in the service to fly on a helicopter crew and then went into CGI when problems with my eyesight bumped me off flight duty.

At the bottom of the message traffic was the thick blue folder Admiral Thorne had given me. Inside were a certificate and the

CITATION TO ACCOMPANY THE AWARD OF THE
COAST GUARD ACHIEVEMENT MEDAL
(GOLD STAR IN LIEU OF A THIRD)
TO
MARTIN L. GALLOWAY
AVIATION SURVIVALMAN CHIEF
UNITED STATES COAST GUARD

Chief Petty Officer GALLOWAY is cited for superior performance of duty while on Temporary Assigned Duty to the First Coast Guard District. Demonstrating exceptional professional expertise and an aggressive commitment to BLAH, BLAH, BLAH, BLAH. The apprehension and subsequent detainment of Petty

Officer First Class Stephen Morgenstern for desertion and BLAH, BLAH, BLAH, BLAH. Chief GALLOWAY's dedication, judgment and devotion to duty are most heartily commended and are in keeping with the highest BLAH, BLAH, BLAH, BLAH.

Like every citation, the official language didn't tell an accurate story. Morgenstern was a yeoman for the chief of Coast Guard operations in Boston back when there was still a substantial fishing industry off New England. I went there to track down whether somebody in the law enforcement branch accepted cash to forget about prosecuting fisheries violations. More boats were being boarded, and there were plenty of violations, but the number of cases getting to court fell way short of what everyone thought it should be. Soon after I arrived in town, many people in the harbor suddenly knew who I was and why I was there. The Boston waterfront has a long history of illegal activity, dating back to John Hancock's smuggling before the Revolution. Rum-running during Prohibition involved everyone from greengrocers to Mafia to Beacon Hill denizens. Didn't take time, just cash, to learn how Morgenstern was involved in all that. Every time the Coast Guard office in Boston opened a new case file, Morgenstern contacted the interested parties and kept them apprised of the investigation, for a modest fee.

When he knew the gig was up, Morgenstern went south. Not hard to follow; he made flight reservations in his own name and used his own credit cards though he had packed a lot of cash. Upon arriving in Zacatecas, I carried no warrant, writ or extradition papers, but I did pack a cheap revolver I had purchased from a pawn shop in Mexico City. That convinced him I was serious. Then I had to convince the Mexican Federales it wasn't a mere kidnapping, which has become, of late, a rather popular source of revenue among ambitious entrepreneurs from Mexico down to Brazil. After two days of negotiations with the State Department and some rough interrogation sessions in a jail cell that left me pissing blood for a week, the Mexicans put the two of us on a plane to Houston, where I turned Morgenstern over to the FBI.

My Mexican jaunt made many people unhappy because the commandant was then negotiating joint operations with Mexico and other countries down the isthmus that would exchange our operational expertise for their narco-intelligence. Several senior officers suggested that hauling me up on charges would demonstrate good faith with our southern neighbors. Admiral Thorne refused to convene a court-martial, largely because of my family name. I'm still trying to repay that debt.

Tuesday 1715

The commandant's jet touched down in Traverse City on the far west edge of Michigan at the start of a warm evening when the *ephemerella lata* hatch would draw trout up from the cold depths, and a quick cast with a slate-wing olive fly could snag a nice catch. We taxied away from the main terminal, distinguishable by the square tower topped by an octagonal control room. We headed toward a remote side of the field away from the hangars and rows of private aircraft; a dozen Piper Cubs, a corporate Bell helo and two unmarked Lear jets – Traverse City enjoyed a positive cash flow.

CG01 rolled to a stop near a line of official vehicles; two Michigan highway patrol cruisers sat fore and aft of a forest green Lincoln Town Car with dark-tinted windows. Somehow I suspected they weren't all awaiting my imminent arrival, other than the tan Dodge sedan with Coast Guard decals parked at the end of the line that had been dispatched to haul me to the air station. The other vehicles were a mystery. A crewman came back from the cockpit to where I sat and helped me with my bags.

The cabin depressurized when we rolled to a stop, and the crewman lowered the small stairway. The engines still whined shrilly as we hustled across the tarmac toward the Dodge, where a petty officer climbed out of the driver's seat and opened the trunk. After he hurled my bags into the Dodge, the aircrewman scooted over to the Lincoln, where a goon in a dark suit and mirrored sunglasses stacked a dozen pieces of matching luggage at the bumper. A second crewman scurried out from CG01, and they whisked the suitcases aboard without delay.

The petty officer slammed the trunk closed and headed for the driver's side without any greeting or acknowledgment of my existence. As I hopped into the passenger's side, a svelte young woman emerged from the back seat of the Town Car. She wore a pale blue polo shirt, white shorts and $200 running shoes. She scanned the area, raised high on her toes by muscular calves and taut thighs, then she shook back her blonde mane and put on a pair of blue-rimmed sunglasses that matched her shirt. A swarm of three giants converged around her. They moved toward CG01 in unison. Each bodyguard kept a hand thrust inside the lapel of their sports coat, prepared for the Gunfight at OK Corral to erupt on the small Michigan airstrip.

"Who's the lady?" I asked the driver as he ground the car's ignition. "The president's mistress?"

"Shit! Try Assistant Fucking Secretary of Transportation." He spat out the words as if trying to dislodge a wad of chewing tobacco from his throat. "Snotty bitch from a rich family. She flies in here all the time to go sailing on Traverse Bay. Heard she wanted to be an ambassador, but her daddy didn't put enough cash into the president's campaign, so we got stuck with her instead. Pure goddam politics is all."

"Whoa, sounds like a serious attitude problem there," I joked. By then, we were headed across the empty airfield toward an open gate in the chain link fence, moving at a speed that must have alarmed the air traffic controllers watching from their glass tower.

"Maybe, but I fucking earned it. Look at me; a first class with a bachelor's degree, pilot's license, medals up the wazoo." He tapped two fingers against the rows of ribbons over his left pocket for emphasis. "You know, I've applied for OCS three times and here I sit."

I examined him for obvious defects that would bar him from Officer Candidate School. He looked like a Coast Guard poster boy; high-and-tight haircut, bulging biceps, trim waist and starched uniform. Whether his brightly sunburned neck was coincidence or irony, I couldn't decide until he spoke again.

"So I read the new OCS list that came out yesterday, and half are women and the other half are Castro or Ho Che Minh. I know they gotta have quotas, but they oughta be fair about it."

I wondered how this conversation would go if Lieutenant Andrews made the trip in my stead.

Poster Boy raged on as we passed through the terminal parking and rental car lots. About a half mile up the road, he cut an abrupt right turn through another gate, slowed to wave his middle finger at a surveillance camera mounted on a traffic island, then made another hard right toward a corrugated-steel hangar. As we rounded the corner onto a wide tarmac, I saw the words U.S. Coast Guard painted on the tall doors. At that moment, the rotor of an HH-3F helo on the far side of the field cranked around.

"An assistant secretary is given protection?" I asked.

"Those goons? Private company. One was ex-Special Forces in Panama."

The Sikorsky H-3 is a big, ugly helicopter with a blunt nose and a square body. Two wide, flat pontoons protrude from either side, enabling the H-3 to land in the water to pick up survivors. With trained rescue swimmers now, the pilots don't do it very often anymore. Instead, swimmers are lowered into the water to affect the rescue – a procedure much safer for the remaining helicopter crew than the rescue swimmer. But risking one life makes more sense than risking four. The H-3's cockpit and the tail vertical are painted fluorescent orange; the rest of the body is white. The most distinguishable feature is a black bulb that houses the navigational instruments poking out from the nose. The H-3s may be an unsightly aircraft, but they are incredibly roomy inside. Like one H-3 pilot said, you can put many people on an H-3, as many as a dozen, and there's nothing worse than leaving someone behind treading water. On more than one occasion, that someone left behind was me.

The number on the tail of the helo looked familiar. CG 9691. After a few moments spent rummaging through the cranium, I remembered flying 9691 while stationed in Kodiak. When I flew them, the service had only about three dozen of those wonderful old Sikorsky birds, so they were passed from air station to air station as they went through maintenance and overhaul. The number was far lower now. Most air stations had already switched over to the H-3's replacement – the HH-60 Jayhawk. Soon 9691 would be retired along with the rest.

"Good timing," I laughed as we headed toward the ready helo, assuming I wasn't getting much of a layover in Traverse City.

"Actually you're late, we originally expected you on the USAir flight at four. Then we were told you were coming on 01 when it came for the Ass Secretary."

"An earlier flight?" I wondered aloud.

"Yeah, they said . . ." He paused and gave me a sidelong look as he stopped the car and shoved the lever into Park. Then he laughed

25

fiercely. "Hey, you didn't think they'd fly the admiral's jet all the way out here just for you, did ya?" He shook his head in disbelief and continued chuckling in glee as we hauled my bags to the open door of the helo.

I've been around choppers for most of my twelve years in the service, but I still hunch down a little when I go under the spinning rotor blades. In Alaska, I once saw a bald eagle make an unsuccessful pass through those whirling guillotine blades, and the pilots needed the wipers to see through the blood-smeared windscreen. Watching that eagle explode into giblets taught me unquestioned respect for helo rotors. We were lucky the carcass wasn't sucked into the turbine intake – the quickest way to drop a helicopter. No doubt a helo pilot coined the expression: Gravity sucks.

An H-3 crewman stowed my gear in the rear of the helo while I climbed aboard. While the crew finished pre-flight checks, I moved to the canvas sling seats along the wall and fastened the seat belt. Through the open door of the helo, I spotted one of the new Jayhawks, another Sikorsky bird, though smaller and sleeker. If the H-3 were an Airbus, the H-60 would be an F-14. Known as the Blackhawk and the Seahawk by other military services, the Jayhawk is built for speed and mobility. I had refused to fly on the new helos – either the Jayhawk or the smaller HH-65A Dolphin – out of principle. Somehow that smacked of adultery or incest – to abandon the old bird that had hoisted me into her bosom from the frothy surf so many times to run off with one of her much younger sisters. Sure, technology changes with the times, but loyalty shouldn't. I still drive the vintage Firebird my father bought while on a state-side leave just ten weeks before his patrol boat was sunk. When I can no longer keep it running, it'll be time to surrender my driver's license.

Another crew member, a young woman with wisps of blonde bangs curling up from under the visor of her helmet, put a headset on me that was wired into the aircraft's intercom network. She tapped one earpiece with a forefinger.

"Have you ever flown on a helicopter before?" she asked, more to check for sound than personal interest.

I adjusted my mouthpiece so the small microphone was below my lips. I pressed the plunger of the talk switch located on my tether and asked, "Does three years on an H-3 in Kodiak count?" I smiled, lifting the lapel of my rumpled jacket to show the silver wings of my aircrew insignia.

Her eyes grew wide. She wasn't expecting anyone sent from Headquarters to come equipped with a clue. She nodded and said into the IC, "Sure, that'll do."

Finally, the crew settled into place and checked their own harnesses; the woman at the communications console that also served as a chart table for navigation, the flight mechanic in the big steel gunner's chair. The pilots were already strapped into their seats in the small cockpit. The engine began to groan louder, and we lifted into the air. Compared with the commandant's jet, the H-3's interior was hopelessly crude. The steel exposed frame revealed hundreds of wires and cables running in every direction. Sure, the H-3 is ugly inside and out, but I miss it sometimes.

The entire crew wore pale blue coveralls, and I felt out of place climbing around a helicopter in a dress uniform, like wearing a tuxedo to a regatta. My old-fashioned green flight suit is now reserved for working under the Firebird.

The pilots heard that I was former aircrew, so they asked when I was in Alaska and who was there at the time. We traded names, and nobody seemed surprised that almost everyone we mentioned had left the service for the money commercial airlines offer aviators and flight mechanics with Coast Guard experience. It had been several years since I'd used an aircraft intercom, and it took a few tries to get accustomed to the squawk and the talk switch on the tether.

"Were you in Kodiak when the H-3 crashed?" the co-pilot asked.

"No," I said, and the subject changed. Talking about accidents is a jinx.

I had left Kodiak before the crash. The H-3, CG-1473, was my old aircraft. I'd flown hundreds of missions on that helo. If I'd remained on flight duty, I may have had duty that foggy evening when the helo slammed into a mountainside, killing everyone aboard. I knew the entire flight crew, and they were fine people. Still, I couldn't stop thinking that if I'd been there, I might have remembered the lay of the islands along the coast, done something, anything – the 'what if' thinking that drives you crazy.

"How'd you go from flying to CGI?" the pilot asked, a slight tone of derision in his voice.

"My eyes went bad. On the duty roster, the senior chief listed me as Petty Officer Magoo," I joked.

They all laughed. The pilot slapped the co-pilot on the shoulder, and the helo took an alarming dip to starboard.

Actually, I didn't go blind or walk into walls. Six months after being promoted to petty officer first class, I began getting powerful headaches during low-altitude maneuvers. The pain radiated from a point on the bridge of my nose, centered between my pupils, as you'd get from looking cross-eyed too long. Soon after the headaches became regular, my peripheral vision shrank as dark shadows edged my field of view. The contract optometrist on the island referred me to Elmendorf Air Force Base outside Anchorage. From there, I was sent on to specialists at Scott Air Force Base and finally Walter Reed, each transfer on a leap-frogging med flight that seemed to exacerbate the problem. Repeated tests, examinations, and scans of my skull revealed that I reported identical symptoms in various conditions.

Unable to find an organic cause, the doctors at Walter Reed called in a psychiatrist. After asking about my flight history for 15 minutes, the dapper young dream doctor told me there was nothing shameful about psychosomatic illnesses. He explained my hidden motives; my fear of failure in a demanding job, my obsessive desire to help the sailor and thus save my father, and my subconscious comprehension of my inadequacy in these tasks and my mortality.

I suggested he was crazy.

He stormed out in anger but returned the next day to apologize. He said that he had described our entire interview to his wife. When he told her my response, she burst into laughter. Then he finally understood my point; being called delusional was more insulting than he first guessed.

I asked how often he violated doctor-patient confidence.

At that point, the specialists surrendered and shipped me back to Kodiak. After four additional months grounded, my normal sight returned without correction or medication. Three weeks after returning to flight duty, the headaches and tunnel vision became so extreme that I felt uncomfortable driving my truck around base. Thus ended my legendary career long before the first balladeer started humming my theme music.

Because I wouldn't ever fly again, I wanted to change jobs. In the wake of special agent school in Virginia, I was assigned to Headquarters. After serving a life sentence at Buzzards Point, I conned the personnel detailer into transferring me to the district office in Juneau. My wife Brenda decided the day before the movers arrived that she never wanted to see Alaska again. She took Toby and Anne back to Ohio, and I had the household goods shipped to her there. Two weeks after I arrived in Juneau, this time as a special agent, CG-1473 went down while flying a doctor to a remote native village on Kodiak Island's south end. My old helo became my first big investigation.

I leaned close to the window and watched the land below.

"Whereabouts are we?" I asked.

"Still over the lower peninsula," the crewman answered.

"Would you like the grand tour?" the pilot asked.

"Sure, if you guys have the time," I said. "It might come in handy to know the terrain a little."

The crewman in the gunner's seat swung back, took off his own harness as he came over to me and strapped it around my waist. I moved to his seat, and he swung me into the doorway. I've ridden at the door many times, but I still feel a rush of adrenaline from the view, the wind, and the noise of the rotors. Though strapped down and held by the tether attached to the waist belt, I felt a touch of acrophobia with nothing between me and the ground but 30 seconds of pointless screaming.

The Michigan countryside below looked pristine, a dark green carpet of forests and fields stretching in all directions; its uneven shag dissected at irregular angles by gray threads of asphalt. We passed over a dozen small towns the crewman identified for me: Central Lake, East Jordan, Boyne City, Burt Lake, Topinabee, Indian River; most no more than a dozen houses surrounding a gas station or a convenience store.

The co-pilot narrated the trip for me. "That group of lakes is the inland waterway – you can sail from Lake Michigan to Lake Huron without going all the way around. It's for motorboats that don't want to risk the Straits of Mackinac; it can get pretty rough up there. I've heard the inland route makes a good fishing trip, too."

My ears perked up at the slightest mention, and I began to plan a vacation for the next time I had a chance to take leave. Exactly when that might be was impossible to predict. The service grants you 30 days of leave each year without guarantee you can take any of it.

By comparison with the hamlets we passed over earlier, Cheboygan was a booming metropolis, with a few hundred houses, stores and buildings. In the Cheboygan River's mouth sat the icebreaker *Mackinaw*, the largest Coast Guard cutter on the Great Lakes. At 290 feet long and 74 feet wide, it looks like a bathtub, but it cuts a swath through ice that any freighter can glide through. As we passed overhead, a dozen crewmen on deck paused to wave their paint brushes. There isn't any ice in those waters during the summer, so the *Mackinaw* pulls three months of public relations duty, hitting every summer festival on the Lakes – the service's showboat in the Midwest. The crew spends the ice-free seasons sprucing up for the tourists or gearing up for the winter months.

We passed over the northern end of Lake Huron. The lake narrows there, with three green islands jammed in the neck. The largest and southernmost island is Bois Blanc; the smallest is a bare knob called Round Island. The island at the north end of the chain is Mackinac, a resort famous for its Victorian-era hotels and lack of automobiles. My ex-wife could watch that movie every night without tiring.

"West of the bridge is Lake Michigan," the pilot explained. "Most of the large traffic past here is headed for Milwaukee or the steel mills in Indiana."

Short in length and low to the water, a small freighter sailed toward the bridge, billowing heavy black smoke from its stack. At first glance, I thought it was on fire.

"Look at that old relic," the crewman called, motioning toward it.

"Yeah, the S.T. Crapo," the co-pilot said, pronouncing it Craypo. "The last coal-burner in the Great Lakes after the state retired their old railroad ferry. The Crapo must be almost 90 years old. It runs cement from Rogers City or Alpena over to Michigan City."

The crewman pointed toward the town of St. Ignace on the northern side of Mackinaw Strait and told me about a small Coast Guard base located there. The pilot banked us around before we reached the Mackinaw Bridge, a huge suspension span across the five-mile gap between Michigan's lower and upper peninsula. We turned away from the bridge and started back east along the northern shore of Lake Huron.

"We're heading for the St. Mary's River," the pilot said. "It runs from Huron up to the Soo locks and Lake Superior."

The co-pilot spoke up. "The river is also the border. East shore is Canada; west is U.S."

The blue water below changed to green and then murky brown as we passed from the lake over the shallow river. The two shorelines drew to less than 200 yards apart. "Pretty narrow through here," I observed. "Is there much smuggling?"

The pilot answered. "Could be some liquor and cigarettes passing back and forth. Most of that action is down in Detroit and Lake Erie – more people down there. Now and again there'll be a big operation, and a lot of people get busted. AirSta Detroit flies surveillance on that stuff."

"What about getting stuff from freighters as they come up river?" I asked.

"That'd be risky. The river's under a vessel traffic system. The freighters that go through are monitored for speed to prevent accidents and wake damage, and the Captain of the Port can fine speeders. If they don't radio in from each checkpoint on time, there'd be questions. They could drop something, but there are a lot of homes along the waterfront. Someone would see it." The pilot knew the area well.

Suddenly the woman at the comms table began scribbling on a tablet. At the same time, a flurry of activity erupted in the cockpit. The co-pilot checked through several aerial charts, and the pilot examined each gauge on the wide, black control panel. He gave the co-pilot the thumbs-up sign. I knew the signs of a breaking SAR case before anyone said a word.

"Sorry to cut the tour short," the pilot finally explained. "The air station is diverting us to a possible sinker off Petoskey. We'll put down here long enough to drop you first."

I wanted to go with them on their rescue case. I miss the action or the adrenaline rush. But this crew trained together and knew how to respond as a team. Depending upon how many people were on the sinking boat, the crew might need to crowd the helo with survivors. I'd get in their way.

The crewman came and moved me out of the gunner's chair and back to the canvas bench seat along the wall. I snugged my seat-belt and asked, "How long before we arrive?"

"About three minutes," the co-pilot replied.

"What can you guys tell me about this search up here?" I hoped they knew something more than the official reports.

A long pause followed before the pilot spoke. "We've been told not to talk about anything, but I guess CGI is OK. We flew all night, low as I could go, excellent visibility, tight track spacing – it's all there in the case file they'll give you when you get to the Soo. If that crew was out there, we'd have seen them. You know how it is when you're looking for your own; you're very careful." He confirmed my analysis of the search patterns Andrews had provided.

"So, what do you think happened?" I asked

"There's got to be something more than what we've been told," the co-pilot said. "Four trained crewmen don't fall off a 44-footer and disappear without a trace."

Through the open door, I saw the outlines of a few buildings as we hovered over the rugged asphalt airfield. There was no other air traffic on a quiet Tuesday evening in late August. Most of the aircraft on the strip looked private except for a mini-jet from an express courier and an excursion airline twin-prop.

The touchdown came as soft as laying an infant in a crib. As I hopped to the ground, the crewman passed my baggage out, and I set it on the tarmac. I unhooked the lifebelt and gave it back. After thanking the pilots, I removed my headset and handed it to the crewman. He hooked an arm behind my head and pulled me close against his helmet.

"You bring them guys back alive, and I'll buy you a fucking beer," he yelled over the roaring swoosh of the rotors.

The airman let go. Then he gave me a thumbs-up. I waved, collected my baggage, and scrambled from under the whirling blades. When I was clear, the engine surged, and the big helo lifted free in a whirlwind of dust, leaves and litter. The prop wash nearly knocked me off balance before the helicopter gained sufficient altitude to start out over the chain link fence and the treetops.

I glanced up at the belly of the helo as it disappeared and spotted the familiar black lettering that spelled USCG. I had seen the bottom of quite a few hovering H-3s as a rescue swimmer, glancing up to get my bearings while thrashing through pounding surf to reach a person in the water, hoping that the helo wouldn't depart scene because of low fuel or an engine problem. Pilots call those in-flight emergencies, but any rescue swimmer who has been left behind adrift can tell you that the emergency is NOT in the air.

I was left behind twice, treading water for days, although the logbooks recorded less than an hour each time before my rescue arrived. Once a survivor went Code Blue in the basket during the hoist. As soon as the patient was in the door, the corpsman began CPR, and the helo banked away, kicking up a frothy white spray that blinded my eyes and swamped my respirator. Watching that Traverse City helo speed off to rescue the people sinking in Lake Michigan, I felt the same sense of desertion.

Tuesday: 1820

Only a few buildings comprised the Chippewa County International Airport, including hangars with a distinctive Air Force motif. A yellow building with a tan roof served as a terminal there, though the large panels of darkly tinted glass around one side gave it the appearance of an adult bookstore. I lugged my bags inside through the glass door and the unattended weapons detector. The small waiting area looked like a hospital lobby, with comfortable upholstered chairs and a pair of vending machines against the far wall.

Service counters took three corners of the room; one airline – Great Lakes Air, "Your Greatest Little Airline" – and two car rentals, Avis and Hertz, still battling it out on the very fringes of civilization. The Great Lakes Air counter sat deserted. Apart from the two car rental agents – both middle-aged women who glanced up as I came in but then returned to their knitting, only one other person sat in the waiting area; a young blond woman sitting erect in a lounge chair. As I approached, I saw she appeared dressed in the familiar light blue shirt and dark blue pants of the Coast Guard summer uniform. She was engaged in a dog-eared paperback of considerable heft. A hot-pink sock peeked out above the high top of her well-polished black work boot where her pants leg hiked up as she crossed her legs.

"Taxi? Can I get a lift into town?" I asked as a joke.

She stood and tucked the book under her left arm. When she faced me, I saw the twin silver bars on the tips of her collar. I realized I'd committed a terrible blunder of military etiquette.

"Galloway? I'm Sharon Dunlay, group operations officer." The lieutenant extended her hand, and I dropped my little black bag to shake it. "I'm glad you're here," she told me, lifting the load so I could balance the other two. She was tall and lithe, the kind of woman my grandmother would try to plump with a few extra pounds courtesy of a home-cooked meal or three. The starch in Dunlay's uniform kept her creases straight even as she moved. When she snugged a blue baseball cap on her head, her short hair stuck out on either side of her head like wings. She led the way out through the front entrance to the parking lot.

34

"This situation is a real puzzle, and we need a fast resolution. The commandant contacted the captain first thing this morning, and the captain made it clear he wasn't happy with our progress. I hadn't considered the need for CGI until Lieutenant Andrews briefed me on his ideas."

"But now you believe it's more than a search and rescue case?" I was starting to wonder if I was unaware of some obvious sinister sign – a ransom note or a bloody horse head.

She stopped and turned on me. "I know this hasn't run like any search I've ever done. I've got excellent coverage, great viz and a high probability of detection. You tell me why I can't find them."

"Could these four be involved in something?" I asked. "Anything illegal?"

"Not these people, definitely not. I know them; I've, uh, partied with them. They would not get involved in anything questionable."

I hedged a moment. "Anything personal between you and one of them?"

She halted again and turned to glare at me, then relaxed a little. "No, there was nothing intimate. In a town like this, Coasties are a close group. I've got plans that I won't screw up with any fraternization charges. But if you don't associate with Coasties here, you don't have a social life."

We walked over to her government vehicle – a nondescript tan sedan – opened the trunk and dropped my bags inside. She remained silent as she unlocked my door and walked back to the driver's side.

"I hope I didn't offend you," I said as she shifted the GV into gear.

"About being your taxi? Or the fraternization thing? No, Lieutenant Andrews warned me about your alleged humor." She smiled for the first time, a lop-sided grin that didn't quite fit her face. Lieutenant Dunlay looked too regulation to smile often.

Adjacent to the airport parking lot was a rusted factory similar to the steel mill in Ohio, where my grandfather worked for 37 years. When I asked about the airport's military look, she explained that the field was once Kincheloe Air Force Base, which closed in 1974.

We headed west from the airport, passing modest cabins and

mobile homes. The road doubled as a scenic tour of classical lawn art, from plastic flamingoes to upturned bathtubs sheltering cement Madonnas. After a few miles, we intersected Interstate 75 and turned north toward Sault Ste. Marie. The titanic recreation vehicles dwarfed the other cars on the highway during the late summer afternoon. The RVs floated across the road like dirigibles. Dunlay seemed apprehensive about passing a few that wobbled to and fro across their lane and, on occasion, strayed across the white centerline. I used the hour to quiz Dunlay about the case, asking for details to confirm my reading of the message traffic. Her recitation of events matched almost verbatim with some of the OPSUMs I'd read. That made sense because, as operations officer, she'd have written that message traffic.

Along the way, I spotted two road-kill deer and dozens of billboards advertising inexpensive hotels, fast-food restaurants, and, most often, the Soo Locks boat tour. The sign for the Sault Ste. Marie city limits heralded the various state championships the local teams had won in the past 20 years. My first glimpse of the Soo was a sizeable red factory with white steam spewing skyward from its towering stack. A tan bridge stretched in a high arc toward Canada.

Along the interstate's right-hand side, I spotted an orange windsock and the peak of a control tower. I asked why the H-3 hadn't come straight into the Sault Ste. Marie airport.

"Traverse City pilots rarely come up to the Soo because the tower here isn't always manned. They prefer Kinross because the approaches are well charted, thanks to the Air Force," she explained.

Dunlay took the last exit before the International Bridge, and after another right turn, we drove through the campus of Lake Superior State College. I might have mistaken the modern construction for an austere apartment complex except for the sign and the gaggles of young women on the sidewalks. The downtown stores were open and crowded, so I assumed mall blight had not yet struck Sault Ste. Marie.

"What's it like living up here year-round?" I asked, shifting on the hot vinyl seat.

"In the Soo? That's what locals call it. It's not too bad if you can tolerate cold and snow. And I like being close to Canada."

"What's around for entertainment?"

"I suspect most people prefer alcohol. Otherwise, it's hunting or fishing."

"Sounds like paradise," I said. "Are you an outdoorswoman?"

"Not me, I'm strictly Book-of-the-Month club." On the seat between us sat the paperback of Michener's mega-book about Alaska, the same thick text she'd been reading at the airport.

We turned onto Water Street and, a few blocks later, pulled up to a wrought iron fence with a sign bearing the distinctive Coast Guard red and blue racing stripe. She waved at the guard as we drove past. The young seaman, dressed in a paint-smeared dark blue uniform, touched the brim of his ball cap in a casual salute but otherwise didn't alter his slouch on a folding metal chair.

"Explain that to me," she said. "The captain stationed guards on the gate after the crew disappeared. You know the expression, closing the barn door behind the horse."

It seemed silly to me, too. "Well, the commandant doesn't want anyone to know about the missing crew yet. Putting a guard on the gate when you haven't had one before might draw unwanted attention."

She parked the car and smiled at me. "Good point. I'll ask the commander to bring that to the captain's attention."

We fetched my bags from the trunk.

"I reserved a GV for you to use here," she told me. "We can put your luggage in it now so you don't have to carry it around."

The car she led me to was another government vehicle, an identical tan Dodge sedan, but this one had "Department of Transportation, U.S. Coast Guard" stenciled on the front doors. "No chance of traveling incognito," I observed.

We loaded my gear in the trunk, and she handed over the keys. I dropped them into my jacket pocket with my Firebird keys and wished it were here instead. Everyone abuses government vehicles, so they never have any pep left. Investigations are never like what they show on television, but sometimes you need a fast car for a pursuit.

It took three good slams to get the trunk lid shut. Rule #17 of temporary duty assignments: Avoid government vehicles; demand a rental car.

Several different units comprised the base, all housed together in one large, tan building; Group Sault Ste. Marie, the Vessel Traffic Service, the small boat station, an aids-to-navigation workshop, and barracks where single enlisted personnel lived. Red, green, and black buoys of various shapes and sizes filled one entire parking lot corner.

As we walked toward the river, she pointed out several black-hulled vessels; a 140-foot icebreaking tug, a small buoy tender and a flat-bottomed utility boat. Three small utility boats were moored along the dock; a 44-footer, a 41-footer and a 22-footer, each with a Coast Guard logo set in red and blue stripes painted on the bow. The engine room hatch on the 41-footer was open, and one of the engineers crouched over it, passing tools down to somebody below. We went a little farther until we stood in front of the 44-foot surfboat.

"That's it, 44323," she said, pointing. I spotted the number printed on the white bow in tall block letters. "The local police dusted it for fingerprints. I should receive their report tomorrow. Otherwise nothing onboard has been disturbed. You can get a better look in the morning."

I followed her back toward the darkened administration building.

"How's the search going?"

"Right now we have the Biscayne Bay on scene. The Air Force is evaluating the film from their overflight, and they'll info us on their report tomorrow. Meanwhile, I've asked Cape Cod to provide a Guardian with FLIR and SLAR."

I felt foolish for not realizing the inconsistency earlier. The Air Force provided a high-altitude reconnaissance aircraft designed to count enemy missiles and tanks that can also spot vessels, sometimes even submerged ones. But we knew where the boat was – I saw it a moment ago. We were searching for bodies, which requires the kinds of equipment Coast Guardian jets carry: forward-looking infrared and side-looking radar – FLIR and SLAR. I asked Dunlay about the decision to request the Air Force plane.

"It wasn't my choice. The Air Force called and said they had orders to fly and they needed coordinates," she explained. "Meanwhile I can't get a Coast Guard aircraft until at least tomorrow because there was – surprise – another oil spill in New York Harbor and now I'm on the standby list. That doesn't help matters with our surface assets, because they think the airdales," she glanced at my rating badge and silver wings, then corrected herself, "the aviators aren't pulling their weight. We've conducted a very intensive search for about 36 hours, and all the crews should be in the bag."

"I read the search reports on the flight over from Washington, but I'd like to see your charts, too."

"Sure, I'll take you up to the operations center. I changed charts every four hours and kept the old ones for reference."

"So you've been awake for the whole search, too?"

She shrugged. "Everyone has except for the captain and the yeomen in admin. There's nothing for them to do."

"Is either the captain or the XO still around this evening?"

"The captain's gone by now, but the commander always works late. Don't get me wrong about the captain. He puts in a full day, but he's also got 28 years in. He'd retire, but I've heard his wife wants to be admiral."

"Well, behind every great man is an ambitious woman. It sounds like everyone I need to talk to has gone home for the night. Except for you."

"With cases like this, there's a high emotional involvement. But we can't quit; there are too many questions." She sounded exhausted. Her shoulders slumped forward as she walked.

"More than if it were four civilians missing?" I asked.

The lieutenant turned on me in anger. "It's not like we don't care if we lose civilians; we search just as hard. But when it's our own asset, we must know what happened. Our crews are taught to handle any crisis. If there's a problem with the boats or our training, we have to fix it so it won't happen again."

"Easy, I'm not from the newspapers."

"Sorry, I'm getting tired." By then, we were standing near a lighthouse replica in front of the administration building. A sign on the admin building door admonished visitors to "Please remove snow and ice from shoes before entering." Sweating in the August evening, I chuckled, but Dunlay reminded me that Sault Ste. Marie is considered permafrost duty. She led me inside, past the seaman standing watch at the desk in the wide lobby, upstairs and down the hall to the operations center. Along the way, she explained that Group Soo monitors Channels 16 and 22 on marine band radio on eleven different high radio towers that funneled into 22 other speakers in the radio room. Channel 16 is the basic hailing and distress frequency, and Channel 22 is the primary Coast Guard working freq. I stopped Dunlay when we reached the door of the operations center.

"Ma'am, I can look at those charts in the morning," I told her. "Why don't you introduce me to the XO and then go get some rest?"

"You're sure? Thanks, I need some sleep."

She led me farther down the hall to the deputy group commander's office. Light shone through the doorway, and soft jazz filtered out, punctuated by the sound of typing. She knocked, and we entered.

The commander sat behind the desk, hunched over an old manual typewriter, but he stood up to greet us when we entered. I was surprised by how tall he was, about six, eight – a prime recruit for the Coast Guard Academy's basketball team some 15 years ago. He leaned across the broad steel desk to grip my hand when Dunlay introduced us. Commander Andrew Fraser wore exercise clothes, sweat pants and a nylon windbreaker. The workday had ended three hours earlier.

Fraser slapped the computer terminal on his desk. "Damn desk anchor is never on line when I need it. I'm typing up some leave papers. Do you think I'll be able to sneak out of here for a few days next month?" the commander asked Dunlay.

"Only if I get a week in Aruba."

"OK, tell me when we're going." The commander smiled at her.

Dunlay tensed visibly. "Sir, if you don't have any tasking for me this evening, I'd like to go home. Mister Jaspers has the duty tonight."

The commander glanced at me, then back at her. "Have you

already briefed Special Agent Galloway? Do you need anything else from the lieutenant?" he asked me.

"We can talk in the morning," I said.

He nodded, and she left after shaking my hand again. The commander settled back down behind his desk and motioned me to take the chair across from him. He was a big guy with handsome features. His brown hair fell almost to his collar, a little longer than regulation and nearly as long as mine.

"Before we get started, you've got to tell me what you did to annoy Captain Burke," the commander said. "He was quite upset when he found out that Headquarters was sending you."

The old expression is true; friends may come, and friends may go, but enemies last forever.

"He might still angry about Miami," I explained. "Somebody was leaking sensitive information about drug patrols, and the district office brought me in because there was a remote possibility it was one of their agents. The captain accused a radioman in the communications center, and he wasn't happy when I proved it was a junior officer in ops. This ensign wasn't even selling the information. He talked a lot in bars to impress women. Bartenders pay special attention to guys like that."

The commander grinned, chuckling. "Yeah, I can see how that would annoy the captain. He'd still like to believe that all officers are also gentlemen."

"Sir, it's not too late to bring in somebody else. There are some fine agents in the district office in Cleveland."

Fraser settled back in his chair and propped his feet on the side of the desk. He wore running shoes without socks. "No, the captain didn't want anyone from Cleveland, and now the intelligence folks in Washington insist that he accept you or nothing. I understand you come recommended by an admiral." He smiled as if he was being discrete.

I asked him to tell me the whole story, comparing details with what I'd heard earlier from Andrews and Dunlay.

"Well, sir, I've read the search reports and the personnel jacket on each of the four crewmen," I said when he finished. "Nothing jumps out at me, except that their performance marks fell about 18 months ago."

Fraser put his feet on the floor, eased forward in his chair and reached for a paper clip which he proceeded to mangle. "I don't think there's any connection. Senior Chief Drucker is tough on his crews. He works them hard, and his evaluations are tough – he never gives high marks. I've talked with him about it, but there's nothing much there. He's one of the old-timers who doesn't give out much praise and who won't put up with any crap."

"I keep hearing about him and about a morale problem here. But you don't think he could be involved?"

"I've had problems with him from time to time, but no, I don't think he's part of anything sinister involving the missing crew. As for morale, I'd say it stinks everywhere these days. You know what they say, 'If you keep doing more with less, pretty soon you'll be doing everything with nothing.' I'm waiting for the day some disgruntled Coastie shows up at Headquarters with an assault rifle and 'goes coastal.'" He wagged two fingers of both hands to make air quote marks.

I decided to call Andrews in Washington and ask him if there was anything else about the senior chief that had aroused his suspicions.

"Well, sir, I'm open to suggestions if you have any," I said.

The commander shook his big head. "Sorry, I haven't got an angle on this, and I've been here since it started. I guess there's a remote possibility that they all went into the water together. Say one of them fell overboard and the others lost their heads and went in after him. They were all wearing their gun belts which weighted them down, so they couldn't swim back to the boat. It's an awful stretch of the imagination though. It doesn't explain why they took the boat out early – before they came on duty. And I have no idea why they headed into Canadian waters, or told the station they were heading down the St. Mary's instead of up through the locks." He paused and then laughed, his mouth open in a wide grin. "I guess it's not much of a theory, is it?"

I smiled. "Sir, I hope you won't be offended if I file it between mass desertion and kidnapping by Martians." If this was the kind of help I could expect, I might need to beg Admiral Thorne for an extension on his 72-hour deadline. "I may have more questions for you after I get a look at the 44-footer in the morning."

The phone rang. I stood to give the commander privacy, but he motioned me to stay while he spoke into the receiver. "Yes . . . yes . . . yes. I'll take care of it. Now get some sleep." He set down the receiver. "You guessed that was Miss Dunlay? She's on duty even when she should be sleeping. But she's a good officer, and it's nice to have a woman around here. She said you thought the guards might draw attention to our operations. I suspect the captain didn't consider that possibility. Besides, I'm sure they can use some sleep, too. What about you? I imagine this has been a long day."

"Too bad Red Tail Airline doesn't offer frequent flyer miles," I joked.

He gazed at me blankly. Fraser wasn't an aviator, so he wouldn't understand that Coast Guard aircraft are nicknamed Red Tail for their bright orange stabilizers.

"Anything else I can do for you, Galloway?"

"May I borrow a copy of the local Coast Pilot, and do you have a spare room in the barracks I can use?"

"The book's no trouble, though mine is a few years out of date," Fraser said, standing and walking toward a bookshelf full of white binders. "But I have to send you elsewhere for the room. We seem to be two-blocked with Reservists doing their two-week obligation. Course it helps to have the extra bodies here for the search. Miss Dunlay said she reserved a room for you at the Superior Hotel. It's a couple blocks down the street. You've got one of our trusty cars, right?" He handed me the thick Coast Pilot with a pumpkin-color cover.

I nodded and got to my feet. "Thank you, sir. I may need to pester you tomorrow."

"That's no problem. I'd recommend you steer clear of the captain. Everyone else should be more than happy to cooperate with you." He gave me a quick smirk and added, "If they're not, I want to hear about it."

He shook my hand again, and I left. Before I hit the hallway, the rat-a-tat-tat of typing resumed.

43

Tuesday: 1930

I aimed the government vehicle toward the hotel, eager to shed the Coast Guard blues. Usually, special agents dress in civilian clothes for work, but I had received strict, permanent orders from the commandant to wear the uniform whenever I visited Headquarters. Admiral Thorne once spotted me in the building wearing a sweatshirt he found offensive. After spending six months compiling a thick file of illegal activities practiced by an admiral in Seattle, I was stunned to learn the fellow was condemned to retirement with full pension and benefits. Feeling recklessly disrespectful, I went to a specialty shop and ordered a custom shirt with the logo: "The UCMJ. It's just not for admirals anymore." Few people found my play on words as amusing as I did. Admiral Thorne seemed even less amused than most.

With rudimentary directions from the gate guard, I found Portage Street and the Savoy Bar, which advertised dancing nightly amidst a row of souvenir merchants. A few hotels had trinket shops attached – a sort of one-stop tourist trap. These were the ultimate convenience for the tourist who doesn't want to stray too far from the damp air conditioning, the fresh-bleached towels and the sanitized toilet they've paid hundreds of dollars to come hundreds of miles to endure. Dunlay had booked me into the Superior Inn, a palace identified by the blue neon outline of the lake on the sign in case you didn't grasp the wordplay. The gray-haired desk clerk took several minutes to reach the door after the bell rang.

"That officer told me you'd be here four hours ago," she complained, hitching her housecoat higher over her shoulder.

I apologized and gave her my credit card. She signed me in, still grumbling about the late hour. I assumed she enjoyed Wheel of Fortune and went straight to bed. Handing over the key and my credit card, she ushered me out the door and slammed it behind me. Room service was out of the question.

Once in room 26, I laid my luggage on the spare bed and checked out the suite. The plaster walls were blue; the curtains bright yellow. Both beds felt a little spongy for my taste, except where the steel coils poked against the thin mattress topper. The legs of the desk and both chairs looked like a rabid beaver had attacked them. The television received only three stations, all pretty fuzzy. The sink had rust stains, and gray mildew ringed the stand-up shower. Just superior.

I hung my clothes on the steel rack behind the door and stowed my empty bags under the bed. I found a soda machine down the hall and came back carrying a ginger ale to settle down with my little bag of tricks.

Whenever I begin an assignment, I always start by checking out my equipment. Unlike Her Majesty's Secret Service, the Coast Guard doesn't have Q tucked in a secret laboratory working on high-tech gadgets. Most of my toys are everyday items that were useful in past cases. Everything I carry fits in a custom-made black leather bag. The locks require two separate keys and a five-digit combination. Between the leather shell and the nylon lining is a heavy steel mesh that can't be cut with a pocket knife.

Emptying the bag, I spread the contents across the bed, examining each as I went: a stethoscope, a pocket flashlight, 200 feet of parachute cord, a miniature tape recorder with telephone jack, an extending law enforcement baton, a pocket-size 35-mm camera with a powerful flash unit, a small video camcorder, four pairs of spare eyeglasses in varying fashions, an aircrew survival knife, a fingerprint kit and miscellaneous other items. Most often, I travel with few weapons, including two pistols, both zippered into a compartment at the bottom of the bag. I like the old government-issue Colt .45 for stopping power, but I strap a Beretta Model 20 onto my ankle for emergencies.

Other agents carry different pieces, ranging from the policeman's .38 Special to the new government-standard Browning 9mm. I prefer pistols that reload with clips, and I've never had a round jam. Even more important to me is how well each fits my hand because I spend so much time on the range. I belong to a gun club and shoot every Sunday morning for an hour, practicing with both hands, but my right hand is still weaker.

I try to avoid situations where I have to draw a weapon because the Coast Guard frowns on it in all circumstances. In five years, I've fired only twice in the line of duty. Once I fired a warning shot to get the attention of a deserter who was driving away. He had played a cat-and-mouse game with us for six months, offering to give himself up and disappearing before an agent arrived. He ran at the sight of my badge but slammed on the brakes and came along in handcuffs after he heard the sharp report of a .45. That incident earned me a charming reprimand now prominent in my personnel record; warning shots are prohibited ashore because of the danger to bystanders. I managed to keep my badge only because I proved that I had fired the round into a sand embankment and that we had already wasted more than 600 man-hours chasing the kid.

The only other time I fired a weapon off the shooting range occurred while working with a dozen Customs agents from the Miami office on an airfield raid in the Everglades when a thwarted narcotics courier started firing off an AK-47. Unlike in movies where people stagger around shooting wildly after being hit, our volley lifted him clear and laid him out flat. I managed to fire off a single round before a Customs agent behind me put a slug into my right triceps. Friendly fire still burns.

With everything checked and stowed back in place, I stripped for the shower. The shampoo barely lathered before the water ran cold. I gritted my teeth and finished quickly.

When working a case, I follow Galloway's first axiom on investigations: Always go armed and always go sober. After my long day of traveling, I could use a cold beer, but I would need to settle for something cold. When I finished dressing, I pulled an elastic holster up my calf and secured the Beretta in place. Then I slipped into a leather bombardier jacket and headed downtown with Fraser's Coast Pilot for the Great Lakes under my arm.

All the businesses along the main drag were closed except a Mexican restaurant and several beer joints. I parked the government Dodge by a bank on a side street to avoid recognition, then headed for the tavern with the most intriguing name; the Horney Toad lounge.

The room was bright, loud and crowded, with a pale blue haze of cigarette smoke lingering in the air. The varnished pine walls were cluttered with flags and pennants, including quite a lot of Coast Guard memorabilia – hats, life rings, pennants and nametags. As I settled on a stool, the perky, lithe bartender asked, quite unnecessarily, to see my ID.

"Increased tips through flattery; I like it." I fished out my wallet, handed over my Alaska driver's license and ordered a club soda with a twist of lemon.

The blonde leaned forward to where she could read the license in the blue light under the bar. The neckline of her loose top opened to expose untethered breasts. "I don't usually need help gettin' tips. But the manager is real strict, especially with all the young Coasties come in here." She handed back my license and gave me a mischievous grin. "And it gives the old farts a real charge." She bounced down the bar and returned seconds later carrying a heavy tumbler with two chunks of lime drowning in tap water. I didn't argue. She extracted a dollar from the money I laid out on the countertop, then sashayed off again, but glanced over her shoulder to make certain I wasn't missing the show. She joined a running conversation with four women at the end of the bar. In another state, she'd have small portraits of Alexander Hamilton tucked under her garters.

I surveyed the rest of the room. The jukebox featured Detroit, not Motown but the industrial rock of Bob Seger and Mitch Ryder, among other air guitar classics. Many years had passed since I'd last heard those immortal lyrics, "Play that funky music, white boy." The place seemed crowded for a Tuesday night; for the most part, a young crowd with a few trying to stay young by hanging out. The standard uniform was flannel and denim, but it didn't seem to have much to do with the grunge thing. A fellow in his early forties had drawn up his shirt, showing the tattoo of a Bengal tiger on his left pectoral to three girls new to legal drinking.

As a trained investigator, I have developed a highly scientific theory about tattoos and what they reveal about the owner's personality. Men tend to go for the masculine: tigers, daggers, galloping stallions. My grandfather had a pair of tall-masted sailing ships, one on each forearm, souvenirs of a drunken liberty in Boston during

World War II while he was on North Atlantic convoy duty. Admiral Thorne's tattooed schooner may have a similar history from a different war. Women seem more creative, even daring with their tattoos, open to the beautiful and sometimes the frivolous. Once, years ago, after a few whiskey sours in the French Quarter, a lithe-limbed yeoman from the district office in New Orleans raised her skirt and tugged aside lacy panties to show me Paddington Bear, outfitted with a pith helmet, scouting into her bush.

A sixth woman joined the giggling gaggle at the end of the bar. She was a redhead – tall and trim, hair fanned over her shoulders like a mainsail rustling under a soft breeze, approaching middle age but still striking even among the college girls in the room. This cluster of women drew the attention of the men in the room for the first time. About four came to hang around the perimeter, like wolves waiting for a young caribou to wander away from the herd.

Pushing my tepid water aside, I opened the Coast Pilot on the bar top. I began to read the encyclopedia of Great Lakes navigation, from local magnetic disturbances to quarantine procedures. After a lengthy discussion of water levels and ice, Chapter 12 described the Vessel Traffic Service that the H-3 pilot had mentioned earlier. "Soo Control" was intended to prevent collisions and groundings in the restricted waterways above and below the Soo locks where you wouldn't want two freighters passing in a narrow turn – big ships don't occupy the same space very well.

As I reached the stirring passage about communications between transiting freighters and the lock operators on 156.70 Mhz and 156.80 Mhz, the redhead detached herself from the barvixen's clique and came down my way. She commandeered the stool next to mine and smiled.

"Hi. I'm Sally Ledoux. Adele said you were down from Alaska. How did you happen to stop in this outpost of hell?"

I put on my most inscrutable look and held out my hand. "Marty Galloway. And I've seen worse dives than this."

She shook back her thick mane and laughed. "No, I mean the Soo. The Toad's the only decent place in town. Trust me, I oughta know."

"Serving a life sentence?" I motioned for Adele to bring a pair of drinks. Barroom seductions are often like pitching baseballs at a carny tent; you pay for the game, not because you want the prize.

"Yeah. And no time off for good behavior." Sally paused and gave me a long, smoldering look. "Or bad." She took a deep swig from her fresh long neck and cooed her thanks.

"I'm passing through on my way to Ohio, may do a little fishing while I'm here," I said, trying to steer the conversation back toward reality. Odds were I'd be deep-selected for admiral before I stroked Sally's inner thighs. The pace was too fast; she wasn't very drunk, and I'm not a hunk. But she was a looker. Under her stone-washed jeans and corduroy shirt was a sturdy body. Her features were delicate, with a light dusting of freckles across the bridge of her nose. Sun streaks highlighted the shaggy auburn mane. She was also smart enough not to obscure her looks under a plaster of makeup. I confess a preference for the attractive over the stunning. If supermodels are so great, why don't they rate a category in the Nobel Prizes?

"This ain't the best year for fishing," she said. "We didn't get much snow, so there's not much oxygen in the water. My brother runs a bait and tackle on the Big Two-Hearted River, and he says it's lousy this year."

"Should I rent a boat and go offshore?" I said.

"Be careful you don't get run over. The Coast Guard has a big search going for some of their guys who fell off a boat."

So much for the commandant's idea about secrecy, I thought. "Has that been on the news? I must have missed it." I asked.

"No, I was talking to a Coastie in here last night. He was scheduled to go out this morning at dawn."

I asked her how many people were missing and how they had fallen off the boat, noticing the way her green eyes watched mine as we talked.

"The guy said four. But he wasn't sure what happened. I guess they weren't even supposed to be out on the boat, and then they disappeared. The Canadians found the boat floating up near Agawa Bay."

Sally knew only the basics, but that was more than Admiral Thorne wanted. No doubt, a talkative seaman hoped to impress her.

49

Soon we started talking about the town and then her. She was a senior bank teller, trying to pay off a house because her husband had signed onto a freighter and never returned. Wife, child and home were too much responsibility for him.

"I should have known it couldn't last. All Floyd talked about was having money and living easy, but it'd take more than a miracle to get rich in the Soo," Sally told me. "So he left. I only get two nights a week to go out when my mother watches my little girl. The other five nights Mom has to go play bingo at one church or another."

"I hear the pope has declared bingo as the eighth sacrament," I said.

She laughed again, so I ordered more water and another beer. She told me about going to the local college for two years to get a business degree before she met her future ex-husband. She wondered if Lake Superior State College would take her back after eight years.

With a hooked finger, she removed her wire-frame glasses. "I hope I'm not boring you." Her green eyes sparkled like a pair of starboard running lights.

"No, not at all. Back in the sixth grade, the music teacher decided I should be a listener, and I've stuck with it."

She smiled. "I'm sorry. I don't have anyone to talk to here. Everyone I grew up with either got out when they could or they're already on their third marriage."

In deference to the women present, the jukebox shifted gears from motorhead music to the pining of REO Speedwagon.

"Hey, you've got one of those old-timey POW bracelets," she said when I reached the bar for a napkin.

I tugged my sleeve back down my wrist. "An old relic I've had for years."

So she asked a few questions about me. I tried to be honest without saying what I did for a living and the real reason I was in town. My grandmother disapproved of fibbing, but simple lies were easier than the complicated truths of my life.

Finally, I pushed my water glass away. "Three's my limit." Best to leave before I broke the rules, quaffed a few suds, and entertained impure thoughts. I thanked Sally for a stirring evening.

"Could you give me a ride home?" she asked. "It's not far."

Sally went to tell her friends that she was leaving. They laughed and stared in my direction. When she returned, I held up her denim jacket so she could slip into it. As we went outside, she put her hand inside my arm and leaned against me slightly while we walked, heading toward the bank.

"You said you were on vacation!" she shouted when she saw the government car. I had forgotten the Coast Guard racing stripes plastered on the front doors of the GV; my mind was still on vacation in Maine. Too late to renege now, but offering a civilian a ride in a government vehicle was a major taboo.

She twisted in front of me. "Why didn't you tell me? You let me ramble on and on about that big search."

"A lot of folks don't like servicemen, that's all. I usually keep quiet about it."

Sally stood about my height, and she stared into my eyes. "Yeah, I thought you were being pretty quiet." Her body moved against mine the way a cat rubs against your legs to get attention. "You seem mysterious."

"Yeah, my mother said I'm a mystery, too. She doesn't know what she did to deserve me."

Sally chuckled. "Sounds like our mothers should get together. They could compare notes." She hugged me a little, then let go. We walked to the car.

She lived in a white cottage on the west side of town, complete with a picket fence and flowers in every window box. I stopped the car by the gate.

"If you're going to be in town for a while, I'd like to see you," she told me. She explained how I could find her bank and when she went to lunch, then kissed my cheek and jumped out.

Her seductive sway as she strolled up the walkway was quite a performance, so I waited until she was safe inside. I turned the car around and drove back to the Superior Inn, wondering how women decide about men. Sally didn't know me except what she saw in the Horney Toad; she couldn't know about the pistol strapped to my leg. Maybe women like the mystery of meeting a stranger, or they're

51

bored with the local clientele and looking for a change. If I saw Sally again, I decided to ask.

On the way back into town, I passed a car rental and also decided to get rid of the Coast Guard advertising as soon as possible.

Wednesday: 0215

Sleep that night was a sweaty, broken voyage of misery. A long parade of bloated corpses trooped through my skull, many with their skin dripping from their bones just the way they slopped across the floor of the helo – the ocean dissolving the body back into water. Snatches of flights replayed through my head in full Dolby and Surround Sound.

The most extended episode began with a fishing boat carrying an Aleut family between Sutwik Island and Karluk. A rogue wave flipped the seiner in a heavy chop, and five people went into the frigid Shelikof Strait. A charter floatplane watched the capsize and radioed a distress call into Kodiak. The H-3 passed over Karluk, heading out to sea within 45 minutes. Unable to land because of the rough open seas, the floatplane circled over the site and vectored us down to the people in the water.

I went into the surf as soon as we arrived on scene. Already the waves had separated the family, and the five drifted helplessly in the bone-chilling waters. I swam for three minutes to reach the closest head bobbing in the flotsam. When I caught the hood of the heavy fur-lined parka, the corpse of an elder rolled against me, and I came face to face with death. His eyes were open and bulging; his tongue clenched between his teeth. Most likely, his heart stopped the minute he hit the frigid water. When I thrust the corpse away and swam toward the next victim, a wave caught up the old man's body and hurled it down on my back. I shoved it away a second time and pushed hard for the drifting person about 15 yards in front of me, but that first body stayed with me, the corpse driven by the waves as fast as I swam so that I bumped against it every other stroke. Finally, I spotted the billow in the parka on the corpse. An air pocket inside the jacket kept the body buoyant and afloat. Grabbing an arm, I pulled the old man close to unzip the front of his rain suit. As the air rushed out, his body slipped into the frothing waves.

Again, I aimed for the next head I spotted in the surf – a smaller head than the first. As I drew near, it seemed to elude me, moving out of my grasp. A rogue wave caught me and hurled me down on the child's body, floating away from me. I wrapped my arms around the child and rolled to bring her face up in the water. The girl was about four years old. Already I was too late. As I felt her neck for a pulse, seawater gushed from her open mouth – water filled her lungs and squeezed the breath out of her.

I thrashed onward toward the next person, kicking with all the strength I could muster but gaining no significant ground toward a figure that receded away from me. Raging because my efforts were useless against the turbulent waves, I took a visual bearing and dove below the surface, thrusting as hard as I could but still pitched by the waves. As I surfaced, I found a woman holding a toddler boy in her arms, their heads barely above the water. At first, they looked lifeless, but then her eyes moved. She made no effort to swim toward me, only a flicker of her eyes in my direction.

When I reached them, I took the boy over my shoulder. It was a mistake; I realized as soon as I'd done it. Relieved of the child, the woman rolled back in the water and sank away from me. Somehow the helo had followed my erratic swim, and the hoist basket dropped into the water a few feet from me. I placed the child inside, waved to the hoist operator that I was clear, then dove after the woman. In what seemed like seconds, she had already disappeared from my sight. I floundered about with my hands, diving deep on a gasp of air rapidly going bad. When I felt the claustrophobia tighten around my neck, I went up. As I broke the surface, I saw the tail of the H-3 as it headed back to Kodiak. I thought I heard the shrill drive of an engine under strain, but it may have been the wind.

As I watched the helo disappear, I hoped the young child would live. I wondered what mechanical emergency had forced the H-3 back to Kodiak, and I prayed in silence that they would make it safely. As I rode the crest of a wave, I saw that the other bodies were already submerged, taken down by the weight of their wet clothing. I felt very alone – five people went into the water, and I had saved only one. My only comfort was an inflatable raft the helo had dropped as it departed. The raft's EPIRB would guide the helo back to my location.

Forty-seven minutes ticked by on my diving watch before another H-3 arrived from Kodiak, with those black letters USCG on its bottom looking like the warmest greeting in the world.

54

Wednesday: 0600

The travel alarm clock went off, and I rolled onto the floor. Once there, I hooked my feet under the bureau and did 100 crunches, reversed and followed with 100 leg-lifts, then finally 100 push-ups. After swallowing a handful of vitamins, I went into the shower. At an early hour, the water ran hot for 15 minutes.

Not knowing what the day would hold, I went fully armed; the Beretta strapped on my ankle and the Colt fastened into a shoulder holster under my right arm. It felt good to be back in my own uniform: loose khaki trousers, a blue button-down Oxford shirt and a leather jacket. Even my feet felt more comfortable in deck runners than polished black dress shoes.

The cloudless sky was turquoise blue except for a reddish hue in the east. Being a prudent sailor, I took warning, especially when the government Dodge refused to start. I popped the hood and scraped some corrosion off the battery terminals with my survival knife. The engine finally kicked over after I pulled off the air filter cover and wedged the choke wide open. It was not a good omen.

I reached the Coast Guard base by 0645. No guard stood at the gate. The senior chief boatswain mate and the small boat interested me most, so I headed first to the white and gray boathouse on the waterfront. A lanky seaman dressed in paint-stained coveralls sat near the door, practicing her knots. She directed me back across the parking lot to the first floor of the main building, where I found the small boat station's office.

Two men talked in the office on either side of a dented gray steel desk, both still wearing civilian clothes as they sipped coffee. Even in civies, the senior chief was easy to distinguish from the first class; Senior Chief Drucker looked older, thinner and paler with gaunt, slack cheeks covered by a slight gray stubble. He stood beside a steel file cabinet, pouring coffee from a thermos into a ceramic mug. I had passed a coffee urn out in the work area, so I reckoned he had enhanced his personal supply for medicinal purposes. The first class wore a plaid hunting shirt, blue jeans and scuffed cowboy boots, but the distinguishing feature was an enormous key ring dangling from a belt loop. He wore his long sideburns in a style no longer fashionable but a mustache clipped well within regulations.

55

He drank out of a white plastifoam cup from the stack by the urn. I wondered if they ever talked about their separate coffees. Did the senior chief ever offer a dollop of his special elixir?

I introduced myself, calling the man with the thermos "Senior Chief," and the one with the keys "Boats," the customary name for a first class boatswain mate.

"How'd you figure us out so quick?" Drucker asked.

"I've never been to a station where the chief wasn't drinking coffee and Boats wasn't carrying the keys to everything from the paint locker to the toilet paper dispenser," I joked.

The first class stood and offered his hand. "Larry Normand, but go ahead and call me Boats if you prefer."

The senior chief shook my hand also. He had a strong grip and a tattoo of a snake coiled around an anchor on his forearm. He wore his mustache clipped tight; his graying hair slicked back from a slender scar across the peak of his pale forehead.

"I didn't know CGI had any real detectives," Drucker said. "The only agents I've met couldn't take fingerprints without covering everyone with ink."

"Well, Senior, you know why there are so many boatswain mates in the Coast Guard, don't you?" I asked.

He shook his head.

"Damn, nobody else does either," I said.

He sat down, chuckling and scowling at the same time. "You got any idea what happened to our crew yet?" he asked in a sharp tone.

"Not yet, but I was hoping you'd both tell me everything you know about the case so far. Senior, if I can talk to you first and then Boats, I'd appreciate the time."

"Nothing more important around here, so you have my full attention," Drucker told me, motioning for Normand to leave the office. "If Boats has something on his schedule, he'll go cancel while we chat."

When Normand departed, I settled on his wobbly chair, which rocked back and forth no matter how I shifted my weight. The senior chief told me pretty much the same story I'd heard from Andrews, Dunlay and Fraser. Galloway's seventh axiom about investigations: ask everybody to repeat the story to see if any discrepancies warrant investigation. The details didn't change, but his reactions were different. I wondered if he was upset because they went out without permission.

"I wouldn't have minded them taking the boat out, if they'd told me what it was all about," Drucker said.

"So, you don't know why they went out?"

"No. As far as I know, they didn't tell anybody, either where or why. They came in early and took the boat. My duty petty officer didn't even know they were gone until they radioed to say they were heading down the St. Mary's River." He sat erect, elbows resting on the edge of the desk, flexing his hands and tugging on his fingers like a third-base coach in spring training.

"But that's the opposite direction from where the boat was found," I wondered aloud for his benefit.

"Yep, but if we followed them, we'd gone the wrong way. Say they waited to make their initial radio call because they figured we'd call the locks and have them stopped. That's my guess, of course."

I wanted to like Drucker; he sounded decent and concerned. Fraser said Drucker drove his men hard, but he seemed like the kind of boss who could make you want to work hard. Still, there were doubts, like Andrew's connection between the crew's performance marks and the senior chief's arrival. And I felt almost certain that he was starting his day with a stiff drink – usually a clear sign of an alcoholic.

When Larry Normand replaced Drucker behind the desk, he wore a uniform; dark blue pants with touches of white paint, a wrinkled pale-blue shirt and deck shoes instead of boots. He couldn't add any new information either. If I believed in conspiracy theories, I might have thought these many versions sounded so similar because they'd been rehearsed at length. That thought ran through my mind when Normand used a few phrases identical to some things both Dunlay and Drucker had said. I attributed the similarities to the professional jargon of the search and rescue business, like the peculiar languages of jet jockeys and computer twidgets. After a while, I became distracted by the way Boats fiddled with the pencils on the desk.

I asked Normand to show me the boat, and we walked down to

57

the waterfront. CG44323 was the only boat at the dock that morning. I assumed the others were already out searching.

"Only three people have been aboard since it was found," Normand told me. "The Mountie went aboard and tied on a tow line up forward. Mister Jaspers was aboard when it came back, and then the detective from the Soo police who did the fingerprinting. Still got that damn dust all over everything, too. Pissed me off because Sunday afternoon I had the duty section scrub down all the boats."

"Who's Jaspers?" I asked, recalling Dunlay's mention of him the night before.

"Chief Warrant Officer Jaspers. He's the assistant operations officer, works for Miss Dunlay."

We walked down the dock and stood beside the 44-footer, its radar antenna on the cabin's roof still rotating. The motor surfboat is one of the most unattractive boats in the Coast Guard fleet, built for seamanship, not showmanship. The superstructure is streamlined, so it will roll completely over and come back upright rather than remain capsized. The cockpit is big enough to hold two or three crewmen. Everyone else aboard sits in a compartment located down on the stern. Ugly like an H-3, but I'd heard 44-footers compared to tanks.

A yellow polypropylene cord fenced off the boat. I ducked under it and went aboard, observing every detail. Normand remained on the dock. He was right about the dust; the gray fingerprinting powder covered every possible surface. First impressions are essential, so I stopped and looked around. Immediately I saw that Normand was wrong about one subject.

"Did Jaspers come back aboard after the detective dusted for fingerprints?" I asked.

"No, the captain restricted all access until you got here."

Across the deck tracked two sets of footprints visible in the gray powder. The clean, smooth prints would belong to the detective's leather-sole wingtips. The other print showed traction, like hiking shoes or construction boots. The tracks were so obvious that I knew somebody had come aboard during the night when they couldn't see the powder. Although curious, it was worthless information: There were thousands of similar boots in northern Michigan – a pair for every hunting license.

I stepped onto the coxswain flat, a small cockpit where the helmsman, radar operator and lookout all huddle together. More dust covered everything; I had to blow the fine powder off the dials to read the instruments on the black dashboard. As Dunlay promised, the 44-footer remained the way it was found. The radio controls above the helm were still illuminated, set to Channels 16 and 22. A thin, yellow line swept around the radar screen, and even the Loran unit in the right-hand corner over the radar still showed a position. Loran stands for Long Range Aid to Navigation. A Loran unit is a radio receiver; the system uses a grid of radio waves that covers most of the globe. Comparing two different radio signals from separate transmitters, the Loran unit determines a position by the intersection of the two wavelengths.

There were no navigation charts on the small bench in the corner, but I assumed Dunlay had taken them to plan the search. I started out and then glanced back at the Loran unit. The two sets of six red digits weren't flashing; someone had locked the unit on a position. Perhaps the Mountie who found the boat did that to record where to start searching. On the other hand, the coxswain may have fixed his position when he got into trouble. I scribbled down the numbers in my notebook.

I walked forward around the bow. Again, nothing seemed out of place. The mooring lines were tied and stowed, hanging on the starboard rail. Aft of the cabin, a canvas tarp still covered the spool of towing hawser. The boat's EPIRB, its emergency distress radio beacon, hung in its cradle. If the boat had capsized or even listed hard, the EPIRB would have automatically begun transmitting its signal. RCC Scott had recorded no satellite hits in the vicinity.

Four rubber fenders hung against the hull, two on each side.

"Do you tie the boats up against each other?" I called to Normand.

"No, each has its own berth."

"Why are there fenders on both sides?" I asked.

"It came in with fenders on the port side. Jaspers rigged those on the starboard when he tied her up."

This presented something of a puzzle. The starboard fenders were put in place before the small boat was moored. If the portside fenders had been used to come through the locks, Jaspers would have hauled them aboard once clear of the locks. So it seemed the original crew had used the fenders to come alongside a dock or another boat after they cleared the locks.

I stepped down to the fantail and peered into the turtleback, a cabin on the stern where passengers and crew sit on narrow benches. Inside were only a few immersion suits and bagged lunches with a two-liter bottle of soda pop.

I climbed off the boat. "What time does it get dark here?"

"About 9:30," he figured.

"And how late did the duty section work last night?"

"Senior Chief had them working on the boats because the search started so early this morning. They finished after 22 hundred."

"And when did the new duty section arrive?"

"The boats left before sunrise, so they were here about zero five hundred."

That left a seven-hour gap when an unknown subject wearing boots with heavy tread walked across the deck. I grew angry with myself; I should have boarded the 44-footer as soon as I arrived in the Soo the night before. I wondered what this blunder would cost.

"Anything else I can help you with?" Normand asked.

"Not right now, but could be later. I may have some more questions about the area and the station."

I started toward the administration building when Normand called me back to ask if I was finished aboard 44323; he wanted to shut the gear down to spare the batteries and also get the seamen busy sweeping off the dust. I told him to have fun. Then I walked up to the group operations center to chat with Lieutenant Dunlay.

While I'd been inside the station talking with Drucker and Normand, a high, thin cast of gray clouds came in. The morning was neither shadowless nor overcast, the kind of day when trout skim the surface during a Mayfly hatch and snag easily on my special nymph tied with the mask of an English hare. I wished I was fishing.

Wednesday: 0950

I found Dunlay talking with Fraser in the hallway outside the commander's office.

"Where have you been?" Fraser asked in an angry tone, his big eyebrows raised like a dog's hackles. "We called your hotel room twice this morning. The captain wants to talk to you."

"Damn, I was having such a good morning so far." I chuckled alone.

The commander frowned. "I'll tell the captain you're here. Nothing personal, Galloway, but coming in late your first day doesn't make a very good impression." He headed down the hall toward the captain's office.

Dunlay's brown eyes looked at me impassively. "I'm not interested in your personal goings-ons, but please don't make things worse around here, OK?"

"Me? I'm the very model of discretion." The commandant would howl if he heard that. "Would you plot these Loran coordinates for me? But I have to ask you not to mention this to anyone else yet. This may tell us something about the 44's last location before the crew disappeared. And please check with your gate watch whether anyone went aboard the 44 during the night."

"So, you've been at the station all morning?" The shock registered on her face.

"Of course, first impressions are important, you know."

"Why didn't you tell the commander? He thinks you were slacking off."

"Because I don't work for him." Sure, I can be obstinate; it's good for the image.

The commander's bulky frame reappeared down the hall. "Galloway! The captain's ready for you."

I motioned that I'd be along soon. "Look, can you do this right away? And also get the charts from 44323."

"What charts?"

"Galloway! Now!" Fraser shouted.

The lieutenant looked befuddled as I headed for the captain's office. But Fraser's opinion of me had changed for the worse that morning. He might wear his hair shaggy, but he wouldn't tolerate

61

the slightest perceived infraction among junior – read enlisted – personnel. If he and the captain were against me, the whole investigation was in rough surf from the get-go.

Rank has more than privileges; it also comes with an interior decorator. Every other office I'd seen on base had only those big steel desks painted battleship gray, but the captain sat behind a massive oak model with a matching credenza behind him. The sofa looked like genuine leather. Worse yet, Captain Burke's office was a shrine to himself. Framed citations covered the walls, along with his degree, commission and photos of the captain receiving various awards. A glass case displayed his medals and sword. Usually, the museum is erected after the great man dies.

My conversation with the captain was brief, tense and uninformative. Even after two years, he sounded miffed about Miami. The captain didn't offer me the use of a car or the loan of his daughter.

"I want to make it clear that I didn't ask for you, and I don't want you here," the captain said gruffly. Burke was a big man with a thick paunch and heavy jowls that moved in unflattering ways when he spoke.

"I appreciate your candor, captain, and I want to assure you that I'll finish as soon as I can and leave immediately." I shifted on my feet. Although it's a custom fit, a leather strap on the Colt's holster poked my back, giving me a strong urge to scratch my right shoulder.

He glared at me with hooded eyes. "If you expect to get out of here so fast, tell us what you investigated in your bed this morning." He smirked in the direction of Fraser, reclining on the couch behind me.

I decided to throw trump cards. "First, somebody went aboard the 44-footer during the night. Second, it appears the crew went alongside a pier or another boat after they cleared the locks. And right now, Lieutenant Dunlay is charting the boat's probable location before the crew disappeared."

Burke snapped out of his lethargy as he came forward in his chair, his meaty palms slapping loudly against the desktop. The captain and commander exchanged stunned looks. Fraser spoke first. "So, you've been to the station this morning?"

"Of course, sir. Like F. Lee said, the investigation never rests," I paused and smiled at Burke. "Now if you'll excuse me, captain, I'd like to see what Lieutenant Dunlay has discovered."

"Hold on a minute there," Burke grumbled, shoving himself to his feet and rounding the side of his desk to face me. "As long as you are in my group, I want to know your exact whereabouts and intentions. I won't have you poking after my officers and fabricating charges like you did in Miami. I've always had trouble with you agents and the way you figure this is your big chance to get back at your superiors. Just because you don't wear a uniform, don't think for a second that you aren't subject to the UCMJ."

No doubt a good strategy at that particular moment would have been a sincere effort at diplomacy. I recognized that option and immediately dismissed the idea. I thrust my hands into my pockets, knowing that would irritate the captain as much as my attitude, long hair and civilian clothes. Factoring in the captain's threat of charges under the Uniform Code of Military Justice, I chose my words to strike a tone midway between disrespect and insubordination.

"Captain, yesterday morning I was on leave. Admiral Thorne recalled me because he felt something happened here that could not be handled by those currently assigned here. If you have concerns about my mission or performance, you should take that up with the commandant personally." I placed in front of Burke one of the business cards I had lifted from Admiral Thorne's office the day before. I executed a proper military salute. "Request permission to carry on."

Still distracted by reading the white card, Burke nodded, so I made a sharp about-face. "Commander, will you set up an interview for me with Missus Desharnais?"

"Absolutely not!" Burke roared. "I will not let you badger that woman."

"The captain's right, Galloway," the XO said. "She's pretty distraught now. I offered to arrange a Mutual Assistance loan if she wanted to go stay with her family while we search."

"You will not disturb that woman, Galloway!" Burke muttered.

"Commander, if you want to sit in, that's fine with me," I said to Fraser. "But she may be the last person to talk to any member of the crew before they left here, and she may know why they took the boat out early. I must talk to her."

Fraser nodded in understanding. He was in a difficult position, knowing I was right, and Captain Burke would never admit he was wrong. Finally, he shook his head. He couldn't afford to cross his CO. I shrugged and went searching for Dunlay. There are always alternatives.

I found the lieutenant in a small, cluttered office down the hall from the operations center. Black and white photographs of light-houses from around the Great Lakes decorated the white walls of her tiny room. Dunlay leaned hunched over several charts spread across a wide table, searching back and forth between two in particular. She straightened up when I entered and closed the door.

"What is this position?" she asked, tapping the eraser of a #2 on the chart table.

"First, show me where it is," I said, taking my eyeglasses from the inside pocket of my jacket.

She pointed to an X she'd penciled on the chart along the southern shore of Lake Superior near Crisp Point, not far outside the normal shipping lanes. She wore chipped pink polish on her chewed nails.

"And where was the boat found?" I asked, peering at a clutter of lines, numbers and symbols she had marked across the chart during the search.

Dunlay indicated a second X close to the Canadian coastline. Using a pair of needle-nosed calipers, I measured the distance between the two Xs and compared it against the chart's mileage scale – about 60 miles apart.

"And where did the Coast Guard take custody of the boat from the Canadians?"

Pulling over another chart, she pointed to the third spot near a small purple dot named Gros Cap Lighthouse at the mouth of the St. Mary's River. "Would you explain what this is all about?" she demanded. "I'm too tired to play games."

"One more thing first." I measured the distance with the calipers and found that Gros Cap was about 60 miles from the position on the boat's Loran unit. "How difficult is it to set a Loran unit to a position other than where it is?"

"I suppose you could recalibrate to show a different reading, but it would be pretty complex. It would require a technician or a factory rep."

I leaned against the edge of the table and looked into her face. "Those numbers I gave you were locked on the Loran in 44323." Her eyes widened, and I continued, "I'd like your electronics shop to check out that unit, but for now we can assume the boat was in that position before or when the crew disappeared."

"Damn it! I've been searching the wrong side of the fucking lake!" she yelled, kicking at a metal trash can beside the table, hard enough to knock it over. A can of soda fell out, pouring its remaining contents on the tile floor in a wavering spout as it rolled over and over. Dunlay watched it go but made no effort to stop the can or clean the dark, foamy spill. Her outburst of obscenity startled me. She had been so clipped and professional; seeing her express human emotions was a relief.

"I don't think it's that simple," I said. "I'd like to see the charts from the 44."

She gave me the same puzzled look as in the hallway earlier. "I assumed they were still onboard the boat. Mister Jaspers said he left them to be fingerprinted," she said.

Then I knew with a sickening certainty that the mysterious Mr. Traction Boot had taken those charts during the night, and they'd already been destroyed. I explained what I had found to Dunlay.

"But the gate was guarded until about 06 when I came in. They wouldn't let anyone on the base who wasn't a Coastie. And no one saw anyone go near 323."

"That figures. If somebody wanted those charts enough, they'd have come from the water or over your fence. But they didn't know they were leaving a calling card behind. Somebody doesn't want us to find that crew."

"You have any guess about who that might be?" She stepped beyond the soda-pop puddle and dropped into a steel and plastic desk chair.

"Well, I figure we can exclude alien space craft. Beyond that I haven't a clue."

Her firm mouth didn't flicker even a smirk. "How do we proceed from here?"

"I'd like you to have a boat search the area north of Crisp Point where that Loran hit indicated, and a shoreline search if possible."

"The boat search is no problem, but that shoreline is very remote. There aren't many roads, and it's definitely four-wheel drive territory. I can ask the Luce County sheriff's department what they can do."

"No, the commandant made it clear we shouldn't request outside help," I reminded her. "Look, could you ask the boat covering that sector to hug the beach as best they can. And if you get one of the Guardians from Air Station Cape Cod, they could run a shoreline search with SLAR."

She chuckled. "And we'd locate every deer within a half mile."

"OK, good point. Skip the infrared, and let's hope a careful visual spots anything there." Using her dividers, I quickly measured the distance between the Loran mark from CG44323 and the nearest point of land. "It's not likely they swam eleven miles anyway, but it's a possibility we can't dismiss either."

"I've wasted the past two days," Dunlay said. Her head and shoulders drooped.

I tried to cheer her. "Look at it this way, now we know where they're not and where they were. We also know that somebody is trying to prevent us from finding them. We cannot stop searching now."

"What are you going to do next?"

"I plan to have a chat with the Mountie who found the 44. Meanwhile will you ask the electronics shop to double-check the Loran unit?"

"I should receive the fingerprint report from the Soo police late this afternoon," she said, regaining her more officer-like demeanor. "Anything else?"

"Well, I'm a little curious about how the 323 could go through the locks without the Coast Guard watchstander overhearing the request on the radio."

"I wondered that myself. I contacted the Corps of Engineers

and according to their radio log, Pelligrini contacted them on Channel 16 at the same time Kunken was talking to our radioman on 21. The watch couldn't hear both conversations at the same time."

"That's pretty clever. You know, ma'am, I know you like these folks, but we have to consider the possibility that they were doing something illegal. That explains taking the boat out without orders, giving the wrong direction to the watchstander and sneaking through the locks. Now somebody has stolen the charts from the boat to hinder our search. It don't look quite kosher."

Dunlay shook her head. "I can't believe that those four individuals would get involved in anything illegal. Kunken's a certified hero, and Pelligrini is top notch. You should see those two dress up for inspection – between them they have any ribbon you can name except the Medal of Honor. Desharnais is a straight arrow – he won't even cheat on his wife and I've heard that he's had plenty of opportunity with the women around here. I don't know Lucas so well, but if she's hanging around with those three she isn't going to get hooked up with anything illegal."

I mulled that over a long while and took another approach to it.

"Well, ma'am, the alternative is that they knew of something illegal going on that they felt they had to stop themselves, without reporting their movements and violating a dozen regulations in order to do it. If they're not the folks doing something illegal, then it would appear that somebody else around here is. And if they didn't share their information with the command, my guess would be that they suspected someone in the command was involved."

Her eyes grew wide as I said this, and she drew her lips into a tight line as she glared at me. "Captain Burke was right about you. He said yesterday that the first thing you would do is make accusations about the officers here. If you have some private agenda, I don't want any part of it."

I had already alienated Burke and Fraser, so I decided to round out the Group Soo wardroom. "I'll be honest with you, ma'am, but if you'd rather not know what I'm thinking then I won't say. I'm not going to make any groundless accusations about officers and end up on the sorry side of the UCMJ. But I won't exclude the possibility that officers can do wrong. I made that mistake once, and I won't ever do anything so stupid again."

"What happened?" she asked, a strong hint of suspicion in her voice.

"While I was assigned to the 17th District, the Juneau police investigated a lieutenant commander accused of sexual assault on his kids' babysitter. He swore as an officer and a gentleman that he was innocent. The police wanted to hold him until the state lab matched blood types with a sperm sample. I suggested that in a small community like Juneau, going to jail was as good as a conviction. Besides Juneau is on Douglas Island; there's only so far you can run. So he was free until arraignment. The only reason I caught up was that his wife couldn't get any money from their teller machine. The bank told her their accounts were empty. So she called me, and I stopped him at the airport."

"How did that go?" she asked.

"About as well as you might expect. He blamed everyone with a badge for his problems. Hit me with a fire extinguisher in the jetway."

"Did he go to prison?"

"Yeah. After the hospital. Then court. And a court-martial."

"Hospital?"

"Mandibular fracture." I shrugged.

"You broke his jaw?" Her mouth gaped open.

"He resisted arrest."

Dunlay smiled to herself, looking toward the closed door. "Sometimes I'd like to break a commander's jaw. So what finally happened to that guy?"

"Last I heard he was editing a magazine for inmates at Fort Leavenworth. I guess hard labor doesn't mean breaking rocks anymore. Look, I'd like to borrow a few personnel records for some evening reading." I tore a page from my notebook on which I had composed a list of names drawn at random from the station and base roster. I handed her the sheet.

She scanned it quickly. "Wait, my name's on here. Am I a suspect, too?"

"I suspect everyone." I've wanted to say that for years.

Wednesday: 1130

Before I left the Coast Guard base, I called the Royal Canadian Mounted Police office in the other Sault Sainte Marie. I arranged an early afternoon appointment with Inspector Peter Thomason, the Mountie who had found CG44323 floating adrift in Agawa Bay. From the number of transfers required – each screening asking more probing and exact questions – I assumed Inspector Thomason was a rather significant link in the chain of command.

Spotting the Coast Guard decals on the government sedan's front doors, I decided to skip lunch and find an alternate means of transportation. I parked the Dodge in the parking lot of the visitor's center for the Soo locks across from the Superior Inn, then caught a taxi to the car rental. The only eight-cylinder model available was a big Ford LTD with every automatic function possible, but I took it anyway. When I'm on an assignment, I want power, not good gas mileage.

Thirty minutes after handing over my driver's license and credit card, I left with a contract for a week, unlimited miles, and an option to adopt. I drove through town and out onto the interstate highway south. With the accelerator pegged to the floor, the needle rose to 85 quick enough for government work. If I needed more power, I could take a wrench and strip 200 pounds of excess metal from the engine.

The big car handled well when I pulled a power spin through a U-turn on a deserted stretch of highway and went back into the Soo. A brief stop at the hotel was necessary to hide away my two pistols – carrying any weapons, especially handguns, into Canada is a hassle, even for an upstanding member of the law enforcement community like myself. After my affair in Mexico, I was a little concerned that the State Department would deny my citizenship if I ever went abroad again.

From the hotel, I headed north across the high-arched bridge. After answering some routine questions at Canadian customs, I asked for directions to the Royal Canadian Mounted Police post. The border guard asked five times whether there were firearms in the vehicle, returning to the question several times during the brief interview as if I might become confused and blurt out a spontaneous confession.

Inside the RCMP barracks, a uniformed constable, looking dapper in his scarlet blouse and blue jodhpurs, watched the front desk. A white braided lanyard fell from his shoulder to the butt of a large revolver secured in a well-polished brown leather holster on his waist. He refused to call Inspector Thomason until I produced my badge. Still, he verified my picture ID and checked the plastic for cuts that might indicate forgery. Thomason proved much more agreeable.

The tall, gaunt inspector came out to greet me, but I could tell by his grip when we shook hands that his slender frame was muscular and wiry. Freckles covered his face and neck, and he had an unkempt shock of red hair. He looked in his early thirties, though I expected someone much more senior based on our telephone conversation. He wore a rumpled brown corduroy jacket with a plaid tie hanging loosely below a white Oxford shirt's open collar. He could have passed for a college professor except for the conspicuous bulge in his jacket from a hip holster over his left kidney.

"Come on in and rest a bit," he told me, leading the way back to his private office. "Tea or coffee?"

I declined the beverages and studied his office decor while he poured a mug of steaming water and added a teabag. An impressive display of historical photographs hung on the walls, including group photos of Mounties, some dating back to the 1890s. Opposite the big oak desk covered with paper stood a gun cabinet and a canvas cot, indicating a man who worked late, maybe too often. The cabinet held an impressive collection of old carbines and revolvers. At last, he sat across from me behind his desk, blowing at his steaming ceramic mug. Who drinks hot tea in August? I wondered.

"I'm sure you've told your story to the Coast Guard a hundred times by now," I said, "but I'd like to hear it again."

"You know it's odd you'd say that because I was thinking that very thing – I should have told my story to everyone. Except no one has asked me about it at all. Once I turned the derelict over to your towing crew at Gros Cap, I've not heard from your Coast Guard again."

"Then you won't mind telling me the whole story?" I asked, quite surprised.

"Don't mind a bit. But will you tolerate a little background history first?" I nodded, and he continued, "You see I've been suspicious about the possibility of smuggling involving ocean freighters for almost a year. I'm not in a position to elaborate yet, except that the price of cocaine and crack has fallen in Detroit, Windsor, Chicago and also here in Sault Sainte Marie as well as Thunder Bay."

"But prices are dropping everywhere," I objected. "Why do you suspect a local operation?"

He withdrew a pipe from his top drawer, filled it with Virginia aromatic, and struck a match against his desk. "Simple economics. Once the drugs reach an entrance port either in America or here in Canada, you expect the price in that city to be the base price. The cost of further transportation, which necessitates greater risk and more people, should add to the price. Since the cost of cocaine in Chicago is almost the same as in Miami and New York, I suspect there is an import source close to Chicago. And what makes more sense than the Great Lakes?" He leaned back and puffed at the pipe.

"So why come here? Why not sail down Lake Michigan, closer to Chicago?"

"Are you familiar with Lake Superior?" he asked, pointing to a detailed nautical chart on the wall near the door. A thousand points and peninsulas jutted into the irregular spread of the expansive lake. Black silhouettes of ships marked the many hundreds of sinkings in the 300 years since Europeans discovered Gitchee Gumee. "Its shores are nothing but hundreds of miles of desolate coastline. The other lakes are much more populated," Thomason explained.

Logical but not substantial, I thought. I needed proof. "Does this connect with the Coast Guard boat you found?"

"Once I had these suspicions, I asked a few people with lake-front homes to keep me informed of unusual activity on the water. One of my look-outs thought it was very unusual for a motorboat to tow a U.S. Coast Guard boat into Canadian waters and then abandon it. Then I borrowed her husband's boat and went to fetch it."

I was stunned. I couldn't imagine how Dunlay and Fraser could fail to mention such a thing; it wasn't the kind of detail you'd forget, even in the heat of a major search. "How much of this did you tell the Coàst Guard?"

"Everything, but they didn't seem very interested." He gazed at the ceiling for a few seconds, then spoke again. "That struck me as quite odd. If my people were missing, I'd consider any information, even if it sounded ridiculous."

"Did your informant get any name or numbers from the motor-boat?" I asked.

"No, too far away I'm afraid, though I had provided her with the best binoculars I could afford out of my own pocket. She lives on a very prominent point. You understand that I can't divulge its location. They didn't tow the boat very near the shoreline, no doubt afraid of being spotted. She wouldn't have recognized your boat except for the red and blue stripes you fellows paint on the hull."

I tried to temper my tone so I wouldn't annoy him. "When you went aboard, did you change anything? Rig fenders, or change the Loran position?" I was fishing for possible explanations to account for the boat's condition as I found it that morning.

"As a professional investigator, I should resent the suggestion that I would compromise a probable crime scene." He took a puff on his pipe and then grinned. "No, when I reached the boat there were two fenders out on the port side. But I neglected to examine the Loran unit at all – it wouldn't have done me any good anyway. I know what it is and what it does, but that's about all. I'm not a sailor."

"Well, as a professional investigator in my position, what would your next move be?" I'm never too proud to accept reliable advice.

"Don't patronize me," he said coolly. "You must be competent or you wouldn't be here. When your local people refused my assistance, I figured your Headquarters was sending their best shamus. I assume that's you."

"I make no claims, but I'm always looking for suggestions and

72

advice. I'm new to this area, and I thought you had a few ideas in mind."

"Well, I'd track down those freighters that cleared the locks recently. Run them through Interpol or your intelligence center in Texas," he paused and puffed again on his pipe reflectively. "And I'd be careful. An operation that can reduce the mean price of cocaine in three major cities is a business whose proprietors will not be happy about any possible revenue loss. In short, expect these people to be armed to the teeth and ready to kill any interlopers."

We stood and shook hands again. The Mountie handed me his business card after he'd penciled his home phone number on the back. "Any time you need assistance, call me. My superiors aren't convinced by my notions yet, so I am somewhat restricted. I'll do what I can, though."

I decided to try a direct query. "Look, I haven't got much time, and I don't want you to take this wrong, but how certain are you about your notions?"

Thomason stood and crossed the room to the gun cabinet. He returned and handed me an old Colt six-shooter, manufactured circa 1880, which was undoubtedly quite valuable. The letters E.J.T. R.C.M.P. were stenciled on a brass inlay in the wooden grip.

"I'll wager my great-grandfather's Peacemaker," he said.

Wednesday 1235

On the way back to the base, I stopped before I reached the International bridge and called Andrews from a pay phone, using my personal charge card and hoping that the travel office would approve reimbursement. The afternoon had warmed, and sweat dampened the back of my shirt under the leather jacket. A slow-witted secretary seemed uncertain of Andrews' existence until I heard the lieutenant himself intercede, and he came on the line.

"Hi, Marty. Have any luck yet?" he asked after the secretary hung up.

"Depends whether you believe in wild conspiracy theories." Then I outlined Inspector Thomason's smuggling notions, his evidence of another boat towing the 44-footer, and my discoveries on board CG44323.

There was silence on the line while he considered the possibilities. "What about Senior Chief Drucker? Have you met him yet?"

"My first impression is that he's not involved. I wanted to know what else you had beside the poor marks on the crew?"

He began a reply, but an old Chevy Impala with a busted muffler roared past on the highway, drowning his words. I asked Andrews to start again.

"Three interesting details. First, he was on a patrol boat in Vietnam. He saw some action, but he was also brought up on charges for stealing drugs and going AWOL. A few years ago, he was treated for post-traumatic stress. He's also had chronic problems with alcohol, and his last commander started a medical board to have him discharged for it. If you're right about the smuggling, this guy has opportunity, past history and motive."

I felt my outrage growing; why was Andrews so eager to hang Drucker because he was in Nam? "OK, I'll check him out again. Later this afternoon, I'll call you with a list of freighter names I'd like you to run through Interpol and our intelligence folks in El Paso."

"Interpol and EPIC; not a problem. I'm waiting here to serve you," he said in a rather bitter tone, sounding unhappy about the decision to send me north instead of him after all.

I climbed back in the rented Ford, now almost furious. When I pulled up to the Customs booth on the U.S. side, a heavy-set inspector with the last brush cut in America asked how long I'd been in Canada, then glanced around the interior of the Ford.

"Where did you get the leather jacket?" he demanded.

"Seattle. Why?"

"Do you have a receipt for it?"

"Well, no. I bought it four years ago."

"Would you step out of the car?" he asked, opening the door for me. "A lot of people purchase leather goods in Canada. Do you still have the bag it came in?"

I climbed out and followed him to the rear bumper. He motioned for me to open the trunk. "I usually don't save shopping bags for more than two years," I said, making no effort to hide my sarcasm.

He peered around the trunk, poking in the spare tire well and feeling along the carpet. "Would you remove the jacket please?" It sounded more like a command than a request. He hooked his thumbs in the belt loops of his green double-knit slacks and tapped his foot impatiently. Near the main building stood a tall security guard with a revolver strapped on his hip. I was in a sour mood, and this fellow's breath wasn't helping my disposition.

"No, but thank you for asking." I fished my wallet out of an inside pocket and flashed my badge. "I would like to see your supervisor, however."

The inspector became flustered, and his pudgy face reddened. "I don't care who you work for. I want you to take off that jacket and produce the receipt immediately."

Over the troll's shoulder, I saw the armed guard growing more interested in our conversation. He heaved his bulky shoulders; his head cocked to one side as he contemplated intervention. I didn't want this confrontation to escalate any further because I might need help from Customs if Thomason was correct.

"Look, Mister Inspector Sir, I am a federal law enforcement officer," I snapped, hoping to intimidate the weathered gatekeeper into cooperation. "I am investigating a serious matter, and I have asked to see your supervisor. If you can't tell that this leather jacket is as old as your deodorant, you can go inspect packages in a very dark warehouse in Lower Manhattan."

His eyes bulged, and he pursed his thick lips. He wanted to slug me; his weight shifted on his feet as he considered the idea.

"Look, if you can't take me to your supervisor, then be a good fellow and point," I snarled. "Can you handle that?"

He jerked his thumb over his shoulder toward a small building with a panel of glass windows facing me. I started for the front door.

"Hey, you can't leave your car there," the guard told me.

I flashed my badge and threw him my keys as I strolled past. "Don't get in an accident," I called.

A sign out front said the senior agent was Peter Schmidt, and I couldn't believe my extraordinary luck. I knew Schmidt from an assignment in Key West. We had spent six weeks together on a fishing skiff, monitoring boat traffic in and out of the main Key West Channel. Later we teamed up on an air-strip surveillance. I went inside and asked the woman behind the counter for Agent Schmidt, flashing my badge once more for good measure.

Schmidt came out of his office while I studied a large relief map of the Sault Ste. Marie area, including the St. Mary's River and the locks. His gruff voice surprised me when he dropped a big paw on my shoulder.

"Hell, I figured you'd be dead by now," he said, gripping my hand. Schmidt was of average height, with a thick waist and gray hair. Thick red and blue veins coursed over his bulbous nose. "I heard about Morgenstern, by the way. Why didn't you shoot that bastard? Nobody would care about a dead American in Mexico" He led me into his office and closed the door. "So, what are you doing up here? Here for the fishing?" He settled into a fancy leather chair behind his desk. The cherry-stained desk and matching office furniture looked rather posh for a civil servant, but Schmidt had quite a few years with the agency.

I draped my jacket over the back of a chair and sat. Every possible space on each wall contained a citation or a photo of Schmidt with somebody famous. His gallery included personally addressed, autographed portraits from five consecutive presidents.

"You know about the missing Coasties – the boat crew?" I asked. "It's starting to look like there's something more to it than a swim call gone bad."

He pushed a cherry-wood humidor across the desktop and indicated I should help myself. "Yeah, I've heard a little about it. Your folks are keeping pretty hush-hush about the whole thing, like the boat was carrying nuclear weapons. What's your thinking on it?"

I could trust Schmidt because our paths had crossed many times before. We had gone to the shooting range in Key West, and I had taken him out to get drunk three days after his wife's funeral in Miami when he could no longer bear the relatives. I repeated everything I had discovered in the investigation up to that point. Schmidt listened, nodding from time to time. When I finished, he tossed a gold-plated lighter over the desktop, and I lighted my cigar.

I puffed. "Havana? Very impressive."

"Special perk of the job," he grinned, proud of his fringe benefits. "All kinds of things come down from Canada. Go ahead and take a few with you. Look, it all sounds pretty plausible to me. Not every upbound ship gets inspected until it reaches port somewhere in the lakes. We're like you guys; we don't have the men, the boats or the money to search everything that floats. Foreign ships get inspected every time they moor, but an American vessel could make several trips, that's all spot inspections."

"So you think Thomason's theory is plausible?" I wanted the opinion of another local expert.

"More than possible, it's damn probable. It could be a very simple operation. We're not geared to intercept serious smuggling here like they are down in Florida and the Gulf. If you could get around the southern interdiction area, say you sailed straight out to the middle of the Atlantic and went due north, you could bypass both the Coast Guard and Customs in the Caribbean. Sail in international waters until you reach Newfoundland. Nobody patrols the middle of the Atlantic. Then you'd risk a Canadian search on the way up the St. Lawrence Seaway or in the locks, but the investment might make it worth it." He threw his head back and exhaled a long series of perfect smoke rings.

I agreed with his assessment, and that sparked another thought.

"Isn't there a real problem with smuggling in the Canadian Maritime Provinces?"

"Sure, sometimes the police up there have found semi-trailers full of coke abandoned on the beach because the smugglers loaded it so heavy the tires sank in the sand. Let's agree that there's a lot of new fishing boats up there, but there's now a lot less fishing going on."

"Bet it's going to get worse now that so much of Georges Bank is closed," I observed. "Going to be a lot of boats sitting idle and a lot of skippers running late on their payments." The situation described by Thomason was beginning to take shape for me, and I felt better knowing Schmidt was in the area. "Can I call on you if I need some help? Be like old times."

He smiled. "Sure, it was fun, but I'm getting a little old for the rough stuff. To be honest, that's why Washington sent me here, though they were nice enough to say that getting my own station was a promotion. They figure all I can I handle these days is undeclared tourist trinkets. I don't mind, it's kind of like an early retirement. I've bought a little cabin out on Lake Superior. Say, we can do a little fishing when you get this thing done."

Studying his face with more care, I realized that Schmidt had not aged well since I had seen him last, when he was the chief of special operations for Customs in Miami. He was only in his early fifties, but most of his hair was gone and what remained was gray. His cheeks sagged; his shoulders slumped. The rough stuff doesn't always kill you straight away; it can wear you down to nothing.

"Don't forget, you've got to stop the huge black market in leather jackets," I said. "I should have shown your barracuda out there the patched bullet hole in the back of my sleeve. Of course, then he'd want to see the receipt for the bullet."

Laughing, Schmidt shook his head and finally wiped tears from his eyes. "I didn't mean to shoot you. You got in my way." He looked through the shaded window to where the anal-retentive inspector was grilling a young couple in a big green Chrysler. "Be glad you don't work with Magruder every day. Everyone around here calls him Mad Dog. Look, I'll talk to him. It won't do a bit of good, but I'll talk to him."

I thanked Schmidt, and we shook hands again. At his insistence, I stowed a half dozen cigars inside my jacket. I told him where I was staying in town and invited him to stop by some evening. When I drove away, Schmidt stood outside chastising Mad Dog Magruder.

Wednesday: 1330

Back in the American Soo, I parked the Ford at the visitor's center and switched back to the government Dodge. I didn't want to drive the rental around the Coast Guard base if it became necessary to travel incognito. Then another quick stop at the Superior Inn for unilateral rearmament. Before heading back to the base, I rolled through a fast-food drive-up for the deep-fried grease combo. If the Coast Guard continues dispatching me on these expeditions, I may investigate buying bulk quantities of liquid protein meals from NASA.

The operations watchstander let me into the OPCEN, then she hustled back to the phone console. Dunlay was running ragged, directing the search while also trying to appease Captain Burke over the telephone. She put the phone down and barked at the watchstander. The radioman thrust a clipboard at her. Dunlay sounded frustrated and venomous. Her mood changed when she saw me, but I had that effect on people lately.

"Where the hell have you been?" she demanded in a rather angry tone. "Things have been crazy around here since you left."

"Then no one can say I'm not a calming influence."

"Except for the captain, who'd still like to see you chained to a buoy anchor." The thought of me bound to a two-ton cement block at the bottom of the St. Mary's River seemed to improve Dunlay's disposition, and she smiled a little. "Give me a minute to clear this UMIB on the search."

"May I take a look?"

Her eyebrows knitted in consternation, but she passed me the radioman's clipboard.

The Urgent Marine Information Broadcast read: A UNITED STATES COAST GUARD VESSEL HAS BEEN LOCATED ADRIFT IN THE VICINITY OF AGAWA BAY. FOUR POB MISSING. THE VESSEL MAY HAVE PREVIOUSLY TRAN-SITED NEAR CRISP POINT. VESSELS IN THE VICINITY OF AGAWA BAY AND CRISP POINT ARE REQUESTED TO KEEP A SHARP LOOKOUT, ASSIST IF POSSIBLE AND ADVISE COAST GUARD GROUP SOO OR THE NEAREST COAST GUARD UNIT.

I returned the clipboard. "I'm not sure this is what the commandant had in mind when he said to keep matters quiet."

"OK, belay my last," Dunlay said to the petty officer. She turned back to me. "We may have a development. Not more than five minutes after you left, a freighter transiting to Duluth reported locating a distress marker light, you know, the small strobe light that boat crews carry on their life jackets."

I indicated that I understood the concept. Coasties tend to forget that special agents had lived in the genuine Coast Guard before earning a badge. "Where was the marker found?"

"Eight miles east of the position you found on the boat's Loran unit." She pointed to a chart. "It was in the middle of the traffic lane; the freighter's lookout spotted it."

"Any way to make certain it came from 44323?"

"No, that's the problem," she said, shaking her head. "These units are not imprinted with serial numbers. Anyone can purchase that model. So, there may not be a connection, but it's all I've got to work with. I'm concentrating a search in that area."

"Anything else?"

"The commander has been in here several times looking for you." She thrust forward a yellow message slip with Sally's name and phone number. "I cannot believe you would waste a minute of your time on some Soo Suzy while those people are missing." Dunlay glared at me.

The petty officer on watch turned to see the fireworks.

I took Dunlay's arm and directed her toward her private office. Closing the door, I said, "Look ma'am, I don't know why you're so angry with me, but the last thing on my mind is bedding down any woman."

She sat on the edge of her desk, arms folded across her chest. "You're here one day, and you've got a girlfriend lined up," she said, still in a harsh tone.

"OK, I met her in the Horney Toad last night. She told me a lot more about your search than anyone in town should know. I didn't sleep with her, and I don't intend to. Now I understand you're having trouble with the XO. And when this is over, I will help you fight that battle if you want. But right now, we have to concentrate on finding those people. Did you know that the 44 was towed into Canadian waters?"

"No!" Her anger turned to shock. "No! This is the first I've heard of it."

"Do you remember who talked to Thomason?"

"Not everyone. First the duty watchstander, and then the call was transferred to Mister Jaspers and I think the commander talked to him. It was pretty confusing around here that day." She slumped into a desk chair. "I guess it's still pretty confusing around here."

"Please don't mention the bit about the towing to anyone yet. I may need to figure out who knew and who didn't and why nobody said anything. While you continue searching, I'm going over to the Army Corps of Engineers to get a list of freighters that moved through the locks Sunday and Monday. I'll be back as soon as I finish." I headed for the door.

"Wait, I forgot about the fingerprints," she said, shifting through the clutter on her desk. She handed over a manila file folder. "I guess it doesn't tell us anything."

I skimmed the police synopsis. The detective found five distinct sets of prints on board the 44323 and four inconclusive partials. Four of the five were suitable matches with Pelligrini and the other three crew members. The fifth was Warrant Officer Jaspers, who'd gone aboard when it arrived back in the Soo. The remaining four were a mystery.

"Actually, this says quite a bit," I told her. "Normand told me the boat was scrubbed down on Sunday, so these prints are likely new. We know seven people went aboard: the four crewmen, Thomason, Jaspers and the detective. If we give the detective the benefit of the doubt and assume he knew enough not to touch anything, we know six names. That means three people we can't identify were on the boat sometime between Sunday's washdown and Monday afternoon when the detective dusted the boat."

"I didn't think about it like that," she said, just as the radioman called for her.

"That's why I get to carry the shiny badge." I grinned and left.

The office that controls the locks' operation was located in a squat sandstone building about 500 yards farther up Water Street from the Coast Guard base. Along the way, I passed the Ira D. Maclachlan American Legion hall, mutely saluted the black POW-MIA flag hanging below the national ensign, and hiked across the lush green lawn of a park. A tan obelisk in the park commemorated the 50th anniversary of the opening of the locks. A sign indicated that the park was the site of Fort Brady, built-in 1822 to claim the Soo for the United States. The black and tan dredges of the Army Corps of Engineers sat moored along the waterfront adjacent to the park.

Atop the sandstone Corps building was a glass observation room like an airport traffic control tower, which I assumed served a similar function of handling the vessel traffic above, below, and through the river's locks. As I approached the building, the locks' maintenance crew raced about on electric golf carts, beeping their horns at slow-moving tourists strolling on the asphalt walkways. Above the main entrance, the Army Corps of Engineers head-quarters was still labeled WAR DEPARTMENT. Though the War Department disappeared years ago, the spirit lives on; it was soon evident that any information I learned there would come only after a battle. Finding the right person consumed 20 minutes. When I finally did locate the alleged expert, she was reluctant to talk.

"Excuse me, Miss Lafser, I need some information about vessels transiting the locks in the past 72 hours," I said after reading the nameplate on her desk.

"That's Miz Lafser," she said, without a glance in my humble direction. "Miz Eileen Lafser." She remained planted behind her desk, wearing a pink polyester blouse and a matching macramé sweater – her frosted hair set in a cheap bouffant.

"Of course, Miz Eileen Lafser. I need some information, please. I need to track any vessel that cleared the locks since Sunday night."

"I'm sorry, I can't look up the names of transiting ships for anyone who walks in the door," she said, adjusting her glasses to see her romance novel better. She was trying to ignore me, but I can be a difficult person to snub.

"Is that information classified? Or protected by the Privacy Act?" I asked, adding a calculated tone of menace.

Miz Eileen Lafser responded without glancing up from her book. "No, but it takes a lot of time to search through the files."

I tried to remain calm yet appear threatening – a delicate balance. "It would seem, Miz Lafser, that you have a surplus of excess time at the moment." I reached across the counter and laid my badge on the open page she was reading. "And may I suggest that you get off your ass before I fetch your supervisor and you find your butt in a sling."

I snatched my badge away as Miz Eileen Lafser slammed her book closed and plucked the glasses from her nose. They dangled on a fake pearl string against her meaty bosom. "Young man, you have no right to use such language with me." Her nostrils flared, and her painted eyebrows knitted in anger.

"At least now I have your undivided attention," I decided a simple, direct appeal to her intellect was best. For her benefit, I spoke very slowly. "I am conducting a federal investigation. You are interfering with it. Aren't you curious about the penalties for that? But why don't we call your boss and get her opinion?"

Sensing she couldn't win, Miz Eileen Lafser laid the paperback aside and rose to her feet with no small effort. "That won't be necessary." She waddled to a file cabinet, exposing the broad, lavender double-knit expanse of her stern. "Have a seat, and I'll look up the transits for Sunday and Monday."

"Gosh, that would be swell." I said. "And don't forget to include ship's name, owner, destination, time of transit and last port of call for each."

While Miz Eileen Lafser searched through the records, I settled on a metal couch with vinyl cushions in the small waiting area decorated with pictures of freighters passing through the locks. I flipped through a two-year-old issue of Sports Afield. Four separate articles listed tips for good bass fishing, and I jotted down a few ideas in my notebook.

Then I wondered why I was having such trouble with people on this assignment. I could understand Burke's annoyance, but the XO and Dunlay were also angry with me. And then came Mad Dog Magruder and Miz Dacron Polyester. What was I doing wrong? I sniffed my underarms for a clue. Yes, Burke, Fraser, and Dunlay were upset about the missing crew. Did the other two realize, as some employees do, that they receive the same pay no matter how they behave toward the public or how little work they accomplish?

Twenty minutes later, Miz Eileen Lafser returned to the main desk with a list of eleven ships, written in delicate scrawl likely perfected under a nun's watchful eye and hovering ruler. I wondered if Miz Eileen Lafser could also type. She had exceeded my demands by including the cargo of each vessel on the list. But even that wasn't enough to merit amnesty.

"Would you do me a tremendous favor and make five copies for me?" I smiled, handing the list back to her.

As Miz Eileen Lafser went down the hall to the copier, I reached across the counter for her romance novel and ripped out the last dozen pages.

Wednesday: 1415

The list of eleven ships that transited through the locks between noon Sunday and noon Monday soon whittled down to a manageable list of suspects. Four of the eleven were downbound and left Lake Superior before the 44-footer departed the station. Two of the upbound had moored at the steel mill in Sault Ste. Marie on the Canadian side, so Crisp Point would have been 50 miles west of their final destination.

Two of the remaining five came from other ports in the Great Lakes and had never been to sea. There was a possibility that one of those could have transferred cocaine or some other contraband from a ship coming in from the sea, but that didn't match Thomason's theory. That left three ocean-going freighters, called "salties."

One of the three suspects had headed to Thunder Bay in Canada after it left Whitefish bay, so I decided to ask Thomason if he could check on that one. That left me with two possibilities, and I figured even I could handle that much, especially since I had help. I called Andrews from a phone booth outside the American Legion hall. He sounded more enthusiastic when he learned about the computer research needed.

"You know, I used to hate computers before I went to the Academy, but they saved my butt there," he said. "Now I play with the damn things all the time. I went out and bought my own last month."

"Careful sir. Next it'll be a fax machine for the car. You'll be so plugged in you'll think power outages are vacations," I joked. "Hey, you got a pencil anywhere in that high-tech office?" I paused while he rummaged. "First on our list of suspects is the *Baltic Express*, and here's a surprise, it's registered in Panama."

"Along with half the ships in the world."

"And next is the *Jersey Trader*. Its last port of call was listed as Madrid, but I don't expect the kind of people we're dealing with to be completely honest about a thing like that. It's American, registered in Wilmington, Delaware."

"I could have guessed that, too," Andrews said. "For the number of ships registered there, you'd think Wilmington was an international seaport."

"The last is the *Chinook*, homeported in Thunder Bay, Ontario. I am going to ask the Mountie to look into that, as well." I gave him the other information I had on each. "I plan to go to Duluth tomorrow, but if you get any information, that'll help decide where I concentrate my time. I'd like you to check with both Interpol and El Paso Intelligence."

"Interpol and EPIC, got it. When will you call me back?"

"I'll shoot for 1800 this evening. If you don't hear from me, leave a message at the hotel and say your name is Jack." I gave him the number at the Superior Inn.

"You take this secret agent business seriously, don't you?" he kidded.

"You know what they say: Just because you're paranoid doesn't mean nobody is trying to kill you."

"It sounds like your biggest enemy right now is Captain Burke," Andrews laughed. "He called here four times today and asked my boss to pull you out. The commander told him you were there under direct orders from the commandant."

"It's nice to have an admiral's support for a change," I replied. "Think you could use it for me? I need you to arrange for Traverse City to fly me out to Duluth in the morning."

"Anything else?" he chuckled. "A limo waiting on the other end?"

"I'll need ground transport, but I figured I could handle that myself. If you're volunteering, though. . ."

When the line went dead, I called Inspector Thomason of the Royal Canadian Mounted Police. He promised to check out the *Chinook*. He had a friend with the local police in Thunder Bay who owed him a favor. I had never met anyone in law enforcement who didn't owe someone a favor and wasn't owed a variety of favors in return.

Then I walked back to the base, expecting to find Burke and Dunlay waiting at the flagpole with a hangman's noose. Instead, Fraser surprised me at the main entrance.

"Come with me, Galloway. I don't have time for questions."

Fraser walked me down to the small boat station and into Senior Chief Drucker's office. Drucker was chatting with a young woman who wobbled on the same chair I had sat in earlier. She was young, tall, and what my grandmother called willowy. Her sun-streaked hair was long, her cotton skirt short. She asked detailed questions about the search; I suspected she was a reporter. When he saw the XO, Drucker excused himself, and Fraser introduced us.

"Melinda, this is Special Agent Galloway. He's investigating the disappearance. Galloway, this is Melinda Desharnais."

Fraser grinned at my surprise. Melinda extended her hand, knuckles up and fingers down, like the bishop proffering his ring to be kissed at confirmation.

"Missus Desharnais, thanks for coming down to talk to me." I sat behind Drucker's desk. Fraser stood in the doorway, his attention fixed on her well-tanned limbs.

"Is there news about Paul?" she asked, glancing up at Fraser.

"No, I'm afraid there isn't yet." I leaned forward to draw her attention. "I want you to know that I understand exactly how you feel. My father has been missing since '68, when his patrol boat was strafed in Viet Nam."

Fraser jumped; it was his turn for a surprise.

"Melinda, did your husband tell you why he was going to work early on Monday?"

"He never talked work when we were on the phone. I only got back from Santa Monica Monday evening. I was home with Mom for two weeks. I figured Paul was on duty till I called Tuesday morning and they said he was missing."

"When you came home, did you notice any changes?"

"Lots of dishes and laundry." She smiled. "But that wasn't unusual."

"Did he ever discuss drug smuggling?"

"Back in Long Beach, sure. But he always said LE up here was boring because the biggest thing they found was a carton of cigarettes."

A seaman came to the chief's office and whispered a message to the XO. "I'll be back," he announced and left.

"Did Paul enjoy working here?" I asked.

"Well, yeah, especially after that big asshole left. What was his name? Banks? Hanks? Sometimes Paul bitched about his marks, but he said he had more respect for Drucker than any officer-in-charge he'd ever met."

"Was your husband good friends with Henry Pelligrini and Walter Kunken?"

"Oh, yeah. They were like the Three Musketeers. They were in the same duty section; they camped together; they all drank Rolling Rock. And Patti Lucas was like that fourth guy, the one who wanted to be a Musketeer."

"D'Artangian?"

"That's right. She was always hanging around them. I started to get jealous, but Paul said she was like their little sister. And I figured she was safer around Paul, Hank and Walt than some of the other guys around here." She glanced at the door where Fraser had stood. "Sorry. Some guys make me uncomfortable – the way they stare."

I nodded. "Have you noticed anything missing around the house since you returned?"

"His sleeping bag isn't in the closet. I didn't see anything else missing." She straightened in her chair and tugged her hem down to mid-thigh. "Can I ask you a question?"

"You bet."

"This is a big deal, right? Four Coasties disappearing."

"Uh huh."

"Why haven't I seen anything in the newspaper or on TV? Every time Paul went out for an overdue there was a little story in the paper. Why is there this big cover-up?"

"I have to be honest with you; there's a lot of politics involved here. The commandant sent me here to find your husband and the others before it gets into the news. There's budget hearings this week, international negotiations – bad publicity could do a lot of damage. I'm sure the admiral appreciates your cooperation."

"That's what he said when he called. But shouldn't I tell Paul's parents? It doesn't seem fair that they don't know. I mean, how am I going to tell them if you don't ...?" She couldn't bring herself to complete the thought, but it was clear she'd spent two days thinking about little else.

"You won't have to tell them. I will find your husband. Give me until Friday; I'll call you as soon as I know something." I tried to think of something more definite I could offer than boasting of my detective skills. "If anyone needs to call Paul's folks, Admiral Thorne will do it. He called my mother from Saigon."

Whispering thanks, she took out her sunglasses, then hoisted her leather pouch by its drawstrings as she stood and tossed her hair and bag over a shoulder in one graceful movement. She held out her hand again, more business-like this time.

"Your husband is alive, Missus Desharnais," I said as we shook hands. "And we will find him."

"I know." She nodded, but as she put on her sunglasses, she wiped away tears.

I tried hard not to stare as she left.

Wednesday: 1510

Back in the OPCEN, I found Dunlay in the midst of a shouting match on the telephone. I gathered that the captain had pestered her all afternoon to mount an air search for the crew and organize a firing squad for me. Dunlay slammed down the receiver in disgust.

"I'm going to lose these yet," she said, tugging at the silver bars on her collar. "The captain figures that if we can locate our crew, that'll get you out of here faster."

"Geez, kind of makes me wonder what he's trying to hide," I mused, rubbing my chin.

"Don't get started. Don't even think about it," Dunlay warned me. "I've got enough troubles around here. The boat crews are exhausted, but I don't have the assets to replace them. The buoy-tender wants to be relieved from searching so it can get back to lighthouse work, and the other cutters want to leave because they're bored." She ran a hand through her short hair in exasperation. "Oh, here's a big surprise. The Air Force didn't see anything on the film from the reconnaissance flight except two freighters and three Coast Guard vessels. How's that for a wise expenditure of the taxpayer's dollar?"

The radioman interrupted her. "Ma'am, the Katmai Bay is requesting permission to return to the Soo for fuel."

"Why didn't they refuel last night?" she asked the ceiling. "Tell them to finish searching their present grid and then return to base." Her face bore an expression of sheer disgust. "Sometimes I can't see how these guys remember to take in the mooring lines before they get underway."

"Sometimes they don't, and that's something you don't want to see," I observed. "Look, I hate to interfere with your fun here, but can we talk for a minute in your office?"

We walked down the hall, and she closed the door behind us when we entered. "I hope you're getting close to something."

"Well, I've got a list of suspects, three upbound freighters that could have been near Crisp Point early Monday morning. Head-quarters is doing background checks now."

Dunlay perched on a metal stool at her chart table. "How long do you figure that will take? Should I plan to continue searching all night?"

"The check should be done in a couple of hours. I'd continue the search though, to keep Captain Burke happy if nothing else."

"I guess all this business about smuggling cocaine up here makes sense, but it doesn't seem possible. I did drug interdiction on the *Northland,* out of Portsmouth, so I'm familiar with smuggling ops. You expect it down in Florida. But I keep thinking it can't happen up here. We're too far north, too remote, too . . . too conservative to break the law."

"I guess we'll put that to the test soon enough," I said. "Different subject. Do you remember a boatswain mate who was discharged a few months ago? He was brought up on charges with Pelligrini."

"You mean Chris Banks. Why? Do you think he's involved?"

"I'm curious. Do you know anything about him?"

"I saw him once in the Horny Toad. Big kid, over six feet, built like a lumberjack, thick beard now that he's out of the Coast Guard. Everybody around here hates him."

"What happened? What were the charges?"

"He got into an altercation with Hank, uh, Pelligrini, outside a bar. Banks pulled a knife, and Hank hit him with a tire iron. The captain was prepared to discharge both of them, but there were enough witnesses that said Banks instigated the whole thing."

"What caused it?" I asked.

"I don't know; nobody would talk about it. I wouldn't be surprised to learn Banks was involved with crime though. I heard he was transferred here about four years ago from the base in St. Ignace when about half the unit flunked a urinalysis."

"Sounds like a charming guy. Any idea how I can find him?"

"No, but he was assigned to the station so you should ask Petty Officer Normand. Have you met Normand yet?"

"Yes, ma'am. I'll talk to him. May I use your phone to call MSO Duluth?"

She looked up the phone number in the district phone book for me. While I dialed, she went back into the operations center.

I had to board the two freighters the next day and figured the best way was through the Coast Guard Marine Safety Office in

Duluth. They inspect freighters for compliance with safety regulations. They also observe the loading of hazardous cargoes. The seaman who answered connected me with the executive officer, Lieutenant Commander Marshall, in short order. I introduced myself and explained that I was investigating the disappearance of the 44-footer crew.

"Sure, I've been following the search in the district OPSUM. Have you found anything yet?" he asked.

"No sir, that's why I'm calling. I suspect that a freighter moored in Duluth is involved in the case."

He paused, considering the situation. "You mean like a collision? I heard the 44-footer was intact."

"Sir, I'm not at liberty to discuss it right now."

"What can we do to help you?" Marshall asked.

"Nothing right now, but I need an excuse to get aboard two freighters tomorrow morning."

"Well, you know that we don't inspect every ship that pulls into Duluth, right?" he asked. "Generally, we only board a freighter if it's American and needs its annual inspection, or if a foreign ship is coming into Duluth for the first time in a calendar year."

"Can't you board a ship whenever you want, to double-check things?"

"Are you familiar with the concept of probable cause?" he asked. "Well, I suppose we could, particularly if you think a freighter is tied in with that missing crew." He paused, thinking it over. "I guess it's possible that one of these guys could hit something in the dark and never even know." He was fishing for the real story.

I didn't take the bait. "Well, I want to poke around a couple of salties that went through the area about the time the crew disappeared, to see what I find."

"So, you have a couple of possibilities in mind?"

"I'm interested in the *Baltic Express* and the *Jersey Trader.*"

"Hang on, let me see where they are." He left the phone for a moment and soon came back. "I've got them listed here. They're both moored at a pier on the Superior side. So, a boarding is a lot easier than if they are anchored off."

"I'm still not certain either of them is involved. Do you think I could borrow one of your inspection teams first thing in the morning to board the most likely suspect?"

"I don't see anything urgent on the schedule for tomorrow. We'll need to sit down with the captain and discuss this whole thing, but we can figure something out. Can you be here by 7:30?"

"To be honest, I'll need some help on that side of things. I figure I'll be at the airport about zero seven hundred. Can you have a duty driver pick me up around then?"

He grunted, a little reluctant to get one of his people out that early. When I finished on the phone, I walked back into the operations center. Dunlay stood drawing out search plans on a chart. The radioman on watch, a young woman with reddish-blonde hair and a wrinkled uniform, complained to the air about the lack of shipboard billets for women and about the poor situation of women in the service.

Dunlay didn't seem to be paying much attention to the petty officer's complaints, but she finally turned and said, "Well, it won't change until we close down the Boys School on the Thames."

"Aren't you an Academy grad?" I asked.

She jumped, startled to hear a male voice. "Galloway! Don't do that! I thought you were the captain."

"Well?"

"Yeah, I went, but I didn't need four more years of kindergarten."

"Sorry I startled you. Did you have a chance to collect the personnel records I wanted?" I asked Dunlay.

She motioned to a large box in the corner. I heaved it onto my shoulder and started for the door. "Would you trust Normand?" I asked her. Without hesitation, she said she would, and I decided to accept her judgment.

The afternoon had grown sunny, with a light breeze off the water, a perfect day to go out trolling deep for pike. After dumping the personnel files in the trunk of the Dodge, I walked down to the docks where Normand stood supervising a crew of three seamen who were busy washing the fingerprinting powder from the decks of the 44323.

"Washing it twice in one week? Gee, Boats, I'll bet that's more attention than you give it all year," I joked.

"Hey, I take good care of my boats," he replied. "Actually, this one ain't even mine. It came up from St. Ignace last week because the snipes were overhauling the engine on our 41-footer."

"You shouldn't call engineers snipes," I told him. "You'll hurt their feelings."

"Impossible, you've got to be human to have feelings. But I've got to give them credit; they worked most of the night to get the 41-footer ready to go this morning. Look, I hope you don't need to go back aboard. Chief told me to wash it down so we could use it in the search tomorrow."

"Thanks, I've seen enough. Tell me, you have any idea where I can find Chris Banks?"

He gave me a look of distrust as if I was asking where to buy a rattlesnake. "Last I knew he was living down in St. Ignace. He knocked up some girl down there and was living with her and the kid. He met her while he was stationed at Saint Iggy before the big drug bust. Of course, he may be in prison by now for all I know."

"Yeah, he sounds like a real hero," I agreed. "I don't suppose he'll be very cooperative."

"With you? Not likely. He got busted from first class back to third because of a piss test down at St. Ignace before he transferred up here. He always blamed CGI for it."

"Yeah, we forced him to do drugs, right?" I laughed. "How about coming with me to go pay a visit?"

"You want someone to ID the body?"

I laughed. "I'm not going to kill him."

Normand laughed, too. "I wasn't talking about his body."

He told the seamen to finish the washdown on the boat and stow their gear. I said I'd meet him at the GV, and he went to change out of his uniform.

I walked along the waterfront, running through the diverse information I'd learned. An 800-foot laker passed the base; its turbulent wake set every vessel along the dock rocking. A ship that big could carry a lot of coke, I thought. How did Thomason's suspicions relate to the missing boat crew? Would I waste a day in Duluth chasing a suspicion? Not that there were any better options.

When Normand returned, he wore his plaid shirt and denim jeans.

"Do you think we should call him before we drive halfway to St. Ignace?" he asked as we climbed into the government sedan. "To make sure he's home?"

"If he hates CGI as much as you say, do you suppose he'd wait till we got there?"

"I'd hate to surprise him. It might piss him off."

Normand's anxiety prompted me to reach inside my jacket and release the safety on the Colt .45.

Wednesday: 1645

The dull drive from the Soo to St. Ignace took less than an hour. Along the way, I quizzed Normand about Senior Chief Drucker, the station's morale problems, and any suspicions he had about smuggling. I rarely reveal information to anyone who wasn't directly involved or that I didn't know well, but Dunlay had vouched for him. I didn't have time to run security checks on everyone assigned to Group Soo before I started asking hard questions.

"What was the dispute between Banks and Pelligrini?"

"I never heard exactly. Banks was a troublemaker. He liked to get drunk and start fights downtown. Sometimes he'd be so hungover when he came on duty that I was afraid to put him on a boat, though sometimes I considered sending him out in hopes that he would tumble overboard. Our waters never get very warm, and with the right amount of preparation time to recover a manoverboard, you know, getting out the stokes litter, and radioing in the distress and planning an appropriate search pattern, a skilled coxswain could leave that asshole drifting until he was a floater. Water up here's cold enough it wouldn't take very long."

I sensed Normand had spent a lot of time thinking about this unique form of murder for this particular individual. He opened the window a bit and fished out a pack of cigarettes. "Mind if I smoke?"

"Here, try one of these instead." I handed him one of Schmidt's fat stogies, unwrapped one for myself, and punched the lighter on the dashboard.

Normand read the band before opening his. "Hey, it's Cuban. Isn't this illegal?"

The lighter snapped out, and I passed it to him. "I'm afraid so. If we're stopped by the cops, you'll have to swallow it."

"Once I swallowed a wad of chewing tobacco and threw up. I was awfully sick for pretty near a whole day." He took a puff and held the cigar up for inspection. "It would take a while to wolf down this puppy."

I gave him my best Cagney. "I'll hold them off as long as I can with my six shooter, see, while you dispose of the evidence, see."

"You agents carry a gun all the time, huh?" His question didn't surprise me; many Coasties don't understand what special agents do. I didn't have an accurate idea myself when I applied for the job after I was forced off flight duty, and there are individuals, including a few who wear stars on their shoulder boards, who will say that I still don't know what agents do – that I sort of make up my own rules as I go along. I prefer to call it my creative investigative prerogative.

"Whenever I'm on a case, except when I'm in the shower," I answered Normand.

"So, you're packing now?" he asked, shaking his head in disbelief. "I couldn't get used to that. I still feel funny strapping on a gunbelt when we go on patrol."

I never think about carrying a weapon until either I need one or having one becomes conspicuous. That's why I always wear a bulky leather jacket to cover my shoulder holster and loose pants to obscure the Beretta on my calf. Contrary to what you'd expect, carrying a gun doesn't always intimidate people. Sometimes an idiot will force an issue to see if you have the testicular fortitude to use your weapon.

"I hope I can remember how to get to Banks' place," he said after a long huff on his cigar. "I only went there once for a party. It's a real dump."

He directed me off the highway, along a winding two-lane, and finally onto a narrow gravel track. I slowed the Dodge because it tended to fishtail on the slag. We stopped before each cabin while he studied it.

"This is it," he announced at a narrow opening in the brush.

I couldn't even see the house through the trees. "You sure you remember this place? I don't want to get shot for trespassing."

"No, I don't remember it at all, but her name is on the mailbox."

"Nobody likes a smart ass," I told him, "and I should know that better than anyone."

We went up the narrow driveway, with pine branches slapping against the fenders. Limbs obscured the path, and soon we were far from the road or the nearest house. The green cabin at the end of the long drive seemed little more than a shack. The one-floor structure didn't look like it could be divided into more than three tiny rooms. The paint was chipped, and several dozen shingles were missing from the roof. A rain gutter hung askew from the porch. Nothing else around the place had been maintained either. An old brown Ford Maverick rested on its axles next to a shed, the tires stacked against the wall. Plastic toys, a busted snowmobile, and a half dozen motorcycles in various stages of disrepair cluttered the yard. The tall grass appeared to have avoided a mower for several weeks or perhaps months.

"I don't see Banks' truck so he may not be home," Normand observed. "He's got this big Ford F-250 jacked up on mud tires. A big roll bar in the back with fog lights. But he might have sold it by now."

I pointed at the open door. "The missus is home?"

"Oh, they never married," he said, then added in a whispered tone, "He used to say he'd never marry a girl that ugly."

"How romantic." Chris Banks sounded more and more like the kind of guy I'd want to shoot as a public service. "Tell me, this guy have any redeeming qualities?"

Normand thought that over for a minute. "Yeah, I once saw him drink a can of beer while standing on his head."

I looked at him in astonishment. "Well, that's worth an invitation to the White House."

We hopped out of the car and waded through the high grass to the porch. I wished I had time to snag a few of the grasshoppers whizzing around us on some excellent pan fishing. I usually prefer fly-casting, but trolling rivers for catfish or carp can be fun, too.

I motioned for Normand to knock while I waited out of sight from the door. We didn't know for certain whether Banks was home or not. If he was as nasty as described, he might not react well to seeing a strange face on his porch.

"Who's there?" a woman called from inside.

"Larry Normand. I knew Chris up in the Soo."

A young woman appeared at the screen door. She was tall and lanky, with long blonde hair that fell to her shoulders from a straight part across the top of her head. She wore a loose flannel shirt, sweat pants, and a large bruise on her right cheek, in all probability from a strong backhand. Her eyes looked puffy, and her lower lip was swollen.

"I work at the station in the Soo," Larry added.

"Yeah, I remember you from the party." Her eyes darted toward me. "Did Chris know you guys was coming by?"

Normand glanced at me. "No. I meant to call, but I lost his number."

"Well, he ain't around. He came by for a while this morning and dropped off some stuff. But he left pretty quick."

Judging by the look of her face, he may have stayed long enough to slap her around a little. I disagreed with what Normand said before; she wasn't ugly. She had strong, handsome features and bright teeth. The woman slouched a little yet otherwise had a solid build. Her grammar was poor, but she seemed bright enough. I wondered how decent women get hooked up with buffoons like Banks.

I decided to try a direct approach and took out my badge. I introduced myself and explained that I was investigating the disappearance of a Coast Guardsman. I asked her name.

"Betsy Kruza. I live here," she said, eyeing me with hooded eyes. "Chris moved out about two months ago."

"Do you know where he's living now?" I asked.

"He's got a cabin up on Whitefish Bay. I think he's got some Indian girl living with him," she explained. "But she drinks a lot and passes out so he comes down here." The purpose of his visits went unsaid, though her dry, bitter tone indicated a certain sordidness she didn't want to discuss. She half shrugged, a gesture of how she was tired of Banks and how he treated her.

"Did he punch you in the face?"

"In the face. In the stomach. It doesn't make much difference anymore."

"Why you let him do that?" Normand asked.

"Like I have a lot of choice. If I try'n stop him, he goes after Jamie. My boy's got welts you wouldn't believe." Her voice quavered, and tears came to her eyes. "I had him arrested once, but he only come back meaner than before."

I wondered why Banks would drive so far out of his way to drop something unless it needed to remain hidden. Unfortunately, I didn't have enough time or evidence to get a search warrant – intuition generally doesn't impress a judge. I had no reason to think Banks was involved except for a chill in my neck. Some agents have little voices or a feeling in their gut; I get a slight shudder. Betsy would have to consent to show me what he'd left, and I needed to gain her confidence to get that permission. "Betsy, if Banks is involved in what I think he is and I can prove it, he will be put away for a long time. I'd like your help, but if he finds out you helped me, he could be that much worse."

She wiped her eyes and gave me a cold, expressionless look. "It can't get no worse. If it wasn't for Jamie, I'd walk away from here."

"Will you show me what Chris left here this morning?" I asked.

Betsy Kruza made her decision. She pushed the screen door open and stood aside so we could enter. Compared with the clutter in the yard, the neatness of the cabin's tiny rooms surprised me. The small living room contained a green couch with a yellow, knitted afghan thrown over the back, a small television, a stack of toys, and an enormous collection of dog-eared paperback romance novels. Betsy was desperately seeking love.

A doorway to the right led to the kitchen and the bedroom on the far side of that. The worn linoleum and antique appliances in the kitchen looked spotless. Normand waited there amidst the little craftsy knickknacks hung on the walls.

Betsy led the way into the dark bedroom, motioning for me to be quiet. She pointed to a crib where a toddler lay curled around a stuffed bear. Jamie looked about two years old, the same age as my daughter the last time I saw her. In a pale cast of sunlight through the blinds, I saw a dark purple bruise – a nasty mark the size of a cue ball – on the boy's bare shoulder. I didn't want to know how it happened.

While I watched the sleeping child, Betsy knelt beside the crib and pulled a wide cylinder of white paper from under it. I carried it into the kitchen and unrolled it across the small table, revealing a wrinkled chart of Whitefish Bay, with a course from the Soo locks to north of Crisp Point plotted in pencil.

A series of X's broke the course line, indicating each time a coxswain had fixed his position with radar. Beside each X, he had recorded the time the boat reached that position. The first mark was made above the locks at 0610 and not far from Crisp Point at 1130.

I knew this was the chart missing from CG44323, but that didn't answer any questions. Why did Banks want the chart? And how did he get on base with a guard at the gate? The most nagging question was why he hadn't destroyed the chart as soon as possible. What justified the risk of keeping stolen evidence?

Normand peered over my shoulder. "Is that the course the 44-footer followed?"

"If my hunches are correct, yes. And this chart came from the boat last night."

Betsy entered the room, carrying her son straddled on her left hip bone. The boy blinked in the bright lights, covering his eyes with an arm but still trying to see Normand and me. "I hope you can nail the son of a bitch for something," Betsy said.

I wanted to take the chart back to Dunlay to help with the search, but if Banks returned to the cabin and found it missing, Betsy would be in serious trouble. Instead, I fished out my notebook and asked Normand to record all the times and approximate coordinates for each position fix.

Then I took Betsy and the boy into the living room. I sat next to her on the sofa to inquire about Banks. I asked about his whereabouts and his connection to the missing boat crew. Jamie played with a fleet of small trucks in the corner, shoving the toys into each other in violent head-on collisions.

According to Betsy, Banks' visit to her remote cabin that morning had been abrupt, brief, and brutal. He hadn't mentioned the missing crew; he demanded money and slapped her when she could produce only food stamps. When he left, she had no interest in asking where he was going.

"Have you ever gone to his cabin so you could tell me how to get there?" I asked.

She shook her head. "I've never went up there. I don't even have his phone number. He comes here whenever he wants." When she brushed her long hair over her shoulder, I spotted a bright red abrasion on the left side of her neck an inch below her jawline. A plum-colored thumb mark about the size of a bottle cap marked a prominent pressure point on the opposite side of her neck. I wondered if Banks had received any Coast Guard law enforcement training on self-defense tactics or whether he dabbled in the martial arts as many thugs do. His type always seemed to ignore the proper form, the strict regimen, and the code of honor, but they want to learn the easiest ways to inflict pain on the human body.

"Do you know where he works or anyplace that he goes regularly where I could find him?"

"Chris can't hold the same job for two days," she snorted derisively. "I'm surprised the Coast Guard kept him as long as they did. Now he spends most of his time drinking."

"What does he do for money?" I asked.

"He does odd jobs, takes some of my welfare check and I think his girl works at the casino in Bay Mills."

"But you can't think of anywhere I should look first?"

She puzzled it over for a few minutes, watching her son's demolition derby. "Yeah, there's a bar over in Brimley or Bay Mills, near the reservation, called the Bear Den or the Bear Cave. He told me about it a while back; I guess he got in a fight there or something. I never been to it."

I wasn't optimistic about searching every beer joint in the Upper Peninsula, no matter how entertaining that might prove. Nor could I spend too much time poking around a Native American reservation without getting a hassle from some tribal cop or the feds; they're both pretty serious about the sovereignty business.

I asked Betsy for a picture of Banks, but she didn't have one.

"I burned everything of his when he moved out," she told me. "If I could afford it, I'd move out of here so he couldn't find us. But Jamie's too little for me to work, and the welfare people won't give me money to move."

The longer I stayed around Betsy, the more I wanted to help her if I could. Like many battered women, she found herself in a rough spot with no easy way out.

"I want you to put the chart back in place, and if he comes back, don't tell him we were here," I said. "Let me find him instead. In the meantime, please call me immediately if you hear from him."

I wrote Dunlay's number on the back of my business card and gave it to her.

Normand finished copying the information from the chart, and I watched Betsy put it back under the crib. While we were alone in the bedroom, I handed her all the cash from my wallet, about $85. "If you have any trouble with Banks, get away from him any way you can. Get to a neighbor's house and get a ride to an inn. Call me from there."

She took the money and whispered thanks.

Normand waited on the porch. He handed back my notebook. "I feel sorry for her," he said. "I left forty bucks on the table."

"We should go into the welfare business together," I observed as we hiked back through the wild lawn to the tan Dodge.

Wednesday: 1815

Normand and I drove back to Base Soo because I wanted to find out how the search progressed and ask Dunlay to plot the coordinates from my notebook onto a chart to compare the new positions with those from the 44323's Loran unit. To our surprise, she had gone home. Chief Warrant Officer Jaspers ran the operations center. Jaspers' build reminded me of a coat rack; his clothes hung on him. His balding head glistened under the fluorescent lights, but huge tufts of hair ringed the collar of his shirt, and the thick hair on his forearms obscured an old tattoo.

"We're running an intensive search in the area where the marker light was found," Jaspers said. "We've got a buoytender, two helicopters and an Air National Guard plane covering the area." He pushed the curl out of a chart and weighted the corner down with his coffee mug. "I brought the small boats home because the crews were getting tired. It's better to bag them now and have them alert for first light tomorrow."

"Have you picked up anything else?" Normand asked.

"No, which seems odd. About everything they carry should float, so you'd think we'd find something else, even if it's a hat." He dunked a piece of cake into his coffee and bit off an end.

Normand agreed with a quick laugh. "Yeah, once I was on a search for a couple of rich kids off Rhode Island, and we found their lunch, a comb, a pair of sunglasses and a wallet."

"Back when I was in New York, we lost a fishing boat south of Long Island, and all we ever found was a pants leg with a thigh bone inside," Jaspers said. "The only way we could identify it was a set of keys in the pants pocket matched the skipper's truck."

While they exchanged gruesome sea stories, I glanced over the charts. Square patterns blocked out in the area north of Crisp Point indicated which cutter or aircraft searched it. Following regular procedure, each unit sweeps back and forth through its own sector, each pass anywhere from a quarter-mile to a mile apart depending upon visibility. A search first concentrates around a particular point like the last reported location or a distress light, in this case, the Loran position from the 44-footer. Factors like how an object would drift or sea conditions complicate things, and as time goes on, you

105

have to cover more area, so you make a wider pass on each turn. Search and rescue is always a trade-off; intensity versus coverage.

Without any reason except my all-consuming distrust, I decided to hold onto the coordinates from the chart in Betsy's house until I could talk with Dunlay. Jaspers tapped my shoulder and handed me a scrap of paper. "Miss Dunlay told me to give you her home phone and asked for you to call. But tell me what you did to piss off the old man. The captain would bring in a Navy sub if he'd thought you'd leave quicker."

"I don't think that's necessary. When I'm ready to leave, I can take a commercial flight out."

Jaspers didn't seem to get it. "You have any ideas about this yet?" he asked.

"I'm still piecing things together." I gave Normand a quick look to keep him quiet about Banks and the chart.

Jaspers took another bite of coffee-soaked cake. "I wish we could find those guys. They were all decent, you know, real good people," he said.

When Normand and I started out, Jaspers turned to the young radioman on watch. "Another time I was on a patrol boat stationed at Sandy Hook, and we pulled up a drowned black dude. He was bleached so white the only way we ID'd him was by his driver's license in his wallet."

As we left the administration building and headed for the Dodge, the crew of the *Biscayne Bay*, one of the 140-foot tugs, was heading for the gate to go on liberty after a long day of searching the open lake. They looked tired and subdued, the kind of exhaustion exclusive to searchers that comes from the extended duration of effort and anticipation. When you're looking for someone missing in the water, you know time is crucial, but you can cover only so much open water on a single pass. So you try to overcompensate – look farther, stare harder, strain to detect any irregularity in the relentless blue waters spread out in all directions around you – but even your best efforts fail at times. And the price of that failure, as any Coastie knows, is a death. The awful antithesis of "search and rescue" is "missing and lost at sea." I didn't wonder why the *Biscayne Bay* crew were headed into town for a couple of strong drinks.

I offered to buy dinner if Normand helped me find a bank machine to replace the cash I had given to Betsy Kruza. The first two we tried wouldn't accept my bank debit card, so I finally made a considerable cash advance on a credit card.

We rolled past a fast-food drive-thru, flirting with the high school girl at the window. Her name tag read Cindy. She wore too much eye shadow and rouge applied in broad streaks along her cheekbones like warpaint. Cindy became flustered at our teasing and gave me an extra five dollars with my change. Then she darkened to a deep red when I returned it.

The delightful desk clerk at the Superior Hotel diverted her attention from Pat and Vanna long enough to thrust seven scribbled messages at me; five from Drucker, the others from Sally and Andrews, using his covert name, Jack. Finally, we settled into my luxurious suite, with quick cuisine for dinner and 57 personnel jackets from the base. Chewing on a greaseburger, I skimmed through each file.

"What are you looking for?" Normand wanted to know.

"Clues are like pornography; I'll know it if I see it."

"Isn't this invasion of privacy?"

"And whoever said you'd have privacy in the service?" I asked.

A knock at the door surprised us. I knew I wasn't expecting guests. Handing Normand the Colt, I motioned for him to wait in the bathroom. Then I slipped the Beretta under the file in my lap.

"Come in!"

The door opened, and Drucker stepped inside. "You're a tough son of a bitch to get a hold of. I left messages here all afternoon."

"My receptionist has the week off. Hey, Boats, come on out."

The toilet flushed, and Normand came out of the bathroom. He handed back the Colt, saying, "I guess we won't have to shoot the chief."

"No, but if he makes any sudden moves, hit him with your sandwich," I joked.

Drucker became very angry. "This ain't no damn game!" He stormed out and slammed the door behind him.

Normand looked startled. "Geez, I wonder what he wanted."

"No, he didn't say, did he?" That made me curious. Did he have something he wanted to discuss? Was he trying to keep track of my movements? That would explain his frequent calls to the inn during the afternoon. I decided to reciprocate.

"Excuse me," I told Normand, as I fastened the pistols back into their appropriate holsters and slipped into my leather jacket. "Would you lock up when you leave? Do you know what the chief drives?"

"An old Dodge station wagon," he called as I pulled the door closed.

A Dodge made a right turn out of the parking lot as I reached the government vehicle. I followed as quickly as I could. Since I didn't know the area very well, I couldn't risk losing him and hope to find him again.

We drove through town on the main drag, made a left and went six miles south on I-75, then finally west on a state Route 28. The sunlight faded, and the road continued across a desolate plain that could have been anywhere in the Midwest farm belt. At first, I thought the senior chief lived outside town and was headed home, but we continued to drive for 20 minutes, then a half hour, and even longer. I stayed as far back as I dared, but close enough so I could catch any sudden turns. There were only a few driveways, marked by mailboxes and red bicycle reflectors, along the dark road. The farther we traveled, the less the houses looked like homes, and the more they seemed like ramshackle cabins, some with pink insulation peeking out of the walls and many with extensive collections of junked vehicles strewn about the property.

After a turn onto Route 221, I saw signs for Brimley State Park. Brimley teams had been state volleyball and basketball champions, proclaimed the sign at the town limits. We rolled past the small post office, the bank, a tiny public park, and the red brick church of St. Francis Xavier. The town of Brimley appeared to center around a Mobil gas station and a flashing yellow traffic light. Drucker stopped at the sign where Route 221 ended, then turned left and hooked another quick left into a tavern's parking lot. Betsy had been right about the bar; it was still called the Bear Den. I wished I felt more surprised when Drucker came to a stop in its gravel parking lot.

I drove past and turned around in a driveway out of sight from the bar. I cruised back and parked the government Dodge about 30 feet from Drucker's car, nosing the GV into the bushes to obscure the front doors. I had rented the Ford for this reason; now, I was stuck with those decals due to exigent circumstances.

Drucker wasn't in sight when I went into the dim, smoky room. An ancient Native American woman with a long braid of white hair down her back tended bar. Most of the clientele looked like they thought professional wrestling was real; lots of flannel, denim, and T-shirts touting favorite concert tours. In my leather jacket and button-down shirt, I felt overdressed. This didn't seem like the kind of place to sip soda water, so I ordered a long neck and slipped behind a table against the closest wall.

The senior chief came out of the restroom and stopped to talk to some pot-bellied bruisers loitering around the pool table. I couldn't hear the conversation, but they shook their heads, and he moved away. Drucker stopped at two tables on his way to the bar, having short conversations and getting the same reaction each time. Finally, he settled at the bar. Halfway through a second beer, he noticed me.

Drucker strode over to me. "What the hell are you doing here?"

"Well, Senior, that's the big question of the evening. It's a long drive for a beer, isn't it?" I asked.

"Why did you follow me out here? Am I a suspect now?" he demanded.

I raised my palms to slow him down. "Let's not attract any attention. First, why don't you get your beer and join me? Then you can tell me why you came out here."

He glared at me and finally walked back to the bar. He returned with three bottles and set one in front of me, then dropped into a chair. "The guys asked me to come here with them Sunday night. I didn't because it was my wife's birthday."

"Who did?"

"Pelligrini, Kunken and Desharnais."

"Did they tell you why? Or did they invite anyone else?"

"No, as far as I know it was only Hank, Wally and Paul. But they never said what it was about, but that they wanted me to come along."

"Why didn't you tell me about this place this morning in your office?"

"Hell, I don't know anything about this place. I've never been here before. I wouldn't have found it but they told me it was about the only place in town."

His story made as much sense as anything else I'd heard on this trip. I decided to level with him. "Well, Senior Chief, Headquarters thinks you may be involved in the disappearance somehow. They told me how everyone's marks dropped after you took over, and about the things over in Nam."

Drucker erupted. "Jesus, won't that ever die. Yesterday the commander called me in and grilled me for 20 minutes about whether I had anything to do with this. Why would I hurt my own crew? What would I get out of this?"

I tried to be tactful. "Well, it looks like this may involve drugs, and you do have that on your record. Wanna tell me what happened?"

"Why?" he demanded. "No one who wasn't there understands anything about Nam. Period."

I pulled the right sleeve of my jacket midway up my forearm and laid my wrist on the table in front of him. "I know some things about Nam."

The chief twisted my POW/MIA bracelet to read the inscription. "Christ, you're Lieutenant Galloway's son? I never met him but I served with a couple of Galloway's Gamblers after . . ." Drucker glanced at me before finishing his thought. "After those shithead Air Fucks sank the *Point Manitou*. Your dad was Number One."

I nodded. I'd heard the same thing from every Coastie I'd ever met who served incountry. Later I learned that 'Number One' was the highest superlative of a war that was anything but. "I've heard. I wish I would have known first hand."

Drucker polished off his second longneck. "OK, let's talk ancient history. I was on the *Point Willis* in 68 and 69. You know about the village adoptions? Patrol boats could visit every other week for three hours if we had a Vietnamese liaison officer with us. We adopted Can Tho."

"Uh huh." I pushed my untouched beer across the table to him.

"We were there for our three hours, and the medic tells us that one of the kids at the orphanage has an infected gunshot wound. We convinced the XO to give the orphanage penicillin out of our stores, but the skipper said it would go to the VC as soon as we left. So I volunteered to stay behind and give the kid the shots he needed. The medic told the skipper that the kid would die of gangrene if the infection spread. So the skipper agreed."

"And the liaison officer didn't?"

"We didn't exactly ask. You know the saying, 'It's easier to get forgiveness than permission'? Well, it came outta Nam. The skipper planned to pick me up in five days. But four days out, they're fighting a pier fire at An Thoi. Well, the VNN officer starts writing his report but the numbers don't add up so he knows someone is missing. He reports it to Saigon, and the Navy wants to know what the hell is going on. And Thorne came down hard on the skipper. Turns out the Navy wanted to kill the adoptions cause the Coast Guard was getting good PR out of it. So I said I would confess to going AWOL and stealing the drugs so the squids and Saigon would back off."

"You made a bogus confession under the UCMJ?" I asked in disbelief. "You're a hell of a sea lawyer. Did you know they could have hung you? Literally. In war, AWOL is desertion."

Drucker chuckled. "Yeah, I was young and stupid." He pointed to the ashtray. "That's smarter than I was back in Nam. But I wasn't thinking about doing the full 20 back then. Nobody thought about careers – one tour at a time." He took a long swig of beer then smiled. "And the village adoptions held till the pullout."

"How many tours did you do?"

"Three. From the *Point Willis*, I was busted a stripe and ended up on the *Taney*. I rode her back to Hawaii and met the *Mellon*. And the *Mellon* went straight back to Nam." He took a long swig on the long neck.

"I'm curious about something. How did you pass the Officer-in-Charge board with those charges on your record?"

"I have a guardian angel. Whenever the charges were brought

up, Admiral Thorne found a way to fix things for me." He pointed toward my wrist. "And I bet the admiral is at it again."

"Could be he's doing this for both of us," I said. "So how did the Gamblers get their name?"

Drucker laughed. "Those sonzabitches would wager on their monthly reports. Whenever they came into An Thoi, they'd bet the other crews that they'd board more junks, grab more VC, seize more rounds; whatever action anyone would take. And they never lost a fin. They tagged me for a case of beer because I figured there was no way they could capture a dozen Cong in one month. They brought back fifteen with another six KIA."

"My dad gambled?" It didn't fit the sterling image my grandfather had created.

"No way, your old man was straight arrow. But he had a standing order that a percentage of the take went to charity. I heard that's how he paid for renovating the Catholic church at An Thoi."

I smiled. "They said a Mass for Dad there. They sent us a picture of his hat on the altar with all the Gamblers around it."

"Yeah, they sure loved your old man. Number One."

Wednesday: 2030

Squeezing the GV between a pair of traveling mansions, I parked at the Superior Inn. I planned a short call to Andrews and a long snooze on the alleged bed.

Two floors up and down the musty hall, I fished the plastic key fob from my pocket and opened the door to my Inn room. The wall switch didn't work, but that hardly surprised me in such a quality inn. I headed for the lamp on the desk and halfway across the room sensed something wrong. In the dim light filtering through the curtain, I saw toppled furniture. Loose paper shifted under my feet. I reached for my Colt, but it was already too late.

A thick arm wrapped around my neck. Two quick punches pummeled my lower back. I tried to yell, but my breath rushed out as my assailant crushed my neck.

This guy was huge. His chin rested on the top of my head, forcing it back so he could get at my throat. His breath stank like a double shot of whiskey. We swung around the room as I tried to get a footing on the sliding personnel files under my feet.

"I'm going to kill you, bastard!" he hissed at me.

By instinct, I stomped my heel back on my dance partner's foot. He didn't flinch. I slammed down again, realizing only then that he wore steel-toe boots. I panicked. I figured this guy had six inches and about 75 pounds on me. He was stronger, and I couldn't budge the arm tightening around my neck with both hands.

His free hand jerked the Colt loose from my holster and tossed it across the room. Then he reached for my throat. I jammed my chin down onto his forearm to protect my windpipe.

"Who's Jack?" he demanded. "Who the fuck is Jack?"

We wrestled around the room so violently I couldn't get my leg up to reach the Beretta strapped in its ankle holster. My head slammed into the wall. Glass shattered, and chunks fell against my face. His weight pressed me over the desk. He gripped my hair, jerked my head back, and shoved my face into the broken mirror again.

He tried to push my head back, driving his weight harder against my spine. If he couldn't choke me, he meant to break my neck.

113

Streams of blood blinded my sight. I grappled around on the desk, looking for a weapon, but found only a couple of pencils and a plastic ashtray. Finally, I touched the lamp and gripped it, hoping for some heft. By its weight, I knew it was plastic. Pulling it close, I twined the cord through my fingers and jerked it free from the lamp's base. Then I shoved the loose end of the wire over my shoulder at my attacker's face.

Sparks sizzled, and he screamed. I twisted, broke free, and jabbed my elbow back into his solar plexus. He staggered away, but I followed, wiping my face with a sleeve and swinging a backhand against his burnt cheek. He howled again. I reached behind me and found the desk chair. By then, he had recovered and started toward me when I smashed the chair against his head and left shoulder. He stumbled, and I got off a kick at his kneecap.

My assailant turned and scrambled out. I fell to my knees, grabbing the Beretta and gasping for breath.

Wednesday: 2110

Ten minutes later, I had enough strength to close the door out to the hallway and stagger into the bathroom. The light there worked, but I couldn't focus my eyes on the mirror. I wrapped my forehead in a bath towel and used a damp wash rag to wipe the blood off my face.

With great care, I removed the towel and examined the cuts on my face. A jagged gash about four inches long ran across the middle of my right temple, with shredded skin peeling back to show meat and bone. Smaller nicks covered my forehead from the hairline down to the right eye, the rivulets of blood sparkling where slivers of glass glinted in the light.

Rescue swimmer training included a great deal of first aid. Unfortunately, I missed the class on self-surgery. I put a wet cloth over the cuts, then wrapped my head in a strip torn from a towel. Finally, I vomited in the toilet.

After 15 minutes had passed, I went into the main room and managed to get the single-bulb lamp on the nightstand to work. I didn't know my sparring partner but judging by the condition of the personnel records tossed across the floor, it was clear he wasn't after traveler's checks. My visitor rifled through my clothes, leaving them spread across the bed and my uniform dumped in the corner. Only my little bag of tricks remained unopened. The locks were scratched, and the leather on one side had been slashed with a serrated blade, but the heavy steel mesh lining still protected my gear. I found the Colt under the oversized cushioned chair in the corner. My head throbbed when I knelt to retrieve it.

Collecting my clothes, I became dizzy and rested for a few minutes until the nausea passed. I couldn't stay in the room, and my head needed professional attention – somebody had to pluck the glass out of my face. The emergency room wasn't an option for two reasons. First, they'd want to keep me for observation, and I had to be underway early the following day to reach Duluth. And second, the hospital would be required to report signs of violence to the police, who'd ask many questions I couldn't answer. I also felt reluctant to give my assailant any chance to find me again or learn that he had hurt me to this extent.

After several more rest stops, I got everything repacked into my luggage. Two extra full clips for each weapon went into my jacket pockets. The jacket itself looked in rough shape from the blood-stains down the front. Even Mad Dog Magruder could see it was no longer new.

With everything packed and the safety on the Colt released, I slipped out my door and down the hallway. Moving slowly and listening for suspicious noises, I went out the back way into a side alley and hustled into the shadows. Then, lugging three bags over my shoulder, I hiked a three-block circuit back to the parking lot of the Soo Locks visitors center where the rented Ford sat.

Settling into the driver's seat, I discovered that a lens of the eyeglasses in my jacket had been shattered. After shaking the loose glass out of the inside pocket, I fished a new pair of spectacles out of my little bag of tricks.

Even as I fumbled with the ignition key, I wasn't immediately certain where to go. The hospital was out. The Coast Guard base as well; it seemed evident that a Coastie was on the wrong side of this mess – at least judging by the missing crew's actions and the disap-pearance of the boat's chart. I felt I could trust Dunlay, but there remained a chance that someone was watching her home as well as tracking my movements. At last, I made my choice.

Street lights and the glaring halogens of oncoming cars stabbed at my eyes like fuzzy white pokers. When I finally got away from the street lights, my eyes wouldn't focus. I aimed the fender of the Ford along the white center lines.

Sally's house appeared dark when I passed it. I parked the Ford in a restaurant lot about 50 yards down the road and left everything in the car but a change of clothes and my black bag. I tumbled in the gravel twice along the walk back to her quaint little bungalow.

Standing on her front porch, I knocked gently so I wouldn't wake her daughter. Sally pulled aside a curtain, the alarm in her face telling me that I looked much worse than I like when I call on a lady. She jerked the door open and pulled me inside. "Jesus, what happened to you?" she asked, taking my bag and clothes. I held the door frame to steady my balance.

"I went dancing with a heavy-weight contender, and he got upset when I tried to lead." I stopped when I saw that she was wearing a skirt – a short black skirt, shiny black shoes with long heels, and a silken blouse that billowed in suggestive ways; an outfit not meant for staying home. "Look, I'm sorry to bother you. I won't stay . . ."

She wrapped an arm around my waist and led me to the couch, touching my makeshift bandage. "You need a doctor. There's glass in those cuts."

I eased down on the couch, and she helped me slip my jacket off. Her eyes widened in surprise when she saw the Colt nestled in its holster under my right arm. "I didn't know the Coast Guard carried guns," she said.

"It's good for the image, makes us look tough." Then I told her a little of who I was and what I was doing – not much, but enough so she wouldn't think I was a homicidal maniac.

"You are mysterious."

"Thanks, I guess. Look, I need you to call somebody for me." I fished Dunlay's home number from my pocket. "Once she's on the phone, I'll talk to her."

"You come here and want me to call another woman for you? Did you get knocked silly?" She gave me a bemused look but went to a small oak desk and started dialing. Her legs were thinner than I would have guessed the night before. As she finished dialing, she turned to face me. "When I said I wanted to see you again, I wasn't expecting this," she teased.

"Look, I don't want to cause any trouble. If you'd rather not get involved, I'll go find her."

She shook her head and held up a finger, indicating I should shut up. "Miss Dunlay? Hi, you don't know me, but I've got someone here who needs to talk to you. Hang on a minute."

Sally brought the phone – one of those cheap punch-button models you get with a magazine subscription – over to the distance the cord reached. I leaned to the right as far as I dared and put the receiver up to the nearest ear. "Hi, Miss Dunlay. This is Galloway. I need your assistance."

"Don't you people have first names?" Sally asked rhetorically.

"Galloway, what's going on?" Dunlay's voice sounded hoarse; the phone had roused her from some much-needed slumber.

Sally knelt on the carpet next to me as though she expected me to topple out of the sofa, and she braced herself to catch me. "I ran into some trouble tonight. I need you to bring the corpsman out to meet me and have him bring sutures," I told Dunlay.

"My God, what is it?"

"It's very small thread for stitching wounds, but that's not important right now." Boy, there's another one I've been itching to say.

"Are you injured?" She sounded panicked.

"Could be worse. I had an unexpected guest this evening. I'll tell you all about it when you come out."

"Give me your location?" I could hear rustling that indicated she was getting out of bed.

"I'll have Sally give you directions. After you pick up the corpsman, go through a couple of drive-up bank windows. Stay in the lot and see if anyone follows you. Do it three times before you come out. If you see anyone behind you, go to the base and I'll call you there in an hour. Please don't tell anyone where you're going."

I handed the phone back to Sally, who gave the lieutenant directions to the house. I interjected that Dunlay should park away from the house, as I had. Sally hung up after assuring Dunlay that I would survive.

"Is there a reason you won't go to the hospital?" Sally asked.

"Do you know what they want for a room these days? The bill would kill me."

She laughed and helped me sit back in the chair. "Are you always such a comedian, or is this a sign of brain damage?"

"I'll have you know that many women have been charmed by my wit," I said.

"So you don't put on this wounded gunslinger act with every woman you meet? That's comforting. I'd hate to think you've bled on other women's furniture."

I lurched forward to see if I was, in fact, dripping on her upholstery. A few red blots stained the flower patterns of the cushion. She pushed me back gently. "Don't worry," she said. "You'll get a bill.

118

Besides, I'm used to blood. My ex always came home from one bar or another bleeding in a dozen places."

She leaned forward and examined my cuts again. At the same time, I studied her; the red hair brushed back from her face, her narrow nose dusted with freckles. She had thin lips that remained parted, showing very white teeth. In the dark bar, I'd underestimated how attractive Sally was. Finally, she realized I was staring at her.

"What's wrong?" she asked. "Is there a hair in place?"

"You remind me of someone I met in a bar last night."

"Yeah, I get that a lot." She stood and headed for the kitchen. "Want something to drink?"

"I'll have a pint of AB positive on the rocks."

She went out to the kitchen, leaving me alone to sit and bleed. The room was decorated with a feminine flair; ruffles and lace with a hint of potpourri in the air. I thought a few bloodstains would add a nice manly touch. Several minutes later, Sally returned and handed me a glass of tomato juice on ice. I grinned up at her, wincing from the pain in my face. "Ah, a woman after my own heart."

"Well, you haven't got much face left," she said, giving me more ice wrapped in a dishtowel. "I was kinda hoping you'd come by the bank today, so I asked Mom to keep Ashley over again tonight." She smiled at me and blushed a little. "I should change before your friends come over. I wouldn't want them to think I'm some kind of dominatrix."

After watching her saunter down the hallway, I eased my shoulder holster off and snugged the pistol next to the seat cushion. It was unlikely that anyone could have followed me, but I wasn't sure if Dunlay would be able to spot a tail. I couldn't take any chances with Sally in the house.

Could it have been Banks in my room? The physique matched the rough description, and my attacker was an experienced scrapper. An awful thought hit me: How had this guy found my room? Who else knew where I was staying other than Normand, Drucker and Dunlay? Did one of them set me up? If Dunlay was involved, then I had been telling her everything, including my present location. I tried to shake off the idea. Sally didn't return immediately, and I closed my eyes, trying to quell the rising paranoia.

A sharp rap on the windowpane in the door startled me. I struggled to my feet and held the Colt behind my left thigh. I worked my way to a window and peered through the curtain. In the dim glow of the porch light, I saw Dunlay next to the door, ready to rap it again. A younger man I didn't recognize stood behind her, obscured in the shadows.

Squeezing my hand around the butt of the Colt, I opened the door and let them inside. Then I shut and locked it.

"Are you all right, Marty?" Dunlay asked, panic in her eyes. "Marty, this is Petty Officer Hopkins, the corpsman from the base," she said, motioning with one hand. She looked odd in a flannel shirt and jeans, but I had only seen her in uniform. It is a rare woman who looks attractive in the Coast Guard uniform, even though Hollywood legend Edith Head designed them.

"Were you in a traffic accident?" the medic asked, peering at my face in a clinical manner. "We could be looking at serious head trauma if you went through a windshield."

"I'm fine. Somebody put my face into a mirror. Twice."

I relaxed my grip on the Colt.

"I'd like to take a look at you under the light," Hopkins said. "It looks like you still have glass in those cuts."

Hopkins wore sweatpants and a football jersey over competition muscles. He was a young guy with lots of black hair and a thin mustache. I would have preferred a veteran corpsman with time overseas. After serving in combat, those medics had as much experience as the average surgeon. My father's friends had introduced me to an Army corpsman who performed three battlefield amputations because jungle rot set in before the choppers could break through the enemy fire. All three patients lived. I've never heard of a combat medic sued for malpractice.

"Do you know who it was?" Dunlay asked, leading me to an oversized recliner in the corner.

"Somebody big, 250 pounds with 180 proof breath," I explained. "Heavy beard, steel-toe boots and no social graces."

Sally returned, dressed in a velvety top and corduroy slacks. She introduced herself to Dunlay and Hopkins. Dunlay eyed me suspiciously.

"Let me get a good look at what we've got here," Hopkins said. I wasn't certain for a moment if he meant my face or Sally.

She and Dunlay held a pair of desk lamps above my head. Hopkins stood behind the chair and pulled me far back into it. Dunlay gasped when Hopkins removed the bloody rags wrapped around my head. He peeled off the wet washrag, pulling the skin up with it. Then he examined the remains of my face.

"This is bad," he concluded. "Normally I'd send a job like this to the ER."

"But you're confident you can handle it," I told him.

"Yeah, I work part-time on a rescue squad, and I've had to sew up bikers who thought that helmets restrict their freedom. Once I put a guy's eye back in the socket."

"Galloway, why can't you go to the emergency room?" Dunlay demanded, her voice a curious mix of concern and disgust.

I shook my head, a move I regretted as new pain rampaged through my temples. "Somebody tried to kill me, and he'll likely try again. I'd prefer to make that as difficult as possible, but right now he's got every advantage because he knows who I am," I explained. "He expects me to go to the hospital. If he looks there and doesn't find me, it'll throw him off guard."

"Sounds pretty macho to me," Sally observed.

"Trying to preserve what little hide I have left intact," I replied. "Besides, I'm not ready to answer questions for the police yet."

"And the commandant instructed you to conduct a covert investigation, right?" Dunlay asked, reaching her own conclusion.

"You've got a future in CGI," I told her.

Hopkins created a makeshift operating room on a small end table. He stacked dozens of sterile swatches on a white cotton square next to a collection of needles and tweezers. He removed a hypodermic needle and a glass vial from his bag. "I'll have to work fast, or the lidocaine may start to wear off. You've got a lot of glass chips left in those nicks."

"Did you bring anything besides lidocaine?" I asked. "Morphine?"

"Oh, I don't see anything that bad. The amount of blood isn't a sign of serious injury. The face has a lot of capillaries, so any facial injury bleeds profusely." He explained all this patiently, thinking I was concerned about the pain. " Lidocaine will be fine," he added in a soothing, professional tone.

"Not on me, I'm allergic to it. Last time I had it, I threw up for two days."

"Wow, that's pretty rare," Hopkins observed as he checked my pulse. "I don't think I can pull this glass without any anesthesia. You could go into shock."

Dunlay set down her lamp. "That's enough; you're going to the hospital."

"No!" I shouted. "I've got four people depending on me. I can't risk the consequences." My outburst was immediately punished by daggers of agony that ricocheted across my forehead from eyeball to temple and back.

"Getting that glass out is going to be painful," Hopkins warned.

"Not as painful as when it was put there," I replied.

Dunlay lifted her lamp again, and Hopkins covered my eyes with gauze. Two spots of brightness glowed through the bandage as the corpsman moved Sally and Dunlay into position. I rested my neck back on the chair, took a deep breath, and closed my eyes, hearing the snap of rubber gloves as Hopkins pulled them on.

Hopkins worked as gently as he could, poking each wound with tweezers, but the fire still seared in spasms until my face grew numb. If I moved, the tip of the tweezers might strike a nerve, and I jolted, jabbing the sharp point deeper into my face. At first, Dunlay winced each time I jumped; then, she gripped my chin to hold my head steady. Compared with plucking out the glass, the sutures went in with little pain.

Halfway through the operation, we took a break. Dunlay and Sally put down the lamps they were holding and stretched their arms. Hopkins helped me limp down the hall to a bathroom full of pink ruffles and doilies. I felt too dizzy from the throbbing in my temples to stand, so I sat on the toilet. When I finished, I glanced into the bowl. The water was bright red.

I pulled up my trousers and opened the door before I flushed. I motioned for Hopkins and closed the door behind him. His mouth gaped open when he saw the blood in the toilet water.

"Jesus, you really did get a work over," he whispered.

"Does this mean I have internal injuries?" I wondered if I had split open an old wound from my Mexican Inquisition.

"Could be a couple of things. Did he hit you in the groin?"

"No, only two good kidney punches."

"That would do it, too. Turn around and let me see."

I turned, and he pulled up my shirttail. When he whistled, I knew it wasn't because he liked my boyish figure.

"You've got a bruise here the size of a hubcap," he said, with an alarming touch of admiration in his voice. "I used to work Golden Gloves matches, but I never saw anything like this. I take it this guy doesn't fight by Queensberry rules."

"Is this something I need to get checked out?" I now worried that I had to go to the hospital after all, which would reduce the past hour of torture to simple masochism.

He poked and prodded at my ribs and back. "Nothing back here hurts, huh? And you're sure you don't remember any blows to the groin? Did he kick you anywhere around the genitals?"

I gave him a brief recap of the one-round fight. I called it a split decision.

"But you've got no pain down there?" Hopkins was puzzled. "I don't know what to tell you. Hematuria with severe pain or a fractured rib, you figure a blow to the kidney. No pain, you're generally looking for something organic, like an infection or a tumor. Either way, you'd better see somebody trained for internal medicine. I've had all of six weeks' classroom time on internal illness."

"Can it kill me?"

"Hematuria? No, but wherever you're leaking blood could, especially...." He stopped and stared hard at my blood-streaked face. "You're not gonna go to the ER, are you? If you're looking for me to tell you it's OK to get stupid about internal injuries, I won't play that game."

I reached over and flushed the john. "What I want to know is my odds. If there's better than 50-50 chance I'll heal, that's a helluva lot better odds than I can give on Pelligrini and his crew right now. I'm not asking for permission or an excuse. I want your professional opinion. I'll decide where to go from there."

"OK, you won't die before morning. As long as you're not hurting, keep drinking lots of water. If the bleeding doesn't let up in 24 hours, haul yourself into the closest ER and fake amnesia about me. I've never lost a patient, so I'll be pissed if you're the first."

He helped me back to the living room. Sally eased me into the chair and propped a cushion under my neck. On the table next to the sutures, Hopkins had piled a small collection of bloody glass shards. He put on new surgical gloves, and the fun continued.

Hopkins worked in silence throughout the procedure, only sometimes asking for more light in a specific position. When he finished cleaning and stitching my wounds, my face stung until I could no longer feel any one wound, only the dull sensation of lingering pain. He wrapped gauze bandages over the worst cuts on my forehead. Sally brought me a tumbler of brandy as a tranquilizer, but Hopkins took it from her and gulped it down.

"That'll dilate his arteries, and he's lost enough blood already," he explained.

"What's next?" Dunlay asked me.

"Well, I'm going to Duluth at first light. I want to board a couple of freighters there as soon as possible."

"You should rest," Hopkins told me. He leaned close and whispered, "I don't have any idea what's so top secret around here, but if you're still pissing blood in the morning you'd better go straight to the ER."

I thanked him. "Next time I need to interrogate an uncooperative witness, I'll be sure to call you."

Hopkins wrapped up his medical gear, and he and Dunlay left after I promised the lieutenant I'd call her at Group Soo before lunch the next morning. As she left, Dunlay looked at me, then at Sally, and rolled her eyes; she had clear notions about my lodgings for the evening. After locking the door behind them, Sally came and knelt before me, a worried look in her eyes. "Are you OK?" she asked.

"Compared to what? Road kill?" I groaned. "Look, I'd like to use your phone again. It's long distance, but I'll reimburse you along with the bill for cleaning the upholstery."

She stretched the plastic receiver over to the chair and placed it in my lap, then dialed the number I recited before she went to get a bed ready. My visitor had been kind enough to remind me to call Jack. Despite the late hour, Andrews picked up after two rings.

"Hey, Marty. Glad you called. I was drifting off to sleep. I left a message because I've got some very interesting things for you. First, looks like the Chinook is clean. El Paso didn't have a listing on it, and the only thing Interpol had listed was a stowaway about six years ago. Some Irish kid looking to come to the New World but he never made it past Liverpool."

"OK, I still have to call Thomason back to see if he has anything else," I said.

Andrews agreed. "But these other guys are a lot of fun. The *Baltic Express* showed up dirty on both EPIC and Interpol lists. For about three years they've been running a regular cargo of grain from Duluth to Brazil, with an added cargo of dynamite. It's used for gold mining and leveling the Amazon Basin. On several return trips, they've brought back native wildlife, specializing in species that are embargoed against import. I talked with a guy in Customs, and you wouldn't believe what some people are willing to pay for a snake."

"Any ties to drugs?"

"No, but I'm still checking. Besides, I'm sure drugs are still more lucrative than parakeets."

"About how long will they be moored in Duluth?" I asked.

"Another few weeks. The Marine Safety Office up there said the ship reported some kind of generator problem, and they'll be anchored off for a while in order to make repairs."

I wondered why Commander Marshall hadn't told me about the mechanical difficulties of the *Baltic Express*. "And the *Jersey Trader*?"

"You're going to like this one," Andrews chuckled. "I couldn't find anything on either list, but I figured that was odd, I mean nobody's that good, right? They didn't even have a bad fire extinguisher on record. So I tried to call the company that it's registered to in New York City. There wasn't a number listed with information so I called the agents on Governors Island and asked them to swing by the company. The address is an old public school, now used as a crack house."

"That's ironic: Close down the school and the drop-outs take over. Do you suppose the dealers pay rent to the city?"

"The agents on GI are going to run down the names on the Trader's registry and the bogus corporation. But you can guess what we'll find. I'm trying to track her sailing agent through the port in Duluth. If that doesn't work, I'll call the St. Lawrence Seaway and ask who paid for the *Trader's* transit."

"Very impressive, sir." I said, not able to think of a thing he had missed.

"I'm not planning to spend a career playing second string while some cowboy has all the fun." Of course, he couldn't know how much fun I had that evening. "What's happening up your way?" he asked.

"All the usual diversions; dinner, drinks, a little moose wrestling." I decided that telling him about my evening bout of fisticuffs would alarm him for no good reason; he couldn't do anything about it, despite his black belt. "And the search continues. They found a marker light this afternoon, and they've got the known world out searching the lake," I explained, wondering how much he'd already learned from the SITREPS that Dunlay or Jaspers filed every four hours. "I'm going out to Duluth in the morning to visit our suspects. Something's got to shake loose around here soon."

"Well, tell me what you need, and I'll do my best."

"Did you have any luck with Traverse City on that flight in the morning?"

"You bet. As soon as I said the word 'commandant' I thought they were ready to launch everything they had in the hangar. I'll tell you, I've gotta make admiral someday. It'd be great to wield that kind of power."

"Careful, sir. The last admiral who used an airsta as a personal taxi ended up with an early retirement."

"Yeah, but even he got off easy. When you send an H-3 from Cape Cod to Maine to fetch fresh lobster for a dinner party, I'd say you deserve a few years in Fort Leavenworth."

"That was a good idea to have the agents check the New York address." I decided that a ship with a phantom owner might be an excellent suspect. And the other would still be in Duluth if the first didn't pan out.

Andrews explained my early morning flight arrangements and signed off.

Sally returned to the room, ready for bed, with a thick blue robe pulled tight around her. "You gonna stay in that chair all night?"

"I can find another place to sleep if you're not comfortable with me staying here."

"You think there's a hotel vacancy within 100 miles of here this time of year? You did get your brains scrambled." When she helped me to my feet, I staggered against her, feeling the pain of every cut and bruise. She slipped her arms around my waist and pulled me close. "Why don't you come to bed?"

Sally led the way down the hallway to her bedroom. Our little parade stopped beside the bed, and I plunked down while she shed her robe. Underneath, she was covered by a sheer white nightgown – a tight bodice that clung to her breasts with a loose skirt dropping away from her slender waist. She helped me out of my shoes. While I stretched across the mattress, she lay next to me and pulled the sheets over us. Hesitantly at first, and then with growing ardor, she kissed me, first on the mouth, then my neck and chest. When I moved to catch her hands, she pushed me back.

"Don't hurt yourself. Let me," she whispered.

I began to laugh. Pain rumbled through my ribs and strangulated the breath in my lungs. As I wheezed, Sally shook me in alarm.

"What's wrong?" she screamed. "Should I call 911?"

My breath returned after I rolled onto my side. I shook my head and wiped away tears. "I'm sorry, Sally," I gasped. "It's been a rough night."

Thursday: 00 Dark

I dreamt that night of a long search over the Gulf of Alaska for a crewman lost overboard from a long-liner. The skipper had pitched a life ring over and reported the exact Loran coordinates to the air station's operations center. We rolled out an H-3 into the 30-knot winds and found 12-to 15-foot seas when we got onscene. After two hours of searching the dark, turbulent waters below us, the fishing boat asked permission to resume fishing.

We kept searching through the night, muttering into the IC about the kind of pals that would leave a 19-year-old shipmate adrift. But we knew; as the helo made pass after pass over darkening seas under a moonless sky, we knew there was no hope. Finally, the co-pilot, calculating our fuel consumption to squeeze the most onscene time out of our tanks, determined that we were at our bingo point. We headed back toward Kodiak.

Back in Ready Crew Berthing, I racked out early, leaving the other guys in the television room. There the dream I could remember from a hundred nights changed. A woman sat on the edge of my bunk and brushed her fingers over my face. I could not see her face, only a thick mane of hair and a lithe, sturdy body, but the details were clear, similar to a girl I knew in high school. She helped me out of the flight suit and snuggled against me. After a long time, she brought her face up to mine and kissed me. Then the dream began to slip away from me.

I woke to find Sally fumbling at my pants in the dark. I brushed her hands away. "I'm sorry," I whispered.

As I drifted back to sleep, I dreamt she whispered, "Oh, you will be."

Thursday: 0430

Exhaustion was my first sensation when Sally shook me to consciousness, but at least my head no longer throbbed in agony. When I stood, I stepped on my wallet on the floor. Seemed odd because my habit is to carry it in a front trouser pocket; at times, I have trouble fishing it out. In the kitchen, Sally covered my bandages with plastic kitchen wrap, and I showered while she cooked up a wonderful breakfast of poached eggs, bacon and home fries. Unfortunately, I still felt a little queasy, so I opted for two glasses of orange juice and a fistful of vitamins with a dash of aspirin. I skipped my daily regimen of calisthenics that morning.

Dressing proved particularly painful because my muscles, especially my lower back, had stiffened during the night. When I couldn't reach my shoes, Sally knelt and tied the laces for me. My jacket looked too blood-stained to wear, so I pulled on a heavy, loose cotton cardigan that disguised the bulk of the Colt under my arm. I pack the sweater for times when the leather jacket is impractical. Somewhere in her closets, Sally had found a couple of hats to cover the bandages on my forehead. The green John Deere ballcap fit tight, and the blue wool watch cap was unseasonably warm. I took both along with me.

As a precaution, I left the Beretta with Sally after explicit instructions on how to load and fire. She laughed at my tutoring, took the pistol, ejected the clip and checked the chamber for a round. Then she reloaded and set the safety.

"Anything else I need to know?"

"Yeah, never shoot a good guy."

Sally kissed my cheek at the front door like sending an accountant off to the office. "Would you call me today?" she asked. "If you need to stay over again tonight, I'll send Ashley to my Mom's."

At least I wasn't staggering when I hiked back to the Ford. With my glasses pushed under the bandages, my vision remained blurred. I chalked that up to lack of sleep. I aimed the car back through town, then south on I-75 toward Kinross.

The purpose of the excursion to Duluth was two-fold. The primary objective was to check out the two freighters that had passed Crisp Point sometime Monday morning. My second goal was to acquire assistance from any federal agency that could spare the manpower or the firepower. The case had begun to snowball around me like the start of an avalanche. From the facts I already knew, and the bruises I wore, I had clearly stumbled into something bigger than the average boating accident. Circumstances indicated that somebody in the Coast Guard was involved. Since I could not determine who that was, I had to get outside help. I wasn't optimistic.

If this operation turned out as substantial as Thomason thought, then most likely somebody in the local police was involved. You can't run a major import business in a small town without at least someone on the local police force building a personal retirement fund by looking the other way. I couldn't trust the state police for similar reasons. They should have detected bulk quantities of drugs moving from remote locations to urban areas. Not all police are corrupt. It only takes one leaking faucet for the criminals to know every move the police are planning.

That left only federal assistance, and the outlook there seemed bleak. I considered Customs, but they concentrate their meager assets along the southern border: Florida, Texas and California. Ten years earlier, Schmidt would have stopped this thing single-handed, but now his goal was to remain healthy long enough to retire. What were the chances of finding a Drug Enforcement Agent within 500 miles of the Soo, unless he was vacationing – hauling up the northern pike that should have been on my stringer? Getting the Federal Marshals from Detroit or Chicago would require more substantial evidence than I had immediately on hand.

So, I settled my hope on the FBI office in Duluth. Although there is an office much closer to the Soo in Marquette, I would spend the day in Duluth. I hesitated to request the FBI's assistance because I knew they would be short-handed. The bureau has a large deficit of agents, and recruiting people into dangerous work with long hours for low pay isn't as attractive now as when J. Edgar first put out the Help-Wanted-to-Save-America sign 60 years ago. It's a warped country where a kid who throws a baseball earns ten times more than a man who risks his life daily. But then I remember wanting to be one of those baseball heroes myself once.

The closer I neared Kinross, the less optimistic I became. I knew

I was up against something big and ugly. I didn't think I could handle it alone. The expression "One riot, one Ranger" was coined before every punk carried a semi-automatic weapon.

A Coast Guard H-60 Jayhawk helicopter waited on the ground at the airport when I wheeled the big Ford into the parking lot. The helo's aerial lights flickered, and a crewman flashed a hand-held beacon around the closed airport. I should have specified that I wanted to ride an H-3 over to Duluth. With the growing number of Jayhawks, there wouldn't be many years left to enjoy the primitive austerity of those beautiful H-3s.

The front door of the airport remained locked at such an early hour. When I tried to sneak around the side of the building onto the airfield, I found an eight-foot chain-link fence separating me from the helicopter. After scanning the area to ensure there was no opening nearby and no one watching, I slung my bag of tricks over the top and dropped it onto the grass. And then I scaled the fence, with more effort than I have expended climbing a 200-foot rock face in the Grand Tetons. When I dropped onto the other side, I felt every suture on my face tug in a different direction. With a handkerchief, I dabbed at each to ensure none had pulled open.

A helo crewman met me halfway across the tarmac. He took hold of my bag and reached to put an arm under my shoulder. "Are you OK?" he asked.

I jerked my arm away and tried to straighten my back a little. "Fine, thanks."

"What the hell happened to you?" he asked in surprise, looking at my face for the first time.

"Nicked myself with a razor." I grimaced. I could see by his confused expression that he hadn't caught the joke.

Within minutes the helo was airborne, heading due west across the Upper Peninsula of Michigan. The Jayhawk is faster and more aesthetic than the H-3. The Jayhawk also rides quieter in the air than the H-3, but the only aircraft I have heard to be louder than an H-3 is the Navy Chinook. Chinooks ride and sound like an old farm tractor with a warped piston and a blown head gasket.

Once we were in the air and headed across the UP, the crew seemed to forget me until I asked if we could fly a little closer along the Lake Superior shoreline to familiarize myself with the search area. The pilots seemed reluctant to fly too near the search until the crewman radioed the Soo for permission. We came out onto the lake over Whitefish Bay in the pale gray of the false dawn, then headed west and southwest past Crisp Point Light, the harbor at Grand Marais, and the cliffs of Pictured Rocks National Lakeshore, all visible through the window on the helo's port side. The sight-seeing confirmed Thomason's observation about Lake Superior – miles of remote coastline perfect for landing contraband.

When the Jayhawk cleared the search area, I opened Fraser's Coast Pilot to Chapter 13 and compared the terrain to the written description. The navigator's guidebook laid out the standard routes for upbound vessels in the lake, from Point Iroquois Shoal to White-fish Point, past Crisp Point, Manitou Light, Copper Harbor, Eagle Harbor and Devils Island. So I thought then about the Manitou – my father's patrol boat and the great Indian spirit. The two repre-sented courage and strength; the powers of the Manitou I would need to complete Admiral Thorne's assignment.

The helo landed at the Duluth airport at what seemed the farthest possible distance from the terminal. The pilot told me over the intercom that the tower had ordered us out here so as not to interfere with Air National Guard maneuvers planned that day. Still, I suspected the pilot didn't mind inconveniencing me in exchange for rousing his crew at such an early hour. I was convinced in my suspicion when the helo lifted away and followed my trek toward the terminal so that its prop wash brought me to my knees in pain.

I reached the terminal as the morning crew unlocked the doors, so I wasn't forced to scramble over their fence. Outside the front entrance, I spotted the distinctive tan sedan favored by government purchasing agents. The driver from the Marine Safety Office was a young seaman who planned to join CGI someday, as he explained at great length. As he rambled, I suspected he might also want to be an admiral someday if his passenger was an admiral or even a pecker checker if he was driving a corpsman. He relieved me of my bag, which he stowed in the back seat. In minutes, we headed down a steep hill overlooking the cities of Duluth and Superior on opposite sides of the bay opening onto Lake Superior. Three bridges spanned the river between the two cities.

When we reached MSO Duluth, I found the front door locked, but a young seaman answered when I rapped, and she led me back to the executive officer.

Lieutenant Commander Tom Marshall sat behind his desk, sipping orange juice and eating a bran muffin. He was one of those trim, athletic officers, no doubt a runner judging by his lean physique. He brushed muffin crumbs from his lap when he stood to shake my hand.

"What happened to you?" Marshall asked, indicating I should sit. "Wrestle a bear?"

"No, bears are smarter than my opponent."

"Well, Captain Seidman won't be in the office today, but when he called in he told me to take good care of you," Marshall said, brushing a napkin against his clipped black mustache. "I guess you did a personal favor for him a few years ago."

The favor had been very personal. When Captain Seidman skippered a Coast Guard 378-foot cutter out of San Francisco, his wife thought a sexy picture of herself would be a nice addition to his cabin. She had some boudoir photography shot as a birthday present. Unfortunately, the captain's wife went to a photographer with cash flow problems. He sold an extra set of Mrs. Seidman's prints to a men's magazine specializing in older women clad in lingerie. The captain was not amused to see his lovely bride on display in the cutter's engine room, and he funded my trip to California to recover the negatives. As a public service, I urged the errant shutterbug to burn the remainder of his files at gunpoint so he wouldn't be tempted to play entrepreneur again. The way I pointed my Colt at his crotch finally convinced him.

"What about getting on the *Jersey Trader* this morning?" I asked Marshall. "Will that be a problem?"

"The teams usually go out after muster, and I've told them to plan on taking you along." He looked me over, frowning at my non-regulation hair and non-uniform garb. "I'm not sure how to get you aboard a freighter, particularly out of uniform."

"If you've got a spare set of coveralls, I'll get dressed. But I also need to take some pictures."

Reaching his conclusion, he smiled and stood. "That's it then. We'll say you're a reporter doing a story about a Coast Guard boarding team. We took a reporter from the *News Tribune* before." He chuckled. "And we'll say your face is from a story on boxing."

He led me down the hall and introduced me to the boarding team I would accompany; a lieutenant and two petty officers, all dressed in identical dark blue coveralls with their names sewn in white letters above the left breast pocket. A chunky, balding lieutenant named Washburn headed the group; I assumed he was prior enlisted, judging by his age. Both petty officers were marine science technicians; the first class was named Haines, and the second class, Cerufetti. Cerufetti had recently returned from a short duty in Valdez, Alaska, and he was busy telling Haines about the hot spot of Valdez, the legendary Pipeline Club where the skipper of the *Exxon Valdez* allegedly drained the tap. I agreed that the steaks there were good. I had been to Valdez three times, twice while on the aircrew taking people to the hospital and once as a special agent from Juneau investigating a drug case at Marine Safety Office Valdez. I couldn't think of a nice thing about the town except that it often had running water.

I fitted Sally's dark watch cap over my bandaged forehead and felt like a washed-up longshoreman. The four of us headed for the state pier. Haines drove the battered government Chevy van. Washburn explained that most of the other piers belonged to individual companies that specialized in one of two cargoes; taconite or grain.

"Have you boarded the *Jersey Trader* before?" I asked.

Washburn couldn't remember, but Haines spoke up. "Yeah, about four months ago, right at the start of the season. They were one of the first ships through the locks but they had some ice damage."

Cerufetti confirmed that. "That's right, they were caught in the ice down in the St. Clair river. Every year the ice breaks loose in Lake Huron and clogs the river when the salties are making the first transit upbound."

The van merged onto the interstate highway, and we soon

crossed a high bridge over the St. Louis River that separates Minnesota from Wisconsin. We were surrounded by freight trains waiting to dump their cargo into ships or silos. We weaved through a maze of streets and railroad tracks toward the towering silos on the Superior waterfront.

"It's always a mess down in the St. Clair," Haines agreed. "They have the *Mackinaw* and the buoytenders escort the freighters through, but some always get stuck."

"Now I remember. The *Jersey Trader* was the one that came in with the fouled anchor chain," Washburn said. The other two nodded. "They didn't have enough power to get upstream, and the ice was driving them back down river. The skipper dropped an anchor, but it didn't help. They were hung up for a day hauling enough chain they could make way."

"What kind of condition is the ship in?" I asked.

"Pretty decent," Cerufetti decided. "You've got to remember that we get everything from newish iron ore carriers to floating rust buckets here."

"What about the *Baltic Express?*"

Haines and Cerufetti broke into laughter. "The snake ship?" Haines coughed.

Cerufetti calmed first. "You know about the animals, right? From South America?" I nodded. "I was with the boarding party that found them. We had this real jerk, Petty Officer Foner; he got transferred out of here last month. We gave him all the shit jobs, and he was opening hatch covers to take soundings on empty tanks and voids. All the sudden, he starts screaming because he pulled off a cover and this 12-foot boa constrictor starts crawling out. Foner almost broke his leg getting off the ship." They chuckled the rest of the way down to the dock.

The dock seemed quiet because of the early hour. A crane on a nearby freighter hoisted loaded pallets aboard from a stack renewed often by a pair of quick forklifts shuttling in and out of an adjacent warehouse. Another ship flew the distinctive solid-red 'Bravo' flag, indicating they were refueling.

To see two or three merchant ships moored along the same pier is an awesome sight. They loom out of the water like steel castles, so large that they seem immovable, that no engine, no power could propel them. They are the largest vehicles in the world; the lakers are as large as aircraft carriers, and the salties are more than double the size of the Saturn V rocket that took the astronauts to the moon.

The *Jersey Trader* rode high in the water, so I figured they were not yet loaded. It was a bulk cargo ship with bay hatches fore and aft of the bridge. The 600-foot hull was painted blue, and the super-structure and rigging were all white. Some rust along the gunwales marred the paint, but it looked well maintained otherwise. I loaded my camera with color film, then followed Washburn and his crew up the steep gangway.

A stout man in greasy jeans and a flannel shirt met us on the main deck and introduced himself as Ed Kucharski, the ship's pilot. Because of the narrow passages and peculiar ways of the Great Lakes, ocean-going ships are required to carry pilots – local experts at sailing the lakes and rivers who handle the vessel's navigation. Becoming a pilot is not simply a matter of being a local resident. Prospective pilots must memorize hundreds of individual buoys and landmarks along the waterways they intend to sail.

As he welcomed us aboard, Kucharski apologized for the skip-per's absence. "He had some business downtown, but he asked me to show you around. I'm afraid the first mate went into town last night, and he's been polishing the porcelain this morning."

Washburn chuckled and introduced us. He explained that I worked for the local newspaper and wanted to follow the Coast Guard boarding team on their rounds. Kucharski shifted his coffee into the other fist, and we shook hands. He seemed in his early sixties and looked like he'd been sailing most of his life. His face was wrinkled, sunburned and unshaven.

"You know the routine by now," Washburn told him. "If you'll take me up to the bridge, we'll go through the papers while the guys have a look around and make sure everything's ship-shape."

"Well, nothing unusual to report, except that we're doing some welding down in the galley," Kucharski explained. "The skipper was by your office Tuesday to get a hot-work permit. Can you guys find your way around or would you like one of the seamen to show you?" he asked Haines.

"No, we're fine. We were aboard back in April when the anchor was fouled across the foc'sle."

Laughing, Kucharski shook his head. "I heard about that. Quite a mess, eh?"

Haines and Cerufetti headed below deck. The pilot led Washburn and me up three steep ladders to the wide bridge. Except for the red smoke stack and the tall mast mounted with a dozen different antennae, we were on the highest peak of the ship, with a view of the whole pier facility through the large windows. On the open decks behind the wheelhouse, a pair of rigid-hull inflatable rubber boats rested in steel cradles located port and starboard and were tied down with wide canvas straps. Hydraulic cranes had replaced the hand cranks crews once used to lower away the boats. There were also two old-fashioned lifeboats with manual boat davits located down on the stern.

Like most freighters, the helm and navigation gear were electronic and very modern. On either side of the chart table stood radar units. Mounted over the table were a Loran unit, a radio direction finder and one of the GPS units for Global Positioning System – the newest satellite navigation system. The radios were mounted so the helmsman could operate them and steer simultaneously. In open waters, the ship could run with only two people on the bridge – the helmsman and the deck officer. While underway, a lookout would stand forward on the foc'sle.

Kucharski laid out the ship's papers on the chart table and then went outside to fix a windshield wiper motor. I snapped a few photos of Washburn studying the documents. He allowed me to skim through the ship's log. The *Jersey Trader* passed Whitefish Point at 0930 Monday morning, putting it at Crisp Point shortly before CG 44323 arrived.

When I asked for the name of the freighter's captain, Washburn handed me the skipper's master license bearing the name Paul Leavitt. Leavitt had renewed his license in New York two years before. The examiner at the Marine Safety Office there was Chief Warrant Officer Gerald Jaspers. The coincidence didn't surprise me. Jaspers had mentioned working in New York when he and Normand were comparing gore stories the previous evening. The Coast Guard has only 38,000 people, and if you stay in long enough, you're bound to see the same names again and again. Sometimes that's a good thing, like the favor I'd done for Captain Seidman that he wanted to repay. Sometimes it's a bad thing like the vendetta Captain Burke stoked years after I visited Miami.

I copied down the names of the first mate and the remaining crew members; Floyd Carver and a collection of names that sounded to me to be Asian. When Kucharski returned, I asked him to pose with Washburn and pretend they were looking at the papers together. He was shy but finally consented. After glancing through the freighter's manifest and other papers, I went to find the other crewmembers.

Haines watched the welder install a new galvanized sink in the small galley on the main deck. I shot pictures of him from different angles, getting as many of the *Jersey Trader's* crewmen in the photos as I could. Aside from the skipper, mate and pilot, the entire crew seemed to hail from Southeast Asia. If you don't mind the living conditions, bad food and being away from home for months, along with the long hours and cruel mistreatment, sailing a merchant vessel is a decent way to make money – especially if home is an impoverished country where the yearly rainfall dictates the standard of living.

Washburn caught me as I headed down to the engine space to photograph Cerufetti with the ship's engineers. "How much do you want us to do?" he asked. "If you want a full-blown inspection, we can spend eight hours here."

"I need to have pictures of the entire crew so I can get them ID'd. If they were dirty, they've had three days to dump the evidence."

"Dirty? You mean smuggling?"

"Yes, I think that the missing crew found a mother ship operation," I said.

"You should have told us before; we'd have kept an eye out for all the major signs, you know, fresh welding, sealed compartments, that sort of thing." He paused and thought it over. "While you go down to the engine spaces, Haines and I will take a quick sweep of the ship and see what we can find."

Clambering up and down the steep ladders set my lower back aflame, and I wondered if my attacker hadn't ruptured all my lower intestines. I found Cerufetti examining fire extinguishers in the main engine room and posed him looking over the shoulders of two crewmen checking lube oil on the big diesel engine. Cerufetti and I walked forward and found three more engineers tinkering with a bilge pump. They all smiled for the camera.

When we went back topside, Kucharski stood chatting with the lieutenant by the gangway. Washburn gave me a questioning look. After I nodded to indicate that I was finished, he thanked the mate, and we all climbed back down to the pier.

"I didn't see anything unusual," Haines said. "Nothing that indicated a smuggler."

"Hell, even their life jackets are new," Cerufetti observed.

"Did you call the freighter to tell them we were coming down?" I asked Washburn as we climbed back into the van.

"No, I thought you wanted it to be a surprise," he answered.

"So how the skipper knew there'd be visitors for the pilot to show around?"

Their gaping looks of curiosity didn't offer any solutions to that minor mystery. I still needed to get a picture of the skipper. If he had left to avoid us, he wouldn't return until we were gone. I asked Haines to drop me by the entrance to the docks. Then I hiked back, dodging behind trucks and railroad cars so Kucharski or another crewman on the lookout wouldn't spot me.

Crouched behind a forest green dumpster with a picture of a grinning hippopotamus on the side, I stayed on the same pier where the Jersey Trader was moored, about 15 yards from its gangway. The slogan painted below the hippo was "Satisfaction guaranteed or double your trash back." The cooks had thrown away last night's leftovers in it and some other noxious things as well – stuff that would wipe the smile off any hippo's face. I mounted a small telephoto lens from my black bag onto the camera body and settled down to wait.

Maybe it's due to many years spent fishing, but I enjoy

surveillance. I don't mind sitting and watching everything that happens around me. Once I clung to an icebreaker's mast overnight to see who was stealing from a warehouse on the moorings. However, the stench of that dumpster could make anyone a little anxious.

Exactly 27 minutes after Washburn's team departed, a taxi pulled up to the gangway. A tall, bearded man climbed out of the back seat, a big guy with a broad chest wearing a green windbreaker and blue jeans. He carried a small valise. I focused and shot some nice full-face portraits while he paid the cabby, then snapped a few profiles as he climbed the steep gangplank.

The taxi had to turn around to leave – a tricky maneuver on the narrow pier, so I ducked behind a warehouse and raced back toward the gate, my battered face protesting every jolting step of the run. I arrived in time to flag the cabby down for a ride to the nearest photography store.

Back on the Duluth side of the river, the clerk at Photo Magic said he was busy and couldn't get to my film for several days. He wasn't swayed when I flashed the badge and explained that I needed a rapid turnaround. Only the promise of a fast fifty bucks changed his mind. I wondered how today's bribery and yesterday's charity would look on my travel claim.

While the young entrepreneur went into the darkroom, I crossed the street to a pay phone and called Lieutenant Dunlay at Group Soo collect.

"How does your face feel today?" she asked.

"Well, at least people appear to have only one head apiece this morning. How's the search going?"

"We found Pelligrini," she said in a quiet, solemn voice. "He was located along the upbound route approximately midway between Ile Parisienne Light and Whitefish Point. A freighter spotted him first thing this morning." Her tone told me that the young coxswain had not been found alive.

"Do you know the cause of death?"

She paused and took a deep breath. "Drowning, but that's not official yet. The helo picked him up and transported him to the hospital. We have requested a full autopsy, but it may not be completed until later this afternoon."

"And no sign of the others in the same area yet?" I asked.

"No, but we're centering the search where he was found. So far, I have an H-3 and the 41-footer onscene. The captain has requested the *Mackinaw* come up from Cheboygan to assist." Her voice sounded hollow. During a search, you try to keep your hopes up; but once it starts to go bad, it's hard to remain optimistic. "What about you?" she asked. "Have you found anything helpful out there?"

"Nothing yet. I'm going to have a little chat with the FBI before I come back to the Soo."

"Oh, that reminds me. Your friend, Schmidt from Customs, called this morning."

"Did he say what he wanted?" I asked.

"No message. He wanted to talk to you before you departed the Soo. And your friend Sally called to ask about your health." She paused. "I am not your personal secretary, Galloway."

"Yes, ma'am. Have you got the phone number of the medical examiner handy? I'd like to give him a call later and see what the autopsy turns up."

She gave me the number and hung up without a goodbye.

I bought a bagel at the bakery next to the photo store and stood outside in the cool morning air. I couldn't eat. Pelligrini's death meant that either I was getting too close to the truth or I was casting a 100-foot leadline into 10 feet of water. Maybe they all did fall overboard. Strange things happen in Lake Superior: Fifteen years later, and still nobody knows exactly why the SS *Edmund Fitzgerald* sank near Whitefish Point.

The prints came out decent for a rush job. I was especially proud of my portraits of the skipper.

I took a taxi downtown to the FBI's resident agent's office in an ugly glass and steel building built during architecture's repressive period. The small reception area looked vacant, as though it had been unoccupied for some time. I felt as though I was in the wrong office or even the wrong building.

"May I help you?" a disembodied voice called.

I looked up because most surveillance cameras are close to the ceiling, making them harder to knock out. "Hi, I was hoping to speak to an agent." I fished out my badge.

"Oh, hell, my kid has a cooler badge than that."

I turned the badge to look at it again. "Hey, I drank a lot of Ovaltine to get this."

"So who are you, Ralphie? What do you want?"

"Do you know Chet Burley, by any chance? He works down in the Chicago office." The voice made an inaudible grunt. "Great. I'd like you to give him a call and ask him about me. Name's Marty Galloway. Coast Guard Special Agent."

"Stand by."

The FBI waiting room sported a worse selection of reading material than even the Army Corps of Engineers in the Soo, including such titles as *Federal Probation: A Journal of Correctional Philosophy and Practice* and *Customs and Border Protection Regulations of the United States.*

"Come ahead," the voice announced.

I found Special Agent Harper-Lloyd waiting for me down a fluorescent-lit hallway. His office looked rather modest, except for the diplomas hanging behind his desk. He'd graduated from law school at the University of Chicago before he signed on. The FBI has been recruiting more lawyers lately because enforcing the law gets very complex at times. He sipped coffee from a mug that read "World's Greatest Lover," and I glanced at the picture of his lovely wife on the desk. The frame faced the visitor, so I assumed he was proud of her cover-girl looks.

"Well, how can I assist you, Mister Galloway?" he asked. "I should warn you that we don't often handle assault complaints." He gestured toward my bandages.

I passed my badge and ID across the desk. Harper-Lloyd seemed more interested in my ring from the FBI Academy at Stafford, Virginia. The Coast Guard nominates special agents for the arduous program, and I managed to get accepted despite my less-than-sterling reputation. Chet Burley was my classmate there.

"Chet told me to arrest you for impersonating a law officer," Harper-Lloyd said with a straight face. "Actually, he said he's been trying to recruit you for a few years."

"Thanks for calling him. See, I know you're busy, and I wanted you to understand up front that I wouldn't waste your time," I explained.

"Very considerate, but the clock is running."

I laid out the photographs I'd taken aboard the *Jersey Trader* across his desk and gave him the list of the crew's names. "I'd like you to run these people through Washington and see what you can find on them."

Harper-Lloyd examined the pictures for several minutes. He finally tapped one. "Don't have to go through Quantico for this guy. Forrest Van Dorn. I'd recognize him with or without the beard."

I leaned forward. He held up my portrait of the skipper.

"So he's not Paul Leavitt, merchant mariner?"

"Oh, no. I'd say the closest Van Dorn ever comes to the water is dumping a body off a bridge." Harper-Lloyd settled back in his chair.

"Forrest Van Dorn, huh? Sounds pretty prestigious for an average criminal."

"That's not his given name, of course. It's a mix of Bedford Forrest and somebody Van Dorn, both Confederate generals. Memory serves, his given name was something like Clayton Pritcher. He changed it after the Army threw him out with a dishonorable discharge. But then again I wouldn't call Van Dorn your average criminal."

"How'd you get to know him so well?"

He tossed the photograph on top of the others. "It's not easy to forget a scumbag like that. I worked on the civil rights squad down in Georgia for a while, and I got to know Van Dorn pretty well. He likes to think of himself as a hero and a martyr. For a while he called himself a general in the One America for Aryans Army. Now he has a group called God's True Patriots. Not a whole lot of difference, but a broader audience appeal for fundraising. He first came to our attention because he was trying to make a name for himself as an enforcer of racial purity, and we thought he was responsible for several attacks on interracial couples. His trademark was a gunshot blast in the groin. His victims, always the male, usually bled to death."

"Sounds pretty perverse. Is there something Freudian about this guy's MO?"

"I never saw his psychological profile, but I'm sure it's full of the usual family violence and alcoholism. But my guess would be that he was clever. Shotgun pellets can't be traced. And even if we could have tied Van Dorn to the crime, we would never be able to prove premeditation. When someone bleeds to death, you always have trouble proving intent. So a smart defense lawyer can plead him in anywhere from murder two down to assault with a deadly weapon." Harper-Lloyd tapped a forefinger against his temple. "Van Dorn is smart that way. He knows that a jury of his peers would figure, 'Shit, I wanna body dead I shoot 'em in the head. I aim doan dere, I's jus' tryin' wing him.'" The agent gave me his best ole boy twang. "Now what Van Dorn knows that his peers may not is that a man's groin has a very large blood supply. If we didn't, we'd be a whole lot more disappointing to women than we are already." Harper-Lloyd gave me a smug grin to show that his wife wasn't the least bit disappointed.

"Sounds like you've spent a great deal of time figuring out Van Dorn's methods."

"Yes, I have. There's a strong possibility that everything I've told you is a bunch of crap, and he's another sick bastard. Weren't most generals in the Third Reich sexual deviants of one persuasion or another?"

"Sorry, I'm no expert on Nazi perversion. Does Van Dorn have any other dirty little secrets?"

"He also worked a little road construction at one time, so he knows about an interesting variety of explosives. Discounting copycat attacks, we figured Van Dorn for maybe four bombings at black churches, two at black colleges, one attempt at a hotel during an NAACP convention."

"How many people has this guy killed?" I asked in amazement.

"Six, five of those were gunshot victims, one was a night janitor at a college. These bombings are intended for shock value so they're middle-of-the-night things, and the colleges lost empty classroom buildings. He's shrewd enough to know that if he wiped out an entire congregation or a dormitory full of students he couldn't knock off a six-pack before we'd put him away for good. And Van Dorn doesn't want to go back to prison with something like that on his record. I hear the boyz from the hood made it pretty rough on him last time he was in the cage – sent him to the infirmary half dozen times."

"What did you finally put him away for, the shootings or the bombings?"

Harper-Lloyd chuckled, shaking his head. "I wish we could have proven any of those in court. No, the Tennessee highway patrol stopped him for speeding. When Van Dorn got antsy, they searched the car. They found two dozen fully automatic M-16s in the trunk, stolen from a National Guard armory in Louisiana. Of course, now he's a lot more careful about his activities. He's much too famous to be reckless. Or infamous. He was on television; one of those FBI Top Ten Countdown shows."

His tone of disdain surprised me. "I thought you G-men liked those shows."

"Oh, we've had some help, but someday a concerned citizen is going to play hero and get his brains blown out." Harper-Lloyd laughed and added, "Or his balls shot off."

"Any conjectures about why a white supremacist like Van Dorn would be on a freighter in the Great Lakes?" I asked.

He puzzled on it for a few moments. "No, but tell me what you've got so far, and I'll see what I can add."

I explained to him Thomason's theory and included the supporting evidence I had accumulated during the past few days. He asked acute questions to clarify a few details. When I finished, he seemed to agree and disagree simultaneously.

"Sounds like you're onto something, but I don't see how Van Dorn or his Patriots could be involved," he said. "I've never seen a connection between these guys and drugs. They usually steal their weapons so they don't need a lot of overhead. Most of their fund-raising is for printing propaganda or buying uniforms. If they came into a major cash flow like a drug deal, they'd have to fix their books. But they know the IRS can nail them for fraud if they ever tried to get cute. Otherwise, I'm not aware of anything the Bureau has on Van Dorn that indicates drug smuggling. Or even drug use for that matter. He's a good ole boy, I'd guess he gets his kicks on a beer and a bump."

"What about through his connections? I've heard a lot of these wacko groups are linked by their own underground networks. Could he be involved in somebody else's scheme?"

"Anyone but Van Dorn, I'd say yes. There's dozens of these groups, each trying to outdo their pals. A lot of misfits; they like the shaved heads and uniforms but they can't take the discipline of, oh, say the Marines. Besides they like their victims unarmed and harmless; they wouldn't know how to deal with an enemy that shoots back. But Van Dorn play somebody else's game? Not a chance. He sees himself as the American Caesar. One reason he had so much trouble in the Army is that he didn't understand why he couldn't go from private straight to major general. Didn't help his case that he was accused of assaulting a sergeant major's daughter outside the NCO club. But now the former private is his own general."

"Well, I'll have to go ask Forrest Van Dorn what he's up to."

Harper-Lloyd laughed. "From what Burley said, I figure you might do something like that. Be sure to leave an address where you'd like your remains sent. In the meantime, I'll make a few calls. And don't worry about my time. Burley said he'd tack it on to what you already owe him."

"So he told you about our running poker game, huh?"

"Of course, and he told me not to lend you any money, either."

"I'm going to have to talk to Chet about all this slander he's been spreading about me. What about the other Caucasians in the photos? The older guy gave his name as Kucharski. Another one unavailable for pictures is a Floyd Carver, DOB and homeport unknown."

Harper-Lloyd picked up the photos and examined each face in turn. "No, don't recognize the old guy. Of course, there are so many good ole boys running around with white sheets in the night or kissing the swastika that he could be part of it. I'd let you run them through NCIC, but my terminal went down last week and I haven't found a repairman who's bonded. You know how the Bureau would react if they found out I had somebody work with it who wasn't cleared. Be helpful for you to read Van Dorn's scandal sheet before you tangle with him."

"What about these other photos?" I asked of the many crewmen below decks on the *Jersey Trader*.

He shuffled through the prints. "Next time, use a better photographer," he groused. "No, sorry. No one stands out to me." He handed the stack back to me. "You think it's part of an international thing? That why all the Asian crewmembers aboard?"

"Come on, don't throw so much at me in the first ten minutes. I'm still trying to fit the racists into it." I wished I could run the entire crew through the FBI's national criminal identification computer. In minutes, a proficient operator can pull up a full individual criminal history based on either a fingerprint, a name, or an MO. The police in California recently made an arrest in a 25-year-old murder case when a computer search turned up a matching fingerprint. Comparing the same number of fingerprints by hand would have taken a human criminologist about 500,000 years, without vacations. "I'll ask Chet for a favor when I finish chewing him out."

"Let me call a couple of friends and see if I can get an update on Van Dorn's activities since I came north," Harper-Lloyd told me as he stood and extended his hand. "Call me at 2:15."

I knew I had been dismissed and that if I called at 2:16, Harper-Lloyd wouldn't be available.

Thursday: 1245

I took a taxi back to the Marine Safety Office, debating whether to investigate the *Baltic Express*. It was past noon, so I had little more than 24 hours remaining before the commandant's deadline. I wondered about the consequences, but I couldn't imagine anything worse than being stationed at Headquarters again. Since no admiral would accept that, I felt a certain impunity. Then I remembered my promise to Melinda Desharnais.

Marshall let me use Captain Seidman's office to make a few phone calls. First, I phoned Chet Burley at the FBI office in Chicago. He sounded annoyed to hear from me.

"I was hoping Harper-Lloyd would be able to keep you off my back," Chet grunted. "Why can't you solve your own cases? You forget everything you learned at the academy?"

"I didn't learn that much in the first place," I retorted. "I was too busy helping you with the reading assignments. Before I came along, you thought Elliot Ness was a Scottish monster."

"If you think this is going to get you a favor, don't forget the two dozen you already owe me. And there's also the matter of $475."

"Funny, it seems to go up every time I talk to you."

"Never heard of interest accrued on principle? So, what do you want this time? The names of every person who ever stayed at the Watergate?"

"Harper-Lloyd was having computer problems so I need you to run a few names for me. Forrest Van Dorn, Floyd Carver and Ed Kucharski. I know Van Dorn is part of God's True Patriots; Harper-Lloyd told me what he knew. I'd still like to hear the whole rap sheet on this guy, and I don't know anything about Carver."

"I keep telling you, Marty, you get yourself a laptop or a portable with eight megs of RAM and an 80-meg hard drive with a 9600 baud internal modem and you could access the national system with a cleared password."

I tend to lapse into a coma when people start talking bits and bytes at me. "Chet, I buy my own rounds for target practice every week. Do you suppose the Coast Guard is going to leave something like a laptop computer under the Christmas tree?"

"Well, I wouldn't want to fund your range time either, not the way you shoot. Are you still using those life-size elephant silhouettes?"

"Next time your wife invites me to dinner, how about I bring along the photos from that luau on Big Pine Key when you met that cute little brunette. What was her name? Misty? Fifi?"

"Check my spelling on that third name. K-u-c-h-a-r-s-k-i?"

With business finished, I dialed Pete Schmidt in the Soo.

"Hey, Marty. I wanted to catch up with you before you left town."

"I'll be back in the Soo later today."

"Well, I figured that since they found one of the crew that you might be ready to wrap up and head home."

"How did you hear about that?"

"It's the Soo. Word gets around. Any interesting developments?" he asked.

"Nothing I want to discuss on the phone, Pete."

"A little paranoid, huh? Do you use code names, too?"

"Only when I forge checks." I wasn't in the mood to discuss my investigative technique, so I told him I'd call when I reached the Soo.

Then I called Sally at the bank as requested. She couldn't stay on the phone long but expressed deep concern about my wounds.

"Any news from the search?" she asked. "I heard they found one of the Coasties."

"Oh? Guess I need to make a few calls," I said. Yes, it was a lie, but I was waiting to call about the autopsy on Pelligrini.

"How did things go out there? Did you get on those two freighters?"

My brain stumbled; when did I tell Sally about my investigation? Was I suffering short-term memory loss from a head injury? Finally, I remembered that she was collecting blood-soaked gauze swatches from Hopkins' makeshift operating table when Dunlay had asked about my plans.

"Yeah, it went well."

"Do you think they're connected to the missing crew?" She sounded excited by the intrigue.

"Nothing says that."

"Yeah, well do you know if you're coming back to the Soo tonight? I need to call Mom before she makes plans with her bingo cronies." Her excitement had turned to exasperation.

When I provided no definite answers, she offered a sarcastic comment about running a boarding house for the infirm, then hung up. I understood her frustration. I had involved her in this, and now I dodged her questions. I had bled on her sofa, slept in her bed and armed her against possible attackers. Why couldn't I tell her the truth? I wasn't sure my answer was sufficient. Next, I called the hospital and learned that the autopsy continued. I decided to pass the time by visiting my second suspect.

Haines and Cerufetti were busy tracking down the source of a small oil slick spotted near the Coast Guard station. Marshall asked Washburn to drop what he was doing and hustle me down to the *Baltic Express*. The lieutenant wasn't much pleased by the assignment, but he went along just the same.

"Why don't you tell me what you're looking for this time?" Washburn asked, impatience clear in his tone.

"I need to find if they were in the vicinity of Crisp Point Monday morning."

"That should be pretty easy to figure out; we'll check the ship's log. To double check, we'll find out when they moored, then subtract passage time across Lake Superior."

I could tell my demands annoyed Washburn, and I apologized for the inconvenience.

"It's no big deal; but it'd make things a lot easier if you told me what you wanted up front."

We drove down to the waterfront and pulled up adjacent to the *Baltic Express*, a tramp steamer that should have been christened *Rust Bucket*. Rivers of orange metal flake covered the black hull, and the deck house was sooty gray. A tattered Panamanian flag hung over the stern.

"Look, why don't you wait here while I run up and check the papers," he said, climbing out of the government vehicle. "That way I won't have to explain who you are."

He walked beyond the gangway and talked with a young man standing on the pier, watching the crane hoist pallets aboard. The longshoreman directed Washburn onto the bow, where he met two other men and then disappeared from view along with them.

Washburn was upset because I hadn't confided in him prior to our visit to the *Jersey Trader*, but I couldn't afford to trust anyone then. Twice somebody had learned my whereabouts or plans; first the hotel ambush and then that morning when the skipper of the *Jersey Trader* had been warned of our visit. Once, it had been an inconvenience; the other time came close to resulting in my untimely death. I had to start playing this game smarter, and that meant alone. I didn't wish to be the cause for my grandmother to dress in black a third time.

About fifteen minutes later, Washburn appeared three decks up on the side of the bridge. He shook hands with the same two men he had met on the bow, and then he climbed down a long steel stair outside the superstructure. He jogged across the deck, scrambled down the gangway and hopped into the driver's seat.

"According to the ship's log, they cleared Whitefish Bay before midnight Sunday," he said. "They were moored here Monday evening so it's got to be pretty close. It's a long trip across the lake."

"Thanks for checking it for me."

"No problem." He started the engine, and we backed down the pier to the first section wide enough to turn around.

"I thought the *Baltic Express* was going to be in port for a couple of weeks making repairs."

"As far as I know they are," he replied.

"Then why are they loading a cargo?"

"Are you kidding? This time of year, warehouse and pier space are at a premium. It'd be cheaper to line the docks with parking meters. A lot of times they'll get towed out to anchorage and make repairs there. Less chance for crews to get into trouble ashore. Or disappear."

Looking south across the river, I saw the pier where my prime suspect was moored. "I could be mistaken, but isn't that the pier where the *Jersey Trader* was moored this morning?" I asked.

"Sure was. Could be they moved out to the anchorage, too."

Another issue confused me. "When Kucharski showed us the *Jersey Trader's* paperwork, it looked like everything only went back

151

like two years. Shouldn't there be more history on a ship running international routes?"

Washburn stopped at a traffic light. "Yes and no. Could be she was sold recently. So the skipper didn't give Kucharski access to the old stuff. Or the dog ate their paperwork."

I sensed that I was treading on the lieutenant's patience. Still, the disappearance of the *Jersey Trader* alarmed me, but there was only one way for that ship to leave the lake. If necessary, I'd sit on the Soo locks and wait until the freighter arrived.

When we arrived at the Marine Safety Office, I called the hospital in Sault Ste. Marie. After several minutes of waiting on hold listening to mood music, the switchboard connected me with the medical examiner. As we talked, Doctor Gauthier sounded more like a general practitioner than an expert forensic pathologist.

"Is this boy one of your missing crewmen?" he asked.

"Yes sir, I'm afraid so." I'd have to explain to the commandant that there's no keeping secrets in a small town like the Soo. "Was the cause of death drowning?"

"Most likely, although he also had some bruises and contusions. And I found fluids in the intestines and colon consistent with dysentery, but that wouldn't be fatal in this case."

"Refresh my memory, doc. What causes dysentery?"

"Could be any number of causes: viral or bacterial. You're familiar with salmonella? That can cause it."

"So, we're talking food poisoning?" I asked in confusion.

"Well, that's the most common cause."

"Were you able to tell how long he'd been in the water?"

He coughed and cleared his throat, causing a harsh static on the phone line. "Excuse me. Well, it's difficult to pinpoint an exact time. Cold water tends to preserve the body longer; however, there was no bloating of the skin tissue or deterioration of the rigor mortis. I'd say no more than 24 hours."

The muscles in my neck tightened. Almost 72 hours had elapsed between the time Thomason found CG44323 floating adrift in Agawa Bay and Pelligrini's body was recovered. "Where were the bruises you mentioned before?"

"On the back of the neck and shoulders. There was another

peculiarity that I forgot to mention; the mucus in his nasal cavity was full of gritty silicon – uh, common beach sand."

I had an awful suspicion, but I wanted the doctor to confirm it. "Give me your best guess, doc. Unofficially, of course. How did Pelligrini die?"

After a long, ponderous silence on the line, Gauthier said, "Given the bruises and the sand, I'd say somebody pushed him into the lake and held his head against the bottom until he stopped breathing."

I thanked the doctor and hung up.

Many years ago, the Coast Guard began sending aviation survivalmen through the Navy's rescue-swimmer training, and I was among the first selected to go. It's a tough course, but the roughest part was a cute little pool exercise. The instructors acted like drowning victims, and the students had to rescue them. Sometimes the instructors would pretend they were panicked and try to pull the rescuer down with them. One big guy held me under so long that I blacked out. A few years later, a student died from asphyxia. My personal experience convinced me that drowning must be the worst possible death; it takes a comparatively long time, and you spend your last moments in helpless, claustrophobic panic.

What the autopsy revealed changed everything. Pelligrini died in shallow water; his murderer had held his face against the bottom silt. The murder scene must be far from the depth of the Canadian waters where the boat was found. If Pelligrini had died within 24 hours, he'd also been alive for 48 hours after Coast Guard 44323 was found empty. Pelligrini was alive when I first arrived in Michigan. Now, he was dead, and I couldn't say who killed him or why. Totaling these things made me angry. I had failed Boatswain's Mate Second Class Henry Pelligrini. He died for it.

The motive behind Pelligrini's murder was not mere cruelty. He had been kept alive for two days, so murdering him had a definite purpose – such as confusing any search or investigation. Captain Burke believed that the rest of the crew were also floaters, and he was bringing up the icebreaker *Mackinaw* to help with the body search. Burke would not support my efforts now. Finding the others became more urgent than any promise.

Thursday: 1415

I watched the second hand tick off exactly two minutes on my diver's watch before I called Harper-Lloyd at the FBI. He was soon on the line, and he sounded excited. "Yeah, Marty, I did some checking, and things sound pretty interesting."

"So, Van Dorn didn't change careers?"

"Not hardly. In fact, it sounds like he has some master plan to eradicate a lot of non-whites without implicating God's True Patriots in any way," he said.

"Are we talking cheap crack or heroin with complimentary AIDS-tainted needles?"

"Something a little more diabolical, like distributing cheap knock-off AKs to gangbangers, hoping they'll use them on each other."

"You mean assault rifles?"

"Bingo! Give any gang a half dozen of those with full auto, and they'll go to war for spit. And these toys are foreign so they aren't registered; that way the serial numbers can't ever be traced back to Van Dorn or the Patriots."

I started to feel dizzy but couldn't decide if it was due to hunger, head wounds or confusion. "So you're saying God's True Patriots are passing out automatic weapons to street gangs hoping they will kill each other off? How did you find out all of this?"

"Like I said, I made some calls. I have a friend in Washington who helps solicit information from people in the Witness Protection Program. This guy my friend was working, a fellow named Larry Gilman, was real eager to hang Forrest Van Dorn out to dry. Seems this guy was a double dipper; he turned state's evidence and went into protection. Then he got bored so he blew his new identity and went back to his old home town. Van Dorn was on the welcoming committee, and this guy barely made it to the emergency room before he ran out of O positive. And guess where he was shot? My friend says the snitch doesn't even look at Playboy anymore." Harper-Lloyd's chuckle wasn't particularly amusing.

"So, the FBI has known about this operation for months?" I asked.

"Not the details, no, only the general idea about smuggling

weapons. The Bureau even put a tail on Van Dorn, but six months ago he climbed on a private jet to the Azores and hasn't been seen until you did his portrait this morning. Also, they were getting information from somebody on the inside, but they haven't heard anything from that source for several weeks."

I thought the whole business over for a few moments, trying to remember everything Inspector Thomason had said. This story explained the freighter's last port of call in Madrid – a free port where many weapons change hands. "Only one thing doesn't make sense to me. Why would the price of coke in Chicago or Detroit fall because some white supremacy group is providing gangs with machine guns? Seems like two completely different things."

"You need to keep up with the news a little better, Galloway," Harper-Lloyd said. "First, more people are smoking crack cocaine, which can be adulterated, or diluted, when it's made. And the synthetics like PCP and meth have gotten popular. So why smuggle it from South America when you can make it at home? So the Columbians switched to growing something even more addictive. Now the drug of choice among heavy users and even the chic dilettantes is old-fashioned heroin. I've heard surveillance pilots say there are so many poppy plants in the Andes now that it looks like flying over the world's largest flower garden. So cocaine drops in price because it isn't as popular these days."

"You're right; I should have realized that sooner – it was in a briefing a few months back." I paused to reflect on this insight. "And why would Thomason think it was drugs?"

"If I had to take a stab at it, I'd guess our DEA isn't sharing their intel with the Mounties. Look, Galloway, I wish I could be more help, but I don't have the extra manpower here. I'll put in a call to the civil rights task force and asked for back-up, but don't expect it soon, middle of next week is the absolute soonest from what I can tell. I can ask the Bureau in Washington if they have anyone they can spare, but I'll have to convince them Van Dorn is up here. I hear BATF is in worse shape than we are."

I hadn't even considered assistance from the Bureau of Alcohol, Tobacco and Firearms. They have fewer people than any other federal law agency, so it's not hard to overlook them. I wondered if Lieutenant Andrews might give their Detroit office a call.

"Well, this is great," I said. "I'm going up against a bunch of guys carrying a load of automatic weapons, and you don't want to play. I don't suppose you loan out body armor."

"No, but if you're going up against Van Dorn," he warned me, "you should get yourself a bullet-proof jockstrap."

Harper-Lloyd's hollow laugh echoed as I replaced the phone's handset. Then I realized another call was necessary.

Thursday: 1430

When Dunlay answered the phone, she sounded surprised to hear from me. "You know, Captain Burke has inquired twice about when you'll be leaving," she said. "I'm surprised you haven't developed a persecution complex."

"Well ma'am, when you've been sworn at by admirals, captains don't seem so impressive."

"You've got to tell me that story sometime," she said, laughing a little. "Speaking of stories, the hotel owner was quite concerned about the condition of your room this morning. She spoke to Commander Fraser about it. So, have you discovered anything useful during your day off in Duluth?"

I hated to ruin her good mood. "Oh, quite a bit. I'll tell you everything when I get there."

"So, you're returning straight here?"

"If I get waylaid, I'll call. But I need a favor. Can you spare an aircraft long enough to locate a freighter named the *Jersey Trader* for me?"

"I've only got a helo and an Air Force C-130 in the air right now. I won't have a Guardian jet here until tomorrow. Where do you think this freighter is?"

"All I know is that it left Duluth earlier today," I explained. "They may be anchored off Duluth, but I can't see them from the waterfront. My guess is that they're heading for the Soo."

"OK, I'll do what I can. *Jersey Trader*, correct? If the captain questions me, I hope you'll have a good explanation ready."

"Like I said, captains don't bother me so much anymore, ma'am. I'll call you as soon as I reach town. That'll be after seven this evening, so should I call you at home?"

"No, I'll be here. Short-handed now. Jaspers went on emergency leave. His mother died. The commander asked the Cleveland office for somebody to help out, but I'll be here round the clock until a new body arrives."

No chance of asking Jaspers about Leavitt's merchant's license, I thought. "Bad timing," I observed.

"Funny, I thought it was pretty convenient myself; Jaspers was never one to work extra hours. But the Red Cross confirmed his mother's death, and we're pretty much obliged to follow their say-so, and the captain signed his leave papers."

"You're doing this for the overtime pay, right, ma'am?" I joked.

"Yeah, you got it. Hey, I've got another call, gotta go." She hung up.

I tried to call the Detroit office of the Bureau of Alcohol, Tobacco and Firearms but reached only a disconnected federal phone number. Finally, I thanked Marshall and headed out to the government vehicle. When the driver dropped me at the airport, I went to the closest counter and asked the clerk to get clearance from the FAA tower for me to go onto the airfield.

She turned to a radio on the back counter. Her shaggy brunette hair reminded me of Brenda, my ex-wife.

We were married before I joined the Coast Guard, but Brenda didn't like moving with each transfer. She hated Kodiak. When the Juneau orders came down, she refused to return to Alaska. The long-distance divorce became a simple paper chore, and I haven't seen her or the kids again, though it's not my choice. The clerk handed me off to airport security.

The Jayhawk was touching down on the far end of the tarmac when I limped out of the terminal. My lower back was stiffening from the previous night's amateur wrestling match. Even though my bag of tricks ran a hair over 20 pounds fully loaded, it hung around my neck and weighed me down like wearing a Yugo. When I climbed into the Jayhawk, the aircrewman reached for my bag, then turned back and hoisted me up into the bay. Gripping my biceps, he wheeled me into a web seat and began to strap me down. I snatched a headset from a peg overhead and lifted the mic to my mouth. "Thanks, I can manage," I said. He backed away and strapped himself into place.

By then, the helo was already airborne. The pilot made a tidy turn to starboard and gained altitude in a swift climb out of the restricted air space. Once the FAA controller cleared the Jayhawk of tower control, the pilot asked me how the search and investigation were going. When I said I hadn't heard much from the Soo that day, one of the crewmen asked why I was all the way over in Duluth. I gave an obligatory non-answer, and the subject changed. The helo crew soon forgot I was even on the IC. They talked about the dense forest of Michigan's UP and how they might return that fall with a gang from the air station in Traverse City for a little deer hunting.

I had some hunting of my own in mind, but where to start my search with three missing people and two missing suspects? I could assume Van Dorn was on the *Jersey Trader* somewhere in Lake Superior because he had no reason to believe he had been identified. But that was only an assumption, and assumptions often have tragic results. Where I found Banks depended on how many sleazy beer halls I could locate. Finally, it turned into an algebra problem: Establish a known quantity – Banks, then solve for the variable – Van Dorn, to find the unknown – the whereabouts of the missing crew. I wished I had been more attentive in Mrs. Hoffman's sixth-period algebra class.

The crew continued to chatter during the flight, and when the helo touched down at Kinross, they seemed surprised to discover I was still with them. The aircrewman lowered me to the grass and dumped my black bag next to me. As I hustled out from under the whining rotor blades, the helo lifted off, and again I felt that familiar down draft of an aircraft leaving me behind. From that perspective, the prop wash of an HH-60 felt like an H-3.

Thursday: 1540

I stopped at a gas station before I-75 and called Chet Burley while the attendant filled my tank. I was stunned when the pump jockey popped the hood and checked the oil; you don't get that kind of service in very many places these days.

"Hey Chet, this is Mar ..."

He cut me short. "Give me a number."

I read off the number from the pay phone, then hung up and waited. Five minutes later, the phone rang. When I picked up the receiver, the pump jockey gave me an inquisitive look.

"Sorry for the delay, Marty," Chet said. "I had to get to a pay phone away from the office." I heard traffic in the background on his end of the line.

"What's going on, Chet? This cloak and dagger stuff isn't like you."

"I got a bad feeling about this one, that's all. Nothing definite, one of those cases of nagging indigestion."

"I get the willies, and you get heartburn. We're a couple of swell detectives."

"Wait till you hear what I've got. This fellow Kucharski is a legit-imate Great Lakes pilot, all right. Seems he went into the FBI office in Cleveland four months ago. He wanted to report a smuggling operation, but when the agent taking his report punched it into the computer he discovered that Washington already knew all about it. They sent Kucharski on his way and told him not to worry, even if he was asked to do something illegal."

"Come again?"

"I called the guy in Cleveland myself. His instructions were that Kucharski should keep the bureau informed because there is a higher priority at the moment."

"Has the Bureau recently rewritten the regulations on putting civilians in danger? How they plan to protect him on a freighter in the middle of Lake Superior?"

"Came from the highest authority. And you'll especially like part two of this. Did Harper-Lloyd tell you he was having trouble getting you some back-up to cover Van Dorn?"

"He said he was going to try to convince Washington that Van

Dorn was involved in something up here," I said. "It sounded like he expected a hard sell."

"Wanna know why?" Chet asked. "Right now, the main focus is on Islamic terrorists, not the domestic groups. There's intel about somebody driving a van loaded with explosives into a major target on the East Coast."

"Have I been missing out on too many briefing papers, lately?"

Chet chuckled. "No, this goes back aways. Remember a few years ago when Oliver North was testifying about Middle East terrorists striking on American shores? What was the guy's name? Abu Nidal?"

I didn't want to go that far back in history. "So the bottom line is that I shouldn't expect any back up?"

"Not unless your admiral can call up a posse of U.S. Marshals or enlist somebody at ATF. Look, my dime has about run out. If I'm out of the office too long, somebody is going to start looking for me. How can I reach you if I have any more good news to pass along?"

I gave him a number to reach Andrews at Headquarters. "Any word on the first mate, Carver?"

"Not even a birth date. I was run off the computer after the first go-round. I'll try to get back on the network before I leave for the night."

When I thanked him, he wished me luck and said he hoped I lived long enough to repay my gambling debt in cash.

Next, I called the only person in the Coast Guard I knew I could trust. There were too many questions to trust anyone from Base Soo. Why didn't the crew tell someone where they were going? Who told my visitor that I was staying at the Superior Inn the night before? And who told the skipper of the *Jersey Trader* about my plans to visit that morning? Andrews answered before the first ring ended.

"Jesus, Marty, I'd give anything to be in your place right now."

"Funny, I have kind of similar thoughts right about now. And I hate Washington."

"You don't know how bad a lot of people would like to get their hands on this bastard Van Dorn. If the NAACP had a ten most wanted list, this guy would be the top three by himself. If you take this guy down, I'll be first line to buy you a drink."

"And if he manages to take me out?"

Andrews laughed, deep and long. "You'll be another dead honky."

"That's an epitaph I hadn't considered. Look, I have a pretty good run-down on Van Dorn. What can you tell me about the others?"

"Nothing special. Kucharski is a registered pilot, qualified from Duluth all the way to the Welland Canal, which is pretty rare. Most of them work a particular waterway, like the St. Mary's River below the Soo or the St. Clair River below Lake Huron. Of course, Kucharski doesn't usually work that much territory because local pilot groups have a hold on who gets the jobs. He lives on Drummond Island, at the south end of the St. Mary's River. He generally works from the river up and over to Gros Cap, or over to Duluth or Thunder Bay if he's needed."

"And Floyd Carver?"

"His mariner papers check out, but I haven't found much more than that, except that he has a current driver's license from Connecticut," Andrews said. "If you're interested, he's got about ten points on his license for a couple of DWIs and a failure to yield. I'll keep checking though."

"Thanks. Any of the other crew on the list come up interesting?"

"You've got me stumped there, too. So far, I can't find an electronic paper trail on any of them.

"I'd appreciate it if you could keep searching on Carver. It would also help to have some background on Van Dorn's people; who are they, how many, how they're armed and how they feel about Coast Guard special agents."

"You sound worried, Marty." he asked, a genuine note of concern in his voice.

"Let me eat my spinach and I'll whip the lot of them," I grumbled in my best Popeye. "Actually, I hoped you could help me in that department."

"What kind of cavalry you looking for? I don't think there's time to airlift the 82nd Airborne from Fort Bragg."

The gas station attendant came within a few feet and flagged my attention. He pointed over his shoulder to where my rental Ford blocked a Chevy pickup from reaching the pump. I tossed him the keys, indicating that I would pay him when I finished on the phone. He nodded and went to move the car.

"The FBI would be nice, but Duluth and Chicago have told me not to expect anything. Could you talk to their field office in Detroit or the resident agent in Marquette. I haven't been able to reach the Alcohol, Tobacco and Firearms folks down in Detroit, but think you can get try? Or jerk a few chains in Washington and get me whatever kind of back-up is available."

"Marty, do you know what time it is?" he asked incredulously. "Nobody will be in the office this late! Not in this city."

Andrews was right. The federal government in Washington closes down at 3:25 p.m. so everyone can catch their carpool. For 40 years, the Soviets could have attacked at 1531 Eastern Standard Time, and the Cold War would have ended with a much different outcome.

"Like I said, I need you to jerk a few chains. Tell the commandant that I need him to kick some bureaucratic butt for me."

Andrews pondered over this dilemma. "But I like being an officer. I don't want to scrub buoys."

I understood his reluctance. The last lieutenant I knew who called an admiral during cocktail hour became a deck officer on an icebreaker bound for the South Pole two weeks before his wedding.

"Yes, sir, but consider my undying gratitude, or at least my gratitude if I don't die. These people have big guns, and lots of them."

"OK, but if this doesn't work, you'll have to answer to Admiral Thorne," he warned.

"No, sweat. I'll take him fishing sometime."

Even after two very enlightening conversations, one thing remained unclear. Banks' obvious involvement still puzzled me. He had taken the chart from the 44323, no doubt to thwart the search, and I believed that he had attacked me the night before. But how would he get hooked up with a big-time operator like Van Dorn? Another piece of the puzzle remained missing.

I didn't know where to look for the crew but decided that if I could find Banks, he could lead me to them. If only I could find

Banks. I made another phone call. Betsy Kruza answered on the third ring.

"Betsy, this is Special Agent Galloway. Have you heard from Banks since I came by?"

"No, he ain't been around. But I get my welfare check tomorrow, so I figure he'll be by to take part of it. I still got that chart, too."

"Any idea where I can find him?"

"Did you try that bar by the reservation? That's the only place I know of where he goes now. He's not allowed in the Toad anymore."

"OK, thanks. Remember what I said. If he shows up and starts getting rough, you and your son get out of there and let me handle him."

"Yeah." Her voice did not sound hopeful.

After buying a soda and a bag of no-salt pretzels from the vending machines, I paid for my gas, climbed back into the rental and headed north. The setting sun fired a few last rays over an encroaching bank of clouds, casting a bright glare off the side mirror. Mists rose from each small pond I passed, and I watched fish hit mosquitoes on the surface, leaving widening ripples in their wake. I sped across northern Michigan into the darkening twilight.

Thursday: 1945

Three sedans and a pair of Chevy pickup trucks sat in the parking lot of the Bear Den when I reached Brimley after dusk. There should have been a bigger crowd on a Thursday night. On the other hand, Betsy said her check would come the following day. Did other checks arrive at the same time?

Unsure what to expect inside, I released the Colt's safety and slipped the law-enforcement baton into the belt of my trousers. The baton is a handy little item; an eight-inch metal tube that extends to an 18-inch nightstick with a flick of the wrist. The lightweight version was replacing the old wooden billy club among some law enforcement, except among the old-timers who still pack snub-nosed .38s and think computers are the devil's work.

A dense blue cloud of cigarette smoke enveloped me when I opened the door. I stumbled inside, trying to adjust to the interior lighting while ignoring the burning sensation in my eyes. Once in the first empty seat along the bar, I ordered a beer. The same Native American woman served me. This evening she had coiled her long gray braid atop her head.

Deciding to fight smoke with smoke, I lit another of Schmidt's excellent cigars, figuring that smoking might draw attention away from the fact that I wasn't swilling the beer in front of me. After a few puffs, my fellow patrons began to shift away from me. With a little elbow room, I could study the room. On my prior visit, I missed the collection of deer head mounts lining all four walls.

Three elderly women, one of them knitting a long green scarf, sat at the bar talking with the bartender. At the far end of the counter, two men in their late forties watched a Detroit Tigers game. Both wore their hair slicked down with more than a little dab of doo gel. A middle-aged couple sat at a table near the dark jukebox, so entwined together they needed only one chair. She stroked his bald crown with affection.

In the back of the room, a late-blooming Lothario tried to hustle a young woman at pool. She wore tight jeans and high heels. Whenever she bent over to make a shot, Romeo maneuvered behind her, grinning in anticipation at what he saw. Exactly why the female

165

coccyx has become such an object of male fascination, I'm hard pressed to explain.

None of the customers matched my description of Banks, and nobody in this crowd carried enough weight to have been my violent visitor the night before. Banks sounded like the typical all-American stud, so I figured if the girl at the pool table was a regular, he would have put the moves on her. I decided to try my charm and see what she knew. And if charm didn't work, I had some cash in my wallet. I ambled back toward the pool table and leaned against the nearby wall.

Romeo pranced about the table, twirling his custom cue stick like a majorette's baton. I've seen better shooting in a game of marbles. He pushed 40 hard, wore his hair in a mullet, and reeked of cheap aftershave. The gold chain looked out of place in the open neck of his flannel shirt.

Under closer inspection, she looked older than she appeared from the bar. Her complexion hid the wrinkles well. She wore a lot of eye makeup but little cosmetics elsewhere. Her low-cut sweater seemed intended to attract admiring glances. Still, I didn't expect to see a girl in northern Michigan with four diamond studs on each lobe and a series of gold bracelets on both wrists.

Romeo missed an easy combination and left the table wide open. Then he taunted her a little. She flashed me a little smile of perfectly even white teeth and cleared the felt in seven tidy shots. He went to the bar to get her another drink.

"Do you shoot?" she asked, nodding toward the table. Her brunette hair spilled forward over her shoulders.

"Sure, but it looks like you've got a partner."

"I'd like a little challenge." She gave me a quick once-over, her gaze lingering too long on my bulky stocking cap. When she turned, I checked to ensure no white gauze spilled out above my eyebrows.

I fished a pair of quarters from my pocket and fed the table. She pulled up the balls and fixed the rack. "Winner breaks – house rules," she told me.

She jammed the cue ball behind the point, scattering the rack across the table and sinking three on the break. Don Juan returned with her beer.

"Hey, what's going on here?" he demanded.

"It's OK," she laughed. "He wagered fifty bucks against my ass."

"Well then, you'd better not lose." He reached over and slapped her buttocks. "I don't share."

I smiled weakly. At that point, I couldn't afford to get in a bar fight over a woman trying to make a date jealous. "Have you seen Chris Banks tonight?" I asked Romeo. "He told me to meet him here, but looks like I missed him."

"Sorry, don't know him." He went to drop a pocketful of coins in the jukebox.

She missed a two-rail bank, and I took three shots before a scratch. I'm not a strong player, so I didn't get fancy. The conservative approach kept me in the game. Pool and darts are essential skills for special agents.

"Have you seen Chris Banks around lately?" I asked her.

"Not in a few weeks. He might be in jail." She spun the cue ball off three rails to sink an impressive double combination.

"Chris? What would he be in jail for?"

She gave me a stern look. "I thought you said you knew him."

Two shots later, she buried the eight ball. She thrust an empty palm toward me. I fished three bills out of my wallet.

"Be sure to claim it on your income tax," I told her.

Placing the stick back in the rack, I headed for the men's room. As I finished at the urinal, somebody came in behind me. When I turned, Romeo caught my collar.

"I said I don't share," he whispered, screwing up his face in an effort to look menacing. "I've had this girl staked out all night."

Holding eye contact, I reached my right hand under my windbreaker and drew the baton from my belt. As he drew his left for a punch, I gripped the hand clutching my shirt with my left and tugged. He tottered off balance. Snapping the baton to full length, I swung the club under his elbow and clockwise back over his right shoulder, smacking it upward against his throat. He staggered, and I stomped down hard on the outside of his right knee.

Romeo collapsed on the floor, coughing as tears welled in his eyes. The knee didn't look broken, but you can never tell until you see the x-rays. My amateur diagnosis: he wouldn't play tennis for a few weeks.

"Try to be a little kinder to strangers," I whispered in his ear. Then I stuffed a handful of paper towels into his mouth before I frisked him for weapons. Finally, I hoisted him into a stall, held his chin up, and back-handed him with a sharp blow. He slumped back against the silver plumbing and began to snore.

When I went back into the main room, the pool hustler sat perched on the wide brown edge surrounding the green felt in one of those poses you expect in every girlie magazine – arms braced behind her and breasts thrust forward – her scuffed heels dangling off her toes. She looked surprised when I emerged instead of her raging Romeo.

"Hey, where's Billy?"

"He wanted to freshen up a little. His hair's a quart low."

She looked me over, and her tone softened. "So why you looking for Banks?"

"He owes me fifty bucks." It was more than $100 between what I'd given to this woman and Betsy on his behalf.

"Forget it. You'll never see it again." She licked her lips. I wondered if she had staged the little restroom wrestling to determine her champion for the evening.

"Can you tell me how to get to Crisp Point?" I asked, figuring to check the last place that had any connection to the case.

"No, but I've got a county map in the car you can have." She smiled. "Do you have to leave right away or can you buy me a drink? There ain't nothing happening out at Crisp Point this time of night."

"That fifty tapped me out." Soon Billy would get off the restroom floor, and I wanted to give him a chance to cool down before we met again.

She led me out to the parking lot and unlocked a white Ford Mustang with a wide blue racing stripe across the hood, roof and trunk. After searching through the glove box, she produced a dog-eared map.

"This is a map of Luce County; that's where Crisp Point is," she explained. "Stay on 221 until you reach 123, then turn right. Follow the signs for the Tahquamenon Park. You'll see a few signs for Crisp Point. It's all dirt and mud from there on in." She followed me back to my car, and I thanked her. She handed back the cash I'd given her earlier. She gave me a seductive leer. "My name's Maggie. Why don't you stop by again some time and buy me that drink?"

Thursday: 2030

Following her directions, I continued north along Route 221.
Dense fog drifting in from Lake Superior filled the lowlands. The
road wound through Bay Mills and the adjacent Native American
reservation, but again there were no trucks on the streets like the
description of the Ford Banks drove. I paused long enough to cruise
through the crowded parking lot of the Club Casino, which advertised blackjack and poker. NEGRES. I continued following the
lake's shoreline, past the old Indian burial ground and the Bay Mills
Community College, which appeared to be a single, one-floor yellow
building smaller than some garages in Northern Michigan. No sign
of Banks anywhere.

If I were back in St. Louis on that August night, I'd have fina-
gled a date to my favorite jazz club downtown. Instead, I fiddled
with the rental's radio until I found a Canadian Broadcasting station
playing a Gordon Lightfoot retrospective. After I calmed down, I
felt a little sheepish for stomping Romeo. He didn't deserve a broken
knee for trying to protect what he figured he rightfully owned. After
all, he had bought Maggie a couple of beers, and he thought that
entitled him to stamp a branding iron on her butt. I could as easily
smiled and walked away. But I was in a bad mood.

Maggie puzzled me, though. Did she like to watch men fight
over her; some girls get their kicks that way. After she went back to
the bar, I unfolded the money she'd returned in the parking lot and
found only thirty dollars. Was $20 the going rate for a county map?

The road outside Bay Mills was rough and patched over with
asphalt. After I passed the Iroquois Point Lighthouse a few miles
outside the reservation, a bright set of headlights appeared in the
rearview mirror. I drove slowly on the unfamiliar road in thick fog,
and this guy came on strong. As he pulled closer, I could distinguish
a rack of yellow fog lights over his roof and decided this was a big
truck. Soon he rode close behind me. He kept his high beams up as
he inched closer. I jogged the mirror up and down, hoping the
reflection would get his attention. He came in tight on my bumper.

When we reached a passing zone, I slowed and eased toward the
side of the road. His headlights disappeared from view, and the car
shuddered. He was pushing me along with his front bumper. I

stomped the gas pedal and pulled away. He came on fast and rammed his bumper into the trunk of the rental. Then he swerved, trying to force my rental off the road, but I pulled the shift lever down to L, gaining some torque. I held the pedal to the floor, concentrating on the highway and looking for an escape. Racing across the twisting road at 75 miles per, I knew I couldn't outrun him. The Ford was built for comfort, not performance. The big truck slowed on turns to maintain balance, but it caught me on each straightaway, slamming the rental's rear end.

I pulled the Colt out of its holster and nestled it between my legs. I could not aim a decent shot back at him while driving that fast, but it would be ready if he pulled alongside. I reached into the back seat and dragged my bag of tricks into the front seat. I was lucky the bag was already open, and the camera was near the top. I pulled out the flash unit and turned it on.

As we went into a series of fast turns, the truck slowed long enough for me to gain some distance. By the time we came onto the next straight stretch, I sat twisted in my seat, my foot poised over the gas pedal and one arm stretched over the back of the seat, aiming the flash through the back window. I eased into the opposite lane, slowed, and waited.

The truck roared around the last turn. The truck's driver had to brake and swerve toward me. I fired off the flash and slammed down on the gas. The pick-up spun sideways as I sped away. His headlights glared off into the woods and shone through the white birch. Then I saw red tail lights in my rearview; the truck spun out of control. Blinded by the flash, he had oversteered the skid. It had worked better than I expected, but I didn't go back to ask if he was impressed. Holding top speed another five miles, I finally slowed when there was no flicker of lights behind me for several minutes. It would have been courteous to turn around and look for corpses, but that wasn't on my playlist.

There wasn't much chance that Romeo drove that truck; about now, he was now getting back the feeling in his toes. The only person who knew my destination was Maggie. Gee, she had seemed like such a nice girl, too. The truck could have belonged to Banks; it was jacked high and carried the fog lights Normand had described.

Did Maggie place a quick call to Banks? Had she followed me outside so she could tell Banks what I drove? Gosh, she was a bright girl, too.

At least it gave me one advantage. If Maggie told Banks I was headed for the light, he would arrange some sort of welcome. Knowing that, I could be prepared.

My attitude changed right then. These people had killed Pelligrini and intended to kill me if they could. Somebody had already tried twice. I would not get a second chance if it came to a fight. Neither would Kunken and the others if something happened to me. I'd never played such a deadly game before, and I needed to convince myself to be ready to kill when the time came.

I had never shot a person, not even the crazy Bolivian with the AK-47 in Miami. Before I could aim to fire back, Schmidt, standing behind me, panicked and shot me in the arm. My slug went into the engine block of a state police cruiser. Many people think they can kill without a thought, but there's always that pause of conscience, a brief wave of doubt. That's why many crime victims are killed with their own weapons. Around criminals as violent and determined as Van Dorn's Patriots, that split-second hesitation would prove fatal. I would have to suspend my outdated notions about fair play to survive.

At the intersection with Route 123, I aimed the Ford north along the straight empty highway. There were no houses, lights, or mailboxes along the road.

Farther west, the roadway improved, and the LTD made less racket, even though the truck had rammed it pretty hard. According to a sign along the highway, that stretch of road along Lake Superior was named in honor of I.L. Curley Lewis. Should the name have been familiar to me? I suspect we skimmed over Mr. Curley in my high school history classes. As I drove on and on across that dark, unpopulated stretch of Route 123, I began to appreciate the genius of a smuggler using Crisp Point as a drop point. The area was miles and hours away from the nearest law enforcement agency. Miles of desolate coastline, Inspector Thomason had said, describing Lake Superior's potential for criminals.

Route 123 turned west in a little town called Paradise. The only place open for business was the Yukon Inn, with pick-up trucks and four-wheel-drive vehicles filling the lot. The few motels in Paradise had their No Vacancy signs flashing that evening. Everyone was here for the fishing except me.

A few miles after passing Lower Tahquamenon Falls, I entered Luce County and stopped to examine the weathered map Maggie had given me. As I studied the black lines, a movement on the road caught my eye. I snatched up the Colt and took aim – on a porcupine waddling across the centerline. My breath returned.

Without that map, finding the way through the backcountry roads that led to Crisp Point would have been impossible. Luckily Luce County maintains its road signs better than their roadway. Homemade billboards before the turn for County Road 500 advertised fishing and canoeing on the Big Two-Hearted River – one of Hemingway's favorite fly-fishing streams – and I wished I had nothing more urgent in mind than an early morning cast.

County Road 500 soon turned from asphalt to gravel, then finally to dirt. Soon it became little more than two deep tire tracks through the thick bushes and small trees. Rocks chunked against the Ford's oil pan; tree limbs slapped the fenders and windshields. I felt vulnerable – poorly informed, badly bruised, only mildly armed, and miles from the nearest payphone. If coming alone was foolish, what choice did I have? There was little choice. I hoped Andrews had arranged for agents from the Bureau of Alcohol, Tobacco and Firearms to greet me if I ever returned from these dark woods for reinforcements. An increasingly remote if.

The road north seemed endless. I lost any sense of direction in the dark night, driving through the woods along sharp curves and unmarked crossing lanes. Crude, handmade signs nailed to trees at the infrequent intersections advertised camps, cabins, and infrequent lodges. More common were markers for the various lakes clustered in the region: Little Two-Hearted Lakes, Betsy Lake, Rat Lake, Pike Lake, Parcell Lake, Muskrat Lakes, Bodi Lake, and Little Lake Harbor.

At Little Lake, County Road 500 became County Road 412. The most obvious change was the road's width, which narrowed to a path through the pines. Tree limbs now raked down the paint along both sides of the rental. At one point, I stopped to size up the gap between two trees bracketing the road like goalposts before easing the Ford through. A pond flooded the roadway in another place, and the Ford's tires spun in the soft mud under the ankle-deep water.

The cowpath ended in a wide sandy clearing circled with dark woods and Private Property signs. A narrow trail continued straight ahead toward the lake. I parked the Ford so it aimed back down the road in case I had to leave in a hurry. With my little bag of tricks strapped over my shoulder, I started down the footpath – Colt pressed against my thigh.

The sky was overcast and moonless. The only illumination was the intermittent glow of the lighthouse as it flashed. When I reached the shoreline, my feet sank into the dunes' deep, loose sand. I didn't know what I was looking for, but the lighthouse stood a few hundred yards east of where the trail emerged, so I headed toward it. I paused to empty the sand from my deck shoes. A cold breeze blew off the lake, cutting through my windbreaker. The wind carried a peculiar scent I couldn't place, a pungent smell that grew stronger as I approached the lighthouse. I tried to stay back along the woods that lined the beach so the beacon wouldn't silhouette me.

As the wide beam of light cast across the water, I detected blunt shapes in the rolling breakers. Several rows of wooden pilings poked above the surface, no doubt the remnants of old piers built by the Lighthouse Service tenders before the road – if those two parallel ruts in the ground could be called a road – reached Crisp Point.

In the dark, I tripped across a cable and went down face-first into the sand. I assumed I had stumbled through a tripwire and alerted a sentry. When 10 minutes passed without a rustle along the beach, I moved far enough to feel the wire. The heavy cable was a thick three-strand wrap, which could be used to anchor the old piers to the shore.

I stood and hobbled toward the lighthouse. The round, white tower stood about 60 feet high. Facing each direction were two oblong windows set vertically, one above the other. The light itself wasn't the traditional big lens set inside a glass cupola. An aircraft beacon poked about 10 feet above the top of the tower. Easier to

maintain, the beacon had been installed when the light was auto-
mated and the lighthouse keeper removed. The windows of the
tower cupola were boarded over.

Nearing the tower, I finally recognized the overpowering stench
as raw sewage. I fought my gagging reflex. Covering my nose with a
handkerchief and breathing through my mouth, I stumbled toward
the tower.

A woman shrieked. I cocked the Colt, but I couldn't see anyone
on the beach in either direction. Then I heard more voices, muffled
but angry. They seemed to come from inside the tower. I crept
across the dune and went up the brick steps to the steel door. A
huge sign on the big gray door warned off trespassers. The padlock
to the door was set inside a round, steel cylinder welded to the door.
The cylinder was intended to prevent vandals from shearing off the
lock and destroying the tower. I leaned against the door and
listened. People were talking inside this sealed lighthouse. I pulled
the stethoscope from my black bag and laid the flat disc below the
sign.

"We can't eat this crap anymore," a male voice said. "That
pork's rancid."

"We ain't even got a refrigerator, and you want fucking room
service," barked a good old boy with a thick Alabama drawl.
"You're welcome to starve."

"Look, Patty is going to die of dehydration if you don't do
something." This voice sounded different from the first one I had
heard.

"Well, at least she ain't scared shitless." The fourth voice had a
different accent than his friend, similar to people I knew from
Tennessee or Kentucky. Then two men laughed; thug humor.

Patty would be Seaman Lucas. Kunken and Desharnais were
concerned about her. They were guarded by two guys with no
sympathy for human suffering.

My little bag of tricks didn't contain anything heavy enough to
cut through the padlock. I backed away, looking for alternatives
when I heard them coming. Two or three vehicles came fast and
reckless down the narrow county road into the clearing where I had
parked the Ford. Through the trees, I saw the glare of yellow fog

lights. Bright headlights illuminated the surrounding woods. I sprinted into the trees for cover.

The lights went out. Car doors slammed shut. Voices were loud but muffled by the woods. The gang sounded like five, or even as many as nine. They weren't charging into the woods, so they could be putting together a methodical search. I felt like the fox listening to the baying hounds.

The sky was black, neither moon nor stars, nothing but the flashes from the lighthouse, about ten seconds apart. I scrambled through the dark forest like moving across a crowded dance floor with a slow strobe light. In the split second in which I could see, I recorded everything in my path, then moved as far as memory took me. Each step became a delicate process of finding solid footing and keeping my head down. A tree limb came close to gouging out my right eye, and I soon tasted a trickle of blood from the wound it left across my cheek.

Crouching behind a thick oak tree, I cocked the Colt and regretted leaving the Beretta with Sally. If these guys carried what they smuggled, I'd need an arsenal or a little napalm to escape alive. Though anxious to move, I couldn't do anything until their strategy was clear.

I considered my avenues of escape and found them all lacking. I was cut off from the rental car. If I hiked out onto the beach in either direction, I'd make an easy target. If I cut south through the dense forest, I might emerge on Route 123 within a week, or hunters might find my corpse after a few years. I hunkered down and, in silence, cursed the commandant for sending me up here without a satellite phone to call 911.

Mosquitoes found me first and zeroed in for the kill. With the hunters so close, I couldn't risk slapping at the nasty parasites even as they crawled on my face, exploring my eyes and nostrils. I draped my handkerchief over my head and listened to the forest, measuring time by nine-count intervals between flashes from the lighthouse. In addition to night-vision goggles, I planned to add a bottle of Old Woodsman repellant to my bag.

The woods grew quiet as the crickets stopped chirping; the boys were on the move. The bushes rustled; limbs and twigs snapped.

They worked their way straight through the trees, the line of men spaced apart to make a thorough sweep of the woods.

I couldn't see them, but I heard them coming, the closest about 30 feet off to my left, moving fast and making too much noise. He fell and cursed often. The others seemed more accustomed to walking through the woods in the dark – no doubt they were experienced deer hunters. They didn't use flashlights because that would give me a target. If they continued to sweep through the woods, I'd have to move and give myself away. Grudgingly, I admired their paramilitary tactics.

They were so skilled I wondered if they were a citizen's militia. An FBI anti-terrorism conference I attended touched on the subject, but the intelligence on the groups was sketchy still. The militias were mostly weekend warriors, and the expert prognosis was that it would be several years before they posed a serious threat. Had Van Dorn allied himself with a gang of misguided minutemen?

I fastened the Colt back into its holster. If I fired, they'd close the line into a circle centered around the noise of the gunshot and soon trap me. If I could somehow take out one of them, that would put a hole in their offense, and I might manage to get away. Whatever I tried had to be very quiet. If my earlier fall on the beach hadn't convinced me to buy NVGs, this jam did. If I could see my enemy, I might be able to slip through their lines unseen and unheard. I'd have given up three paychecks for that option right then.

The minutethugs finished their first arcing pass at the beach and headed back into the woods on a long whistle. I fished out the parachute cord and tied a 25-foot length to the wrist cord on the minicassette recorder from my bag. One hunter aimed to come within about 10 feet or closer to the oak where I knelt. He stumbled, then veered away, crashing through the brush. Then he turned and headed straight for my position.

I pressed my body against the oak's rough bark, waiting for a chance to strike. His footsteps halted, then I heard a zipper and the sound of water spraying on the rocks. Bingo! His hands were busy, and he was preoccupied. The light flashed, and I began counting. On the count of four, I started spinning the recorder on a three-foot leader, picking up speed until it hummed on the cord. On the count of eight, I spun around the thick trunk, brought the swinging bolo over my head, and let go at the dark silhouette against the passing glow. I felt the cord tighten as it wrapped around him. The recorder sounded a dull thud when the slack ended, and it struck his body.

"Shit!?" His voice came out choked and guttural.

With a hard jerk on the parachute cord, I brought the guy off balance so that he sat with a thud on his butt. I scrambled across the rocks toward him, reeling the line taut as I went.

"Don't move," I whispered. "Don't yell." I pressed the muzzle of the Colt into the soft flesh under his chin. "I won't kill you unless you make me. Clear?"

His chin bobbed up and down against the barrel. I stuffed my handkerchief into his mouth, stripped off his jacket, and bound his hands with the remaining cord so they looped between his legs. He didn't struggle. With my aircrew knife, I cut the recorder off the line wrapped around his neck and put it away in the bag.

"You all right, Mike?" a nearby voice called.

I kicked at the loose rocks, then muttered a loud curse. In the dark woods, several people laughed.

"Quiet! Listen!" somebody yelled.

His bulky jacket stretched over the black bag strapped around my shoulders. His rifle lay on the rocks where he had dropped it. Mike carried an M-16 with a banana clip – a good American weapon, not some cheap foreign knock-off. I took it and went in the same direction the others were headed, back toward the clearing where I had parked the rented Ford. As I moved, I made a little noise so the rest of the gang wouldn't come looking for Mike.

I stumbled across a log and went down in a thicket of briars. When I stood, the whip-like strands of thorns raked across my face, tangled in my clothes, and ripped at my hands. I plunged through, the rifle held low in front of me, trying to drive the brush down. I studied the dark ground but couldn't see through the thick grass. Tree limbs grabbed at my head and poked my eyes.

I calculated the distance to the clearing at less than 30 yards, but I wanted to stop and wait for them to find me. My body grew sore and tired. With 20 rounds in the extended magazine, I thought I could take them one at a time. My heart raced, my temples throbbed, and my breath came in gulps. I felt claustrophobic. If I could rest a few minutes . . .

Stupid thinking, I knew. I panicked, which was the most dangerous way to play their game. They were quiet and organized, hunting me down like flushing grouse out of a thicket. If I didn't calm down and start reasoning straight, I could save time and trouble by putting the Colt's barrel in my mouth and swallowing a live round. I had never faced anything so deadly before. From here on out, none of my past training applied.

Concentrating on a plan helped steady the nerves. Already the odds were better; one down, a maximum of eight to go. When I reached the clearing, I'd wait until they were well back into the woods and drive away in the Ford. Or there might be a working phone in a nearby cabin, and I could call for help. That way, I could maintain surveillance on these fellows and the people in the lighthouse at the same time. Boy, the possibilities seemed endless.

The dense tree cover thinned as the ground turned to gravel. Approaching the parking area in the woods, I saw the shapes of two trucks and another car near the rented Ford. When I cleared the trees, I could make out dark figures on either side of me, forming a rough, uneven line along the forest's edge. I counted six. A sharp whistle pierced the cool night air, and the stormpunks marched back into the trees.

I went with them, then stopped after a few yards and retreated toward the parking area. With the M-16 level at my waist and a forefinger resting on the trigger, I moved toward the rental car.

One of the trucks was a big Ford pick-up, jacked high on mud tires with a roll bar and a toolbox mounted across the bed behind the cab. I couldn't recognize it as the same one that had tried to run me down or whether it belonged to Banks, yet I reckoned it was a safe bet on both counts. Behind the Ford was an old Willy's pick-up with oversized tires and three radio aerials on the cab's roof. The third vehicle was a late model Chrysler. I didn't have time to disable all three, so I went straight for the LTD.

The Ford listed hard to port, so I traced my hand around one of the tires on the lower side. The rim rested flat on the gravel, but I couldn't find a knife slash in the rubber. Feeling the valve stem, I discovered they had let the air out by loosening the core. Later they could inflate the tires and drive the car away, so there'd never be any connection between my death and the lighthouse. My admiration for these guys trying to kill me continued to grow.

The gravel crunched behind me. I spun and saw a bulky shadow moving toward me, a rifle dangling from his left hand.

"Hey, Mike, whadya doing?" he asked.

He kept coming toward me until I could discern his face in the dim light from the tower. Without warning, he stopped walking, and the long gun in his hand started to come up fast. His legs moved into a firing stance. He was aiming. My finger squeezed around the trigger of the M-16. The shots sounded like dynamite in the quiet of the dark woods, a quick burst of five rounds that splayed across his chest. All other noise ceased until his shotgun clattered on the gravel, and he pitched backward, carried by the impact. His limbs flailed as he tumbled to rest on his side. The rapid gunfire surprised me; I didn't expect Mike's M-16 would be set on full auto. I should have checked the safety when I relieved Mike of his weapon. Negligence was a luxury I regretted as the men in the woods started shouting and crashing back through the scrub toward me.

I ran for the Ford pick-up with the rack of fog lights, but there were no keys in the ignition. The steering wheel clamped locked when I touched it, making hot-wiring useless. I heard footsteps on the gravel and figured I didn't have time to make a run. To create a distraction, I threw the M-16 into the weeds on the far side of the clearing and slipped into the truck's cargo bed. With my Colt cocked and ready, I pressed myself into the eight-inch gap under the toolbox and squeezed as far forward against the front wall of the bed as I could go. Unless somebody looked from over the tailgate, they wouldn't be able to see me.

The voices grew louder and more distinct. They sounded about 15 yards away, just beyond the Willys. Six or seven distinct voices, all male.

"It's Bobby. He's down."

"He's dead, shot in the chest."

A loud voice yelled out from near the truck, "Hey, break up the huddle; you're making a perfect target."

Why hadn't I thought of that?

"Come on, team up in two's. Find that sumbitch and kill him before he gets away," the same strong voice commanded. A born leader of men. "Check out these cabins and see if he's holed up in one of them. He ain't going far without wheels."

"Hey, where's Mike?"

"A couple of you check out the woods where Mike was. Could be he fell and broke something," the leader said. "If that agent's on the road, I'll find him. I gotta go see how he knew to come out here."

The driver's door on the truck opened and then slammed shut. The engine kicked over and roared as we spun around the clearing fast and headed down the two-track I had followed earlier.

The odds had changed to one-on-one. I should have felt better about those odds than I did.

Thursday: 2245

We bounced down the gravel road at high speed, slamming into every bump and pothole along the way. I braced my arms over my head against the side of the truck bed, hoping to avoid a severe concussion. Tree limbs smacked against the cab and body. The relentless pounding of the truck bed jarred my kidneys without mercy, and the pain in my lower back roared to life like the previous night.

I assumed the driver was Banks. The truck and temperament matched. His role at Crisp Point sounded like chief of security, and he seemed eager to kill in the line of duty. I had no idea where we were headed, but I felt safer dealing with Banks alone than with the six angry gunmen backing him.

At least Kunken, Desharnais, and Lucas were still alive, even if they couldn't be released from the lighthouse soon. That would take a little more planning and manpower than a lone, bandaged special agent carrying a .45 Colt and a baton.

Finally, pieces began to fit together. The crewmembers weren't captives; captives can become witnesses. This was not an operation that sought publicity. Unlike political groups or other terrorists, racists thrive in the dark – they attack at night or throw firebombs from speeding cars. The crew had been kept alive for a reason; they were hostages intended to achieve a specific goal. What could Van Dorn want? Not a ransom; he would realize the government could trace any payoff – money, bonds, gold or weapons. Van Dorn would also know that killing these three Coast Guardsmen now would be a mistake. It was too late to think anyone would believe they were victims of a boating accident, as someone intended Pelligrini's murder to appear. Nor could God's Patriots get much popular support from publicity about the murders; no spin would justify the murder of Patricia Lucas, a 20-year-old woman serving in her nation's armed services. Van Dorn had a plan for the crew. Whatever he intended, he would have to bring them out of the lighthouse alive. My mission was to be back there waiting.

The evening's events answered a lot of questions. Crisp Point was an ideal landing for smugglers: a prominent landmark, a remote location, few witnesses, and limited access. The lighthouse had also become a perfect prison; who'd look for missing Coasties in a Coast Guard lighthouse? However, the tower was not intended as a residence, so it lacked amenities like sanitation or a refrigerator. Pelligrini's dysentery symptoms were likely caused by spoiled food; the same illness currently afflicted Seaman Lucas. That explained the awful stench. They used a bucket for a commode and then dumped the waste from the top of the tower. Locking the door from the outside prevented the crew's escape from their two captors, but it also avoided suspicion. The tower appeared locked and secure. Who would question it?

If I needed any more proof that a Coastie was involved, the lighthouse cinched it. True, the smugglers could have cut the lock and replaced it with their own, but they wouldn't know when a Coast Guard maintenance team might come to the tower. Somebody in the Coast Guard provided keys to the tower and guaranteed its privacy.

Dunlay. As an operations officer, she would have access to lighthouse keys and be able to keep people away from Crisp Point. She had made my room reservations, and an attacker found me there. She knew I went to Duluth, and the skipper of the *Jersey Trader* learned about it, too. She searched the wrong area, even though Thomason had told the Coast Guard that the 44-footer had been towed into Canadian waters by a motorboat. I cursed myself for not investigating Dunlay more completely. After the personnel files carpeted the floor of my inn room during the scuffle, I never glanced at them again.

My stupidity stunned me. Sometimes the people most helpful are the most guilty. In the 1920s, Richard Loeb helped Chicago police investigate the kidnapping and murder of the 10-year-old boy he had also helped murder and stuff into a storm drain.

I had to proceed with caution now. I couldn't make wild accusations about Lieutenant Dunlay's involvement in criminal activity. If I couldn't substantiate my charges against a Coast Guard officer, I'd face charges myself, and I cannot risk a court-martial. Given my reputation and unpopularity among certain officers, I might be convicted of conspiracy if anyone ever alleges I was on the grassy knoll. However, I was only a child at the time of the assassination. I know the nuns at St. Stephen's won't back my alibi.

Dunlay had been dealing from the bottom of the deck, but I still had a couple of aces. She didn't know what I had learned about Pelligrini's death, Crisp Point, the *Jersey Trader*, or Van Dorn. She was not aware of the BATF agents Andrews was trying to enlist. The key to turning the thing around was the guy behind the wheel of the big Ford truck as we sped through the Michigan woods.

The truck was broad but not enough for me to lay flat across the bed. My knees were cocked up at a painful angle. My spine and tail-bone grew sore from jostling on the ribs of the steel floor; the muscles along both shoulders started to cramp. I felt a searing fire where my attacker had punched my lower back the night before. I tried to relax as best I could, calculating my next move.

In all honesty, I wasn't in any condition to confront Banks. My face throbbed, my muscles ached, and I was exhausted. If he got his hands on me, Banks would kill me. To even the odds, I decided to shoot him in a limb as soon as I could. The thought sounded cold-blooded even as it came to me, but I knew I had no choice. He'd recover from a well-placed flesh wound, but even a slight injury would give me an even chance in a fight.

Depending upon what Banks told me, I would decide how to handle Dunlay. If I thought she might cooperate in exchange for special consideration during prosecution, I'd confront her and ask for details of how the crew would be removed from the lighthouse. To use the crew as hostages, the smugglers would have to put them aboard the *Jersey Trader*. Dunlay would know how that operation would happen. Would she tell me enough to stop the transfer? If she refused to talk, I'd need Fraser to arrest her and take charge of the search himself. Still, I wasn't confident I had enough proof to convince him. Fraser might arrest me instead.

When I closed my eyes, I remembered the sentry in the clearing coming toward me as he brought his shotgun up to aim. He stopped as the impact of my shots took him full in the chest, lifting him off his feet and carrying him over backward. I hadn't seen his face, only the form of his body, and I didn't know who I had killed, only that he was named Bobby. That took a while to register – that I had killed a man, gunned him down without hesitation. Though I wanted to convince myself there had been no choice – that he meant to kill me – it still felt wrong. After the monster truck tried to run me off the road, I told myself that I was playing the kind of game you survive only by striking first, but all my training as an agent rebelled against the notion. Don't fire unless you are in imminent danger, I remembered. Justify every bullet. I didn't enjoy the thrill of the kill, and I fought back the bile rising in my throat.

The rough jostling subsided when we reached the state road. The adrenaline rush ebbed, and the long day zapped my stamina. As my thoughts drifted, I dozed to the steady drone of the engine and the dull, monotonous roar of the wind over the cab. As hard as I fought it, the monotonous ride over asphalt lulled me to sleep.

Friday: 0025

The truck sat with the engine off when I woke. I peered out but saw no lights behind the truck and heard only distant, muffled voices. Pushing my body from underneath the toolbox proved excruciating – muscles straining as they unfolded from their taut positions.

After listening for any rustle of grass or clothing nearby, I poked my head over the tailgate. The pickup sat parked at the edge of thick woods, limbs of a maple tree hanging down into the truck bed. The only visible lights shone through the windows of a small house about 20 feet away. The rest of the scene was so dark I saw only the outlines of another vehicle and a small outbuilding. Recognition came as my night vision improved; I was back at Betsy Kruza's little cabin in the woods.

I eased over the side of the truck bed, stretching my muscles as best I could. My legs felt like fire, and when I lowered my weight to the ground, they collapsed under me. I fell, chunking my head against the fender. I saw no movement inside the house to indicate anyone there heard. After massaging my thighs and calves, I tried to stand again. I tottered, gripping the truck for support. As feeling returned, I could walk, with effort.

To reach the porch, I had to cross the cluttered yard. I closed my eyes and shuffled my way along inch by inch, sliding my feet through the tall grass while feeling for toys and other obstacles as I went. I wondered how her son had toys left after losing so many in the weeds. The voices grew more distinct: Betsy, timid and whining; the other was the same voice as at the lighthouse, a booming half-shout. I finally had a chance to meet Chris Banks face to face.

After removing the jacket I'd taken from Mike in the woods, I slipped my bag of tricks off my shoulder and laid it in the grass. I released the safety on the Colt.

"This chart is like insurance, to make sure I get paid. That asshole ain't going to stiff me this time, and I don't care who has the key to that damn lighthouse," Banks shouted. His voice carried an angry edge. "Did you tell anyone it was here?"

"No, Chris, nobody knows. I didn't know what it was. I never even opened it."

A sharp crack sounded, the harsh thwack of a powerful back-hand. "Then how'd that agent know where to go?"

"It wasn't me," she wailed.

Another slap, followed by the sound of breaking glass. "Tell me, damn it!"

I eased onto the porch, stepping on the wooden slats to where I could see the people inside through the screen door. They were in the front room, Betsy curled on the sofa, her eyes dark and swollen. Banks towered over her, waving a broken beer bottle at her face. He stood well over six feet and weighed about 250 pounds, his big frame in dark pants and a gray sweatshirt with the sleeves cut short to show a naked woman tattooed on his wide bicep. He began to laugh and tossed the jagged glass aside.

"Come here, babe. You always liked things a little rough." As I put my hand on the doorknob, he jerked his pants' zipper down and reached for the back of her head. She struggled to pull her face away from his crotch. They were so close that if I shot him, the round might strike her too.

"Freeze, scum!" I yelled, jerking the door open and moving inside, my post and pumpkin aimed between his shoulder blades.

Banks spun, knocking Betsy away with a fist to her chest. I lowered my aim and fired. He collapsed to the floor, clutching his bleeding right knee and screaming in agony.

"Are you OK?" I asked Betsy. She nodded, coughing again and again. "What about you, Banks? Feel well enough to talk?"

"Go to hell. I shudda killed you last night." He lay on his left side; both hands clamped around his wounded leg. He wore tan calf-high construction boots with thick traction on the soles. A large, pink welt covered his left cheek.

"But you couldn't. And I seem to have a distinct advantage this evening." I stayed near the door, far enough away that I'd get two clear shots if he lunged for me. "Say, how'd you get that nasty burn on your face?"

"I'm gonna kill you, fucker," he hissed.

"You know for a guy with his pecker hanging out, you sure talk mean. Although it's not much of a target." I pointed the Colt for effect.

"You hurt me, and that crew is dead. The guys holding them have very exact instructions."

"What kind of instructions?"

"I ain't telling you shit!" he yelled.

A child's piercing scream came from somewhere off to my left. I glanced toward the bedroom where Betsy's son slept and almost did not see Banks grab the small coffee table and hurl it at me. I knocked it away with my forearm, but he was already on his feet, scrambling toward me, one hand holding his trousers up. Before I could bring the Colt back down, he caught my arms, slammed me against the wall, and jabbed a knee at my crotch. His whiskey breath stung my eyes.

The pistol came loose and fell. Banks shoved me away and went after it, but I kicked at his wounded knee, then tackled him around the waist, driving him against the sofa. Banks fell like dead weight so that I tumbled past him, then he rolled up and straddled my chest. His knees pinned my arms to the floor. He laughed as his fists beat down on my head and neck. Blows came so fast they didn't record as individual hits but as a torrent of agony in the flesh raw from our last fight. Banks punched my throat twice. Then he wrapped those meaty paws around my neck, twisting my head back so he could crush my windpipe.

I couldn't move except for my legs. I slammed my knee against his lower back. He didn't flinch but continued to tighten his constricting hold. With my head shoved back, I couldn't see his face. Gripping my neck in a two-fisted vice, he pummeled my head against the floor, once, twice – again and again, until I lost count. My chest burned, but no air came to cool the fire. Once more, I felt like I was drowning, unable to breathe, limbs useless. My sight went black.

A woman screamed, shrill and incoherent.

The first thunder sounded muffled – loud but indistinct. I tried to focus on it, place where I'd heard such a noise before. Wetness, something on my face, I could feel, but from where? I gasped for air; it came in little gulps. Another boom seconds later, and my neck was free. Gunshot! Coming groggily back to the present, I lifted my arms to shield my face. The weight rolled off my chest, and I could breathe again. I opened my eyes.

Betsy stood over me, my Colt dangling from her right hand. Banks lay crumpled in a bloody mess beside me, the left half of his face gone, replaced by oozing red and gray tissue, his skull gaping open. Betsy sobbed, gagging and holding her hand over her mouth, unable to look away from the convulsing body. Her stare was fixed where his pants had fallen open, exposing his twitching erection.

She dropped the pistol finally and rushed outside. I heard her retch, then cough and groan between choking dry heaves. Banks lay sprawled on his side, one leg heavy and limp across my waist, what remained of his head flopped into the dark morass of his blood and brains, two black wounds each the size of a dime behind his right ear. Powder burns on his neck showed that she had rested the barrel against his skull when she pulled the trigger the first time. I pushed Banks' leg off me and pulled the green afghan from the sofa over his body.

Then I heard the screams of Betsy's son again, shouting for his mother from the bedroom. In the kitchen, I wiped Banks' blood from my face with a dishtowel. Entering the dark bedroom, I lifted the boy from his crib and carried him out to the porch, shielding his face with a bloody hand when I carried him through the front room, past the ugly corpse.

When Betsy finished heaving, I gave her a damp towel to wipe her face and pulled the door shut. Carrying the child, I led Betsy by the arm to the truck, then doubled back through the grass to find my black bag and Mike's jacket.

The big tires crushed a few plastic toys in the high grass when I turned the truck around in the yard and headed down the narrow driveway. Empty beer cans rattled under the seat, and a half-drained whiskey bottle rolled under my feet as we bounced onto the main road.

Friday: 0110

Most accommodations in St. Ignace were motor lodges with No Vacancy signs illuminated out front, so we drove south across the Mackinaw Bridge. A lake freighter with bright deck lights running down the gunwales port and starboard passed under the span as we crossed. Betsy's son stood on her lap, his face pressed against the passenger window so he could see the big ship. She didn't say a word but sat staring straight ahead, one arm around the boy's waist. The big Ford swayed in the strong crosswinds.

In Mackinaw City, we found a Ramada Inn. I wore Mike's bulky jacket to cover my blood-stained clothes. Still, the desk clerk recoiled in horror when she saw me come through the front doors. She was one of those petite brunettes with a China doll face and a tiny figure you wouldn't hug hard so she wouldn't break. Cute, but too much green eye shadow poorly applied. Cute name on her tag: Callie.

To calm her concerns, I flashed my badge and explained that I needed a place to hide a federal witness for two days – room service mandatory, maid service optional. She took my plastic after examining it for excess blood. Why do so many hotels act snobbish if a guest arrives in the lobby covered with human tissue? I explained the need for absolute secrecy and hinted that she might do hard time in federal prison if she even mentioned the subject to her husband, boyfriend or lover. Callie smiled the cherubic, frozen smile of an overwhelmed robot.

I ushered Betsy and Jamie upstairs to a room overlooking the pool and the interstate, telling her to stay put until I returned for her. She wasn't to call anyone, but I gave her enough cash to go shopping downtown the following day for new clothes and a few toys. Betsy sat on the bed as I told her these things, with dull eyes watching me. Jamie lay beside her, his head in her lap.

"Did Banks say if there was another Coastie involved?" I asked. "Do you know who has the keys to the lighthouse?"

Her head moved side to side, but the effort seemed to drain her of all energy.

"Everything is going to be OK, I promise," I told her, putting my hand on her knee and trying to peer into her eyes. Her sullen face looked pale gray.

"Will it? Ever?" she asked. "Am I going to jail?"

"No! You saved my life, and you were defending yourself. Even if you hate somebody, that doesn't make it murder."

Betsy raised her head, tears coming to her eyes. "I'm not sure I did hate him. I don't know why I pulled the trigger. I couldn't stand the craziness anymore."

She pulled the boy onto her lap, hugging him to her chest and sobbing into his hair. I left the remainder of the cash from my pocket on the nightstand. Back in the lobby, I stopped for a quick phone call. After five rings, a sleepy woman came on the line.

"Missus Desharnais, this is Marty Galloway. I found your husband."

"What? Where? Is he OK? When can I—?" The stream of questions continued as she woke.

"I can't tell you anything else right now. Will you trust me?"

"Yes, I . . . want him home. Is there anything I can do?"

"If you believe in prayer, now might be a good time."

Waving to Callie on the way past the front desk, I went out to the big pickup, then headed north on I-75 and across the Mackinaw Bridge. The only sign of human life along the route was the smiling blond woman with round spectacles in the toll booth on the St. Ignace side. As I drove up, she launched into a conversation about the chill in the air but halted as her eyes popped open. Her mouth hung wide but mute as she took the cash from my blood-covered hand. She didn't say a word as I drove away. The highway north to the Soo stretched through barren miles of night; few exits, no houses, few lights visible in the dark forest on either side of the four-lane highway.

After seeing the bruises on her face, I couldn't imagine how Betsy might still love Banks. He had beaten her, stolen from her, and left her. Worse, he beat the child. Anyone who could do those things had no right to either affection or mercy.

The things Banks said while I listened from the porch struck me. He had saved the chart as insurance so he'd get paid by whoever held the keys to the lighthouse. If Dunlay had kept back money from him, he would have gone after her, beaten her senseless, and taken what he wanted. Banks would not be intimidated by any woman, no matter what leverage she held over him.

Loud wind roared through a missing vent window in the truck. Banks' collection of cassette tapes was scattered across the dashboard. Among the heavy metal clones, I found a vintage recording of Jimmy Buffett, which seemed out of place. At that moment, I wished I was a boat bum myself, working tuna charters or skippering a yacht for the idle rich. Even if Banks had odd tastes, his stereo sounded excellent.

With Banks dead, I had no choice but to confront Dunlay about the crew. The only chance to rescue them alive would happen while the laughing thugs moved them out of the lighthouse. They had to come out sometimes, especially if they were already eating spoiled food. Of course, an ambush would be dangerous for Kunken, Desharnais and Lucas. Any information I had going into the play would improve their chances.

The pickup ran rough at 80 miles per. The valves tapped angrily on hills, and the steering wheel shimmied from a bad alignment. Seemed Banks didn't treat his trucks any better than his women.

Still, what Banks had said gnawed at me, eroding my conviction about Dunlay's involvement. Banks was the enforcer. He had come after me twice, and he was in charge of the shooters at Crisp Point. Had he selected Pelligrini for death because of their prior feud that resulted in Banks being discharged? Dunlay couldn't have controlled Banks, given his violent temper, especially if he wanted money.

The alternatives weren't reasonable: Drucker, Normand, Jaspers, Fraser, or Burke. Neither Burke nor Fraser would have any call to ask for the keys to a lighthouse. As far as I knew, neither of them was aware of my plans in Duluth. Both Drucker and Normand could get a key to Crisp Point. If Normand wanted, he could have searched my room after I followed the senior chief Wednesday night. Then there would have been no need for Banks to stop by that evening. And Drucker had convinced me at the Bear Den of his innocence.

All of which left only Jaspers, and I felt a sudden chill on my neck. Jaspers had signed the master's license of a man who had never walked on a ship's bridge before. Of course, it was impossible to guess what kind of documentation Van Dorn presented when he applied for a certificate as Paul Leavitt. Was Leavitt a legitimate sailor? Had Van Dorn stolen Leavitt's identity and contacted the Coast Guard for a duplicate certificate, claiming the first was lost? Still, it was an interesting coincidence. Jaspers could get the keys to Crisp Point whenever he wanted. As Dunlay's assistant, he could divert maintenance teams away from the tower. And now he was missing from action.

I thought that I was once again alone in a raging ocean without a helo hovering overhead to rescue me. Was I in beyond what training had prepared me to handle? If I could not ride the surf, what other options for rescue did the three hostages have? I considered the alternatives: ATF, Michigan State Police, Luce County Sheriff, the Boy Scouts . . . Ultimately, I remembered the one reason I could not simply walk away now; I promised Admiral Thorne.

Off the highway on an exit for Kinross, I stopped in a closed gas station and used the payphone. Seven rings. As I prepared to give up, Thomason came on the line. His first words were, "Do you know what the hell time it is?"

"I've got 2:07 a.m.," I answered, then identified myself.

"Galloway? I'm afraid I haven't heard back from Webster in Thunder Bay," Thomason said.

"That's OK, I've got a full scorecard already. I need one last name. Who in the Coast Guard did you tell about the motorboat?"

"An officer, no, a warrant officer. Jessup?"

"Close, how about Jaspers?"

Thomason grunted, clearing his throat. "Why is that important? At this hour? Is he involved?"

"We'll see."

After thanking him, I called the Base Soo. A tired Dunlay answered the phone.

"Where the hell are you?" she demanded. "You said you'd be here hours ago."

"I met a girl named Maggie and got busy. Did you have a chance to find the *Jersey Trader*?"

"The Air Force C-130 spotted them before sunset off the Keweenaw Peninsula. Your freighter's heading east."

"Time to sound general quarters, ma'am. This is not a drill."

"Marty, I don't understand what this is all about, but there's a couple of ATF agents in Fraser's office. And they're pissed."

"Good. I hope they are so angry they won't mind facing automatic weapons. Look, I need you to call Fraser and Burke and have them come in, too. I need a couple more hours though."

"Automatic weapons? Galloway, what's going on? I can't call the CO and demand his presence."

"Honest, ma'am, I'll explain everything when I get there. But if we're going to save Kunken and the others, we have to move fast." I hung up and started for the truck, realized I didn't know where to go, and then called Dunlay back to ask how to get to Jaspers' house. When she understood that I would not explain myself until the meeting, she gave me directions.

A mile north of the Kinross on-ramp, the Ford's oil light began to glow a constant red. Chugging up the next hill, the engine's racket drowned out the stereo, and the tachometer's needle began to keep rhythm with the tapping of the valves. Switching on the dome light, I searched the cab for an extra quart of heavy-weight oil. Banks hadn't carried any tools or a single quart in reserve. I considered pulling into a service station in Sault Ste. Marie, but I figured that with Banks dead, the condition of the Ford made little difference. My concern was finding Jaspers.

I exited at the Three Mile Road sign and bore to the left. In the dark, I missed a few of Dunlay's landmarks but found 12th Avenue and followed the numbers on the infrequent mailboxes to a simple one-story ranch with white aluminum siding. As I neared the correct address, I eased off the gas and idled past so no one could hear the Ford's death rattle. I parked the truck farther down the street, halfway to the nearest house about 300 yards away, and walked back on the opposite side of the dark road.

The windows of the Jaspers' home were dark. On the first pass, I missed the two-car garage set outback. Bright lights shone through an open bay door. Jaspers hadn't yet left for his mother's funeral.

I crossed the street and went up the cement driveway, staying close against the row of young fir trees along the right side. Both the front and rear doors of the house were closed. A Chevy Blazer sat parked in the driveway, its tail end half inside the open door. I eased along the closed garage door, keeping my head below the row of lighted windows.

When I poked my head around the corner, Jaspers stood about eight feet away, busy hooking a boat trailer to the Chevy. A heavy wool sweater and down vest gave his scrawny frame a bulky look. Fluorescent overhead lights cast a glare off his bald crown.

Sitting on the trailer behind the Chevy was a 25-foot open boat, a wide, flat skiff perfect for nosing into shallow lakes after bass and muskie. Not a cheap model either, judging by the metal-flake paint and the big Mercury outboard. Dozens of wooden crates, cardboard boxes and metal footlockers labeled or stenciled with the typical federal nomenclature cluttered the two-car garage. In a far corner sat a lawnmower and a cross-country motorcycle caked with dried mud.

I slipped the Colt out of my holster and stepped into the light. "Hey there," I called.

Jaspers jerked upright, rather tense. "Galloway! What are you doing here?" The hatch of the Blazer was open, and several shotguns rested against the back seat.

I decided to bluff. "I came to ask why you got involved with Van Dorn and God's Patriots, or whatever."

Jaspers stared at me, a look of bewilderment on his face. He was deciding whether to play dumb but seemed to realize I knew too much. Then he nodded. "Banks, right? I never trusted that stupid bastard."

I strolled farther into the garage, back along the trailer to the boat's transom, luring him away from the shotguns. He followed along in curiosity.

"Scum like Banks I can see getting involved in this mess," I observed. "But you're only a year or two away from retirement. Why screw up a good thing with a bad deal like this?"

"This ain't nothing to do with money," he growled. "Can't you see what's happening? Aren't you old enough to remember Watts? I was stationed at Group Miami back during the Liberty City riots in '80. That was a hell of a mess. We gotta stop them. These people got a jungle mentality. We can't educate them into real Americans."

I turned to stare at him, stunned. My mouth gaped open.

"You can't see it, can you? This plan is genius," he bragged. "We give 'em the guns, and they kill themselves off. These gangs are the best thing we coulda hoped for. This way they die off young before they breed more."

I stepped toward him and swung backhand, pistol-whipping him across the face with the barrel of the Colt. Jaspers screamed in pain, falling to his knees and covering his head with both arms. I aimed the Colt at the smooth skin over his skull, then lowered my weapon and shook my head in disgust.

"Tell me how to get the crew out of Crisp Point," I demanded.

Jaspers moved quicker than I expected as he came up fast and snatched a long wooden boat hook from the floor. He smashed the brass hook down against my left shoulder and jerked hard, wrenching my arm out of place. I screamed as my left hand fell loosely at my side, and the Colt clattered on the floor, skittering away from me. He swung the thick pole again, aiming for my skull, but I ducked and lunged for him, trailing my dislocated shoulder to protect it. He kicked me off and ran for the open door of the Blazer.

The .45 lay under the far side of the boat trailer. Jaspers loaded a shotgun at the rear of the Blazer, forcing shells into the loading port. I glanced around the cluttered garage for cover, gripped the rail of the boat with my right arm, boosted myself against the trailer tire, and pulled myself over the gunwale. The fiberglass hull wasn't much protection, but I hoped he wouldn't shoot through it if he intended to use the boat that morning in Van Dorn's plot.

He slammed the rear door of the Chevrolet closed; I couldn't reach one of the remaining weapons. I crouched between the twin seats of the boat, trying to hold my loose shoulder from shifting while looking for a weapon among the fishing rods, tackle box, first aid kit, and life jackets. Jaspers prowled through the cluttered garage, searching for me. Once again, I wished I carried the Beretta strapped to my ankle. The shotgun thundered, and I heard something bulky fall. The gun rattled as he jacked another shell into the chamber. I hoped the neighbors heard the shot but realized it was far from the nearest house. I needed a more definite plan than the waiting game.

"Come on, Galloway, give it up. Since Banks killed Pelligrini, you can be the fourth hostage." He moved through the garage, working his way around the boat. "We'll trade you for safe transit down the St. Lawrence. No harm, honest."

There was the truth – the crew from the 44-footer were bargaining chips to get the freighter back through the locks and rivers to the Atlantic. With the three Coast Guardsmen aboard, neither the American or Canadian government would be eager to launch an assault. Moving ships make challenging targets for even trained tactical units like Navy SEALS. Whether or not he was descended from a Confederate general, Van Dorn was a shrewd strategist.

I continued searching for a weapon or an escape route. A flare gun lay under the steering console. I slipped a small rocket into the barrel and snapped the gun butt back in place.

"There's no way out of the boat," he called. "Shudda taken the deal, cause now I gotta kill you." He stood somewhere off the starboard side.

I threw two life jackets over the transom. He fired at them recklessly. I popped over the gunwale, aimed fast with my right eye, and fired the flare into his torso as he pumped another round into the shotgun chamber.

Wild, inhuman shrieks echoed in the garage – guttural cries of agony. I couldn't see Jaspers through the blinding light and smoke. Ducking behind a seat, I heard his shotgun clatter on the cement as it fell. The acrid smoke filled my lungs, choking me – carrying the smell of burning flesh. The screams turned to groans and finally whimpers. Only then I peered over the lip of the cockpit.

Jaspers lay slumped against the wall with his legs sprawled away from a gaping hole that was once his abdomen. The smell of bile gagged me, the putrid stench of intestines, like the bloated, sickly yellow floater that exploded after nine days in the ocean when we hoisted it into the H-3, spewing liquid guts and tissue across the helo's cabin floor.

I eased myself over the side of the boat onto the garage floor and picked up the Colt.

Somehow Jaspers remained alive. Above the ugly red and brown cavity, his chest heaved; bright pink foam gurgled from a ruptured lung. Flesh and tissue sizzled as a residue of phosphorous burned away. Breathing shallow through my mouth to avoid gagging, I knelt beside him and lifted his head.

"Tell me how they're taking Kunken and the others out to the freighter."

His voice came in a shallow whisper. "Fuck you." He coughed, and dark blood ran down his chin.

"Jaspers, you're dying. Tell me, and I'll make it go fast." I rested the barrel of the Colt against his temple, uncertain about how the UCMJ treated mercy killing. When he didn't respond, I nudged him with the Colt's muzzle, hoping he hadn't yet expired.

"Bastard," he choked, followed by more blood and an exhausted groan. "My boat, at the tower by seven."

"Do the guards at the tower know you?" I asked.

He moved his head to the side once, an answer that appeared to require near superhuman effort. I closed my eyes and pulled the trigger.

"Very generous, Marty," came a familiar voice behind me. "I'll kill you as quick."

Friday: 0250

Schmidt stood by the passenger door of the Chevy 15 feet away, his revolver aimed uncomfortably close to my heart. Since he wasn't wearing a tie, I didn't figure this was official business.

"Don't move, Marty," he said. "Put the gun on the floor and slide it under the boat."

It went; I stayed and felt very naked.

"Come on, Pete, you can't shoot me." The shotgun lay four feet away, next to Jaspers' right foot, its butt in the growing pool of his blood.

"Why's that? I've already done it once; this time I'll aim." His smirk didn't offer any comfort. "I told those idiots that drowning Pelligrini wouldn't stop you, but they underestimated you. I never did."

I thanked him, starting to rise. He waved me back down with the barrel of his pistol.

"I never figured you for a Nazi," I said.

"I don't believe in that crap. Hell, I had a black cleaning girl in Miami, and I'd slip it to her now and then for an extra $20."

"How enlightened," I observed. "So what got you into this mess?"

"Don't be stupid. The money. Tell me, Marty. Did you ever know that I was involved?"

"Never had a clue." Did Jaspers finish cocking the shotgun?

"You disappoint me." He crouched into a combat-firing position, lifting his aim to my face. "What? No last jokes?"

"*Et tu*, Brute?"

Schmidt narrowed his right eye down the barrel, and our stares met over the front sight. His fingers flexed and tensed around the gun butt. I watched him. Squint, breathe, aim, squeeze, fire: the same way he practiced at the firing range. I waited, counting to five. Squint, breathe, aim, squeeze . . . at four, I lunged for the shotgun.

Pain exploded in my injured shoulder when my chest hit the floor, sliding in Jasper's blood. I lifted the barrel, shooting with my right hand at the same time Schmidt fired a round into my thigh – a fiery iron thrust under the skin. Everything else stopped except for the intense, excruciating pain; my sight darkened, my breathing stopped, and my entire consciousness revolved around a six-inch area midway between hip and knee. I was helpless on the ground, unable to hold onto the shotgun, incapable of firing another round even if Jaspers himself rose from his exploded corpse. For long, senseless minutes that seemed like hours, I lay still, seeing yellow sunbursts explode on a red sky.

Sound revived me. Schmidt screamed as he staggered and fell against the truck; his chest turned to raw meat. A siren wailed. He brought his pistol up and aimed, but his legs gave out, and he collapsed onto the cement floor.

From my butt to my knee burned like molten steel, burning pain searing through my hamstring as I tried to stand. I scrabbled across the floor, my left arm dragging uselessly at my side. The back of my leg bled more than I could spare this week. The .38 caliber pistol lay in Schmidt's lap, and I tossed it outside. The siren sounded closer. If I stayed, there'd be a lot of questions and no way to reach Crisp Point in time.

I grabbed Schmidt's shirt collar and tugged him away from the Chevy's back wheel. He moaned when I moved him. After shoving the Colt into my belt, I limped to the driver's side. My left arm dangled as I crawled inside. The keys hung in the ignition.

Headlights stayed off as I pulled away from the driveway. I headed out of the Soo, away from where the Soo police likely came. Five miles later, I found a large intersection and turned the Chevy around, the boat trailer swinging along behind in Bristol fashion. When I passed back in front of the small ranch house, two cruisers with blue lights whirling sat in the yard I'd left a few minutes earlier.

I felt betrayed and fortunate. If anyone else had held that pistol, I'd be dead. But Schmidt had always been a very methodical shooter; great on the firing line, lousy in combat. He accidentally shot me in Florida because his reactions were too slow. He wasn't able to kill me this time for the same reason.

Schmidt had sold more than his silence. When we met after my encounter with Mad Dog, I had told him what I was doing in town and that I was staying at the Superior Inn. He had passed the information along to Banks, who came calling that same evening. I wondered what else he had provided to the conspiracy. His betrayal left me angry and confused, a hollow feeling in my gut like putting down a favorite old dog turned rabid.

I was grateful Jaspers' Chevy came equipped with an automatic transmission and power steering, sparing me shifting or wrestling with the wheel in the downtown streets. Everything looked dark when I drove down the main drag, even the Horney Toad. Two more cruisers and an ambulance raced past in the opposite direction, sirens blaring. On base, I parked the Chevy in front of the mock lighthouse at the main entrance. I crawled out of the truck, climbed with great effort into the boat, and raided the first aid kit for gauze to wrap my leg. With the boat's marine radio, I called Group Soo on Channel 22.

Dunlay's voice crackled on the speaker. "Vessel calling Coast Guard, this is United States Coast Guard Group Sault Sainte Marie, go ahead with your transmission." She thought I was a late-night recreational boater.

"Coast Guard, this is Galloway. How's your evening, ma'am? Better than mine I'll bet."

"Marty, where are you?" Her sharp voice pierced the quiet night. I twisted the squelch knob down five notches.

"On the only boat in your parking lot. I could use a little assistance. I've been shot."

Thirty seconds later, she burst out the front door, followed by Fraser and the radioman on duty. I leaned against the steering wheel and waved.

"Is there a doctor in the house?" I asked, straddling the gunwale. "Or even better, a surgeon?"

"That's Jaspers' boat, isn't it?" Dunlay demanded.

"Until very recently. He's dead, along with Banks and also Pete Schmidt, from Customs. I think the crew will be too, if we don't act soon." I swung my wounded leg over the gunwale, and the three of them helped me down.

Fraser jerked his hand away and looked astonished at my blood covering his fingers. "Jesus, what's happened?"

With the radioman under one shoulder and Dunlay cradling my useless arm, I limped toward the admin building. "Well, I came close to being killed six times, but you don't sound interested in that."

"You found smugglers?" Dunlay asked. "Did they kill Jaspers and Schmidt?"

"No, they were working with the smugglers," I explained. "I killed them."

"This doesn't make any sense. Jaspers left on emergency leave," Fraser objected.

"I think he was planning to go away until things cooled down a little. Or he was deserting. Tomorrow morning he was heading for Crisp Point. The police will find his body in his garage, along with Schmidt." We climbed the stairs into the admin building one painful step at a time.

"You did kill him?!" Dunlay exclaimed in surprise.

"Yes, ma'am. He came after me with a shotgun. Look, can you call Hopkins to come fix me again?"

As we came into the fluorescent lights of the building, they saw the blood that covered me. The radioman shrieked. I tried to explain that it all wasn't mine, but the distinction seemed meaningless. For the first time, I had a vague concern about exposure to AIDS. I pushed the idea to the back of my mind, where it festered in quiet moments for months.

We went at a slow pace up the inside stairs and down the hall to Fraser's office. While Dunlay settled me onto the cheap vinyl couch, the radioman returned to the operations center. The commander went to get Captain Burke and the two BATF agents. Blood ran down my leg and dripped onto the carpet.

"Will you be OK?" she asked.

"Well, I hope so. Will you call Hopkins?" I asked with more urgency than the first time. "I'm a little short on blood this week."

The commander returned as Dunlay went out. Fraser instructed her to wake one of the seamen to make coffee. As he turned away, she rolled her eyes at me and left.

"These federal agents are being pretty tight-lipped," Fraser said. "I guess they were told to report to you. But neither the captain nor I authorized a request for outside assistance. The commandant gave specific instructions against it."

I shrugged my good shoulder. "My guess would be Cleveland. You know how the district office loves to interfere."

He gave me a suspicious look, but then the captain came in, followed by two linebackers in cheap suits wrinkled from several hours in a car. Both looked in their early forties. One was sandy blond, and the other had dark hair, but both were gray in identical places on the temples. The dark-haired fellow had broken his nose several times, and it angled off toward the left side of his face. I wondered if it was a souvenir of Golden Gloves or Marine Corps.

The captain appeared startled to see me covered with blood, and he glanced at Fraser for answers.

"You Galloway?" the Special Agent Probiscis asked. "Some guy named Thorne called the director in Washington and asked for us to come help you."

"Some admiral named Thorne," Burke growled.

The blond agent turned to Burke. "Captain, we need to speak with Galloway in private."

The request shocked Burke. No doubt, the captain was rarely excluded from any meaningful conversation.

I interrupted, "It's OK, the captain and commander aren't suspects."

Blondie shot me a nasty look. "I still think it's best we speak alone," he said.

After some hesitation and foot shuffling, Burke and Fraser left the room. The agents introduced themselves: the blonde guy was Olsen; the one with the misaligned nose, Siggly. They didn't offer badges or IDs, and I didn't ask.

Siggly came over and leaned close. "It's after three in the morning, we're tired, we drove six hours and some guy we never met claims to have a handle on Forrest Van Dorn. You'd better make good or your right arm won't work either."

Olsen rushed over, squeezing between us. "What Mark means is that he hopes we're not wasting our time."

I leaned back on the couch and smiled at them. "Come on, guys, this is no time to play good cop–bad cop, especially with another cop."

Siggly reached down to grab the cloth once filled by my left shoulder and lifted me with a grip of fabric. He brought his sneering face too near mine. "Wanna see how bad this bad cop can be?"

Not completely feigning agony, I lifted my right hand toward my dislocated shoulder, slipped it inside the windbreaker and jerked the Colt out of my belt. My little sleight of hand worked, and Siggly jumped in surprise when I pushed the muzzle up under his ribs. "Wanna see how dead?" I asked, grinning to cover the spasm of pain.

Olsen pulled the bulldog off, and they stared at me with thinly veiled hatred. I dropped the weapon to my lap and decided to be as pleasant as the pain allowed.

"You guys think I'd make this up? You think I'd break my shoulder and shoot myself in the leg to jerk your chains and keep you up all night?" I shook my head in disbelief. Their glares didn't flicker. "Wow. OK, then. Look, I'll tell you what I know. If you don't like it then run along home, and I'll take care of it myself."

"Looks like you couldn't take a piss by yourself right now," Siggly cracked.

I ignored him and explained how I'd come to Michigan looking for a missing Coast Guard crew and ended up with a positive ID of Van Dorn on an ocean-going freighter in Duluth. "Harper-Lloyd did some checking, and the FBI suspects the Van Dorn and his Patriots may be smuggling automatic weapons to street gangs."

Olsen glanced at his offensive tackle. "That'd explain why we're finding so many unregistered pieces recently."

"The FBI informant hasn't been in contact for months," I continued. "Meanwhile, the Bureau's principal focus is Islamic terrorism on the East Coast."

Siggly wasn't happy. "But you think the FBI is wrong, and you're the only one who knows what the hell's going on."

"Look, all I care about is three Coasties held hostage. But I also have a location on this Van Dorn your people are hot for aboard a freighter in the Great Lakes. I don't think he's on a pleasure cruise. I've also seen some pretty serious security around a lighthouse – guys with automatic weapons, set on full auto. They're not back-woods thugs either; they've had some training in dense cover searches, like those citizen militias. And the lead Customs agent here admitted he was taking money to keep quiet about the arms shipments. What do you want, Van Dorn's personal diary?"

They thought about the possibility for a moment and finally decided that some guy they didn't know might have a clue.

"Where's Van Dorn now?" Olsen asked.

"As far as I can tell he's somewhere between here and Duluth, heading our way," I answered.

Siggly opened the door. The commander came back, followed by Burke, Dunlay and Hopkins.

The corpsman examined me with less effort than some people select vegetables. "Your life insurance premiums must be outrageous," he whispered. "Let's get you up to sickbay."

"Work on him here," the commander said. "It sounds like we have some planning to do."

"Imagine that, two house calls in one week," I told Hopkins.

"OK, let me go get my bag," he said with a nonchalant shrug. "If you ask nice, I'll bring back something besides lidocaine."

"Did your cadaver at corpsman school sue for malpractice?" I asked.

Hopkins chuckled and gave my dangling left shoulder a heavy pat. "I hope I can get that back in place on the first try or so."

The medic left as the coffee arrived. The Coast Guard runs on java, as much as JP5 fuel and archaic tradition. A sleepy seaman left the pot and white foam cups on the commander's desk and exited. Dunlay closed the door behind him.

In the next hour, I told them all that had happened and everything I knew, from my interview with Thomason to killing Schmidt. Hopkins returned during my summation of Pelligrini's autopsy results in time to affirm my conjectures about the sand and dysentery. Everyone left the room while the medic prepared to set my shoulder back into place.

"I want you to know," Hopkins warned, "that this is going to hurt you a hell of a lot more than it's going to hurt me."

Putting my arm back in its socket registered as close on the pain scale as when it came out. I let out a yell that brought Dunlay running. The rest of the group returned after the rough part was over, and I continued outlining my evidence of the conspiracy while Hopkins stitched and bandaged the deep flesh wounds in my thigh left by the passage of Schmidt's shot through my hamstring. After 45 minutes, he finished strapping me back together again.

I tried to be as thorough in explaining the case as possible, leaving only one question unanswered.

"So what do we do now?" Dunlay asked.

Friday: 0615

The sky looked asphalt gray, and a bitter wind roared in off the lake. The thick clouds forecast heavy rains that would drive even stout fish like northern pike deep, and you'd need a heavy plug or a lead sinker to carry a rubber wiggler down to them. Senior Chief drove because he knew the way and the bulletproof vest made it difficult for me to steer with my bad shoulder.

We were on a wide gravel embankment at Little Lake Harbor, a rounded inlet that opened onto Lake Superior. The state game dock sat deserted, with only a single dark green boat moored against it. I felt tempted to call my mother from the single payphone near the state pier to say goodbye, but I glanced at my watch and thought better of it. If we hurried, we'd nose the boat ashore near the Crisp Point Lighthouse a few minutes after seven. While Drucker backed the trailer down the ramp, I scanned the fog-shrouded lake to the north for freighters. NEGRES.

Drucker released the canvas straps and cranked a handle on the trailer, paying out a steel cable that eased Jaspers' sleek bass boat into the water. He used the slack to pull the skiff around the side of the ramp, then tied a mooring line to a steel spike pounded into the beach. When he finished offloading Jaspers; boat, Senior Chief parked the Blazer and trailer back along the tree line.

Given the weather and our plans for the morning, we had dressed as best we could for the occasion, both wearing waterproof jackets over bulletproof vests that could stop shotgun slugs. Drucker wore knee-high boots and a heavy yellow slicker in anticipation of the predicted storm. I had borrowed a shirt and trousers from Hopkins. He carried about 20 pounds on me, so I cinched the belt tight to gather the slack cloth around my waist. Dunlay had carried my blood-stained clothes to the dumpster to get them out of her office.

We had a plan, one being revised often as we went along. The *Mackinaw* waited 10 miles northeast of Crisp Point, ready to intercept the *Jersey Trader*. A helicopter hovered off Whitefish Point, standing by to airlift the three Coasties to the hospital as soon as they were free. Normand drove Dunlay, Hopkins, and the two

BATF agents straight on to Crisp Point, where they would wait in the woods.

Drucker led the way to the boat, carrying a shotgun and an M-16. I packed my Colt inside a green foul-weather jacket with Jaspers' name stamped on the black leather patch over the left breast pocket. Dunlay had found the jacket while searching Jaspers' office for a spare key to Crisp Point Lighthouse. Hopkins had altered the holster straps to fit under my left shoulder, where I could get at it with my remaining good hand.

The wind whipped the lake into irregular waves that crested with white spray. The senior chief sat at the small console, and the engine roared alive when he hit the ignition. I cast off the forward mooring line and settled next to him as he steered through the channel between the rock breakwaters marked with red and green daymark panels set on steel towers. Once we were out on the lake, Drucker gradually accelerated until we skipped across the chop. I held my sore arm as the rough waters pounding the hull jarred us.

Fraser orchestrated the whole show from Group Soo, and everyone stayed in contact on Channel 83 marine band. After we left the Soo, the commander received a call from the local police. They had found Jaspers dead and moved Schmidt to the hospital in critical condition. They wanted to know if any Coast Guard operation might be pertinent to their homicide investigation. Fraser stalled, saying he needed clearance from the Cleveland district office before discussing ongoing law enforcement efforts. I had no proof that the local police were involved, but I had no way to exclude them. Meanwhile, the fewer people who knew what was going on, the better the chance of rescuing the three crew members alive.

The light fishing boat bounced over the rough waves, causing the fishing rods to rattle so loud they competed with the outboard motor. Drucker kept the throttle wide open. The cold spray covered the windshield and pelted our faces. I double-checked the Colt.

The little sleep on the ride from the Soo to the Little Lake was all I'd had that night. When bandaged, my leg stopped bleeding. Surgical tape held my shoulder in place, helped by the heavy vest and the straps of my pistol holster. The cold air woke me; the rising adrenaline flow made me more alert. We covered the six miles from

Little Lake to Crisp Point in about 40 minutes. When the stark white tower came into view, I fidgeted, flexing the fingers of both hands on the console. Drucker eyed me with suspicion.

"LT told me it was a pretty rough night. You OK to go into this?" he asked.

"I don't see much choice at the moment."

"This ain't about your dad. The Gamblers never started a fight they couldn't finish."

I gave him my best John Wayne grin. "I'm going to finish this."

Drucker scowled. "Don't get dead. Admiral Thorne won't forgive me."

Scanning the gray horizon with a pair of binoculars, I spotted the white hull of the *Mackinaw* crashing through the waves to the east. Other Coast Guard cutters and small boats waited out there beyond the horizon. Although I couldn't see the helicopter, I heard its occasional position reports on the radio. Far to the northwest, I spotted a merchant ship hull down, sailing a downbound track that would pass some 10 miles north of Crisp Point.

I wished I was more optimistic about the outcome. In Fraser's office early that morning, I had proposed the current plan, despite the objections of everyone present. The BATF agents wanted to board the *Jersey Trader* at dawn and arrest Van Dorn immediately. Of course, they had no substantial warrants or any ideas about how to free the hostage crew from the light tower. Burke wanted to let the FBI handle the whole thing and remained obstinate until I called Harper-Lloyd at home, and he confirmed that his office didn't have the manpower to stake out a men's room stall.

Simple. I planned to impersonate Jaspers until I could lure the laughing thugs out of the tower and bring Kunken, Desharnais and Lucas into the open. Dunlay's team would come out of the woods, armed for bear, preventing the hoods from hurting the crew. With the missing people recovered, the *Mackinaw* would stop the freighter and arrest the crew – nice and easy. If things went sour, Admiral Thorne would explain to my mother in short, solemn sentences what had gone wrong. I would become the last of Galloway's Gamblers.

At 0706, Jaspers' shallow boat ran up to the pebbly beach.

Drucker raised the big Mercury and used a small electric motor to set the bow hard in the sand, about 20 yards east of the tower, away from the tangle of wood pilings, cement abutments, and steel cables in front of the lighthouse. After leaning the rifle and shotgun – both cocked and ready – against the console, Drucker wished me luck. I hopped over the gunwale and waded ashore in the shallow water.

The beach looked deserted. Dozens of seagulls clustered around the tower's lakeward side, picking through the raw sewage along the waterline. The strong wind carried the smell away from me. I hoped for a signal from Dunlay to tell me that she and the others were in position and ready. The dunes and surrounding woods were quiet except for a few scattered bird cries. A white mist hung in the trees. For reassurance, I touched the foul-weather jacket covering the holstered Colt. Remembering the dozens of hours I had practiced my right hand without improving my accuracy, I wished I carried an automatic rifle myself.

I came up onto the slight rise where the lighthouse stood. In the heavy gravel there, I saw the impressions left behind by wide truck tires. A Coast Guard maintenance crew could have left them, I thought, or smugglers moving out contraband weapons. The voices inside the tower were quiet when I climbed the brick steps. A sign on the steel door read "U.S. Government Property." Past visitors scrawled their names and dates in black marker on the gray wall. I rapped several times and reached inside the vertical steel cylinder to unlock and remove the padlock. When the steel door swung open, the thin barrel of an AK-47 reached out and brushed my nose, inviting me inside.

Blinking at the darkness, I stumbled along until my eyes adjusted to the dim light inside the light tower. Under the dark steel stairs, I saw three Coasties in blue work uniforms pressed against the wall, each hunched over. I realized their wrists were handcuffed between their legs, the same way I'd tied Mike the night before, a position that made running especially difficult.

The thug with the long gun grabbed my collar and slammed me against the wall. He looked as big as Banks, with thick, greasy black hair and a week-old beard. He jabbed the barrel of the assault rifle into the soft flesh under my chin, aimed into the back of my brain.

His partner stood about my height but weighed better than 50 pounds heavier, a difference of muscle, not fat. He shoved the door closed and grabbed my groin. When he squeezed my testicles hard, I felt a wave of nausea.

"Good morning, Mister Jaspers," he said in his heavy Alabama accent, jerking my crotch forward. "You look real good for somebody dead." He laughed and added, "I guess you ain't heard of police scanners. Or satellite phones. A friend in the Soo called about an hour ago and said Jaspers died during the night. A lethal case of heartburn, you might say." His other hand searched my chest and found the Colt. He tucked it into his belt.

The one with the AK-47 poked the slender barrel harder into my neck. "Mister Van Dorn said you were worth an extra 20K, dead if possible."

In a minute, everything had gone wrong. This time I was unarmed, opposed by two professionals unburdened by moral compunction. The best I could hope for was to be left in the tower castrated and brain dead. Can I lure them outside? Can Kunken and the others run at all? Is Dunlay in the woods, ready with Siggly and Olsen?

The stout thug squeezed hard on my crotch and grunted. "Time to take a little walk on the beach. Gonna be your last so try to enjoy it."

The other took his gun away from my throat. "Yeah, ignore the smell." They both made similar snorts.

"And if you give any signals to your pal on the boat, my friend will kill one of your friends," the fire hydrant said with yet another firm yank at my groin. "Have I made myself clear enough?" He opened the door and shoved me outside. The other bruiser herded the crew, prodding them outside with the rifle barrel. We walked down the steps and across the open dunes. Farther down the beach, Drucker waited in the boat. I went in the lead, followed by the thug who had fondled me. Then came the crew, limping along as best they could. The big guy with the assault rifle followed up the rear, nudging Desharnais forward with the weapon's muzzle.

The northwest wind felt cold, wet with misting rain. Drucker stood behind the console, his hands slack at his side. I glanced over the dunes but couldn't see any movement in the woods. Where is Dunlay?

When the parade approached within 10 yards from the boat's bow, Drucker snatched up the M-16 and brought it to his shoulder. I turned and tried to distract my groping buddy with a ragged round-house kick to the face, but my heel fell short when my wounded hamstring refused to stretch the distance. I was too late; already, the thug had spotted Drucker. A small automatic pistol in his left hand spit two quick bursts; the first aimed at Drucker, the second …

The impact knocked the wind out of my lungs like a punch in the chest with a baseball bat. I staggered and fell, landing on my back in the pebbles and sand, gasping for air.

More gunfire followed, distant this time. The seagulls screeched, and a light rain fell on my face. I felt paralyzed, and somehow everything around me seemed to slow as if time had come to a full stop. My breath finally came again in little bites. Each time my chest moved, pain exploded through my ribs.

The short thug towered over me, pointing his weapon into my face. For no obvious reason, the model was critical to me – I didn't want to die cheaply. I couldn't see much of the weapon beyond the stubby barrel. A woman shouted. More gunfire. I heard a single gunshot, then another prolonged burst. The guy jerked and swayed; his ugly face skewed into an expression of horror. He pitched over backward and tumbled down the dune.

I lay immobile, listening to the world pass me by – bird cries, shrieks, howling winds, shouts, and breaking waves. The churning clouds unleashed a torrent of rain that pelted my face and drowned out the distant voices. I rested without moving, waiting to breathe again.

Dunlay knelt beside me, supporting herself with the stock of an M-16. "I didn't want to kill him," she said. "He was going to shoot you."

"Thanks," I choked. "I'm glad you changed your mind." I tried to sit up, but the pain in my chest felt dizzying.

"No, I meant. . . Dammit, you know exactly what I meant."

Normand came running up the beach from the skiff. "Drucker's dead. He was hit in the neck."

Dunlay helped me sit, then the two of them pulled me to my feet. I scanned the beach. The BATF agents each knelt over one of the thugs. The one Dunlay had shot before he could kill me lay sprawled on his back about a yard away, the sand around him growing dark with his blood. Siggly leaned over him, conducting a body search. Closer to the tower, Olsen inspected the bigger corpse, feeling through his coat pockets. I assumed both were dead. Patricia Lucas knelt on the crest of the dune, vomiting, as Hopkins held her head. The other crewmen sat on the ground nearby, working their legs free from their bound arms. All three looked filthy and disheveled.

My chest felt better when I stood, and breathing came easier. Three slug holes were grouped in the chest of Jaspers' jacket I wore. If I hadn't been wearing the bulletproof vest, the holes would have been in my sternum. I took the M-16 from Dunlay and leaned on it as I limped down to the boat, still gasping in pain with each breath. The drizzle turned to a heavy downpour.

Senior Chief Drucker sat slumped in the driver's seat, two small holes in the neck of his yellow slicker marked by thin trickles of watery blood. His head hung back; vacant eyes stared into the rain. I reached over and closed them with my fingers. Then I crossed myself and asked for mercy on his soul. Dunlay stood behind me, calling the Coast Guard helicopter on a small hand-held radio.

"I told the *Mackinaw* that we're finished and asked them to stop the freighter," she told me.

The rain came down in torrents, driven by the wind off the lake. I leaned over the boat's console and turned on the marine radio. On Channel 16, I heard the *Mackinaw* hailing the skipper of the freighter.

"Motor Vessel *Jersey Trader*, this is the Coast Guard Cutter *Mackinaw*, request you heave to and stand by to be boarded."

"*Mackinaw*, this is the *Jersey Trader*, apologies, but conditions are too rough to receive a boarding party at this time." The voice sounded like Kucharski.

The *Mackinaw's* reply came abrupt and curt. "*Jersey Trader*, thanks for your concern. For your information, the hostages are free

213

and your two accomplices at Crisp Point are dead. If you don't stop your vessel now, we are prepared to take action."

"What you got in mind, captain?" The voice on the radio had changed, and I assumed Van Dorn was now speaking.

"*Jersey Trader, Mackinaw*. We're not playing games. You are an American vessel, sailing in American waters and subject to my jurisdiction." Another voice changed as the Mackinaw skipper took the microphone as well. "I will aim my fire hoses down your stack to disable your engines, and if that fails, I am prepared to order my crew to open fire into your deck house."

"What's the *Mackinaw* carry for firepower?" I asked Dunlay.

"Pistols and long guns for law enforcement. Because of a treaty with Canada, she doesn't carry deck guns."

"I don't think an M-16 or a shotgun will do much damage to a freighter," I said, feeling helpless.

The skipper of the *Jersey Trader* finally answered. "*Mackinaw*, play your little games if you want. I'm heading for the Soo locks. If anyone tries to stop me or hold me, I'll ram the gates, flush my tanks and torch the locks. The same goes for the Seaway canals. You can imagine the damage if I shut down the locks and close off the lakes."

"Do you realize what that would do?" Dunlay asked in disbelief. "Our grain feeds half the world; there'd be massive starvation. Without iron ore, it'd shut down Pittsburg and Detroit. It'd start another depression." Her mouth gaped open in horror.

Normand spoke. "If the *Mackinaw* can't stop them here, we'll have to let them go."

The radio in Dunlay's hand crackled as the helicopter answered her call. "Coast Guard Mobile One, this is Coast Guard 9691. ETA your position approximately ten minutes. How many passengers do you have?"

I snatched the black microphone away from her. "Coast Guard 9691, this is Mobile One. Request a change in plans. I need you to drop your basket 50 yards east of the light. Two people will climb in. Then I want you to leave the basket down and fly to the freighter near the *Mackinaw*, her bow reads *Jersey Trader*. The two people will board the freighter."

Minutes passed as the radio operator relayed the message to the pilots and waited for a reply.

"Mobile One, negative on your request. First, we don't fly with the basket lowered. And we hoist only one person at a time." The crewman's voice told me that his pilot was reluctant to break the rules.

"I understand that, but there won't be time to hover over the freighter for two individual hoists. And I expect there will be shooting, so the quicker you drop us off, the better your chances to escape."

A long pause followed as the pilot and co-pilot debated their defense options at court-martial. "Mobile One, CG 9691. OK, 50 yards east of tower, two people, bucket down, straight to the freighter. But don't tell our C.O. about this."

"There's, what?, 20 guys on that freighter," Dunlay objected. "Anybody who tries to go aboard now is gonna get killed."

I agreed. "That's why I'm taking somebody I don't like with me." Then I called Siggly over. He came at a jog, carrying two shotguns. He was out of the wrinkled suit, wearing jeans and a regulation windbreaker with the BATF department logo on the chest. The jacket looked drenched, and he tugged at the thin material where it clung to his bulky arms. His bulletproof vest was visible. He handed back my Colt that he had retrieved from the dead man.

"Want to go flying with me?" I asked, handing him the M-16 from Drucker's lap. I pulled the clip out of Dunlay's rifle and replaced it with a fully loaded one Normand handed me. "The *Mackinaw* needs a little help stopping the freighter."

Siggly checked the clip in Drucker's rifle, then snapped open the cylinder on a large-caliber revolver tucked into his belt. He added four bullets and snapped it closed. "Only if I get Van Dorn," he said, a perverse smile on his lips.

"Finders keepers."

Friday: 0750

The violent downdraft from the helo rotors kicked up beach sand in a small whirlwind, and the raindrops felt like hail against my upturned face. The helicopter's basket dropped within 10 yards of where we stood. Siggly and I stood under the helo, ready to climb into the litter. Dunlay and Normand helped Hopkins get the crew back to the government van parked at the clearing where I'd left the rental car. Olsen went to investigate the light tower.

Neither of us knew what to expect onboard the *Jersey Trader*, but each carried an M-16, a shotgun, and a pistol. Rainwater made the stocks slick and dripped off the long barrels. Siggly packed his revolver under his jacket, and I again carried my Colt.

The steel mesh basket was about four feet long and two feet wide. Siggly was built big, so the two of us would make a tight fit. We let the litter touch the ground before we grabbed it because the helo rotors create a static electric charge in the steel cable. I instructed Siggly not to get out of the basket until I had grounded us against the freighter's deck with the shotgun barrel. He looked dubious but nodded.

We climbed in and sat with our backs against each other, legs dangling over opposite ends of the cage. I held the M-16 and shotgun between my legs and waved at the crewman leaning out the helo door. The engine surged, and we lifted off the ground, heading out over the water. The basket swung like a pendulum, spinning us in the heavy wind like a carnival Tilt-a-Whirl. Siggly was heavier, and the cage tipped toward him, giving me a perfect view of the bottom of the helo. Thick black letters read USCG.

Twisting and swaying in the rain, I became disoriented. The only way I could be sure which direction we were traveling was to glance up at the black bulb on the helo's nose. As the basket swayed and twisted, at times, I saw the lighthouse at Crisp Point growing more distant.

The storm seemed more severe out on the lake. The wave crests were regular, about six to eight feet, each capped with white foam. The winds picked up too, and the basket swung farther to and fro. We hung about 100 feet above the lake's choppy surface.

Before I could see either ship, I saw the smoke billowing from their stacks. While we waited for the helo to arrive on-scene, the *Mackinaw's* skipper had tried to disable the *Jersey Trader* by aiming his fire hoses down the freighter's stacks. When that failed, he warned Van Dorn that he would direct machine-gun fire at the bridge on his next pass. That had also failed, and the freighter continued to steam eastward.

"What the hell is the Coast Guard ship doing?" Siggly yelled.

I pushed myself up in the basket so I could see better. The *Jersey Trader* rolled in the waves, steaming away from the *Mackinaw*. The thick exhaust indicated they traveled at maximum turns, making about 15 knots.

The *Mackinaw* was farther north, about a half-mile from the freighter. Black smoke rolled out of the icebreaker's massive mustard-colored stack, and the *Mackinaw's* bow aimed to cross the freighter's course at a 45-degree angle.

"The *Mack's* going to ram it," I yelled back, then shouted into the hand-held radio, "9691, Mobile One, stand by. Let's see what the *Mackinaw* is doing."

The helo crew saw the action, too. We stopped and hovered 500 yards astern of the *Jersey Trader*, putting Siggly and me into the billowing gray cloud of exhaust trailing behind it. We both coughed violently, and my eyes watered. The fierce wind knocked us about, dangling at the end of the steel tether.

As it neared the *Trader's* stern, the *Mackinaw* seemed to accelerate, the black plume growing and glowing with bright sparks that showered its upper decks. The wide, white hull rose and fell in the rough surf, sheets of heavy spray washing across the *Mack's* wide foc'sle.

Twisting the volume knob as loud as it would go, I switched the radio back to Channel 16. The *Mackinaw's* captain was calling the freighter.

"*Jersey Trader*, this is *Mackinaw*. Prepare for collision, port side. Repeat, collision imminent, port side."

The bow of the freighter turned hard to port. Instead of evasion, the *Jersey Trader* now crossed the *Mackinaw's* course broadside.

The basket spun and swung as the helo pulled away from the

two ships. I strained to peer over the side of the basket, as did Siggly, both of us watching in amazement.

The icebreaker's blunt bow slammed the *Jersey Trader* on the freighter's port side aft of the bridge house, the jackstaff on the *Mackinaw's* bow riding higher and higher as it crushed forward through the steel decks until it reached the freighter's amidships. In a quick maneuver, the *Mackinaw* reversed course, pulling itself away from the damaged ship and sliding back into the lake. The white paint on the hull was scraped and blackened, but otherwise, the *Mackinaw* looked undamaged. The *Jersey Trader* continued steaming eastward, though its stern sagged as the lake rushed in and filled its rear compartments. Finally, the freighter stalled, sitting dead in the water, rolling with the rough waves. The black exhaust turned to white steam.

The helo flew closer to the sinking ship. I strained forward, and my hand slipped. The basket lurched. The pouring rain made everything slick and cold.

Two dark figures burst out of the *Jersey Trader's* bridge, both tall and bearded, each wearing dark coveralls. They scrambled across the listing deck and began to release one of the freighter's two lifeboats. The other lifeboat sat on the portside where the *Mackinaw* had struck, and it looked badly damaged – twisted in its own hoist rigging.

"Van Dorn!" Siggly yelled, pointing at the two men. No one else came on deck, and it became clear that Van Dorn meant to launch the only lifeboat for himself and his partner.

I turned the radio back to 83. "Take us in!" I shouted into the mike.

The helo dove toward the freighter's bow, where it could drop the basket without tangling the cable in the ship's rigging. As we passed over the bridge, another crewman came out on deck. Siggly and I watched, unable to intervene, as Van Dorn turned and gunned the man down with a small automatic.

"Do you know what you're doing?" the helo pilot shouted over the radio.

"Do it! Do it!" I hollered back.

The basket went down fast, swinging and twisting among the

hatch covers on the freighter's main deck. In the wild winds, the pilot couldn't control how we landed on the pitching surface. We hit hard, bounced twice, and spilled out as the basket toppled on its side. An electric shock jolted through my hands, numbing my forearms. Siggly howled in surprise.

"I didn't think you were serious," he yelled at me.

After fetching the long guns from the basket, I waved up to the aircrewman looking down at me. The helo pulled away, hoisting up the litter at the same time. Our weapons survived the landing, but the small hand-held radio had shattered on impact. We ran aft along the port side, ducking low behind the wide deck coverings. Already the freighter carried a 10-degree list. The heavy rainwater ran over our feet, pouring over the low gunwale. For balance, Siggly kept one hand along the steel cable that ran the length of the main deck, juggling both long guns in the other hand.

Two steep ladders led up to the bridge house; one on the port side, the other starboard. Siggly raced across to the starboard side and climbed to the top, crouching below the edge of the upper deck, his M-16 ready. Slipping on the wet steel rungs, I went up the port ladder – one hand for the ladder, one high up around the stock of the shotgun with a finger hooked around the trigger, the M-16 slung over my back.

The steel deck around the port side of the bridge was buckled and twisted. The bridge house walls were pock-marked from small arms fire on the *Mackinaw's* last pass, and most portside windows showed bullet holes. Twenty feet astern of my position at the top of the portside ladder, the crumpled deck gave way to a vast, jagged cavern, and through the rising steam, I looked down into the lower tiers. The lake rushed in two levels below the main deck.

The portside door into the bridge house gaped open, and I eased inside, the shotgun leveled at my waist. Kucharski hung slumped over the helm, his arms tangled in the steel wheel – the tile floor slick with his blood. I stepped behind him, felt for a pulse on the cold skin of his neck and found a small slug hole in the middle of his back.

From a window on the starboard side, I saw Van Dorn working the controls on a small crane while the other man struggled to start the outboard motor on the lifeboat. Already Van Dorn had lifted the lifeboat from its cradle, and the long hydraulic arm was swung out over the open water, obscuring my view of the man in the boat. The cable started to pay out, and the fiberglass boat began to descend. A small machine gun that looked like an Uzi rested on the top of the crane's control panel.

I crouched inside the corner of the open doorway. Five feet away, a Korean crewman lay sprawled on the gray steel, his face pock-marked with small red wounds and the back of his head blown away. The drizzling rain washed his blood across the listing deck.

The lifeboat disappeared, dropping below the level of the deck. Through the roaring wind, I heard the whine of the crane's motor. My finger tensed on the trigger. I wanted to kill Van Dorn and be done with the whole conspiracy. I looked at the young Korean again.

"Van Dorn!" I shouted. "You're under arrest!"

He spun, snatching up the automatic and spraying the bridge with a burst of gunfire. I fired, pumped, and fired again. The quick rattle of another gun told me Siggly was firing his M-16. Van Dorn stumbled back, falling behind the crane.

An explosion far below rocked the freighter, knocking me against the wall and slamming the steel door shut. The deck pitched farther to port, and another loud burst of gunfire sounded outside. The glass in the windows above my head shattered. I kicked the door open in time to see Van Dorn scrambling across the empty lifeboat cradle. I fired again from the hip. He jumped over the side, wrapping his arms and legs around the steel cable dangling from the crane arm. Spinning around the wire, he slid out of sight.

Dropping the shotgun, I ran to the gunwale. Van Dorn stood in the rocking lifeboat, releasing the crane hook. I snapped off two rounds with the M-16 before the man working the engine jerked a pistol out of his jacket and aimed it at me. As I ducked away, three rounds ricocheted off the steel superstructure.

Siggly shouted, and I crawled to the top of the ladder. He dangled by one hand off the side of the ladder 15 feet above the main deck, scrambling to get a footing on the wet steel. Climbing halfway down, I hooked a leg around his body and pulled him over to the railing.

"You didn't tell me that sinking ships explode first!" he shouted.

By the time we reached the upper deck, the two men were speeding away in the rigid rubber boat, bouncing across the six-foot waves. Siggly aimed from the shoulder and fired a few rounds with his M-16, but neither man reacted. I raced inside to call the helo on the ship's radio, but there was no power on the bridge. The last explosion may have destroyed the ship's generator.

Siggly stood in the doorway, shaking off water like a wet retriever. "I can't believe that sumbitch got away."

"Don't worry, he's got to come ashore somewhere," I told him. "I figure Fraser has all available Coast Guard units waiting to intercept him." I wasn't very optimistic. "I don't suppose you recognized his friend in the boat."

"I didn't get much of a visual. One of the crew?"

"No, he wasn't aboard in Duluth," I mused. "I've got pictures of the whole crew."

"And some guys collect baseball cards." Siggly laughed at his own wit.

"Here comes our ride," I observed. Through the portside windows, I saw two small boats from the *Mackinaw* approaching. The icebreaker waited about a quarter-mile off, and crewmen on the bow were busy draping rescue nets down the hull.

"Hey, how many guys does it take to sail one of these?" Siggly asked.

"Two or three dozen."

"And where are they?"

I looked out and saw no one swimming away from the freighter. "Good question. Let's go have a look below and see where everybody is."

Siggly eyed me with contempt. "Jesus, this thing is sinking, and you want to go snooping around."

I started down the ladder into the narrow hall between the radio room and the skipper's cabin. I heard Siggly clatter after me, slipping a fresh clip into his M-16 and springing the cocking lever. "I'd better go, too; you never know what you might find," he called.

As we moved from deck to deck down through the freighter, I checked each compartment. Siggly stood behind me with his M-16 at the ready. At the bottom of the ladder on the main deck, we stepped into eight inches of lake water. Everything open to the ship's stern was filling with dark water, but as we moved forward, the flooding grew shallower. We found the bodies of two more Asian crewmen slumped over a table on the crew's messdeck. From their postures, it appeared they had been shot, execution-style, in the back of the head.

When I opened the hatch to go below the main deck, thick smoke rushed out, a dark fog that smelled of burnt plastic. When the generator blew, the fire spread throughout the ship's electrical system, melting the plastic coating on the wires. I assumed the gas was poisonous.

"We're gonna need OBAs," I told Siggly.

"What?"

"O-B-As. Oxygen breathing apparatus, you know, gas masks!" I yelled.

Siggly shook his head and motioned toward the fire hose coiled on the wall. The ship's deck now listed to almost 25 degrees, and walking was rapidly becoming more difficult. I waded across the messdeck and dragged the hose off the rack. Passing the nozzle to Siggly, I cranked the spigot open. The hose filled with water, stiffening in my hands as I ran back toward the ladder down to the engineering spaces. Holding a rag over my mouth and nose, I climbed down the dark stairs behind Siggly.

At the bottom of the ladder, my lungs were ready to explode. Siggly opened the nozzle and inhaled near the rushing water. He passed the nozzle to me.

"I learned this in the Navy," he yelled. "It's an old fireman's trick."

The cold spray carried with it enough oxygen to inhale. It would last only as long as the water pressure remained, so I shut the gate and crawled down the narrow passageway after him.

The hallway was dry and dim, illuminated by emergency lights every 20 feet. With my bad leg and sore arm, I had trouble getting down the passageway. We crouched below the thick cloud of smoke, as low as the Kevlar vests allowed. After two more stops to breathe from the nozzle, we reached the main hatch to the engine room – a wide, flat square door on the deck with a round scuttle port in the center. The hatch cover itself was bolted down, but the scuttle opened with a quick-release wheel. I heard banging below me on the other side, the tinny noise of metal on metal. The scuttle shuddered but didn't open. The crew was trapped below, unable to open either the hatch or the scuttle.

"Why can't they get this opened?" Siggly yelled.

The steel wheel in the center of the scuttle cover moved freely, so it wasn't battened down. The hatch cover slammed up and down as the crew pounded at it from below. Feeling around the edges of the scuttle cover in the dark, I found a padlock binding a clasp on the right-hand side.

After sharing a breath of oxygen from the nozzle with Siggly, I took out the Colt. The problem stumped me. If I moved back to shoot from a safe distance, I couldn't see in the darkening hall. If I held the muzzle against the lock, a ricochet off the steel deck or bulkheads might make my fifth gunshot wound for the day. The loud clamor from the engine room reminded me there wasn't much time to think about it.

I motioned Siggly to move behind me. Pressed as tight as I could against the shuddering hatch, I poked the barrel of the .45 into the U-bolt of the lock and fired. The padlock shattered, and with the gunbutt I knocked the steel hook out of the clasp. The steel cover swung open – the wheel inches from hitting my face – and an anxious crewman burst through the scuttle.

Hauling him to his feet, I put the hose into his hands and pointed back toward the ladder I came down. "Go! Follow the hose! Go! Go! Don't breathe! Run! Go!"

More men clambered up from the engine room, each shouting back instructions in Korean or Indonesian to those still below. After hauling up the last of them, Siggly and I took a final hit of air from the nozzle. The spray turned to a dribble as the water pressure in the hose dropped. I lurched back up the passageway and climbed the ladder; Siggly came a stride behind me.

Five crewmen stopped and picked up the bodies of their two

dead comrades from the messdeck. They carried the corpses out onto the main deck. The other men were already there, hanging on the lifelines and waving to the Coast Guard boats. The deck listed beyond 20 degrees. The *Jersey Trader* would sink in minutes now.

The *Mackinaw's* fiberglass small boat nosed up next to the freighter's port side, bobbing in the chop. The ship heeled so far over that the crewmen stepped from the main deck onto the small boat's bow when the waves brought it up. Twelve crewmen crowded aboard the 26-foot boat before it pulled away. A smaller rigid hull inflatable already carrying three other *Jersey Trader* crewmen came alongside next. The crew passed the two corpses down and then climbed over themselves. Siggly stepped aboard. Including the three Coast Guardsmen manning the small rubber boat, I made the twelfth body. In a loud voice, the coxswain instructed everyone to sit still and hold onto the rope on the boat's orange pontoon. Puttering at a painfully slow speed, we turned and made our way back to the *Mackinaw*.

Friday: 0945

When I climbed the hemp rescue net draped down the *Mackinaw's* bow, the skipper stood talking with Siggly. The captain's leather bomber jacket looked drenched; his wet hair was plastered against his head.

"I've already alerted Group Soo that Van Dorn escaped," Captain Hayden said. "The group has called in the state police, and they've put out an all-points bulletin for him."

"What about the freighter's crew?" I asked. "How many survived?"

"According to MSO Duluth, there was a total of 24 aboard. We've got eighteen alive, two dead, and Van Dorn and another one got away, that's 22. We're missing two," the captain explained.

"They're both on the bridge of the freighter. Van Dorn shot them dead in cold blood, same as the two we found on the messdeck," Siggly said. "And he locked the main hatch into the engine room to prevent the crew from escaping."

The bodies of the two dead crewmen were laid in steel mesh litters and covered with wool blankets. *Mackinaw* crewmembers lifted the stretchers and carried them aft along the port side. The remaining men from the *Jersey Trader* sat silently on the gray deck as a corpsman moved among them, examining their injuries. They looked shell-shocked by these events.

The skipper turned to watch the freighter slip into the stormy lake. The entire bridge was submerged, and the notched bow jutted high out of the water. "And I thought this was going to be a quiet twilight tour," he said. "Something like this can really foul up a retirement."

I wished I could offer him some encouragement, but without Van Dorn or the weapons, we had only a sunken freighter and eleven dead men.

"That was a hell of a thing to see," Siggly told Hayden. "Weren't you worried you might sink yourself?"

Hayden smiled. "No, a skipper always knows what his ship can do. I've got more than an inch and a half of steel on my hull. I could cut a frigate in half."

A voice boomed on the loudspeaker. "Special Agent Galloway, lay to the bridge."

Captain Hayden led us aft along the starboard rail, and we climbed the steel stairs to the expansive bridge. The ship's executive officer, Lieutenant Commander Weston, met us, saluting the captain. "Group Soo wants to talk with Galloway, sir."

The XO led me away from the main bridge house into a small shack equipped with an engine order telegraph, a fathometer and a bank of radios. The telegraph's brass handles were well-polished. The bridge wing had windows that opened, and the conning officer would come out here to maneuver the ship during docking. Weston turned on a radio and switched it to Channel 83. "Group Soo, this is *Mackinaw*. Galloway is standing by."

Fraser's voice came on the speaker. "*Mackinaw*, Group Soo. Galloway, the helo is refueled and sitting on deck in Kinross. Captain Burke wants to know if you or Siggly are hurt and need to be taken to the hospital."

I took the microphone from Jacobs. "Group Soo, *Mackinaw*. Negative. We're fine. Some of the crewmen from the freighter may be suffering smoke inhalation or hypothermia. You may want to alert the hospital."

"*Mackinaw*, Group Soo. The hospital's getting crowded fast. Our people haven't arrived yet."

"Will Schmidt survive?" I asked.

"*Mackinaw*, Soo. Doubtful, he lost a lot of blood. Before he went under, he named a detective in the Soo police who was involved. That may be how the guys at the lighthouse knew Jaspers was dead."

"Group Soo, *Mackinaw*. Got any good news?"

"*Mackinaw*, Soo. About Van Dorn and company? No. Although I heard the last thing Schmidt said was that you could have his tackle box."

What was so crucial about Schmidt's tackle box? I wondered. And why was I having trouble breathing? "Group Soo, *Mackinaw*. Thanks. I'm going ashore to look around for the weapons. Can you have a vehicle meet me there?"

"*Mackinaw*, Soo. Very well. I'll send Normand back out for you."

"Soo, *Mackinaw*. One final request. Would you call Mrs. Deshar-nais as soon as you can. I made a promise."

When I finished with the radio, Jacobs said he'd arrange to have the rigid-hull inflatable run Siggly and me to Crisp Point. The *Mack-inaw* would sail straight for Sault Ste. Marie to get medical attention for the rescued crew. The *Jersey Trader* had already vanished into the depths, leaving only loose debris – a few boxes, papers, books and clothing – that bobbed in the rough waves. The wind carried the sour scent of diesel fuel, but I couldn't see the familiar blue-green sheen in the storm-driven chop.

When I returned to the bridge, Hayden asked Siggly why the *Jersey Trader's* crew was locked in the engine spaces.

"Cause Van Dorn is one evil son of bitch," the BATF agent said. "He planned to kill every one of them. It wouldn't have made a bit of difference to him cause they weren't part of his master race."

"Let's go renew his subscription to *Prison Life*," I said.

Friday: 1145

During the rough ride to Crisp Point on the *Mackinaw's* rubber inflatable boat, the coxswain and the boat engineer talked in excited tones about the morning's events, recounting the captain's angry reaction when the freighter refused a boarding team. They were shocked that the captain had not only opened fire with the M-16s but had rammed the freighter. They each described the collision three times.

Siggly spoke only once on the forty-minute trip. He leaned over and said to me, "There's only one reason why Van Dorn got away. We have to say 'Freeze' before we shoot, and he doesn't."

He was right; I could have killed Van Dorn while he worked the crane controls, shot him down the way he'd killed Kucharski and the other crewmen. I didn't because my job is to arrest criminals. In self-defense, I had shot two men dead and wounded two others, but I could not commit either premeditated murder or murder of opportunity. A slight difference, but one that made me a lawman and Van Dorn a killer, though sometimes I could agree with Siggly that being practical is better than being right.

The Michigan state police combed the beach as the small rubber-hulled boat dropped us ashore. A sergeant took us up the sandy road – through a dense cloud of mosquitoes – to where the lead detective sat in a squad car parked in the clearing not far from my rental Ford. Olsen was with him. While the BATF agents conferred, Detective Moreau told me they'd found Banks dead, then asked if I knew where the automatic weapons were stored at Crisp Point.

"We've been all through the area and haven't found anything," he explained. "We're trying to get search warrants for the houses back there and the cabins up the road right now." He scratched his balding head as he studied his clipboard.

"Which cabin belongs to Agent Schmidt?" I asked.

He pointed toward a tarpaper-roofed shack, and I told him to give me a two-minute head start before sending a search team over.

Schmidt's little cabin looked very simple; a little shack covered with red shingle siding built on a fieldstone foundation – the kind of one-floor clapboard shanty popular with thrifty outdoorsmen and producers of slasher films. The windows weren't boarded and had no shades, only sheer curtains. I saw little furniture inside. I walked up on the rickety porch and opened the screen door. The wooden door had a heavy padlock, but the clasp looked old and rusted. Balancing myself against the screen door and the roof support, I slammed my right foot above the doorknob. The screws ripped out of the jamb on the second kick, and the door swung open.

The three rooms had little furniture. A table and two chairs were pressed between the stove and sink in the kitchen. The small sink – designed for a bathroom – was stacked with dirty plates and glasses. The bedroom had a cot and a small dresser. A folding lawn chair was shoved up close against a small portable television on a folding table in the sitting room. Schmidt hadn't spent his hush money on an interior decorator.

Two uniformed troopers came to the door. I motioned them in, but they seemed reluctant to enter.

"What happened to the door?" one of them asked.

"That's how I found it. Could be kids, or strong winds. Nothing here worth stealing."

They looked at me with calculated suspicion.

I spotted two fishing rods and a tackle box against the bedroom wall. While the troopers poked through the kitchen, I opened the box and found four bundles of $100 bills wrapped in cellophane. I stuffed two of them into my coat pocket and then called the officers in to show the rest of what I'd found. They became very excited.

Normand stood in the clearing, leaning against a tan Dodge government vehicle. He said Fraser told him to drive back from the Soo to give me a ride. I walked over to where the hired Ford rested on two of its four rims, removed my luggage from the dented trunk, and put the bags in the government Dodge. Once in the Soo, I'd call the rental agency, tell them where their car was, and explain that they could put the charge for the tow truck on my bill. When Normand and I hopped into the government vehicle, Olsen and Siggly came over and asked for a lift. They climbed into the back seat, complaining about the circus the state police were running. We started back down the two-track.

"Van Dorn is too smart to keep the guns out here," Olsen said.

"He'd put them where he could move them, someplace more accessible."

"Instead of looking for the guns, the police should be hunting for Van Dorn," Siggly added. "Those guns will be here until things cool down, but he's gonna be on the next flight to Europe."

"No idea where Van Dorn dropped the boat, huh?" I asked Normand.

"A 41-footer from Station Grand Marais chased them up the Big Two-Hearted, but they beached the lifeboat and ran into the woods."

As we wound down the two-track, I realized how dangerous my trip the previous night had been. In the daylight, I saw all the turns, false trails, and near misses I had avoided in the dark while driving the oversized LTD through the thick brush and dense woods.

Normand drove the GV more aggressively than I liked, not using the brake but only altering his acceleration to meet each turn or hill. I found myself clutching the armrest and pressing hard on an imaginary brake pedal into the floorboards. I remembered reading in his personnel file that Normand had grown up in the Ozarks, so he was accustomed to roads that lacked graded pavement. Under Normand's steering, the Dodge wagged across the loose gravel and dirt, sometimes not even aimed in the same direction as the road. Siggly and Olsen continued airing their grievances in the back seat.

Somehow my plan had all gone awry. We had saved the three survivors of the 44-footer crew, but Drucker was dead. We managed to stop the freighter, but Van Dorn had escaped. We had prevented the *Jersey Trader* from damaging the Soo locks, but Van Dorn had murdered four innocent crewmembers. We had blown the smuggling operation apart but didn't have the contraband. In baseball, you can bat .350 and earn millions. In law enforcement, doing 50 percent will get you a court-martial.

We pulled up on the hardtop of Route 123 and headed east. Olsen and Siggly continued to debate the possible hiding places for the weapons. Normand tuned to a radio station called Q-Lite, a station dedicated to middle-aged housewives in polyester frocks scouring the oven while imagining that David Hasselhoff would come to read the meter. The afternoon disc jockey seemed especially fond of the bubble gum music of the late Sixties.

I tried to tune out both noises – the heated discussion in the backseat and the noxious music – watching the lush green countryside we sped by. We passed the upper and lower Tahquamenon Falls and drove through Paradise. The road south stretched along a perfectly straight line. Normand pushed the government sedan up to 75 mph. Fifteen miles south of Paradise, we passed a string of three state police cruisers – their red lights whirling and sirens screaming – heading north, no doubt on their way to Crisp Point.

When we reached Route 28, Normand headed east, back toward the Soo. About a quarter-mile down the road, we drove by a used car lot with an old Willy's pickup parked out front. The four-wheel-drive truck was set up on enormous knobby mud tires. How many of those antique trucks are there in the UP? I wondered.

"Turn around," I told Normand, sitting up and releasing the safety on the Colt. "Go back to that car lot."

"Did you see something?" Siggly asked as Normand made a wide U-turn.

"I recognized a truck back there. It was at Crisp Point last night."

Normand stopped the Dodge behind the tiny white trailer that served as a sales office. The agents took their shotguns from the trunk, and Siggly gave Normand his revolver. We split up and walked around the building. Olsen and Siggly crouched behind a Jeep Grand Cherokee parked about 15 feet from the front door. I motioned for Normand to wait by the corner of the trailer.

Through the big plate glass window, I saw two people in the trailer, a man and a woman, both seated behind desks. I went up the wooden steps; Colt held in the air and my badge hanging around my neck on a chain. I turned the knob, then kicked the door wide open.

"Freeze!"

The woman screamed, and the man jumped from his desk, hands in the air. They were both in their mid-forties and overweight. He wore a plaid jacket and brown double-knit slacks. Her dress was white, with green and yellow flowers.

"We have no cash here," the man stammered. "We only have my wallet and her purse." He thought I meant to rob the place.

Keeping the Colt aimed, I waved my badge. "Federal law officer," I said. Trying to explain Coast Guard Investigations Special Agent always sounded cumbersome. "Please come outside."

"I don't understand, officer," the man said to Olsen as they went down the steps into the gravel lot. "What's this about?"

As I expected, Olsen and Siggly both gave me looks of disgust. "We're not sure ourselves," Olsen told him.

"Look, sir, I'm sure you run a legitimate business, so you won't mind if we look at a few of your cars," I told the salesman. "There's been a terrible problem with people rolling back odometers."

He paused. "That's a federal law?" he asked.

"You won't get in trouble yourself. If we find anything, we'll go after the wholesaler who sold you the car." Olsen and Siggly gave me very concerned looks as I said this. "On the other hand, we could go get search warrants," I offered.

"No, go right ahead and look." The salesman glanced at the woman.

Putting the Colt away, I went back into the trailer and came out with the rack of keys, a flat board covered with sets of car keys hanging from brass hooks. Late-model sedans packed the lot, so I went to the nearest Buick, unlocked the driver's door, and looked through the glove compartment. I found a trunk release where I expected. The lid came up, and I walked around the back.

"Mister Olsen, could you bring our two good citizens over this way?" I shouted.

The couple edged around behind the rear of the Buick in fear. I smiled at the man in plaid. "I seem to have opened the trunk by accident. Would you happen to know how a crate shipped from Korea to Spain turned up in a used car on your lot?"

The BATF agents moved closer and peered into the trunk. The wooden box was about a yard long and 20 inches wide, its destination in Madrid stamped on the side. Olsen grabbed my injured arm and pulled me a few yards away.

"Does the expression illegal search mean anything to you?" he asked. "We can't touch these people now."

"Who cares about them? They're fronts. You can't even prove they knew the guns were in the trunk. We've got the guns, and they could tell us something about Van Dorn if they think we won't arrest them."

Olsen groaned. "I hope we don't get our dicks stomped over this," he said in exasperation.

When we returned, Siggly had pried the lid off the crate with the tire tool. He handed Olsen a long machine gun that looked like an AK-47. "Look familiar?" Siggly asked. Olsen scrutinized it and glanced up for an explanation.

Siggly described it matter of factly, "Same thing the guy out at the lighthouse was carrying. It's Korean, all right. Five and a half millimeter, 30 rounds per clip. The folding stock makes it particularly attractive to street punks because it fits into a gym bag."

Olsen nodded, handing the weapon to me. "Oh, yeah. I know this piece. We've found two dozen of these little bad boys in the past six months."

Siggly and Olsen looked through the trunk as I turned the weapon over in my hands. The rifle felt light, almost like a toy – and it was deadly because so many kids treated it like a toy.

"Legal retail on this kind of weapon is about four hundred, but fully automatic and unregistered, we're talking as much as two grand," Siggly said.

I turned to the pair of forlorn car dealers. "Look folks, I'm sure this little discovery surprises you as much as it does us. And in return for your absolute cooperation, we'll do our best to make sure the two of you don't go to prison for a very long time."

The terrified looks they exchanged were encouraging. "What do you want?" she asked.

"For starters, permission to go through the rest of your lot and collect any other weapons. Of course, we don't have a search warrant, but we will make the court aware of your cooperation. Then we want to ask you some questions about a man named Paul Leavitt or Forrest Van Dorn. And I'd like to use your telephone."

After a little persuasion, Olsen agreed to share the bust with the state police. While he questioned the couple, Siggly and Normand opened the trunks of the remaining used cars. They stacked each crate they found next to the trailer. Among the 33 vehicles on the lot, they found 28 cases, five rifles in each or 140 total. Twenty-two more crates were stacked in a small brick garage behind the lot, bringing the final tally to 250 assault rifles. By Siggly's estimate, they were worth roughly a half million on the street.

From the sales office, I called the local state police barracks, identified myself, and asked them to contact Moreau out at Crisp Point to have him come down to the car lot on Route 28. I explained that we'd need a large truck and an armed escort.

The couple couldn't tell Olsen much more than the basics about how the operations worked. Each load was brought in from Crisp Point and hidden in the cars. During the next four weeks, drivers brought cars from downstate and swapped them for vehicles with a trunkload of automatic weapons. All the cars showed dealer plates registered to a phantom corporation, so they were untraceable to an individual owner. Each of the first two hauls contained only 30 crates apiece. This was only the third batch, but things went so well that it was much larger than the first two. Due to the alarm my investigation raised, fifteen cars had gone downstate in the past three days, each carrying a crate. So a third of the cargo had reached the streets already.

The couple proved quite cooperative, though they had never heard of Van Dorn. According to Lionel and Ellen, all the details were handled by a fellow from Sault Ste. Marie named Floyd. I believed them because it seemed unlikely that Van Dorn would want too many people to be able to recognize him or testify against him.

The yelling started when Moreau and his posse arrived, a conversation similar to the one I had with Olsen earlier but at a much higher decibel. He used ugly terms like 'legal jurisdiction' and 'false arrest.' While Moreau and Olsen argued, I shook Siggly's hand and thanked him for his help all day. Smiling, he told me he hoped never to see my ugly face again.

I strolled over to where Normand leaned against the tan government Dodge. He watched the state troopers load the crates onto the back of a flatbed truck.

"Bet you're glad this is over," he said.

I thought about Van Dorn and his co-conspirator running loose. "No, it ain't over until the fat lady sings," I quipped.

"Hey, what's my wife got to do with this?" he asked.

When I laughed, a sharp pain shot through my chest. "Would you mind driving me to the hospital? I think I broke a rib."

Friday: 1745

The x-rays showed only a hairline fracture in my sternum and a slight crack in my ribs, no doubt from being shot at close range on the beach at Crisp Point. One of the slugs still lodged inside my shirt fell to the emergency room floor when I undressed. I put the flattened slug in my pocket. I still have the one doctor removed from my arm after Schmidt shot me in Florida. The Soo police likely collected the slug Schmidt fired into my thigh at Jaspers' garage. Quite a collection of lead. I may start a museum someday, like Dick Tracy's wall of bullet-riddled hats.

The doctor who wrapped my chest also examined my other bandages. He gave Hopkins high marks for his tidy work. When one of the nurses called the doctor by name, I realized that he had also performed the autopsy on Pelligrini.

"We couldn't have done any better here," Gauthier said of Hopkins' patchwork on my face, shoulder and knee. "Especially today, with all those guys from that sunk freighter taking up our time. Most of them are fine, but they are all shaken up a bit. A few inhaled too much smoke. Nothing serious. Wouldn't mind having a translator around to help us figure out their symptoms."

"I'll mention it to Lieutenant Dunlay at Group Soo. She could try to get the Immigration and Naturalization Service to send somebody up," I said. "How's Schmidt, the Customs agent?"

"Still in a coma; doesn't look good." The old doctor was pretty straightforward. "It's a good thing you patch up so well, because I don't have a spare bed for you right now. I hope the Coast Guard can put you up somewhere for a few days."

"What about the three Coast Guard people who came in today?"

"Well, the woman suffers from dysentery and malnutrition, but she'll be fine in a few days. The men are very weak. I suspect they had mild food poisoning combined with stress." He cut one last strap of surgical tape and wrapped it around my chest. "Let's put that left arm in a sling to immobilize it. Come back Monday, and we'll rewrap everything."

I thanked the doctor, and a nurse helped me put a shirt over the bandages. Normand sat in the hallway, waiting for me. "Another case like this one, and you'll get out of the service on a full disability," he joked.

"Another case like this and you won't have to give me a pension to get out. Look, I need you to do me another favor. Betsy Kruza and her son are staying at the Ramada in Mackinaw City. She can't go home because Banks' brains are smeared all over the floor of that shack. Can you go take her wherever she needs to go? And give her this." I fished a thick pack of money I found in Schmidt's cabin out of my jacket. "Tell her to move wherever she wants and start a new life."

He thumbed through the thick stack of cash. "Damn, where did this come from?"

"It's better that you don't know, and that you forget about it as soon as you give it to Betsy."

Normand glanced down the hallway. "Hey, turn your radar on. Your relative bearing 180." I made a clumsy about-face and spotted Sally walking toward us, my valise and suit bag slung over her shoulder. She wore a skirt and heels, so I assumed she had come straight from work. I told Normand I wouldn't need a ride and appreciated his time. On the way to the exit, he passed Sally and then glanced back to check her out from behind. Normand flashed a thumbs-up at me. I smiled at Sally.

"Miss Dunlay told me you'd be here," she explained. "How do you feel?"

"Well, for a man who has been shot and beaten up, I'm in dire need of a beer or two."

She fished into her purse and handed over the Beretta, butt first. "Look, my ex is back in town so you shouldn't come by for a couple days."

I nodded. "Thanks for your help. I wish I could repay you before I leave town."

"Where you gonna be staying?"

I didn't have a clue and told her so. She asked me to call when I knew. When Sally walked away down the hall, it was hard not to think of Dunlay and Melinda Desharnais as I watched Sally's hips sway under her brown skirt. So Fraser wasn't the only jerk around.

I phoned the Superior Inn from the hospital cafeteria, only to learn my room had been given away. I made a few more calls searching for a vacancy, working my way up the price scale. Finally, I made a reservation at the Holiday Inn south of town. The taxi driver obliged me and waited outside a convenience store while I bought a six-pack of Molson Canadian. The driver also helped me carry my luggage inside. I tipped well beyond 15 percent.

The hotel didn't offer room service, but the young man clerk at the front desk handed over a small collection of take-out/delivery eateries. He assured me I could take them to my room to peruse at my leisure. I couldn't blame him for wanting me out of the reception area; I was bandaged, unshaven and rather odorous. I went back upstairs and ran the water ankle-deep in the tub. Stripping off Jasper's jacket and Hopkin's uniform, I stepped into my first bath in four days. With a damp washrag, I wiped clean the skin not covered with bandages. Then I tried to rinse the heavy chemical smell of smoke from my hair.

A sharp rap sounded on the door as I emerged from the bathroom. I wrapped the narrow towel around my waist and peered into the hallway through the peephole. The delivery woman raised her hand to knock again.

"I'm just out of the shower," I called. "Give me a moment to find my wallet."

Opening the door wide enough to extend my hand, I passed out a $20 for a $12 charge. "No change," I told the young woman. "Please leave it on the floor. And have a safe evening."

When I finally opened the door, my dinner sack sat on the floor. I carried in an order of fried chicken and a green fibrous material purporting to be a vegetable. The milk came in the familiar half-pint carton I remembered from St. Stephen's. I washed down each bite of food with a swig of beer until I gave up on the food altogether. With five bottles down and one left unopened, I sprawled back across the bed.

Bright sunlight woke me the following day. Glancing at my watch, I calculated that I had slept twelve hours, a personal best. I stumbled into the head. As I brushed my teeth, the telephone rang. I spat out the mint gel and went to the nightstand.

"Mr. Galloway, I have a call for you," the desk clerk said. "She sounds pretty upset."

"OK, thanks for the warning."

The operator patched the call through.

"Martin, are you OK?" a hysterical woman asked. "Art Thorne called and said you were hurt."

"Relax," I said. "I'm fine, Mom, I'm fine."

Saturday: 0925

After reassuring my mother that I was healthy and would visit very soon, I called Andrews. He was at home for the first time in several days, but he remembered most of the information he had for me. He had researched Kucharski with the Great Lakes Pilots Association, Leavitt/Van Dorn through the Organized Crime Task Force, and Jaspers by walking down the hall and reviewing his personnel jacket. He'd even gone over to the Customs building on Constitution Avenue to request a peek at Schmidt's record. No joy.

The lieutenant's most exciting discovery came courtesy of the Immigration and Naturalization Service. From interviewing the surviving crewmembers, INS learned that the *Jersey Trader* and her crew had been literally hijacked. Christened *Bintan 3* and flying a Malaysian flag, the freighter was a day out of Singapore carrying electric equipment and computers when a small boat came alongside during the dog watch. Six pirates came aboard using grappling hooks. Once on the bridge, they demanded the first mate summon the captain to the bridge. When he arrived, the skipper and mate were both summarily executed. Of the six pirates, two disembarked at Port Klang in Malaysia; two more helped sail the freighter as far as the Welland Canal in Ontario, and the remaining two pirates were Paul Leavitt and Floyd Carver. Somewhere at sea, the *Bintan 3* became the *Jersey Trader*.

In appreciation for his help, I told Andrew I owed him a beer. He figured a case sounded more reasonable.

After dressing, I repacked my luggage and cleaned up my equipment. The Colt was in rough shape from the rainwater of Friday's adventure, but I always carry a cleaning kit in my black bag. With a spare bath towel spread across the top of the dresser, I stripped the pistol apart and scrubbed each piece with solvent.

Shortly after I finished reassembling both weapons, Dunlay called from the lobby and asked if I wanted to visit the hospital with her. I pulled a sweater over my shoulder holster and the wool cap over my bandages. When I met her downstairs fifteen minutes later, she led the way out to the same government sedan she had brought to the airport Tuesday evening. The day was hot and humid. The air conditioner in the Dodge GV didn't work, and we rode through town with the windows open.

"The commandant's aide called Captain Burke after you left," she said. "They want you to fly to Washington today and brief the commandant this evening."

"No time off for a little fishing?"

"The captain spoke up for you and said he wanted you here until Tuesday. He told me you needed a little rest."

"Wow. You know the captain's been down right cordial to me the last couple days. Think he's trying to lull me into a false sense of security?"

With an amused smirk, Dunlay parked the Dodge and led me into the hospital, down to the intensive care unit. "Don't worry, Patty's doing fine. It was the only bed they had available," she told me.

She pushed open the door, and we found Patricia Lucas propped on a raised bed, her blonde hair spread across the pillow. Her skin seemed somehow paler than the white linen. She smiled, holding out an arm toward me. I went and hugged her, feeling her tears against my neck. When I pulled away, she caught my arm and held me close. "I'm glad you killed Banks," she whispered. "When he dragged Hank outside, I knew he was planning to kill him. I wanted to see Banks die after that. There was no reason to kill Hank."

Then I saw the other two, Kunken and Desharnais, dressed in loose hospital-issue green pajamas. Kunken was shorter, his hair prematurely gray. Their faces looked haggard and pale.

Kunken shook my hand and held my wrist. "Thank you, from all of us. We, uh, I thought they'd kill us, well, I guess they would have."

Desharnais stepped over, taking my other hand and gripping it. "Hank would be happy to know you stopped it. All the kids that would have died; I hope you know what it means."

A matronly nurse shoved the door open. Over her white smock, she wore a fuzzy pink sweater that seemed as out of place on that steamy afternoon as my wool cap. She carried a translucent rubber bag with clear liquid attached to a long, thin hose. "I'm sorry, but you folks can't stay," she told us. "Patty needs to rest. We have got to get some fluids back into this girl."

We filed out as the nurse rigged the intravenous feed on a rack over the bed. Lucas waved goodbye. Kunken and Desharnais walked with us to a small waiting area where we sat together.

"How did you figure there was a smuggling ring working out of Crisp Point?" I asked them.

"Hank was the one; he kept putting little things together," Kunken said. "Like one week Banks was begging money off everyone at the station, and the next week he goes out and buys a Ford pick-up with cash. That's what started the fight between them. And once Hank and I were out riding motorbikes and we heard some automatic weapons. Those babies aren't cheap, and we'd heard that some of the drug gangs in Detroit were carrying autos, so it figured that they were up here waiting for a drug drop from a freighter. I guess we had it backwards; they came here for the guns and fought over the drugs down there."

"Why did you guys go to Brimley Sunday night?" Dunlay asked.

Kunken shrugged and looked down. "Hank said he ran into a crewman from a freighter a few months back in the Horney Toad. The guy was pretty far gone and told him the whole thing. Hank said this guy was slugging whiskey. He let loose with everything; names, dates, places. I guess he mentioned Banks, because Hank would have killed him the next day if we had found him."

"And Pelligrini also knew about Jaspers, and that's why you guys slipped the boat out Monday morning before anyone was awake," I guessed, putting the last facts of the case together. "You didn't want Jaspers tipping off Van Dorn on the freighter."

"Well, to be honest, we didn't know who else was involved," Desharnais said. "We only knew that somebody was keeping Coasties away from Crisp Point."

Kunken glanced at Dunlay with a contrite smile. "To be honest, ma'am, we even thought it might be you for a while, or Commander Fraser."

Dunlay blushed the color of winter sunsets in Key West. Then she laughed, and the three of us joined her. Kunken and Desharnais had nothing else to offer, and both seemed to grow tired as we talked. I broke off the interrogation by standing and asking Dunlay for a ride. Both men shook my hand again. As we went out to the car, she walked in silence for a few minutes, mulling over the events of the past days.

"You suspected me, too, didn't you? That's why you didn't call me all day Thursday, isn't it?"

"I couldn't be certain. The bad guys were finding out too many things. They found me at the hotel; they knew I was going to Duluth."

"Why didn't you question me?"

"I had no time. But I came very close to asking Fraser to arrest you."

She glared at me, then laughed. "Yeah, well then I wouldn't have to deal with all these investigations we've got going on. I think the only people who I haven't talked to yet are the United Nations and NASA."

"Well, at least there won't be many criminal trials," I observed. "Nobody left except Dunlay and Floyd, thanks to Galloway – cowboy and executioner."

She blocked my way. "Stop feeling sorry for yourself," she said. "You saved those people – three lives. You're not the only one who feels bad about this mess, you know. I haven't slept for two nights, thinking about that guy I shot. I see the way he fell and the bullet holes." She paused as a strong shiver coursed her body. "Look, you saved twenty crewmen from going down with the *Jersey Trader*, and a few hundred more kids who won't be gunned down. You did your job, and if you can't deal with it then you should go be a plumber."

She walked to the car and yelled for me to hurry. On the drive to Group Soo, she asked if I had suspected anyone else on base.

"Captain Burke. First, he was trying to get rid of me, and now he's being nice to throw off suspicion."

Dunlay grinned at me. "Don't you have any respect for officers?"

"To be honest, ma'am, the only people who should be called 'sir' are knights and admirals."

"Your problem is that you're too smart to be obedient and too arrogant to hide it," she observed.

"I think; therefore, I'm screwed," I quipped. "You know what kills me though?"

"A wooden stake through the heart?"

I laughed. "True enough, but I was thinking about how Burke is going to write all this up on his next evaluation and get selected for rear admiral."

"I'm putting it on my OER," she said. "My dad wants me to be the first woman to make admiral in the Coast Guard, and I can use all the attaboys I can get."

"And that's why you haven't brought the XO up on charges," I observed. "Whistleblowers don't make admiral?"

"Boy, you are a detective. OK, since we're getting so personal, let me ask you a question. Who is your father? I heard the XO and CO talking about him."

I told her the story of the mistaken attack on the *Point Manitou* and explained that my father remains one of only two Coast Guard MIAs from the war. I only learned the whole story at boot camp from a film called "Operation Market Time." When the movie ended, I went out between the barracks and vomited chow into a snowbank.

"I think that's what changed the captain's mind about you. He acted like your family was legendary, and he couldn't believe you were part of it."

"He's could be right on both counts. I'm fifth generation Coastie. My grandfather flew on the very first helo. My great grandfather ran smallboat stations on Lake Erie. And his father sailed on the *Bear* in Alaska. Now I read police reports and complete background checks."

"Hey, I saw your uniform Tuesday. You've got a whole row above the Achievement Medal, and that's the highest I have. You don't get a Coast Guard Medal for papercuts."

I liked Dunlay when she relaxed; she had been so serious during the search that her forehead furrowed into a dark crease. Now at ease, she laughed, showing wide, irregular teeth. But she'd be all business again when she returned to work Monday morning.

I spent the rest of the afternoon in a crowded office on the Coast Guard base answering questions from Moreau, Olsen, and the local chief of police, a big, muscular guy named McDuggan. McDuggan's thick handlebar mustache would not have met Coast Guard regs. Everyone wanted to get the story straight, and we went back over every minor detail without mercy. I was surprised they accepted my version of the deaths when there was so little evidence.

Dunlay stopped by my hotel room, bringing a case of Canadian beer and a large pizza. She had spent the entire day working with the INS to get the Asian crewmen back home. Fraser had gone out with the inspectors from Duluth's Marine Safety Office to where the *Jersey Trader* sank to determine whether its fuel tanks were leaking. They had found the body of the Korean crewman Van Dorn had shot to death floating in a sheen of diesel. Kucharski remained missing. Divers from a salvage team were scheduled to examine the freighter early Monday to determine if it could be refloated. A Coast Guard buoy tender had already put a marker buoy over the wreck to warn off other ships. If the *Jersey Trader* could not be salvaged, it would be pumped of any remaining fuel and then demolished where it sat on the bottom of Lake Superior so it wouldn't create a hazard to navigation.

"Do you have plans for the evening?" Dunlay asked.

"Other than bad television? No."

"What about your friend Sally?"

"No, I won't be seeing her."

"Already got someone else lined up?" The disapproval in her voice was not subtle.

"No," I said, "and I don't always think with my marlinspike."

"Look, I'm sorry, Galloway. I get tense around some men who...."

"You mean you don't always sound like the perfect cadet?"

"Why, what do I say?"

"Around the OPCEN, you sound like a Coast Guard manual."

She blushed and changed the subject. "Look, it's no big deal. I only asked because I thought we might get a few people together here tonight. It's been a hell of a week."

The small gathering soon filled my hotel room, and folks sat on the twin beds as they gobbled pizza and quaffed beer. Siggly and Olsen stayed at the same hotel, and they were glad to get out of their rooms, even if to a different room. Normand brought his wife, Linda. She wasn't as big as Normand had insinuated, but she had a wicked sense of humor. Fraser stopped by, bringing word that Schmidt had died without regaining consciousness. Everyone in the room seemed subdued out of respect for the eleven men, good and bad, who had died that week.

"I guess the only person who didn't die in this whole mess was Jaspers' mother," the commander observed. "Turns out the number he gave me was bogus, and the Red Cross contacted a phony nursing home for confirmation."

"The one thing I can't figure out is why the *Jersey Trader* turned and crossed the *Mackinaw's* bow," Dunlay said. "To get away, they should have gone to starboard, not port."

"Kucharski did that, and it was intentional," I explained. "My friend at the Bureau said Kucharski called the FBI in Cleveland, but he was told to go along with the scheme. When he realized that Van Dorn might get away, Kucharski saw a chance to stop him. My guess is that's when Van Dorn killed him."

Nobody understood how Van Dorn had escaped with every cop in the Midwest looking for him. His picture had appeared in the newspapers and on all the television reports. The airports and border agents were on special alert. The toll booth attendants on the Mackinaw Bridge had his description and were instructed to be on the lookout.

Olsen shook his head, musing about the possibilities. "Do you suppose he went to a plastic surgeon?"

"Not many of those in the UP," Linda Normand said. "You'd have to go to the lower half for that. The only things the upper peninsula has are fish, deer and casinos. We don't even have fudge like Mackinaw City."

"There is the Bay Mills reservation," I observed, feeling a now familiar chill on my neck. "And reservations are sovereign, right?"

Fraser objected, "Well, the tribal police can invite the state police if they need help, and the FBI has jurisdiction. What's your point?"

"If you needed a place to hide, wouldn't you go where the people looking for you can't?" I asked.

Siggly put it all together first. "Where would Van Dorn stay on the reservation?"

I knelt and rummaged under the bed for my bag of tricks. "With an accomplice," I said. When I stood, Siggly was already on his feet. "Want to go for a little drive?" I asked as I positioned the modified holster straps around my chest.

Fraser blocked the door. "We should call for assistance. You have no authority on the reservation."

"I don't think we'll get permission from the tribal council to roust one of their residents, and we don't have time to wait for a federal marshal." Then I tapped the pistol butt under my shoulder. "You know what they say about a kind word and a gun."

Normand's wife laughed. "Gunbelt diplomacy."

"Galloway's right, sir," Dunlay said. "If Van Dorn's on the reservation, let's stop him before he escapes. We'll deal with the consequences once Van Dorn's back in prison."

"How can I help?" Fraser asked.

"Call McDuggan and tell him we've got a federal prisoner for his jail," I told her. "Then give Harper-Lloyd and Moreau a heads-up."

"

Saturday: 2215

Siggly drove a big Chrysler, and Olsen sat up front next to him. I was in the back, gazing at the full moon – those benevolent features frozen in a somehow sardonic grin that night. We went into Brimley and rolled past the crowded parking lot of the Bear Den. I spotted Maggie's white Mustang shining in the moonlight – parked near the street – and asked Siggly to drop me at the bar, then told him to wait in the closed gas station next door.

I went into the bar's heavy smoke cloud on the lookout for Maggie or her friend Romeo – I didn't have time to get in another fight. The dim room was crowded, many senior citizens perched at the bar and the tables packed with younger couples in various stages of mating; a flood of black leather, denim and Harley-Davidson insignia. While trying to get the bartender's attention, I saw Maggie standing at the jukebox talking with a leather-clad moose. Squeezing my way through the crowd, I eased up next to the big guy. Maggie wore a white blouse and a denim mini-skirt.

"Excuse me, could I talk to Maggie alone for a moment?" I asked the hulk.

He turned to look down at me. "Why don't you get lost, asshole?"

"Are you circumcised?" I asked. "If not, you're going to be."

He glanced down as he felt my survival knife pressed against his crotch. With my other hand, I opened my jacket so he could see the butt of the Colt hanging in my armpit.

"I only need a minute. Promise." Pressing the blade against his groin, I looked at Maggie. "I wanted to say thanks for the map. Do our friends know you told me exactly where to go? You might consider Witness Protection. But you do what you think is best." I turned back to the ugly bumpkin. "See, that wasn't so bad, was it? And you still have testicles."

I backed off, grinning, until far enough away that the steroid-enhanced stud couldn't reach me. Then I turned and strode outside. I jogged over to the Chrysler, and we crouched below the dashboard.

Ten minutes later, Maggie came out, her thin legs and white high heels flashing in the glow of the neon light. She scanned the lot several times. When she didn't see the Ford rental car or me loitering outside, she went to her white Mustang and started it.

"Cute," Siggly observed. "I'd like to pat her down."

Olsen set down a small monocular and picked up a radio microphone. "Let's call her plate in and see what we get."

Siggly started the big Chrysler's engine and shifted into gear. We rolled onto the highway about a quarter-mile behind Maggie.

"Keep a safe distance," Olsen said. "We'll have her address in a few minutes, so let's not spook her."

From that point, Siggly stayed a few hundred yards behind Maggie, shadowing her every move so we never lost track of the Mustang's taillights. We followed her through Bay Mills and headed out of town. When her headlights flickered on the Hiawatha National Forest sign, she turned a sharp left off the asphalt of the state road and onto a dirt two-track. We tagged along at a comfortable distance. The Mustang swung into a dark driveway.

"Don't stop!" Olsen said. "Go on past, or she'll see the brake lights."

Siggly took his foot off the gas, and we rolled to a stop about 20 yards farther down the road. I reached up, popped the plastic cover off the inside dome light, and removed the bulb before Olsen opened the door.

"Stay here," Olsen told me. "This has to be a clean bust."

Siggly grinned at me. "What he means is no more odometer shit."

They cocked their weapons and headed down the dark gravel driveway together. I climbed out and leaned against the Chrysler's trunk, where I checked both the Colt and the Beretta. There were few other noises in the dark woods than the constant chirps of crickets and the irregular cries of loons as I walked to the driveway entrance.

In the quiet night, a loud engine started, a small block without a muffler. I heard Siggly and Olsen yelling in the darkness. The engine roared, coming out of the dark drive toward me. I saw a small headlight in the forest. A motorcycle roared down on me. A dark figure leaned close over the handlebars behind the bright headlamp.

I crouched and fired twice. The rider popped the bike up on its rear wheel, using the engine as a shield, the light glaring into the treetops, still coming straight for me. I shot at the speeding shape again and again – now less than ten yards away and closing hard – firing as I scrambled aside.

The explosion knocked me flat, and I rolled fast to escape the speeding fireball. The bike and rider roared past, both engulfed in a blinding, fiery mass. I stood and reloaded. My shoulder and chest throbbed in biting pain. The burning motorcycle lay on its side about five feet from the rear of the Chrysler. A spasm racked my whole body when I gagged on the strong smell of gasoline. One of my last shots had hit the bike's fuel tank.

I couldn't see the rider. But I heard the groans and followed them, the Colt aimed along the beam of a small flashlight, sweeping across the dark ground in broad strokes. When I came closer, I followed the scent of burnt skin, now familiar from Jaspers. Van Dorn lay on his back in the driveway; most of his clothing burnt off, and his skin blackened beyond recognition. He whimpered the high-pitch cry of a hurt puppy. The smell sickened me. When I shined the flashlight over him, only one eye flickered. The other was gone. I cocked the pistol in case he moved, but then I saw that his limbs were only blackened, bleeding stumps. Forrest Van Dorn would never again blast a helpless victim with a shotgun.

"Please," he begged in a hoarse voice. "Do it. Shoot. Please do it. Sweet Jesus, it hurts."

I thought about Pelligrini gasping for breath that wouldn't come, inhaling water and sand as the panic and darkness crowded his brain. I thought of Drucker's empty stare into the rain. I remembered Kucharski hanging in the wheel of the Jersey Trader. I saw again the young Korean on the boat deck of the sinking freighter, dead from Van Dorn's quick burst of gunfire.

"Suffer," I said to Van Dorn. Walking toward the cabin, I heard him muttering behind me. I stopped to listen.

"Our Father, who art in heaven," he whispered in the dark. "Hallowed be thy name ...."

Sunday: 0020

Siggly and Olsen came running down the narrow drive. They stopped when they saw the smoldering motorcycle.

"Christ, you packin' a bazooka?" Siggly asked.

"Maybe he'll talk," Olsen said, kneeling next to Van Dorn. "Tell us who your accomplice is? Where is he?"

Van Dorn continued to mumble his deathbed novena.

"Why won't he talk?"

"Cause you didn't say 'Simon says'!" Siggly exploded. "You think he'll rat out one of his loyal disciples? Hell, right now he's praying that heaven is segregated."

"I'm sure he'll find plenty of his kind where he's going," I observed.

Siggly turned and chunked his fist against my bad shoulder. "I might learn to like you after all."

"We'd better call Moreau." I said, heading up the driveway. "He won't be happy."

Maggie had disappeared while I was dodging Van Dorn's last motorcycle ride. She'd run off into the dark woods. Searching the entire forest would be futile. When I finally located the telephone under the cabin's accumulated trash, I called the state police, described my location as best I could, and requested a mortuary team and Detective Moreau.

Van Dorn died before the ambulance arrived. I would have preferred to see him endure months of painful burn treatment before he went to prison.

Moreau came about 45 minutes later, dressed in gray sweat pants and a blue turtleneck. His hair was uncombed and his face unshaven, so I figured the call woke him. He seemed unhappy about being disturbed at such a late hour – his greeting to me was, "Does the word 'jurisdiction' exist in your vocabulary?" – but his mood improved when he saw that he could call off an exhaustive manhunt. He explained that his department did not have the money for overtime anyway, so a simple dental check would make his budget people happy.

"Fingerprints are even cheaper, so in the future don't roast 'em beyond recognition," Moreau said.

Olsen, Siggly and I stayed two hours, observing the investigators examine the crime scene and answering hundreds of questions. They examined my Colt and fired a test slug. A K-9 unit searched the woods around the house for Maggie with NEGRES. One of Moreau's boys found more than $100,000 in non-sequential bills stashed in stereo speakers. A detective unearthed a dozen computer disks among the pornography and hate lit in a back closet. Moreau fed them one by one into a computer the state police found in a closet. The files revealed the League's mailing list, sources, contacts, assets and contributors.

Moreau was pleased with the haul but unhappy when he realized we were still around. "I've got your statements, so why don't you get your friends out of here before I find a reason to arrest all of you." He shook my hand and walked away.

"What about Van Dorn's friend in the freighter's small boat?"

Moreau turned to me and shrugged, looking bored. "Seems kind of pointless to keep looking. We've got no name except Floyd, that's from those car lot people, not much of a description – he could be anyone. Besides, Van Dorn was leader of the pack."

The BATF agents were happy to let Moreau take full credit for the demise of Van Dorn and his conspiracy. They were quiet during the long ride back to Sault Ste. Marie. I turned things over and over in my mind to answer all the questions about the plot. Every seam looked tight. Van Dorn met Jaspers in New York and bought a forged master's certificate. Jaspers asked to be transferred to Group Soo to watch things and assist as necessary. Jaspers brought Banks into it when they needed somebody violent and ruthless to handle security at Crisp Point. And Schmidt extorted a payoff in exchange for minimal information and silence. He'd also told Banks where to find me at the Superior Inn.

If Pelligrini and the others hadn't become suspicious of Banks, the operation might have continued for quite a long time. Detroit and Chicago would have turned into war zones, rival gangs armed with plenty of automatic weapons. Moreau and Olsen thought they might locate more weapons that had slipped into the country via Crisp Point if they tracked down the cars that passed through the dealership. Eleven men were dead, but there was no guessing how many lives we had saved.

All the questions seemed answered except for who was this Floyd Ledoux? Thinking about him created a whole new set of questions. How was Floyd so crucial to the operation that Van Dorn decided not to kill him as he had Kucharski and the Asian crewmen?

The smuggling operation fit together in a neat package; the virtual lack of customs enforcement on the Great Lakes compared with Florida or the Gulf Coast, the remote location of Crisp Point, and the used car arrangement. And all the people involved – Van Dorn, Jaspers, Banks, Schmidt, Kucharski, the detective in the Soo, Banks' enforcement team, the car dealers, and whoever ran the boats out from Crisp Point to the freighter – they all came from diverse backgrounds without a common thread. How had this grand conspiracy converged on Crisp Point?

The answer could only be a single person with lots of local knowledge, somebody with smarts, savvy and immodest greed. The local expertise eliminated most of the prime candidates except the detective on the Sault Ste. Marie police force, but he lacked any apparent connection to Van Dorn. There was someone else involved, and that I concluded was the second man in the lifeboat as it sped away from the sinking freighter, a tall, lanky man with brown hair wearing dark coveralls whose face I never saw. And his name was Floyd. Moreau was right; such a manhunt would be pointless.

Sunday: 0520

I woke in a heart-racing sweat from more dreams of death. Before the mirror in the head, I toweled off my neck and examined the new flaws on my face for the first time since I pulled on the watch cap in Duluth.

Duluth.

The word echoed in my mind, nagging me about something unsolved. I opened a beer and drank it warm. Pulling the curtain open, I stood before the growing dawn in my boxers and thought about Duluth.

How did Van Dorn know I was heading to Duluth?

I fired up the last of Schmidt's Cuban cigars. Who knew? Dunlay. Marshall. Andrews. Half the officers at Air Station Traverse City. Jaspers? Sally?

Thoughts rolled like thunder in my brain. Her ex had signed onto a freighter and disappeared. He was home from nowhere, and Sally didn't think I should come around. And Tuesday night, she'd said his name. It came back to me on a bolt of lightning: Floyd.

Andrews wasn't happy with my wake-up call. His reluctant tone and another voice in the background suggested he had already made plans for a quiet Sunday breakfast.

"What was the last address you had for Carver, the first mate on the Jersey Trader?" I asked him.

"From what I can remember, it was Danbury, Connecticut. His seaman's papers were renewed in New York about a year ago."

"About the same time as Paul Leavitt?"

"You suspect they're forgeries?"

"No, they were signed by the proper Coast Guard authority. But I don't know how much he was paid."

"Jaspers?"

"Uh huh. Now I need you to run a name for me. Floyd Ledoux. Place of birth is Sault Sainte Marie. He's about 30, if that will help."

"Is this our boy?" Andrews asked.

"I don't know. I hope not. If so, his ex-wife may be in danger."

"I need some time. I'll head to the office now. I'll call as soon as I have something."

I looked across the foggy morning and saw a steeple a few blocks away. "No, let me call you. I'll be out for a little while."

Sunday: 0748

The sparse attendance at early morning mass at All Saints consisted of gray-haired matrons and a few old gentlemen in outdated suits. I came in during the sermon on charity and sat three pews from the back. The priest reminded me of a great uncle who had taken the vows; stout, balding and baritone. I dropped the remainder of Schmidt's money into the collection basket, and I was the only member of the congregation who did not go up to the altar for communion. The recessional hymn was "A Mighty Fortress is Our God," my grandfather's favorite. The organist played only the melody, and few voices rose above the general murmur.

I lingered after services until the crowd left. Then I caught Father McNeely as he came back up the aisle toward the altar. He smiled and shook my hand like a recruiter meeting a young prospect.

"I was hoping you might have time to hear a confession."

Father McNeely seemed taken aback. He glanced at his watch. "I, uh, . . . confessions are scheduled for Friday night and Saturday afternoon."

"I'm afraid I've been busy, Father."

He nodded. "Shall we sit out here or would you prefer the traditional ...?" He nodded his head toward the confessional against the back wall.

I had never said confession face-to-face with a priest, and this didn't feel like the best time to start. We went into our separate compartments of the ornate wooden confessional. I knelt in the dark on a padded edge. He pulled up the divider and mumbled the traditional greeting. I started at the beginning.

"Forgive me, Father, for I have sinned. It has been nine years since my last confession. I ask forgiveness for the grievous sins I have committed. I have killed four men."

Father McNeely gasped, and I knew a lengthy explanation was necessary before absolution.

Sunday: 0825

When I called Andrews at Headquarters, he gave me a lot of interesting information about Floyd Ledoux. Floyd had sailed on lake freighters for a few years before he moved east. He'd upgraded his merchant seaman's papers as he moved, advancing from the basic seaman's Z license to first-mate qualified.

Along the way, Ledoux also upgraded his criminal record from miscreant to felon. Using the Coast Guard's computer link into FBI files, Andrews discovered an assortment of illegal activities in Floyd's past; drunk and disorderly charges, a concealed weapons charge, trespassing charges stemming from a protest outside an abortion clinic, and conspiracy to murder a federal judge.

"This guy's a real sweetheart," Andrews observed. "In some states, there's an open season on varmints like him."

Switching computer links, Andrews had downloaded a series of Associated Press stories about the incident involving the judge. He explained the intricacies of the computer network and the varying log-on procedures to me. Still, his description was no more intelligible than Burley's description of the perfect pocket computer. I know not RAM from ROM.

The judge considered a petition to ban protesters from blocking public access, such as streets and sidewalks, leading to an abortion clinic. Ledoux's female accomplice phoned the judge three times to tell him exactly how he would die if he decided against the anti-abortion forces. The FBI had recorded the last two calls, and they were waiting for Floyd in the basement of the federal building the day after the judge returned his decision against the protesters. Ledoux got 7 to 10 in the Federal Correctional Institution at Danbury.

"Hey, guess who shared Floyd's cell in Danbury," Andrews challenged.

"Give me a hint: Congressman or savings and loan executive?"

"The illustrious Forrest Van Dorn. He did three years of a ten-year stint for a weapons charge. He was caught with 22 fully automatic M-16s stolen from a National Guard armory in Louisiana."

"I heard about that. You know, that guy had a thing for automatic weapons. Figure it was too much sugar or too much television?" I asked. "Wait. Two years for stealing two dozen M-16s?"

"He started with five to ten. Then good behavior, and add early release for overcrowding. Technically a non-violent offense, because he didn't have a chance to use those weapons," Andrews explained. "I called Danbury this morning and talked to an assistant warden. He remembered them very well; he put together a white gang to fight the blacks and the Hispanics."

I mulled over everything he had told me. "Still one thing I can't figure. How did Floyd go from Mr. Right-to-Life to 'Let's kill those black folks'? Doesn't seem like a Christian attitude to me."

"If Van Dorn was as popular in this white supremacy movement as everyone says, he had to be a real politician. I can see somebody like Ledoux getting caught up in the zeal. They're stuck in the same cell for two years, one of them is going to rub off on the other – depends on which personality is stronger."

"Is this jailhouse psychology?" I asked.

Andrews laughed. "OK, you caught me. I picked up a lot of that from the assistant warden. Besides, it sounded pretty convincing, didn't it?"

"Sure. Listen, you have any whereabouts on Ledoux?"

"The only permanent address I have is a box office in Duluth."

"What about outstanding warrants?"

His fingers tapped on the keyboard. He whistled in astonishment. "How many you need?" Andrews asked after a long pause.

"I may need all of them."

Sunday: 1020

Dunlay dropped me in front of Sally's house. Drawing the Colt from under my windbreaker, I glanced back as she parked the GV in the same lot where I'd left the rented Ford Wednesday night. She would direct McDuggan's men in when they arrived. I hoped to get Sally out before Floyd showed up; the Soo PD could host their own homecoming for Ledoux.

Colt at the ready, I went up the cobblestone path. Sally's front door was ajar, and I called her name. From the porch, I shouted for her again. When the doorbell brought no answer, I suspected the worst. Crouching as best I could manage, I checked the perimeter, peering in each window of the house. All the curtains were drawn closed. The kitchen door had been locked with a deadbolt. Had Floyd come and gone already? Back out front, I went up the front stairs and eased through the open door, holding the barrel of the pistol level with my eyes and sweeping my glance and my aim across the room.

Nothing in the living room had been disturbed since I bled onto her delicate furniture. With my back against the wall, I eased down the dark hallway – careful to avoid bumping the pictures hung there – and checked the kitchen, the bathroom and her daughter's bedroom in turn. I moved at a snail's pace to avoid creating any noise, looking for odd shadows. I carried the pistol in my right hand. The weight of the Colt began to drag on my arm, and my wrist grew tired.

Spying through the hinges of the door, I examined the master bedroom. Nothing. I moved into the room, spun fast, leading with the Colt, and stared into the dark muzzle of a .12-gauge shotgun. The thick blue barrel led to the trained eye of a tall man in jeans and a flannel shirt standing in a recessed alcove behind the door.

I eased down the Colt's hammer and let it dangle from my finger by the trigger guard. Resting the muzzle of his weapon against my chest, Floyd Ledoux reached over and snatched the pistol away. He was now clean-shaven and well-groomed. His sunburnt face broke into a gleeful grin.

"Looking for Sally?" he asked with a cackle.

"Or a good French restaurant." I smiled. "I'd say you have

about four minutes left before the police arrive. You wanna get a beer or something?"

Floyd stopped grinning. "You fucked my wife. Now you're gonna die long and hard. Turn around!" he ordered. Seemed like the wrong time to correct her story.

He poked my back with the barrel, prodding me toward the bed where Sally had stroked my bandages a few nights.

"Drop you pants. Ever hear of a lead enema?"

I did as he instructed, thinking for no reason about the first inning I pitched in Little League. The second batter smacked a line drive into my left ankle, putting me out of the lineup for a week.

"Spread your legs and bend over," Floyd snarled.

Negotiations were hopeless. I leaned forward and put my hands on the side of the bed. This sadistic bastard planned to blast my groin with a load of pellets and leave me to die, to bleed out in pain. After two years of studying under Van Dorn in prison, Floyd learned the benefits of this particular execution style.

"Farther!" he shouted. "Grab your ankles!"

I dipped closer to the floor, my chest and ribs now bursting with pain as I reached for my ankles. My right hand slipped inside my left pants leg, where it fell below my knee. I found the Beretta strapped to my calf. Without any time to aim, I fired off three rounds from between my legs before the vermin knew what hit him. Floyd staggered and fell, firing a single booming shot into the ceiling as he slumped against the wall. I came up fast, twisted around to aim, and snapped off two more. He slipped to the floor, trailing two broad streaks of crimson across the pale blue paint. The shotgun dangled from his hands. One of my shots struck high in his forehead, and the others were grouped on his torso.

Pulling up my pants, I kicked the shotgun away from his lap. Then I heard the shouting outside.

"Get the fuck off me, you cunt!"

As I burst out the front door, Dunlay put Sally on her knees with a quick twist of her arm – a basic move from law enforcement school. Then Dunlay drove the screaming woman face down into the lawn with a knee planted between her shoulders. Dunlay held

Sally's arms twisted up behind her back. When she saw me, Sally let loose a new string of venom.

"If you hurt Floyd, I'll kill you, you son of a bitch!" Her voice was already growing hoarse from the shrill screams. "You asshole! Even your friend sold you out!"

I stared at Sally. Why was she so angry? Why did she care so much about her ex-husband? What was it Floyd had said? His wife? I felt nauseous and confused. Finally, my mind accepted the contradictions, and the whole miserable week made sense.

McDuggan's squads arrived with sirens blaring, but even that did not drown out Sally Ledoux's obscenities. She cursed my heritage and questioned my ancestry. Dunlay still rode Sally's back, keeping both elbows pinned behind her. The cops weren't eager to grapple with a hysterical woman, and they hung back at a safe distance.

I pulled off the watch cap Sally had given me three days earlier, knelt, and shoved it into her mouth. "You have the right to remain silent."

Sunday: 1710

McDuggan didn't know what to make of me. I had admitted killing five men within four days: the guard at Crisp Point, Jaspers, Schmidt, Van Dorn, and now Ledoux. To protect Betsy Kruza from legal hassles, I had worded my statement to dramatize her cooperation by showing me the chart Banks had left in her cabin and, simultaneously, to diminish her role in his death. If the D.A. didn't concur that killing Banks was justifiable homicide for various reasons, Detective Moreau thought he could get her immunity in exchange for the risk she'd taken. McDuggan watched from behind his desk, with hooded eyes that indicated he felt I needed to be either put away as a menace to society or shot like a rabid dog. McDuggan's eyes never left me as Moreau explained what they had learned from questioning Sally.

"I'd say you were a marked man from the minute you hit town," Moreau said. "It seems Jaspers told your friend Schmidt you were coming, and Schmidt figured you were enough of a threat that they had to neutralize you."

"Well, I told Schmidt where they could find me."

The detective shook his head. "They already knew. You meeting Sally Ledoux wasn't a coincidence. She followed you to the Toad."

"How would she know I was going …?"

McDuggan interrupted. "Easy. Jasper told her where you were staying and what you were driving. It wasn't hard to follow you in a Coast Guard vehicle. Once you were in the bar, Missus Ledoux moved in for the kill."

"So, it wasn't my dashing good looks?"

They laughed a little too hard.

"Didn't they teach you down at that fancy FBI Academy that there's no such thing as a coincidence?" McDuggan asked.

Moreau gave me a somber look. "Marty, I understand exactly how all this happened, but I'll bet the prosecutor is gonna have some troubles with it."

"I didn't know they were still married. She told me they were divorced."

"The DA isn't interested in adultery," Moreau said. "He's going

262

to say that you killed a lot of people, and we should take a careful look at each death."

I tried to think of something to say in my defense, but there wasn't much that would stand up in court, as they say. From the ambush at Crisp Point to meeting Floyd in Sally's bedroom, I had ignored the fair warning and adopted the first-strike attitude. With malice aforethought, as prosecutors like to say. If I had paused to offer Jaspers, Schmidt or Ledoux a chance to surrender, they would have shot me dead. Those deaths weren't a problem because each knew who I was. But Banks' sentry at Crisp Point never had a chance. I hadn't said a word but fired before Bobby could. His rifle was coming up, and I moved quicker.

"You know, I never failed a shoot, no-shoot test before," I said.

Moreau leaned back in his chair and put down his notepad. "I'm not saying you weren't justified. But there's going to be questions. Some guys go through entire wars without killing five people. And this isn't the best time to cover for you. We've got a D.A. now with a Harvard degree and a Boston wife. He's looking to move to Lansing or even Washington. You could be his ticket."

The police chief came around the desk and motioned for Moreau to leave us. McDuggan sat in Moreau's empty chair and pulled it close to mine.

"I've been watching you," he said, leaning close. "I know you weren't gunning for anyone, but you could hang yourself if you're not careful. Trouble is there are no witnesses. Nobody on the reservation has seen that Indian girl, or if they have they won't tell us about it. If we can talk to Betsy Kruza, she might be able to tell us about Banks' death."

"I didn't see Betsy during the fight. I think she was with the boy." I didn't explain that I couldn't see anything after Banks began bashing my head on the floor.

McDuggan exhaled long and sat up straight. "Moreau's right for once. An eager prosecutor could play this to a grand jury, and you'd be facing indictments from manslaughter to murder one. These days a badge means that everyone gets to second guess you. The way things are now with so many dead, there's going to be stink. And ask me, I say bad people stink worse than most."

The door opened then. McDuggan turned quickly, ready with a snarl. Moreau came in with Captain Burke and a tall, thin Black man wearing a three-piece suit. Moreau closed the door behind them and tugged the paper curtain down over the glass window.

"Chief McDuggan, this is Special Agent Ralph Tinker, Justice Department," Burke said. "He was sent out here by Washington to handle the whole Van Dorn business. And this is Special Agent Galloway."

McDuggan and I both stood and offered our hands. Tinker shook McDuggan's hand. He nodded toward me. "Yes, the amateur." Somehow, I controlled the urge to embed my FBI Academy ring on the bridge of his nose.

Tinker walked behind the desk and sat in the padded chair. He picked up the phone receiver, listened for a moment, and then placed it back in the cradle. He finally gestured that we should sit. McDuggan moved near the door and leaned against it, arms crossed. Moreau and Burke sat on the sofa behind me.

"Gentlemen, Washington sent me here to help avert a serious disaster," Tinker said, rocking in McDuggan's desk chair and pressing his palms together as if praying. "What we have to avoid here is unnecessary press coverage. If this little plot of the Van Dorn and his Patriots leaks out more than it already has, there could be serious problems among our minority communities. No one wants a repeat of Watts or Detroit."

I realized as Tinker spoke that he was the assistance from the civil rights office at the Justice Department that Harper-Lloyd had offered to request. I was not sensing the help.

Moreau objected first. "There's no suggestion that the government was involved in anything here. Van Dorn's people are extremists. How can stopping this look bad?"

When I glanced at McDuggan, I saw that he had affixed Tinker with an ugly stare.

"You don't understand the feelings of minorities," Tinker said. "Not everyone would see that we stopped a dangerous group here. Some might think that we allowed it to continue far too long. Right now some elements of our minority communities are led by individuals who are willing to distort the truth to achieve their own goals, same as there are people on the far right who will no doubt say that what happened here was an attack on the Second Amendment. It would be unfortunate if this incident received the wrong spin in the media."

"What do you want?" McDuggan asked, his angry resentment evident in the tone of his voice.

"We must restrict press access to this story. From now on, DOJ will be the chief press contact. Justice will release any news necessary regarding the Van Dorn case. No personal interviews whatsoever."

McDuggan moved to where he could lean down and whisper between Moreau and Burke. After a short discussion, they broke their huddle.

"Can you protect Galloway from prosecution for any deaths related to this?" Burke asked.

"I can't make any blanket promises at this point immunity would seem impossible," Tinker said. "If the FBI finds the kills were justified, we will discourage prosecution. Does that sound fair enough?"

Moreau glanced at me for approval, then he nodded. McDuggan and Burke grunted in agreement.

Tinker stood, rebuttoning his jacket. "If there are no other questions, gentlemen. I hope you will agree that public safety is more important than grabbing a few headlines."

Something clicked for me right then. "Ledoux, or Carver, or whatever you called him, was an informant, wasn't he?"

Tinker gave me a baleful look. "The interest of Justice here is preventing civil unrest."

"And a little damage control?" I asked. "Ledoux shared a cell with Van Dorn and told you what the Patriots were planning. You had his sentence shortened by years and helped him create a new identity. But Ledoux started passing you bad information. That's why you didn't know Van Dorn moved his guns through the Great Lakes. Because of Ledoux, Kucharski was told to play along, and that got him killed. Now you're trying to put the right spin on this mess in order to save somebody's ass."

Tinker never blinked. "I suggest, Galloway, that you keep your comments to yourself. Wild accusations can be very, very dangerous."

McDuggan moved to place his bulk between Tinker and the office door. The police chief's hefty frame loomed over the agent, and when McDuggan spoke, the rest of us strained to hear him.

"The next time you threaten somebody in my office, you'd better bring the firepower to back it up." McDuggan paused, and Tinker looked him over, measuring the chief's size as a yardstick of his meaning. "Now you get yourself out of here. I've heard all I want to outta you."

Tinker glanced to Moreau and Burke for support but didn't find it. Both were too stunned by McDuggan's outburst to react.

When Tinker brushed past McDuggan on his way out of the office, the agent shot a glare that made me glad I didn't have a single outstanding parking ticket anywhere.

Sunday: 1940

With questioning done, McDuggan directed one of his officers to drive me back to the Holiday Inn. After ordering dinner from the restaurant, I bought four bottles of beer in the lounge, happy to pay bar prices. While waiting for the food to arrive, I packed the beer under ice in the bathroom sink and took a quick shower. Television was dismal, and I opted against rereading the Old Testament courtesy of the Gideons. As I debated the merits of cleaning my weapons again, the phone rang. When I picked up the receiver, Andrews asked if I was safe. I tried explaining that Van Dorn and Ledoux were dead.

"Marty, you've got a bigger problem than the Patriots now. The commandant got a call from the White House Chief of Staff. The U.S. Attorney General now thinks you're a threat to national security up there. Admiral Thorne told me to change your return flight from Tuesday to the next flight out. And your friend Chet thinks you should pick an alias and defect to whatever's left of the Soviet Union."

"Sir, you're gonna have to slow down to 33 and 1/3 rpms for me to follow all this."

"Do you recall mouthing off to somebody named Tinker? First Tinker screamed at Washington about your behavior. Then he requested a couple of agents to examine how you handled the investigation. According to Chet Burnley, these were very specific requests. One of these guys is a forensic specialist."

My mind and body slumped as I considered the impact of those words. Forensics would reveal that Jaspers was already dying when I shot him with the Colt. From there, it would be easy to second-guess every move I'd made since Tuesday afternoon. I didn't need to be told about the second agent coming to the Soo.

"Tinker asked for a civil rights lawyer, didn't he?"

"How did you know that?" Andrews asked.

Tinker was clever, planning his second punch before landing the first. He knew I hadn't said 'Excuse me' and 'May I?' in every situation. Tinker had been more than willing to promise McDuggan and Moreau that the FBI wouldn't push for criminal charges against me. He knew that he'd need their support, and he also knew he wouldn't get it. Instead, Tinker planned to pursue civil rights violations in federal court, outside the jurisdiction of McDuggan, Moreau and the state prosecutor. Even if I escaped Tinker's retribution, defense costs would bankrupt me. Tinker was very clever.

"Marty, what's going on up there? It sounds like you're in real trouble. Listen, your friend told me to tell you something else that sounded pretty strange. He said it was very important that you know he was calling from the Montreal Indian's stadium, and that he had tickets to a White Sox game for tonight. What's that all about?"

"That means I'll be at National Airport in a few hours."

I didn't know how serious the situation was, but Chet thought it was very bad. Chet had driven down from Chicago to a payphone outside a ballpark in Indianapolis so that no one could connect the call to Andrews back to him. Then he had to drive home to make the White Sox game. I concluded that if he took those kinds of precautions for his career, then there must be something substantial in his warning.

It was time to get out of Dodge.

Monday: 1045

Dressed once again in Coast Guard blues with my left arm in a pale blue sling, I sat near a group of six captains, all waiting to see Admiral Thorne with pressing business that couldn't wait until he returned from his diplomatic trip around the world. They occupied two flowered couches situated on either side of a teak coffee table near the double glass doors of the commandant's suite of offices. I sat perched against the wall on a plastic and steel desk chair designed by a sadist with no concept of lumbar support. The condition of my dress uniform hadn't improved while it remained rolled in my luggage during the past week. Neither the remaining patch of gauze on my forehead nor the sling on my arm met uniform regs. Consequently, I tried maintaining a low profile around the senior officers on HQ's second deck.

All six captains were white males, which struck me as odd for the first time since enlisting. From the Academy to flag rank, the officer corps is still dominated by alums from the Boys School on the Thames. In time, people like Andrews and Dunlay will shatter the glass ceiling, but it won't come easy. When Dunlay dropped me at the Chippewa County International Airport that morning, I wished her luck on her quest for a star. She will make a hell of a commandant.

Admiral Thorne's aide called my name, and I jumped. It's not polite to doze outside an admiral's office, so I expected a stern reprimand. He motioned me over, then led me into the admiral's office. When I glanced back, the captains gaped in confusion. Rank may have privileges, but it doesn't always have priority.

Admiral Thorne sat behind his desk, scratching over page after page of a thick manuscript. He glanced up when we entered, then went back to work. "Pete, do you have Galloway's orders ready?" he asked.

"I'll get them, admiral." The aide turned and left.

I posted myself at attention in front of the commandant's desk, my garrison cap tucked inside the strap of my sling. The admiral marked up a few more pages before he looked up again.

"At ease, at ease. Hell of a job up there, Marty. I ask you not to start a war with Canada, so you start one with the Justice Depart-

269

ment," he chuckled, then glanced back to the papers in front of him. "But those three crewmen are safe, and that's what's important. You did good, Marty, and I'm proud of you."

I said my thanks and assured him that Lieutenants Dunlay and Andrews deserved a great deal of credit. I described the delightful cooperation I had received from Commander Fraser and Captain Burke. The commandant appeared to ignore me as he edited the text. The lieutenant commander came in without a word to leave a bulky brown envelope on the desk blotter. Admiral Thorne continued to scribble for a few more minutes. I felt foolish like I had been summoned to the principal's office for misbehaving in class. Finally, Admiral Thorne leaned back in his oversized leather chair and removed his reading glasses.

"Pelligrini will be buried tomorrow up in Pennsylvania. I'm going up tonight," he said.

"Respectfully request permission to accompany you, sir."

He nodded. "I figured you'd ask. We've made the arrangements for you." He paused and punched the intercom on his desk.

"Yes, Admiral?" the aide asked.

"Would you see what we can do about the condition of Galloway's uniform before we leave? He's going to need a mourning shroud. And something more suitable than that blue sling. See what the Honor Guard might have in black." That task all but accomplished, Thorne turned his attention back to me. "After we get back, I'm sending you on assignment to Florida."

"With all due respect, Admiral, I was on leave. If I don't get back to Boston soon, the airport will declare Dad's Firebird abandoned. It's costing me $10 a day as it is."

The commandant waved aside my protests with his right hand, the one wearing the gold Coast Guard Academy ring. "Put the charge on your travel claim. You're finally going to get some of that time off you've got coming. I talked with the chief of medical this morning, and he agreed that you'll need some convalescent leave to let your wounds heal. How's six weeks sound?"

"Didn't you summon me for another case?" I asked, now completely puzzled.

Thorne opened the envelope and removed a blue oblong box

used to present medals. Pretty quick approval from the awards board, I thought.

"No, I said assignment," Admiral Thorne corrected. "You are to report to the lighthouse at Hillsboro Inlet in Florida for rest and recuperation. The quarters are reserved for captains and above, so don't have any wild parties that will get me in any trouble." He smiled at that thought. "If we're lucky, in six weeks all this mess you stirred up will die down." He stood up from his desk to hand me the open blue box. Inside, rather than the usual military decoration, dangled a long saltwater jig covered with silver and gold tinsel. Pointing to the fishing lure, he said, "But you've only got two weeks to find the marlin before I join you on vacation."

– BT –

Made in United States
Cleveland, OH
15 January 2025

13471910R00154